MAGIC OF WIND AND MIST

ALSO BY
CASSANDRA ROSE CLARKE

Our Lady of the Ice

The Mad Scientist's Daughter

Magic of Blood and Sea

MAGIC OF WIND AND MIST

THE WIZARD'S PROMISE

AND

THE NOBLEMAN'S REVENGE

CASSANDRA ROSE CLARKE

SAGA PRESS

LONDON SYDNEY NEW YORK TORONTO NEW DELHI

SAGA PRESS
AN IMPRINT OF SIMON & SCHUSTER, INC.

1230 AVENUE OF THE AMERICAS, NEW YORK, NEW YORK 10020

The Wizard's Promise copyright © 2014 by Cassandra Rose Clarke
The Nobleman's Revenge copyright © 2017 by Cassandra Rose Clarke
Cover illustrations copyright © 2017 by Dane Cozens

SAGA PRESS and colophon are trademarks of Simon & Schuster, Inc.

For information about special discounts for bulk purchases, please contact Simon & Schuster Special Sales at 1-866-506-1949 or business@simonandschuster.com.

The Simon & Schuster Speakers Bureau can bring authors to your live event. For more information or to book an event, contact the Simon & Schuster Speakers Bureau at 1-866-248-3049 or visit our website at www.simonspeakers.com.

Also available in a Saga Press hardcover edition

The text for this book was set in Perpetua Std.

Manufactured in the United States of America

First Saga Press paperback edition October 2017

2 4 6 8 10 9 7 5 3 1

Library of Congress Cataloging-in-Publication Data
Names: Clarke, Cassandra Rose, 1983, author.
Title: Magic of wind and mist / Cassandra Rose Clarke.
Description: First Saga Press paperback edition. | New York : Saga Press, 2017.
Identifiers: LCCN 2017004921 | ISBN 9781481461702 (trade pbk.) | ISBN 9781481476423 (hardcover) | ISBN 9781481461719 (eBook)
Subjects: | GSAFD: Fantasy fiction.
Classification: LCC PS3603.L372 M34 2017 | DDC 813/.6—dc23 LC record available at https://lccn.loc.gov/2017004921

CONTENTS

THE WIZARD'S
PROMISE

CHAPTER ONE

I was picking ice berries for Mama's start-of-spring cake when a spark of magic smacked me in the side of the head. My basket hit the ground and berries rolled out over the mud, and I scowled at the little trail of amber lights darting back and forth through the air.

"Larus!" I shouted. "What do you want?"

The light flickered and coiled in on itself. For a moment I thought it was going to extinguish, since Larus doesn't exactly have the most reliable magic in Kjora. But instead it just zipped off to tell him where I was.

I cursed under my breath and knelt down in the soft, cool earth to gather up the escaped berries. A trail of light from Larus meant one thing—somebody had a message for me. Larus, untalented wizard though he may be, was still the only person in the village who had trained at the academy in the southerly seas and officially been named a wizard by the capital, and thus the only one people ever hired to do tracking spells. He took that job seriously, too, the prig. Like carting weather reports around the village made him important. It wasn't as if he had even trained someplace renowned, like the Undim citadels.

So someone was looking for me. I knew it wasn't Mama or Papa or my brother Henrik, since they all knew this little road leading away from the sea was the best place to pick late-season ice berries. My friend Bryn never hired Larus for anything after he ruined one of her best dresses with a love charm. And nobody else in the village had any reason to send for me.

Except Kolur, of course. I'd bet my entire basket of berries Kolur was the one looking for me.

I cursed again.

The wind, still sharp-edged with winter's cold, blew through the bushes. I stuck my hand in the brambles and pulled out another handful of berries. This would probably be the last time I'd get to harvest them before next winter, and I wanted to collect as many as I could before Kolur's message ruined my day. That you could still pick the berries this late in the season was why Mama used them in her start-of-spring cakes, since she always said spring was as much a goodbye to winter as it was a hello to summer. Mama liked winter, for some reason. Papa always said it's because she grew up in the south, where heat is dangerous. I could never imagine it.

Larus took a long time following his tracking spell back to me. I'd managed to clear out most of the remaining berries by the time I spotted his tall, gangly figure up on the road. He raised one hand in greeting, the embroidered sleeve of his red wizard's cloak billowing out behind him.

"Hanna Euli!" he called out, as formal as if he were a wizard from the capital. "I have a message for you."

"Yeah, I noticed." I sighed and hooked my basket in the crook of my arm and hiked through the mud to the edge of the road. Larus watched me, his eyes big and blue and round. He wasn't much older than me, although I was still expected to treat him like an adult, given that he was an official wizard. I didn't, though.

"Is it Kolur?" I said. "It's Kolur, isn't it? Couldn't he have let me have a few days of spring?"

Larus cleared his throat and made a big show of pulling a scroll out of the cavernous depths of his sleeves. I sighed and shifted the

4

basket of berries to my other arm. Larus unwound the scroll. It was a short one.

"Get on with it," I muttered.

Larus drew back his shoulders and held his head high. Delivering messages was pretty much the only wizardly thing there was for him to do around the village, so he always took it too seriously. "Kolur Icebreak wishes you to meet him at the village dock at the start of longshadow. He wishes to set sail for the Bathest Chain, as he—"

"What?" I tossed my basket to the side and stalked up to Larus, reaching to grab his scroll. He jerked it away from me and sparks of magic flew out between us, stinging my hand.

"Don't touch the scrolls," he said.

I glared at him and rubbed at my knuckles. I called on the wind, too, stirring it up from the south, but Larus just rolled his eyes like it didn't impress him.

"Tell Kolur I'll sail with him next week," I said. "I've got to help Mama with chores today."

"Let me finish, Hanna." Larus struck his messenger pose again. "For the Bathest Chain, as he's thrown the fortune for the coming weeks and found that the fishing will be excellent for the next few days. He's already spoken with your mother and knows that she can spare you."

I glowered at Larus. He coughed and looked down at his feet. I made the south wind stir his robes, tangling them up around his legs.

"Stop that," Larus said. "You know some child's trick doesn't make you a real wizard."

"Is there anything else?"

"No." Larus pulled a quill out of his sleeve. "Would you like to send a reply?"

"Do I have to pay for it?"

"All messages cost one common coin." He glared at me. "You know that."

"No thanks, then." I picked up my basket. Sometimes you can wheedle a free message out of Larus if he's in the right mood, but I should have known better than to try after teasing him with the wind. He doesn't like being reminded that I'm a better wizard than him, even if I am a girl.

Not that I needed to send a message. Kolur knew I would show up whether I wanted to or not, because I was his apprentice and he was friends with Mama, and between the two of them there was no way I could ever slack off work. I mostly just wanted to send him something rude so it would annoy him.

"Has the message been received?" Larus asked, back to playing the village wizard.

"Yeah, yeah." I ran my fingers over the ice berries, relishing the feel of their cool, hard skins against my fingers. The last crop and I probably wouldn't even get a slice of Mama's cake, since Henrik would eat every crumb by the time I got back. It was always that way, fishing with Kolur. He didn't go out for just one day—no, he had to go out for three or four at a time. Only way he could get a decent haul.

"Well, if there's nothing else," Larus said.

"There's not. Thanks for nothing."

He made a face at me. I didn't bother trying to retaliate, just left him there, making my way down to the road, toward the little stone house where I lived with my family.

When I walked up the muddy path, Mama was out in the garden, tending to the early-season seedlings she'd finished putting in the ground a few days ago. She waved, her hands streaked with dirt.

I figured she'd been out here waiting for me, seeing as how she received word from Kolur before I did.

"Did you get the message?" She sat back on her heels. Mama's accent was different from mine and Papa's and everyone else's in the village, since she'd grown up speaking Empire her whole life. Normally I liked it, because it gave her voice this pretty melody like a song, but today even that wasn't enough to sway my annoyance.

"You knew!" I tossed the basket at her and she caught it, one-handed, not spilling a single berry. "Why didn't you just come tell me yourself?"

She smiled. "Oh, I don't like stepping in between your arrangements."

"Larus said he checked with you first!"

"You know what I mean." She stood up and tried to shake the mud from her trousers, although it didn't do much good. "It looks like you have a good crop of berries here."

I scowled.

"Oh, don't be like that." She came over to me and draped one arm over my shoulder. "You know you'd be bored if he hadn't sent for you."

"It's only just starting to get warm! The sun's out"—I gestured up at the sky—"and the south wind's blowing. I was going to practice my magic."

Mama gave me one of her long sideways looks. "You can practice aboard the *Penelope*." She paused. "You know, when I served aboard the *Nadir*, there were no days off, warm sun or not."

I'd heard this story before, and a million like it besides. "That's because the *Nadir* was a pirate ship. Fishing boats have rules. He can't just run me like a slave driver."

"And he's not," Mama said sharply. She lifted up the berries.

"Come, let's go make the start-of-spring cake so you can have a piece before you leave this evening."

She strode out of the garden, and I shuffled along behind her, my hands shoved into the big pockets sewn into my dress. It was nice to be back inside, since for all my protestations about the warmth, the spring cold had been starting to get to me, and our house was always warm and cozy from the fire Mama kept burning at all times. Henrik was sprawled out in front of the hearth, pushing his little wooden soldiers around. He ignored both of us, and Mama stepped right over him to get to the tall table where she did all her hearth work.

"Are you going to help me, or you going to sulk?" she asked over her shoulder.

I crossed my arms over my chest and didn't answer. Mama took that as a yes to helping her, the way she always did, and handed me the berries. "Clean those off for me while I mix up the batter."

The basket dangled between us, and she was already pulling the little ceramic jar of flour toward herself with her free hand. She'd hold the basket there all day if she had to. I knew I'd lost. No fisherman's ever gone up against a pirate and won, that's what Papa's always saying. Although in his case, she just looted his heart.

I sat down on the floor next to the fire and started separating the stems and leaves from the berries. Henrik kept on ignoring me, he was so involved in his toy soldiers. Mama hummed to herself as she worked, an old pirate song about stringing up the sails. She'd sailed under one of the greatest pirates of the Pirate's Confederation, Ananna of the *Nadir*, and when she was my age, she was living on board Ananna's ship and sailing to all ends of the Earth, fighting monsters and stealing treasure and basically having a far more interesting life than I could ever hope for. Sometimes I tried to imagine what it would be like to sail the seas in search of adventure instead of fish. I wondered about the sort of people I'd meet outside of Kjora, if they'd be as strange and different as all the elders in the village claimed, with antlers growing from their foreheads and cloven feet tucked inside their boots. Mama told me once that was a silly northern story, but I wanted to see for myself.

Mama met Papa when the *Nadir* blew off course and wound up in the waters off Kjora, where she and some of her crew hijacked Papa's fishing boat. Apparently, Papa had been so handsome back then that she'd taken one look at him and decided to stay on the islands—at least, that's how she told it. Papa said the story was a bit more complicated than that, but he never gave me any details.

At any rate, when Mama decided to stay, part of the deal to convince Ananna to let her go was that Mama'd name her firstborn daughter after her. And that turned out to be me. Of course, no one in the village could say "Ananna" right, so the name got distorted to Hanna. I didn't mind. I liked having two names, a fisherman's name and a pirate's name. I took it as a sign that someday I'd do something more with my life than work for Kolur, that I'd sail beyond the waters of Kjora and see the rest of the world and all the excitement it held.

I finished stripping the berries and then carted the basket over to the ice melt we kept next to the stove so I could rinse off the dirt. By the time I'd finished that, Mama had the cake batter all whipped together in a bowl, and she let me stir the berries in before dumping the whole thing in the long, low pan she used for start-of-spring cakes. Henrik was still occupying the space in front of the hearth, and Mama had to shoo him aside like a fly so she could stick the cake into the heat.

"Did I ever tell you about the time Ananna and I stole a cake from the emperor's own bakery?" Mama asked me. She turned to Henrik. "Sweetling, why don't you dry off the bowls?" He sighed and tossed his soldiers aside and did as she asked. I was already stacking the mixing and measuring bowls for cleaning myself.

"Yeah, all the time," I said.

Mama smiled and went on like I hadn't answered. "It wasn't an ordinary cake, of course. It had been enchanted. Anyone who ate even a single bite could be controlled by the person who had served it to him. A dangerous thing." She lugged over the bucket of ice melt and set it on the table, and together we set to cleaning. "And worth a fair price, too, on the black market, which is what Ananna wanted with it. Of course, as a cake, we only had a few days to steal and sell it—there was no use trying to go after the emperor's magicians to try and learn the spell, they're too highly protected. So we had a few of the crew disguise themselves as guardsmen, and Ananna and I dressed up like noble ladies, and we walked right into the emperor's palace." Mama laughed, plunging a mixing bowl into the ice melt. "We were able to get ahold of the cake easily enough—it was in the kitchen, and the kitchen crew ran scared when they realized we were pirates—but carrying it while being chased through the streets of Lisirra, that was no easy task. The cake wound up falling and melting in the sand." Mama and I lined up the mixing bowls to dry, and I waited for the usual final line. "I supposed it was all for the best. No good could come of magic like that existing in the world."

I nodded in agreement, my expected response. I thought it sounded fantastically exciting, running through Empire streets in a lady's dress, trying not to drop an enchanted cake, but I knew my life didn't have anything like that in store for me.

Mama settled down in her favorite chair to wait for the cake to be finished. "I remember learning how to make start-of-spring cake. Your grandmother had to teach me."

I'd heard this story too, but I didn't say anything. I liked listening to her stories.

"I gave up on the second try and stomped out of the kitchen, cussing and shouting, just as your father was coming from his fishing. He hadn't caught much that day either." She smiled again, and the hearth light made her brown skin glow, and I wondered if that was how Papa had seen her that day as he walked in from the gray, cold sea. She must have been a shard of Empire sunlight here in the north. "And he told me it didn't matter to him one whit if I could bake a cake or not, that he had married me for me, and if it was such a problem, then he'd bake all our cakes himself."

I gave the expected titter. Henrik wiped off the wet mixing bowl with a scowl.

"Would you ever make a cake for your wife?" I asked him.

"Wives are stupid." He set the bowl aside.

"Spoken like a man of the Confederation," Mama said gravely. "As it happened, your father was the one who finally taught me how to make a start-of-spring cake, the next year. It was quite the scandal for a few days, a man teaching a woman how to cook." She winked at me. "But I taught him some tricks myself."

I'd heard all those stories too, about how Mama'd gone aboard Papa's fishing boat and showed his crew a better way to string up the sails so that they could move more quickly through the water. That had generated a scandal for more than a few days, from what I gathered.

We finished cleaning up the bowls. Henrik went back to his toy soldiers, Mama went back to her garden, and I went into my bedroom to pack up my things for the fishing run with Kolur. The sweet berry scent of the start-of-spring cake filled the house, and I told myself it'd only be two or three days' time before I'd be back home, ready to practice calling down the wind and finally welcoming spring to Kjora.

I rushed down to the docks, my hair streaming out behind me, a couple of slices of start-of-spring cake dropped in my pockets. It was already past longshadow and the sky was turning the pale purple-blue of twilight. I figured I could give Kolur a slice of cake for waiting.

The *Penelope* was the only boat in the dock, its magic-cast lanterns throwing a pale bluish glow over the water. Kolur waited for me on land, his arms crossed over his chest, the lanterns carving his rugged face into sharp relief.

"You're late," he said.

I reached into my pocket and pulled out a piece of cake wrapped up in a scrap of old fabric. Kolur stared at it.

"I said longshadow," he told me. "Not the middle of the night."

"And it's not," I said. "The stars aren't even out yet. Are you going to eat the cake or not?"

Kolur's pale eyes glittered in the lantern light. Then he plucked the cake from my hand and dropped it in his satchel.

"Get on board," he said. "If we don't leave soon, we'll miss our window."

"I hate night fishing." I sighed. "I've been up since this morning, you know."

"You can sleep once we get to the islands." Kolur gestured at the gangplank. "Go on, then."

I squared my bag on my shoulder and walked aboard. The *Penelope* was small and sturdy, the sails knotted in the pirate style— Papa wasn't the only one Mama taught Confederation tricks to. There was a narrow cabin down below where Kolur let me sleep, since he preferred to stay out on deck in case of emergencies. We had a storage room too, and a galley for preparing meals. I went down to the cabin and dropped my bag on the cot, then joined Kolur up on deck, where he was already plotting the navigation that would take us out to the open sea, toward the Bathest Chain.

"Unmoor us," he told me without looking up.

"Aye." I pulled up the gangplank and unlooped the rope tying the *Penelope* to the dock post. She floated free in the bay, the frozen twilight shimmering around us. I called on the wind before Kolur could cast one of the cheap charms he always bought in the capital—it was easy work, since the wind was already blowing from the south, pushing us where we needed to go.

The *Penelope* glided forward, her sails snapping into place. We drifted silently through the moonlit water as Kolur steered from the wheel and I tended to the sails and all our fishing equipment, ensuring that everything was in its place. It was dull work, but at least I got to practice a bit of my magic. Besides, there was something calming about the rhythm of moving through the boat, going step by step to make sure everything was perfect. Like arranging the parts for a spell or a charm. If I used my imagination, I could pretend I was apprenticing for a wizard and not Kolur.

We sailed on toward the northwestern corner of the sky. I dropped the fishing nets at Kolur's feet and then sank down in them, quite prepared to get in a nap before we started fishing. But Kolur was feeling unusually chatty. Just my luck.

"Saw a big school of skrei in the bones," he said, looking straight ahead out at the starry night. "Last of the season."

I pulled out my cake slice and nibbled at it while he droned on about throwing the old fish bones he kept in a pouch around his neck. "Odd to see them this time of year, you know. Usually we're just pulling up ling and lampreys. That's why I wanted to give it a go. Bones told me they'd be gone by next week."

I made a muffled *humph* sound, my mouth full of cake.

"You need to be learning this, if you want to take over your father's boat someday."

He paused, waiting for my answer. I took my time chewing.

"Henrik can take over Papa's boat," I finally said. "I've got other plans."

Kolur laughed. "Taking cues from that friend of yours? You'd be better served learning how to dance than learning how to fish, if you've got your eye on a husband."

He was talking about Bryn, who was quite beautiful and already had a handful of marriage prospects. Good ones too. Elders' sons and even a wizard from Cusildra, two villages over. Most of the girls in the village planned on marrying, but Mama had pushed me into fishing with Kolur. She said I needed to make my own way. I didn't disagree with her, but fishing wasn't where my future lay. I knew that. I was going to be a witch.

"Nah," I said. "Not unless I can marry someone from outside the village. The boys here are dull." I didn't bother telling him my real plans. Kolur didn't talk about much, and I didn't think he'd understand. All he needed to know was that I didn't want to be a fisherman or a fisherman's wife. Ideally, my future would involve as few fish as possible.

Kolur laughed again. "Ain't that the truth? Glad to see you've inherited some of your mother's good sense." He tilted the wheel, and the *Penelope* turned in the water, splitting open the reflection of the moon. It was full and the stars were out, but the night still seemed too dark, like it was trying to keep secrets.

"Here, take over for a bit." Kolur jerked his chin at the wheel, and I hopped to my feet and gripped the smooth, worn wood while he knelt down on the deck a few paces away, rubbing the space with his hands.

"I just keep going straight?"

He nodded. I tightened my grip and steadied the wheel. Kolur took off his pouch, dumped the bones in his palm, and muttered one of the old fisherman's incantations. As far as I knew, this was the only spell he'd ever attempted.

The bones leaped and rattled in his hand, a tinny, hollow sound, as they charged with enchantment.

He tossed them along the deck like dice. And then he gasped.

Now, I'd learned to read fish bones when I was a little girl, hanging around down at the docks while Papa tended to his own boat, the *Maia*. It's easy, easy magic. So I knew what I was looking at when the bones scattered into their preordained patterns. A twist of tail curving out from jawbone: times of strife. A tooth inside a chest cavity: stranger coming to town. And two skulls facing away from each other: romantic troubles.

Not a single thing about the state of the ocean. Not a single thing about skrei.

"What the hell?" I dropped the wheel. The *Penelope* swung out from under me, and Kolur cursed and I shrieked and realized my mistake and jerked us back into position. The bones scattered over the deck. Kolur slid with the boat and gathered them all up in one clean motion.

"Pay attention, girl!" He squeezed his hand into a fist and when he opened it, the bones were jumping again. "I didn't tell you to play fortuneer; I told you to take the wheel. You know what happens when sailors don't do their assigned job? Your mama ought to have made that clear."

"I'm not a sailor," I said.

Kolur threw the bones again. This time, they fell in more common patterns, twists and squiggles that gave us a direction, northwest, and the promise of a good catch.

"Told you," he said. "A school of skrei in the northwest." He pointed at a scatter of teeth that looked like islands in the Bathest Chain. "There's our destination. Getting all worked up over nothing."

"That is *not* what I saw the first time."

"Because the moonlight was playing tricks on you. It's what I saw the first time, until you tilted the damn boat."

"Then why'd you gasp like that?"

"I didn't gasp like nothing." He gathered up the bones again and dropped them back in his pouch. When he stood up, his face had a hardness to it I'd never seen before. A determination. Kolur never looked determined about anything except the ale down at Mrs. Blom's inn.

"Let me take that." He grabbed the wheel away from me, and I knew enough to let go. I was still seething about what I'd seen in the bones. He was lying. Which he did often enough, but it still annoyed me.

"Where are we going?" I glared at him, my hands crossed over my chest.

"Told you, girl, the Bathest Chain. Now go set up the nets before we sail right over the damn things."

He wouldn't look at me. Kolur was already pretty old, older than Papa at any rate, but in the darkness he seemed ancient. Like the capital wizards who have cast so many spells that the magic keeps them from dying.

"Do it," he snapped, and this time I did, because I knew if I didn't, he'd tell Mama and I'd be washing out the outhouse for months. But I wasn't happy about it.

Kolur and I worked well into the night, the *Penelope* slipping through the water with the nets splayed out behind her, the fish glinting silver in the moonlight. The air turned colder, and I was lucky I had one of my old winter coats stashed down below so I wouldn't freeze. Trawling like that was dull work, but with the waters as smooth and calm as they were, it wasn't dangerous. Most of the night, I just sat around on the boat, waiting until Kolur decided it was time to heave the nets aboard and check the catch. We worked together to get the fish on the deck, and then Kolur had me cast the charm to keep them fresh for the two or three days we'd be out at sea, sailing a wide circle around the Bathest Chain.

When the *Penelope* couldn't hold any more fish, we'd sail back to Kjora, and I'd be free until the next time Kolur decided to drag me away from home.

I thought about home as we sailed through the cold, shivering night. Kolur didn't go in much for talking if he could help it, but he was unusually quiet tonight. Withdrawn. I didn't mind the silence; I'd gotten used to it since becoming his apprentice, but it could get tiresome, being alone with my own thoughts all the time. Bryn would probably have some news about her suitors when I got back—she liked to tell me all the details about their weird habits and conversational topics. Mama'd probably make me help in the garden, and we'd sing old pirate songs as we worked. Papa'd come home with stories about his own fishing trip—all of them dull compared to Mama's stories, even the ones I'd heard over and over. But still, he'd pick Henrik up from the floor and swing him around and then give Mama a big hello kiss. Maybe the sun would even dry up the mud by the time we made it home, and I could go out in the fields and practice my magic without anyone watching.

"Check the nets," Kolur told me from his perch up at the wheel. I pulled myself away from my thoughts and did as he asked.

"Everything's fine." My voice carried with the wind. It was definitely stronger now, the sails snapping and pulling tight on their ropes. I frowned up at them. There hadn't been anything in the fish bones about bad weather in *either* of the castings, and generally I had an easier time controlling the winds than this.

I glanced up at Kolur. He held the wheel tightly and didn't look at me.

"You think a storm's coming?" I shouted. "You said the weather would be smooth."

Silence. The wind was howling now, cold and sharp as knives, the *Penelope* tilting back and forth in the water. I reached out for it, trying to call it back through me so I could work my magic, but it was as slippery as the ocean.

"Kolur!" I shouted.

This time, he glanced over at me, his dark hair flying into his eyes. "Yes," he said in an odd, flat voice. "Yes, a storm is coming."

Storms had never scared me much, not even out here on the open sea—I've got my affinity with the wind, and I knew enough protection charms to keep the boat safe. But I didn't like Kolur's behavior at all. It wasn't like him. Normally, when a storm blew in, he'd be fussing and fretting over his precious *Penelope*.

"Do you want me to bring in the nets?" The wind zipped my question away as soon as I spoke it. Kolur looked at me again.

"Yes. The nets. Of course."

Fear gripped me hard and cold. Kolur wasn't much of a fisherman, but he never forgot the nets.

I didn't like this at all.

I pushed my alarm aside and grabbed the nets with both hands and hauled them aboard. If I stood around feeling scared, then that'd be the end of us for sure.

The nets were empty save for the glitter of old fish scales. Ice water splashed over the railing, slapping across the boards and leaving a pale froth in its wake. It was too dark to see anything but the confines of the boat, even with the magic-cast lanterns swaying back and forth. Kolur was still at the wheel. He might as well have been a statue.

I ran up to him and grabbed him by the arm, steadying myself against the podium. "Kolur!" I shouted. "What's going on? The storm!"

He looked at me, and he looked almost normal. Maybe a little older than usual.

"I'm trying to keep the boat steady, girl. What do you think I'm doing?" He sounded like himself. "Put a charm on her for us."

I nodded, taking deep, shuddery breaths. Maybe the strangeness earlier had just been my imagination. A little bit of fear creeping out to blind me. That could happen.

I rushed down below to gather up the lichen powder and the mortar and pestle. The *Penelope* tilted wildly, and everything slid back and forth. Dark seawater dripped down through the ceiling from the deck and stained the cot. I caught a few drops of the water in the mortar and braced myself against the wall as I sprinkled in the lichen powder. As I mixed them together, I muttered an incantation in the language of my ancestors, guttural and sweet at the same time. Magic thrummed through me. All that power of the islands, all that power of the winds, all that power of the north.

The boat tilted again, lifting up on the starboard side. I cried out and covered the mortar with one hand. For one long and terrifying moment, I thought we were going to flip, and then we'd freeze to death in the black and unforgiving sea.

But then the *Penelope* righted herself, and I cried out in relief and rushed up on deck to finish the rest of the charm.

The winds were worse now and laced through with tiny pellets of ice that struck my bare face. Kolur was still at the wheel, as calm as if the water was flat and the skies were clear. I smeared lichen paste on the masts and the railings, shouting the incantation against a storm. I was so cold, I could hardly think. When I finished, I slumped down next to the small, scattered pile of skrei, trying to steady myself as the boat rocked and the magic flowed out of my veins and into the wood of the *Penelope*. I could feel it working, distantly, like an overheard conversation. We kept rocking and swaying, but thanks to the charm, the ocean no longer washed over the railings, and the water already on deck was no longer frigid. The storm crashed around us but it didn't touch us.

I was exhausted.

Kolur looked over at me and gave a short nod of approval. "You did good," he said. "Kept calm under pressure. Very good."

He turned back to his sailing.

Yes, calm under pressure. He'd been *too* calm. But I was too tired to say anything about it. My limbs ached, and my eyelids were heavy. I pushed myself to my feet, leaned up against the mast.

"I need to rest," I said.

Kolur nodded again, this time without looking me at me. "Figured so. You go on down below, rest off the magic. I'll see us through the storm."

Something tickled in the back of my mind, a phantom thought that maybe I shouldn't trust him. But that was absurd. I'd trusted him for three years, and besides, he was Mama's best friend.

So I went down below and fell asleep immediately.

CHAPTER TWO

I woke up with a headache. Not a bad one, but painful enough to remind me I'd done magic the night before. I'd heard the more spells you cast, the fewer headaches you got, but I didn't see any of that improvement this morning.

I spent a few moments lying in the cot with my hands folded over my stomach, staring up at the ceiling, trying to sort out my thoughts. Because I was so bleary, it wasn't until I stood up that I noticed the *Penelope* wasn't moving.

Odd.

I shambled into the storage room and pulled out a skin of water and drank it down. That cleared my head some. We still weren't moving. Had Kolur turned around and gone back home to the village after the storm? It didn't seem like him. We hadn't even brought in a full load of fish yet, and he didn't like pulling into the docks without one.

I pulled out another canteen, along with a jar of salted fish and a hunk of dark bread. It was the usual food we kept aboard and not really that appealing, but recovering from magic always makes everything taste better. I savored each bite, licking the salt from my fingers. I was feeling much brighter about the whole idea of being awake, and so I ran my fingers through my hair a few times and climbed up on deck.

The *Penelope* was moored at the docks, nestled in between a pair of unfamiliar red-tinted fishing boats. Kolur wasn't anywhere to be found: not at the helm and not up in the masts, either. Our small catch from last night was intact, encased in the soft blue glow of the preservation charm.

Well. Looked like I'd be getting to celebrate spring after all, although I knew Kolur would have it out for me if I left without helping him haul the fish down to the market. He must have walked over to the Eel's Eye Inn for breakfast. I dropped the gangplank and made my way down to the docks.

And froze.

These were not the village docks.

They looked near enough to them from up on the boat, but now that I was on land, I found that they were much busier, crowded and bustling like the docks in the capital. But these weren't capital folk—they didn't even look like Kjoran folk. Not that they had antlers growing out of their foreheads, but the men wore beards and long embroidered coats, and the women had their hair up in elaborate braids woven through with pale ribbons. As often as Bryn dressed up for her suitors, and as fond as she was of capital styles, I'd *never* seen her wear braids like these.

Panic gripped me again, cold and icy like the storm. I realized how foreign the voices chattering around me sounded. We all speak the same northern tongue, but from island to island, the accents change, and here the vowels were long and distorted, as if they were being shouted down a tunnel.

We weren't in Kjora.

When she was angry with him, Mama called Papa an "ice-islander," a phrase from the language of the Empire, of which I could speak a little. Papa always retorted that he was a Kjoran, and I'd gathered over the course of my childhood that in the south, they saw the north as one place, the "ice-islands," and not a collection of places, as we did. I had grown up in Kjora and so was familiar with

Kjoran customs and practices. As far out to sea as I went with Kolur sometimes, I'd never stepped foot on another island.

Until now.

My head spun. I wasn't sure I could breathe anymore. Why had Kolur brought me here, to this foreign place? Had we been blown that far off course? I thought of the carved map Papa kept aboard the *Maia*. Akel was the closest to Kjora, a half day's sail. We must be there.

My initial panic receded then, and excitement rippled through me instead. My first time off Kjora. My first time having a proper adventure, just like Ananna of the *Nadir*.

I took a deep breath and wove myself into the crowd. I received a few strange looks, and I wasn't sure if it was because I was Kjoran or because I bore the imprint of Empire features. As I walked, I thought about how strange Kolur had been in the moments before the storm, like a man possessed. I'd say it was by magic if I didn't know better. Kolur couldn't call down the winds like that—my magic was the reason he brought me on board the *Penelope* in the first place.

And yet here we were, arrived safely on land by no action of my own.

I made my way along the narrow wooden walkways until I came to a trapper selling furs out of a cart. Vendors dotted up and down the docks, but he was the closest to the *Penelope*. I strode up to him and remembered the stories I'd heard about the bravery of Ananna of the *Nadir*. I reminded myself that Ananna was my true name.

"Excuse me," I said. "How long have you been set up here?"

He gazed at me over the stacks of pelts. "Why you asking?"

"I work aboard that fishing boat there." I pointed at the *Penelope*. "My apprentice master's awfully forgetful, and he didn't tell me where he was going when he left. I was hoping you might have seen him."

"He Empire like you?"

I shook my head, even though my cheeks burned. I wasn't used to people pointing out my ancestry. Everyone in the village had gotten over that urge a long time ago.

"Hard to say, then. A lot of folks came this way."

"He'd be dressed like a Kjoran. Brown hair. Only a little taller than me."

The trapper frowned. "A Kjoran, huh? I seem to recall spotting a fellow like that. Early this morning. Going into the city. But then, they all are." He grinned. He was missing a couple of teeth. "A bit far from home, aren't you, for your master to be leaving you on the boat?"

I scowled at him. "I'm not Empire! I'm from Kjora too."

"I know. That's what I mean."

My stomach felt suddenly heavy. "What?"

The trapper jerked his head back toward the bustle of the town. "Kjora's a couple days' sail from here, ain't it? Never been off the island myself."

"A couple days? No." I shook my head, refusing to believe him. I told myself he was a typical landsman, that since he had no reason to sail the seas, he'd no reason to know the distances between islands. I only knew because of Papa's carved map. "Just half a day. We got blown off course."

"Half a day. That certainly ain't true." The trapper leaned back on his stool and gave me a long, appraising look. "Where exactly do you think you are?"

"Akel," I said, although my voice trembled.

The trapper stared at me for a moment longer. Then he laughed, his great shoulders shaking beneath his shaggy coat. I took a step back, glancing around, not liking this one bit.

"Stop laughing at me," I said.

"You ain't in Akel," the trapper said. "You're in Skalir."

Skalir. The whole world tilted the way the *Penelope* had last night. I grabbed onto the edge of the trapper's cart to steady myself.

"That's not possible," I said.

"No idea what's possible or not," he said. "But you're in Skalir."

My ears buzzed. Papa's map appeared in my head—the islands raised up in relief, the stain sunk deep into the wood. Skalir, past the Bathest Chain, past Akel, heading up toward the north, toward the very top of the world. The trapper was right; it was three days' sail, not even from Kjora but from the spot in water where the storm had hit us.

"Not possible," I said again.

The trapper squinted at me with suspicion, and I pushed away from him before he could say anything more. At first, I headed in the direction of the *Penelope*, but then I started worrying that it was still doused in whatever magic had brought us here in the first place. *That* magic—that must be why I slept so late. Working a simple protection charm had never worn me out so thoroughly before.

I turned away from the boat and walked toward town, my heart pounding. Something must have happened to Kolur; he wouldn't have left me alone otherwise. I could work a tracking spell on him but I didn't have the materials, and I wasn't sure I'd be able to find them here. Or even afford them. Or if my magic would even work. Everyone said that magic changes as you cross the seas, and so the spells of Skalir might be spells I could never understand. I couldn't risk it.

I shivered and left the docks.

As crowded as the docks were, the town itself seemed small, little more than a settlement growing out of the cold, rocky ground. The wind blew in from the sea, smelling of salt and fish and the peculiar scent of late winter. There weren't as many people here, as if everyone wanted to cluster close to the ocean. I trudged down the main street, trying to be as inconspicuous as possible. It didn't much seem to work. Anyone out on the street stared at me as I walked past, and whispers trailed behind me like clouds.

Mama and Papa had both taught me pride. So I kept my head high and refused to look away if anyone caught my eye. But it was hard, not so much because I was ashamed but because I was scared. Scared that Kolur was gone for good, that some foul spell had stolen him away as I slept. Every child raised in the north hears stories about the Mists, those creatures from beyond even the uppermost part of the world. I didn't remember seeing any of their mist last night, that cold, gray blanket that can swallow you whole. But it had been dark and difficult to see.

Sea and sky, I wished I wasn't so far from the soil of my home. There's magic to keep the Mists at bay, but I still didn't trust that it would work here, even with the south wind.

So when I came across a wizard's shop, I ducked through the heavy, carved wooden doors, relieved at the sudden weight of magic around my shoulders. It was a small shop, dark, smelling of incense and blood. A girl stood behind the counter, chopping up dried marsh violets. She lifted her head when I walked in and frowned like she didn't know what to make of me.

"I'd like a protection charm." I pulled out the small pouch of gold discs Mama had me carry whenever I went sailing with Kolur. For moments like this one, I supposed. Papa always thought it was silly, that I should just carry Kjoran money, but Mama always insisted that he was shortsighted.

"We don't have many." The girl pulled out a tray, only half of the pockets filled with charms. They were basic things, built of lichen and stone. I ran my hands over each one, feeling out the magic. Even these simple premade charms work differently from person to person, and you have to make sure you're able to channel the charm's power properly before you buy.

The girl nodded approvingly.

When my hand passed over a bracelet made of twisted-up asphodel and threaded with tiny seashells, my whole body blazed.

"This one." I plucked it off the tray. The girl nodded and named her price. It was reasonable, and I was glad, because I didn't know the customs for haggling here in Skalir.

"Do you feel you're in danger?" she asked after I paid.

I slipped the bracelet onto my left hand. "I'm not certain."

She tilted her head at me. "If you're in trouble, the wizard could help you." *For a price.* She didn't say it aloud, but it was implied.

"Not necessary." I lifted my arm and shook the bracelet. With each movement, its power pulsed through me. Comforting. "But I am looking for someone. Another Kjoran. An older man. Brown hair."

"No one else has been in here for some time," she said. "I'm sorry."

I frowned and thanked her. I'd hoped that Kolur might have come here to gather up more premade charms for the boat.

Unless the *Penelope* had been damaged. Then the simple charms wouldn't be enough—

"Is there a repair yard here?" I asked. "Or a supply shop?"

"Are you *sure* you're not in danger?"

"Quite. I've just lost my apprentice master." I flashed a smile at her. "He tends to drink."

My answer mollified her curiosity. "The repair yard's not far from here. Walk left from the shop, and then turn toward the sea when you reach the prayer stones."

I thanked her again. When I walked back out on the street, I really did feel safer with my bracelet. The air was brighter, and I had a good feeling about the repair yard.

It didn't take me long to walk there. The prayer stones lay at the outskirts of town, a great pile of rocks worn smooth by the ocean, arranged in unfamiliar patterns in the frozen mud. We had prayer stones in Kjora, too, but the patterns were different, based on runes from the ancient tongue.

The repair yard was as small as the town, just a rickety wooden fence hemming in some broken-up lumber and a shack built of gray bricks. A single boat floated out in the water, one of its sails dangling at an unnatural angle. It hurt me to look at it, like I was seeing a broken arm.

This time, no one came out to greet me. I went up to the shack and banged on the door until a shriveled old man answered, his white hair tucked up in a startlingly red cap.

"Empire girl!" he cried when he saw me. "Do you like my hat?"

"What?"

"My hat. It was crafted from the finest Empire fabric over twenty years ago, by a sailor who lost his way. I helped repair his ship when no one else would, and he gave it to me as a gift of thanks."

"Oh." I pretended to study the hat like I had knowledge of Empire fabric. To me, it looked tatty and worn, but then, it was twenty years old. "It's quite lovely, yes. Wonderful workmanship." I had no idea if this was true. It was a hat.

The old man beamed. "What can I do for you, so far from home?" he asked. "Do you have a ship that needs repair?"

"Not exactly." The wind blowing off the water was as cold as the ice from last night's storm. I fiddled with my bracelet. "My apprentice master's gone missing. I thought he might have come here. We were in a storm, and he'd probably be seeking repairs."

The old man studied me, rubbing at his chin, his stupid red hat jumping in and out of my line of vision. "An apprentice master? So you aren't from the Empire."

"I was born in Kjora."

"Kjora! Still a long way from here." He nodded. "And your apprentice master, he's Kjoran, too?"

I nodded, not daring to get my hopes up.

"Aye, he did come by here, looking for parts."

I sighed with relief. "Not too short, not too tall? Brown hair?"

"And dressed like a Kjoran, yes. A bit grumpy."

That was definitely Kolur. "Oh, thank you, sir," I said, grinning wildly. "Do you know where he went? Did he mention anything?"

"He wasn't terribly chatty, but he did rush me about. Said something about having to meet someone."

My good mood evaporated. Meet someone? Who could he possibly be meeting? We had been blown here by accident.

I pushed the doubts aside. Maybe he had a friend here. Granted, I didn't know how, since no one befriends those from the other island, and besides, he hardly had friends in the village, save Mama. Perhaps he was asking around for a way to get us home.

"Did he say where?"

The old man shook his head. "But there aren't many places to meet here in Beshel-by-the-Sea. There's the lodging out on the edge of the woods, and Mrs. Arnui's inn, in town."

I considered the two options. Kolur never liked to venture too far from the sea, so I figured it was safer to put him at the inn.

"Thank you," I told the old man. "That was very helpful."

His smile brightened. "If you need repairs, you know where to come."

I left the repair yard and made my way back to the village. The wind had picked up, blowing in from the north, cold tricky gusts that stirred up my hair and sent all the shopkeepers rushing to latch their shutters. I wrapped my arms around my chest and kept my head tilted down, checking the sign of each shop as I passed, looking for an inn. The wind blew. It didn't feel like Kjoran wind; it was sharper, and with a sweet scent to it, like ice berries or frozen flowers. A pleasant change from the brine of fish.

I found the inn easily. It was tucked down close to the docks, marked by a pair of thin, spindly trees that were out of place in the rocky landscape. INN, the handpainted sign read.

I went in. The wind ripped the door from my hand and slammed it up against the wall, and every face in the room looked up at me. All the murmuring stopped. I froze, feeling vulnerable and afraid. I was in a strange place, and these people were all strangers.

"Shut the door!" A woman bustled up to me, her sleeves pushed up to her elbows. "You're letting in the Abelas." She grabbed the door and slammed it shut. "When they get like this, blowing down from the mountains, they'll stir up anything bad enough if you let them."

"Oh, I'm sorry." I straightened up my spine. "I'm looking for a friend. He's Kjoran."

"In the back." The woman sounded bored and harried at the same time. I wondered if she was Mrs. Arnui. "If you want something to eat, let Addie know. We've got elk stew today."

And then she scurried off to a nearby table, the benches lined with bearded fishermen.

I went toward the back of the room, looking for Kolur's brown hair. When I found him, he was facing away from the door, hunched over a bowl of that elk stew, talking to a woman. She glanced at me as I approached, the candlelight flickering in her eyes.

"Got a few weeks' time——" Kolur stopped and looked over his shoulder. "Hanna! You found it."

"Found it?" I stomped over to the table and slid into the bench beside him. "I've been looking for you all morning. I went to the repair yard and a magic shop and I had *no idea*—and why are we in Skalir? How is that even possible?"

My ranting was met with silence. The woman kept staring at me with a dark, hollow expression.

Then Kolur laughed. "Oh, you stupid girl, you didn't see my note."

I glared at him.

"I pinned it next to your bed. Told you exactly where to find me." He laughed again. "Guess you were in a hurry to get home? Thought we were in Kjora?"

The woman sighed and lifted one hand. A girl appeared. She was a smaller, shorter version of the woman who had yelled at me to shut the door, and she immediately refilled the woman's glass with frothy amber-colored ale.

"No," I said. "I thought we were in Akel. How the hell are we in Skalir?"

Kolur turned back to his stew. The woman took a long drink of her ale. Then she spoke. "You ought to just tell her, Kolur."

Her voice vibrated inside my head. It was rich and sonorous, like the bottle of Empire wine Mama opened up on her birthday one year.

"What's there to tell? Are you hungry, Hanna? I imagine you are, after that charm you cast last night. Addie!"

The girl appeared again.

"Bring Hanna here a bowl of this elk stew. And a glass of milk." Kolur peered at me. "Milk does wonders, helping you get over the magic exhaustion."

I wondered how the hell someone like Kolur would know that.

"I'm over it," I said. "I just want to know what's going on." The woman watched Kolur and me both. She was probably Kolur's age, but she didn't look as worn down by life as he did.

"To answer your question," Kolur said, stirring at his elk stew, "We're in Skalir because that ice storm wasn't just a storm. There was magic in it."

"I figured out that much. What sort of magic?"

"The wild sort. It's of no concern to you. Just know that it brought us here. Probably would've blown us farther, if I hadn't cast a quick redirection charm. I knew Frida here could help us."

"Redirection charm?"

The woman flashed a quick, hard smile. "It's lovely to meet you, Hanna. I apologize for Kolur's rudeness." She held out one hand, long and tanned and graceful. "He should have introduced us right away."

I took her hand, hesitantly, and shook it. When our skin touched, my blood sparked; she was some sort of witch, to have such strong magic running through her body.

She smiled again, dropped her hand, and took a drink.

"Frida's an old friend," Kolur said.

"You don't have friends," I said. "And how did you cast a redirection charm? You can't do magic."

Kolur looked down at the table and didn't answer. Addie reappeared and set down a bowl of stew and a cup of milk. As much I didn't want to admit it, the smell of the stew made my mouth water and my stomach rumble. I really did need to eat.

I picked up the bowl and took a long sip. Kolur nodded approvingly. "Told you."

"When are we going home?"

There was a pause. Voices hummed around us, all speaking that strange, foreign dialect.

"You that excited to be back in the village?"

"No. I'm just curious." I gulped down my stew. It was delicious, the meat tender and falling apart, the broth flavored by herbs like the ones Mama grew in her garden.

"A couple days' time, most like." He stared down at his own stew as he spoke. "We'll get started repairing the boat tomorrow.

There was a bit of damage, mostly magical. Frida should be able to take care of it."

"Not you? Since you can cast redirection charms now?"

"That was a fluke." Kolur took a drink of ale.

I kept eating my stew. A couple days' time on an island I only knew from the carvings on Papa's map. It was a sort of adventure, like the ones Mama used to have. Hanging around the Skalirin docks wasn't exactly the same as sailing a pirate ship through Empire waters, the way I used to pretend when I was a little girl, but it was as close as I was likely to come.

Still, doubt niggled at me. As excited as I was to see beyond the shores of Kjora, I couldn't shake the discomfort that something was wrong. Kolur couldn't do magic beyond the same few charms everyone can do, and it was strange that Kolur, who aside from his friendship with Mama was one of the most conventional Kjorans in the village, would have a friend on another island.

That his friend was a witch, well, that was even stranger. Exciting, too. But mostly strange. And I didn't know why.

Kolur set down his ale and leaned back on the bench. Something in his expression was off—not wrong, exactly, but *different*, the way the wind had felt as it blew through the town. It gave me the same sort of chill. He looked across the table at Frida and I followed his gaze, peering at her over my soup bowl. She stared back at me with eyes like oceans. They were just as unpredictable.

CHAPTER THREE

As it turned out, the repairs were even more minor than Kolur had suggested, and by the next afternoon the *Penelope* was fit to sail again. I hardly had to do anything at all, mostly just hand Frida foul-smelling powders and unguents as she made her way around the ship, casting unfamiliar spells. It was the closest I'd ever come to apprenticing as a wizard, and it was a disappointment to learn that it didn't feel all that different from apprenticing as a fisherman.

I could sense Frida's power crackling against my own, but there was a restraint to it. She wasn't showing me everything she could do. Every time I handed her something—some ground-up shells, a bit of dried seaweed—that magic would arc between us and then fizzle away, and I wondered what she was keeping from me. All her spells were sea-magic, something I was familiar with but hadn't really seen, and it was frustrating to sense her power but not be able to fully experience it.

I wondered if proper witch's apprenticeships were this frustrating.

Kolur watched the repairs from his usual place up at the helm, eating dried wildflower seeds. When I asked about them, he said they were a Skalirin specialty.

"How do you know about Skalirin specialties?" I said. "Are you telling me you've been off Kjora before?"

"I'm a fisherman," he said.

"That doesn't answer my question. My papa's a fisherman and he's never sailed out of Kjoran waters."

Kolur just ignored me, though. "Here, try one." He handed me a wildflower seed. It was a small, dark dot in my palm. I glared down at it, angry with Kolur for keeping secrets.

"You wanted adventure," he said.

I wanted answers, too. Still, I tossed the seed into my mouth, figuring I could ask him again once we made sail. The seed burned my tongue and I spat it out on deck. Kolur laughed at me.

"Ass," I said, wiping at my mouth. "Is this really all I'm going to get to see of Skalir? Some burning seeds and a shabby dock town?"

"It's probably for the best," Kolur said. "Skalir's a backward little island. Isn't that right, Frida?"

She glanced up at him from her place at the bow, where she was finishing the last of the repair spells.

"Not so backward when you leave the shore and go into the mountains." She blew a swirl of glittering powder out into the water, and the ocean churned around us. "For good luck," she added, looking at me.

I'd never seen that kind of good luck charm before, but before I could ask more about it Frida was walking back toward Kolur.

"Too many fishermen around," she said. "That's why Skalir seems so backward."

She grinned, so I took it for a joke and laughed, even though I was technically a fisherman. But Kolur didn't find it so funny.

"Fishermen are honest folk," he snapped. "Unlike your lot."

"My lot?" Frida said. "You would know——"

"Hanna." Kolur stood up and shoved his package of wildflower seeds into his pocket. "Check with the shop to see if our supplies are ready."

I looked back and forth between Kolur and Frida, wondering

what Frida was going to say that got Kolur all worked up. Kolur jerked his head at me. "Go on," he said. "Frida's done here, and I want to get to the water as soon as we can."

Frida crossed her arms over her chest. "You best do what he says," she told me. "Kolur never liked being disobeyed."

I scowled at both of them but I knew she was right, even if I didn't understand how. It still didn't make sense that Kolur knew so powerful a witch, that we just happened to land on the island where she lived, three days' sail from where we ought to be . . .

I didn't like it.

The supply shop was a little store right at the point where the docks gave way to Beshel-by-the-Sea proper. The owner recognized me when I walked in, even though I'd never met him before. Kolur must have told him to be on the lookout for a Kjoran-Empire girl. Not a lot of us around.

"You Hanna?" he asked, straightening up from where he'd been wrapping packages in rough tunic fabric.

"I'm picking up Kolur Icebreak's order." I stood in the doorway, fidgeting, looking around. It wasn't much of a store, just a room stacked with packages. I wondered what was in each of them. Goods from all over Skalir, probably.

"Certainly." The shopkeeper turned to one of his stacks. It was a dull sight, his hunched-over back, and I knew it was likely the last non-Kjoran sight I'd see for a good long while. "Here you are."

He dropped the packages on the counter. There were about ten of them, rather large, all wrapped in the same rough fabric. He read off the list—food mostly, dried fish and some sea vegetables, skins of fresh water. An awful lot for a three-day trip.

"Need any help carrying it to your boat?"

"No, thanks." I scooped the packages up by their tie strings and staggered out of the shop, where I called on the south wind to help lighten my load. Those ten packages felt like two as I walked back down the docks, the wind bearing the bulk of their weight. So far, adventuring was pretty dull. About the same as being in Kjora, all things told.

I carted the supplies back to the *Penelope* and set them up in the storeroom. The sun was sinking pale gold into the horizon, and I figured Kolur was anxious to be out on the open sea. So it was a surprise, when I climbed up from down below, to find Frida still on board.

And a bigger surprise still that she was standing over the wooden map with a sextant.

"What's going on?" I whispered at Kolur. "I thought she was finished repairing our boat."

"She is." Kolur stared straight ahead, out at the water. "I didn't ask her just to repair the boat, though. She's coming with us."

"What?"

Frida straightened up from the map and brought a roll of parchment over to the helm and handed it to Kolur. I fell quiet and watched her the way I would the poisonous spiders that crept through our house. But Kolur just glanced over the parchment once, nodded, and then rolled it up and stuck it in his coat pocket.

"Route calculations," Frida said to me.

"I know what they are." My confusion spiraled out like some unwieldy plant. Why was Kolur bringing a powerful witch back with us? Why would she agree to leave her home so easily?

What did they expect to *happen*?

"How are you going to get back to Skalir?" I said.

"Excuse me?"

"We're going home to Kjora. Don't imagine we'll ever come back—it was just a fluke that brought us here. So how are you going to get home?"

Frida glanced over at Kolur.

"Make sail!" he hollered out. "That means you, Hanna."

"Are we coming back here?"

"That ain't anything you need to worry about. Make the damn sail, girl."

"I'm on this boat, so it is something I need to worry about."

"I'm the captain, and I'm telling you it's not. So make the sail."

I glared at him, but I knew it was pointless; he was going to ignore me. So I did as he asked, dropping the sails down and tying them into place, my anger bubbling up under the surface. It was hard to concentrate. I kept glancing over at the helm, where Kolur and Frida stood side by side like old friends.

"Which direction for the wind?" I shouted at Kolur, my voice snappy with irritation.

"Oh, don't worry, I can do it." Frida strode to the center of the boat. My anger flared again. She lifted one hand. The direction of the wind shifted, filling up our sails and pushing us out away from the docks.

I gaped at her.

"You conduct through the air," I said, my anger with Kolur vanishing. "But earlier—"

"I do." Frida smiled. "I find simple water charms work best when repairing a ship. I can do both."

Both? That was a rarity. And maybe it explained why she was willing to leave Skalir so easily. That sort of power didn't make her typical of the north.

The wind gusted us out to sea. Frida walked back over to the map and looked over it again, nodding to herself. So she wasn't just a witch, she was a windwitch. Same as me.

Maybe that was why Kolur brought her on board: because I wasn't good enough at magic, because I wasn't a proper witch. Ass.

I walked to the stern and leaned against the railing as Beshel-by-the-Sea drew farther and farther away. Their lanterns were already switching on, pale blue like the lanterns back at home. *Home.* Maybe when we got back, I'd convince Mama to send me to the academy to apprentice as a witch the way I wanted. I'd tell her Kolur was a liar. She didn't abide liars.

Frida materialized beside me, the wind blowing the loose strands of hair away from her face. A northern wind. She seemed to have an affinity with it, the way I had an affinity with the south. This fact irritated me for some reason.

"Have you left before?" I hoped I could get some information out of her if I came at it sideways.

"What?" She looked at me. "Oh, you mean Skalir. Yes, of course."

I looked down at the dark ocean water and shivered. She was so nonchalant about crossing the waters. I'd always wanted to try it, of course, but I was my mother's daughter, and that made me different from most island folk.

"I'm not from there, actually." She glanced at me out of the corner of her eye and smiled mischievously. I wondered if I looked surprised. "I was born farther north."

Farther north. I looked at her more closely. Her accent wasn't the same as mine, of course, but now that I thought about it, it wasn't the same as the Skalirins', either. More lilting, like a lute. And her black hair, that was unusual around Beshel-by-the-Sea too.

"My mama sailed far north once," I said. "All the way to Jandan-var. She said it was full of wonders."

"Wonders." She nodded and looked back out at the land slowly diminishing into the sea. "Yes, I suppose you could call them that. But it's dangerous there too. The Mists are closer, the cold is crueler. The people are further from human than in the rest of the world." She let out a long sigh. "I much prefer it here."

It rubbed me raw that Kolur had brought another windwitch aboard, especially one who kept her power close by. But at the same time, I wanted to ask her about the north, about Jandanvar, about all those wonders Papa never expanded upon.

Kolur called her over to the helm, claiming he needed her advice. He didn't call me. So I stayed put, long past the moment Beshel-by-the-Sea vanished into the darkness, until all that surrounded us was water.

The next day, the ocean was as calm and smooth as glass, which meant there wasn't anything to do. Kolur handled the wheel and Frida tended to the wind and the sails, and that pretty much took care of all the morning chores aboard the *Penelope*. Under normal circumstances, I would have appreciated the chance to laze about on deck, maybe practice my magic. But every time I tried, I'd start dwelling on all of Kolur's and Frida's secrets. The fact that I'd been so neatly removed from any duties aboard the ship didn't help.

Midmorning, I gathered up the nets, preparing to cast them out into the sea.

"Girl!" Kolur barked. "What the hell do you think you're doing?"

"We're a fishing boat, aren't we?" I held up the nets. "Gonna do some fishing."

Kolur glared at me. "We already got a catch."

"Yeah, hardly anything. And it'll be all dried out from the preservation charm by the time we get home." I hooked the nets into place. "Might as well see what else we can find."

Frida watched us from the bow. Kolur stared at me for a few minutes, then pushed one hand through his hair.

"Liable to be disappointed in these waters," he muttered.

I pushed the nets into the sea. They fanned out and sank below the surface. Now I was back to where I started. Waiting.

Waiting.

Waiting.

Lunchtime came around and the nets still weren't full. We ate up on deck despite the cold, huddled around a little heat charm that Frida had cast. I'd never seen anything like it before, a perfect glowing ball the same color as the summer sun. It radiated warmth for a few paces, but it never got too hot, the way a fire would. The really remarkable thing was that it didn't seem to drain anything out of her. She'd fixed up the ship and she'd drawn down the wind and now she was heating the deck, too, and she didn't seem pale or worn out or anything.

I didn't know what to make of Frida. She was probably the most interesting person I'd ever met, and if she'd wandered into the village one afternoon, I bet I would have tried to be her best friend. But out here on the cold water, with all those looks between her and Kolur, and all those *secrets*, she left me nervous. Unsettled.

"That's some pretty interesting magic," I told her between bites of dried fish, trying to find out answers.

"Thank you." She smiled. "It's a northern charm. The winters are much longer up there."

"Northern?" I frowned. "Is it Jandanvari?"

She laughed. Kolur shifted a little in his place and stared off at the horizon.

"There are places in the north besides Jandanvar," she said.

I blushed. "I know. I just—" I tore angrily at a hunk of bread. "I was just curious."

"No, this particular charm isn't from Jandanvar." She drew her knees up to her chest. "I can show you some Jandanvari spells, though, if you'd like—"

"No." Kolur stood up and tossed his half-eaten fish back in the jar. "There'll be none of that on this ship."

"You're no fun." She winked at me, which I found startling. It made me feel like she and I were conspirators against Kolur.

"You're too reckless." Kolur stomped over to the wheel and whipped off the premade steering charm he'd bought from a wizard in the Kjoran capital. "Keep to the winds. What I brought you aboard for."

I frowned. My control of the winds was enough to get us home. It wasn't as if I'd never been aboard the *Penelope* before.

Frida laughed. "Is he always like that?"

Her question jerked me out of my thoughts. "Don't you know?" I said. "I thought you were friends."

"Oh, but that was a long time ago. He had a sense of humor then."

"How long ago?"

"Too long to count." She laughed. "We did have our adventures, though."

I looked over at Kolur. It was like I'd never seen him before. I'd always assumed he'd lived in Kjora his whole life, like everyone else in the village. He was a fisherman. Fishermen didn't have adventures. That was the whole problem with them.

Frida stood up and stretched. The wind swirled around her, its magic glinting in the sun. Back at home in the village, I would dream about looking like that, a proud windwitch who had seen the world. It was one of my favorite daydreams this past winter, when the night crept in early on and the snow froze around our little cottage. Henrik would be playing by the fire, making nonsense noises to himself, and Mama would be singing pirate songs, and Papa would be repairing his fishing nets, and I'd look at all of them and know I wanted something more to my life. And so I thought about my future.

But looking at Frida didn't feel like looking at my future. It just made that future seem even further away. Her life wasn't going to be mine; my life was going to be more like Kolur's, a bit of adventure in the past and nothing more. That's what comes from growing up in the north. Your life is bound by the rocks and the cold and the sea.

It was depressing.

I gathered up the leftovers from lunch and put them back in the food stores down below. Then I checked on the nets. They weren't full yet, but I was so bored, I pulled them up anyway. The catch wasn't *too* bad—mostly seaweed, although a few ling flopped among the ropes. I sorted them out and cast a new preservation charm over them. Kolur watched me, but he didn't say anything.

Night fell. We ate another meal by the light of the heat charm. I went down below and fell asleep.

The next day was the exact same. Still no chores for me to do, so I cast out the nets again. This time, I left them floating for longer. The wind gusted and swelled, ruffling my hair so badly, I finally combed it into two thick braids.

The wind was a true wind, not anything that Frida had manufactured, and it smelled sweet, the way the Abelas had back in Beshel-by-the-Sea. I stood up at the bow and let the wind blow over me, my eyes closed, feeling for the enchantment veining through the air. This was an old wizard's trick, meant to bring you more in tune with the world's magic. I tried to practice it as often as I could.

But today, I couldn't feel the magic, not exactly—or rather, I did feel it, but it seemed different, more of a presence than magic usually is. Like a predatory animal watching you from the shadows of a tree.

I didn't like it.

I opened my eyes and pulled myself back into my own head. The wind swept around me, although it no longer smelled of flowers. Maybe we were too far north. Maybe it was the Mists—

I shivered. No. The presence hadn't felt frightening; it hadn't felt dangerous. It was just *there*.

"Kolur," I called out, turning around to face him. "How long till we get back to Kjora?"

"You know better than to ask me that." True enough—never asking him if he were home yet was one of the conditions he'd set forth when he brought me on as his apprentice.

"Yeah, but there's nothing to do. You're not interested in fishing, and Frida calls down the wind and fixes the sails before I can—"

"Three days ago, you were griping about having to work. Now you're griping about not having to work."

I scowled at him. "I'm still trapped on your boat."

"That's because you're my apprentice," he said. "Now go on. Stop bothering me."

"You didn't answer my question."

"'Cause you ain't supposed to ask it. Go check your nets."

I knew I'd lost, but I stalked over to the helm to see if I could glare an answer out of him. Kolur didn't even acknowledge I was there. As far as I could tell, he thought the only things that existed in the whole world were the *Penelope* and the vast shining expanse of the sea.

Eventually, boredom got the best of me in my standoff. I went back to my nets.

Still not full, even though I'd left them out for a couple of hours longer. I sighed and hauled them in. Less seaweed this time, but there was a hunk of glacier ice. I frowned. There weren't any glaciers this far south, and the water was too warm this time of year for the ice to have floated down—

And then I saw something else, something that froze all the air out of my body.

A capelin, long and thin and gasping for air on the deck. I knelt down in the tangle of nets, not noticing the cold seawater soaking through my trousers. I scooped the capelin up in my hands. It slapped against my gloves, leaving a scatter of scales in its wake.

You couldn't catch capelin in our waters. They were northern fish, and they never came this far south. Skalir was farther north than Kjora, certainly, but we should be firmly in Kjoran waters by now, and this fish, this narrow, gasping fish, should not be here.

With a shout, I flung it back into the nets. Tears prickled at my eyes.

We weren't going south to Kjora.

We were going north.

"Kolur!" I screamed. "What are you doing? Where are you taking me?"

My voice bounced off the cold. The air vibrated. Over at the navigation table, Frida set down her sextant. Kolur kept staring at the horizon.

"Kolur!" I scooped up the capelin and raced over to the helm. He looked at me, looked at the fish.

"What is this?" I hissed, shaking it at him.

"It appears to be a capelin."

I hurled the fish back out into the water. "It doesn't swim this far south. Which means we aren't south at all, doesn't it?"

Kolur fell silent and my anger coursed through me. Not just anger, though—fear, too, a little prickle of it. I'd trusted him. Mama had trusted him. And now he had spirited me away. Even if I had always wanted to go on an adventure, I wanted to do it on my terms. Not Kolur's.

"Frida!" he called out. "Do you think you could take the wheel? Don't like using the steering charm unless I absolutely have to."

A pause. The *Penelope* rocked against the waves. That cold, sweet-scented wind ruffled my hair.

"Of course," she finally said, and she set down her sextant and walked over to the helm. I recoiled from her when she passed, no longer admiring her magic but fearing it, fearing what she might be capable of.

She didn't do anything except take the wheel from Kolur, who turned to me, not looking the least bit guilty.

"I suppose we should talk," he said.

"Talk?" I shrieked. "*Talk?* What are you doing to me?"

"Nothing." He walked over to the port railing and leaned against it, the wind pushing his hair away from his eyes. I joined him, my whole body shaking, and not from the cold.

"I'm not doing anything to you." He glanced over at me. He looked older than usual, like the last few days had drained the life out of him. "You are right, though; we're not sailing back to Kjora."

It was a strange relief to hear him admit it. I slumped against the railing and wrapped my arms around my chest. "So, where are we going?"

"North." Kolur squinted into the sun.

"Well, that's obvious. *Why* are we going north?"

"Just an errand I have to take care of."

"An errand? An *errand?*" I threw my hands up in the air in frustration. "You couldn't have told me about it?" Then I peered at him, considering. "Why'd you bring me, anyway? You clearly don't need me."

Kolur hesitated.

"Well?" I snapped. "I know it's not just because you thought I'd have a good time. You're the most unadventurous person I've ever met." Even though I wasn't so certain of that now.

Kolur let out a deep breath. "I didn't know about it until after we had made sail. I had to make a quick decision, and I chose to bring you."

I stared at him. "The bones," I said, remembering the way they had scattered across the deck, foretelling times of strife and strangers coming to town. "I knew what I saw."

Kolur looked away from me.

"And you lied to me. You said they spelled out the same thing both times."

"I know what I said." He ran a hand over his wind-tangled hair. "I didn't handle it as well as I should have."

"You think?"

He gave me a dark look. "Well, you're always saying you wanted an adventure."

"You still lied to me." I pointed back at Frida. "Besides, you don't even need me. That's why she's here, isn't it? 'Cause you need someone trained to do magic? Real magic?"

Kolur gave me a long look and didn't answer.

"Sea and sky, why didn't you just say from the beginning—"

"It's difficult to explain." He gave me a weak half smile. "If I'd turned around to take you home, I'd never have made it. But I swear I'll have you back home in only a few weeks' time."

"A few weeks?" My chest tightened. "Mama will be worried sick. Papa, too—they'll come looking for me."

"I sent word that we were delayed."

"You *what?*" The whole world spun around. Kolur kept staring at me, as unperturbed as if we were arguing about the fishing schedule or repairs to the boat. "You told *them* but you didn't tell me?"

"I had my reasons," he said quietly.

I tore away from him, shaking with fury. Frida looked at us from her place at the wheel, the wind tossing her braid around. Everything was falling into place. The extra supplies. Frida joining us on the trip. Kolur's strangeness during the storm—

"You caused this." I whirled around to face him. "You made all this happen. I don't know how, but you—you're planning some-thing."

He didn't deny it.

My eyes were heavy, and my face was hot. I raced over to the stairs and climbed down below. As soon as I was off the deck, the tears spilled out. I thought about Mama receiving word that I'd be home in a few weeks. It was from Kolur; she wouldn't think any-thing of it.

He'd betrayed me. He'd betrayed *her*.

I slammed the door to my cabin and shoved the trunk of old sails up against it. I hoped that would be enough to hold him—I hoped he wouldn't get Frida to use magic. Then I dug through my stack of clothes until I found that charm I'd bought in Beshel-by-the-Sea. I'd taken it off when I'd boarded the boat, thinking I was safe.

I slipped on the charm, and its thin protective spell rippled through me. I collapsed down on the bed and took deep breaths as tears dripped down the side of my face.

I didn't know if the bracelet would keep me safe from Frida's magic. It certainly wouldn't take me home, where Papa could soothe me the way he had once when I was a little girl, telling me that all liars are punished by the ancestors. But it was better than nothing. Even so, I lay there weeping, with no idea what to do next.

I woke with a jolt in the middle of the night. My face was sticky with dried tears, and the charmed bracelet had twisted tight around my wrist. I couldn't see anything. I was in a void.

No—I just hadn't activated the lantern before I fell asleep.

I crawled out of the cot and felt around until I found the lan-tern's familiar round curves. "Light," I whispered, and it blinked on. The cabin looked as I had left it. My clothes were flung across the floorboard; the trunk was still shoved up again the door.

The *Penelope* rocked and creaked, sailing us to whatever fate awaited in the north. My stomach rumbled. Of course. I'd missed dinner.

I shoved the trunk aside and eased the door open. Kolur usually slept up on deck, next to the helm, but Frida had been sleeping down in the storeroom. I wanted something to eat, but I didn't want to see her. I supposed that was the trouble with hiding on a fishing boat—there aren't many places to hide.

Still, I crept into the storeroom, taking care not to step on the noisier boards. The storeroom was flooded with dark blue light from the lantern, and I could just make out the shape of Frida curled up in a hammock in the corner. Moving quickly, I grabbed a jar of dried caribou and some sea crackers and jam, along with a skin of water, and then hurried back to my room to eat.

It was a satisfying enough meal, since we hadn't been at sea long enough for me to be sick of it, but when I finished, I had no desire to fall back asleep. My thoughts kept swirling around, churning and anxious. I imagined Frida sneaking into my cabin and casting some dangerous curse on me, and I rubbed at my bracelet, trying to make the image go away. It didn't.

Plus, my chamber pot needed emptying.

I held out as long as I could, not wanting to risk facing Kolur up on deck. I resented him for keeping secrets from me, for keeping his magic from me. In the gentle rocking of the boat, I had the unnerving thought that maybe Mama'd known about his past too, and maybe that was why she'd arranged for me to apprentice with him.

Or maybe not. I took a deep breath, grabbed the chamber pot, and left my cabin.

The *Penelope* rocked back and forth, and I pressed one hand against the wall to steady myself. The wind was howling outside, a low, keening moan that sent a prickle down my spine. I'd have thought it was Frida's doing if I hadn't just seen her sleeping.

With practiced movements, I climbed up on deck without spilling the chamber pot. The wind gusted around the boat, slamming into the sails and kicking up the ocean in frothy peaks that appeared now and then over the railings, illuminated by the magic-cast lanterns. At the horizon, Jandanvar's lights cascaded across the night sky, swirls of pink and green. You could see them even in Kjora, and it was a comfort to see them here, in unexpected waters.

The first thing I did was check for Kolur. He was over by the helm and sleeping, a blanket tucked around his shoulders.

I made my way to the starboard railing and chucked out the mess in the chamber pot. It all disappeared into the churn of the sea. I set the pot down at my feet and leaned against the railing. The air had that scent again, sweet like berries and flowers. Except nothing about it made me think of spring.

It was cold.

Death-cold, Papa would say, but I stayed out in it anyway. There was a crispness to it I found refreshing after being cooped up in my cabin. I wasn't used to being inside, and I'd always preferred to be out-of-doors. I did understand why Kolur would rather be at sea than back in the village, trapped in his shack on the beach. But that still didn't explain what we were doing out here, why we were sailing into the north. Maybe it had something to do with his old life in Skalir. A fisherman's debt? Payment to a former apprentice master? Perhaps he'd gone too far into unfamiliar waters before I met him, and he had old ties to sever.

A lot of possibilities, to be sure. None of them made me any less angry with him.

The lanterns cast long shadows across the water that rippled with the waves, moving like the ghosts in Papa's warning stories. It was mesmerizing, the inky black of the night sea, the blue glow of the lanterns, the stars glittering overhead. My thoughts unwound from me, still conjuring up reasons for Kolur to sail us north with a trained windwitch. Maybe he was cursed and finally found a cure. Maybe *she* was cursed, and he was the cure. It would be just like the story Mama had told me about Ananna—I used to pretend I was Ananna before she was a ship's captain, traveling across the desert to cure the curse placed on Naji of the Jadorr'a. Maybe I was on the same sort of journey now.

Something splashed in the water.

I jumped back from the railing, startled. Or maybe this was about the Mists. I hadn't considered that possibility. I hadn't wanted to.

Another splash. This time I realized it came with a shadow, one that moved differently from the others. I leaned over the railing, peering close, my heart racing. In truth, this didn't seem like the Mists. They always came with omens, with mist and gray light. Maybe this was just a whale. Even though we were too far north, and too early in the season, to see one.

Another splash. I grabbed one of the lanterns and dangled it over the water, trying to get a better look.

There was something below the surface. Too small to be a whale and too thin to be a seal.

I took a step back. Under other circumstances, I would have called for Kolur. But not tonight; I was still angry with him. I touched my bracelet instead.

A head emerged from the water. A young man's head, pale hair plastered to his skull, seawater running over his skin in rivulets.

I shouted and dropped the lantern overboard, then immediately turned to Kolur, afraid I'd woken him—but he slept on.

The lantern's glow sank all the way down into the ocean's depths. I cursed. I'd have to explain that eventually.

"Oh," said the young man. "You dropped something."

His voice was strange, melodious and reedy, like a flute. I was too scared to move. He swam alongside us, his face turned toward me. It was almost a human face, one with all the marks of beauty—sharp cheekbones and a long, thin nose and large, pale eyes. But that beauty was what made it unnerving. I'd seen handsome men before, and I'd seen exquisite women, and it wasn't until this moment, in the shivering dark, that I realized every single one of them possessed some minor imperfection that let you know they were human. The more I looked at this young man, swimming like a dolphin alongside the boat, the more inhuman I found him.

"What are—" I started in a fierce whisper.

The young man dove beneath the waves.

The wind surged. I clutched the railing so tightly that my knuckles turned white. My bracelet was freezing against my wrist. I waited for gray mist to curl off the water, for a gap to appear in the sky filled with unearthly light. I waited for danger.

But nothing happened.

Kolur slept on.

The *Penelope* continued on her path to the north.

The ocean was empty.

CHAPTER FOUR

Three days passed and I didn't see the boy again. I wasn't frightened of him, exactly, but when I crept up on deck at night, I wasn't certain I wanted to see him. I thought he might be part of the reason Kolur was sailing us north.

After those three days, I decided not to keep myself locked in the cabin during the day. It was too much, being alone with my thoughts like that, with all my anger and frustration and confusion swirling around inside my head. I didn't want to hide—I wanted answers. Besides, fuming in my cabin was even more boring than doing chores.

When I finally wandered up on deck, nothing had changed: Frida still mapped out our path through the water. Kolur still steered at the wheel.

"Decided to join us, huh?" Kolur grinned. It was colder now than it had been a few days ago, despite the sun shining up in the clouds. No heat charms burned on the deck. I thought about Mama's garden back in Kjora, all the seeds tucked into the mud and waiting for the air to turn so they could punch their way up to the surface. Henrik and I had helped her plant them, the way we did every year. She never told us what seeds we were given, and it was a surprise every spring when they revealed themselves.

It was almost spring there. But it didn't feel like spring here.

"Are you going to tell me where we're going?"

"North." Kolur pointed up to the sky, as if the world were a map.

I glared at him. "Well, if you're not going to answer my questions, do you at least have anything for me to do?"

Kolur shrugged.

"Maybe you should have thought of that before you dragged me out on your errand."

Over at the navigation table, Frida lifted her head, the wind tossing strands of her silvery-brown hair into her eyes. "I do," she called out.

I frowned. Glanced at Kolur. He was staring out at the water, lost in the motions of the *Penelope*.

"You can come over," she said. "I won't bite."

I walked across the deck, rubbing at my bracelet. It held the warmth of my skin, so I knew I didn't face any immediate harm.

"Our path is going to get dangerous," Frida said.

"I thought this was just a simple errand."

Frida smiled. "The danger isn't the errand; it's the path." She pulled the cover over the carved map before I could see where that path led us. "The ice hasn't completely broken up yet, so we run the risk of icebergs. Kolur tells me you can do a bit of magic? I may need help with spells, and I thought we could practice."

"You want me to help you but you won't even tell me where we're going?" Heat flushed in my cheeks.

Frida looked at me, her head tilted like a bird. "Kolur asked me not to."

I twisted around and looked at him through the blustering wind and the flapping sails. He was ignoring us both, as was his way.

"Why?" I turned back to her. "What harm could it do? It's not like I have any choice here."

Frida smiled knowingly. "That's what I told him. But he's worried about you doing something that could get yourself hurt."

I hugged myself, trying to conjure up some warmth.

"Shall I show you the magic we'll be doing?"

"On what? There isn't any ice around here."

"Ah." Frida nodded. "Yes. I see what Kolur was worried about now."

"What?" I hated this, the way they both kept talking around me, dropping hints. Like they were playing some stupid game.

"There is ice here. Come." She walked over to the railing. I waited a moment to be contrary. Then I followed out of nothing better to do. The water was choppy and dark green, almost black: a color that made me think of emptiness. "It's hidden, drifting beneath the surface. I have a spell working to melt it away before it hits the boat." She glanced at me out of the corner of her eye. "That's why I'm not burning the heat charms."

I had wondered, but she didn't need to know that.

"Kolur worried that you would run off when we next made port, that you'd try to steal a boat to sail your way back home." She laughed. "I told him you seem capable enough. You're his apprentice, after all."

I squeezed the railing and wondered where we were going to make port. It was hard to remember the carved map from Papa's boat, but I was pretty sure there were chains of smaller islands this far north. Not that I'd ever heard anything about them. Papa was always saying that there was enough wonder in the waters of Kjora to last a lifetime.

"Where are we going to make port?" I said.

"Ah, already plotting your escape, I see."

"I'm not going to steal a boat," I snapped. "Kolur's going to take me home, isn't he?"

"Of course." Frida smiled. "But your mother is a pirate."

I rolled my eyes. "You can't sail these boats alone, even with magic. I'm not an idiot."

Frida laughed. "It's been done before, I imagine. But yes, you'd be safer with a crew. Honestly, his real concern is that you wouldn't know this part of the world. It's dangerous, more dangerous than the southerly islands. Not just because of the Mists"—she gestured at my bracelet and I covered it protectively with my other hand—"but because of the land and the sea themselves. You're not used to it. Now watch." She braced herself against the railing with one hand and lifted the other in a slow, graceful gesture. Her wrist swirled and swayed, and her fingers rippled.

The wind shifted.

It had been blowing in from the southeast, the sails catching it so as to propel us northward, but now it was blowing entirely from the north, and there was a melancholy to it from the magic.

Over at the helm, Kolur cursed. "You'll break the masts!" he shouted.

"Ignore him," Frida said. "Look at the water."

I did. Spots of brightness appeared on the surface, like spangles of sunlight. Except they didn't line up with the sun.

Frida exhaled slowly.

The spots of brightness glimmered. For half a second, I saw what Frida saw—ice. The bright spots were chunks of ice, invisible in the swirl of the waves without the aid of enchantment.

And they were melting.

Their light bled into the ocean water, bright on dark, a beautiful swirl of color, like Jandanvar's lights, like the moon dancing with the night sky.

And then it was gone.

Frida let out her breath again, this time in a long unpracticed rush. She grabbed the railing with both hands and leaned back, stretching.

"So that's how you melt the ice." She straightened up and

grinned at me. "You can do it with sea-magic as well, but I thought you'd prefer the wind."

I felt a twinge of annoyance because she was right, but it passed quickly enough, swallowed up by a lifetime of dreaming I could become a witch.

"I was curious which direction, though." Frida's eyes sparkled. "Do you know yet? It took me a bit of exploration before I figured it out."

I didn't want to answer at first, but at the same time, it was a chance to talk about my magic with someone who understood, and I didn't get that opportunity often. I sighed and braced myself. "I'm pretty sure it's the south wind." Everyone always laughed when I told them that, and said how obvious it was, since I had Empire heritage. But I'd actually inherited it from Papa. Mama's magic was all based in the soil.

But Frida only nodded. "You should find this charm easy, then. When we sail across more ice, I'll show you how to do it."

I stared out at the dark water. It was good to have a job aboard the ship again.

Even if I had been dragged out here against my will.

I went up on deck that night, late, long after everyone had gone to sleep. It had become a habit these last few days, a way of having the *Penelope* to myself, even if just for a little while.

The wind was calm, nudging us gently along our way. I walked over to port side and leaned over the railing, staring down at the water. The lanterns' light reflected back at me, but I didn't see anything swimming alongside the boat.

I still thought that I might have imagined him. But I walked around the perimeter anyway, checking the water. Kolur snored, a soft rhythm that lined up with the motion of the *Penelope*. At the stern I stopped and let out a deep breath. No boy. Maybe I really was going mad out here. Maybe it was the far north making its way into my thoughts. Changing them.

Water splashed against the side of the boat.

I leaned over the railing immediately, gripping tight. A shadow flickered through the water.

"Hey," I snapped, forgetting the possibility of madness. "Hey, are you down there?"

A pause. The wind shifted directions; the sails swiveled into place, their magic crackling around me with the same melancholy I'd sensed before.

Then that pale face appeared, glowing in the water like the moon.

"You were casting magic earlier," he said.

I shivered. My heart pounded.

"Not me," I said in a low voice. "The witch on board."

"You mean you're not a witch?"

I shrugged, nervous but a little pleased, too, that he'd mistaken me for a proper witch.

He dropped below the water. I was certain I wasn't imagining him now, and all the many explanations for his existence passed through my head: he was a ghost; he was a water spirit made manifest; he was a merman, a new kind that lived in icy waters.

Or he was from the Mists.

He reappeared without warning. I gasped and stepped back. The boy frowned.

"Don't be scared of me."

It took me a moment to find my voice. "Why not?" I leaned closer. Sprays of freezing water splashed across my face. But the boy didn't seem cold at all.

"Because I'm here to help you." He bobbed with the waves. "My name is Isolfr."

"What *are* you?"

"Does it matter?"

"Yes!" My answer came out louder than I'd intended, and I glanced over at Kolur. He was still asleep. "Yes," I said, more quietly. "I don't make a habit of trusting boys who can swim in ice water."

Isolfr gave me one perfect, dazzling smile. "I'm not a normal boy."

"I can see that."

A wave crested and he rode with it, rising up alongside the boat. The water sparkled around him like it was full of stars.

"You still didn't answer my question," I said. "What are you?"

"What are you?"

"I'm human! You have to know that. Are you from the Mists?"

I spat out the question without meaning to—it's dangerous to be so forthright with someone from the Mists. I regretted it immediately, too, and my whole body went cold, and I took a step backward, shaking in the wind. But my bracelet remained lifeless, inactivated, on my wrist.

Isolfr looked scandalized.

"The Mists?" he said. "No, never. It's true I'm not human, but you don't need to be human to live in this world, do you?"

Quiet settled around us, and I eventually shook my head.

Isolfr smiled again, although not as brightly as he had earlier. His smile was lovely, like the paintings in the capital, and I didn't like that I thought that.

"You never told me your name," he said.

I hesitated. I got no sense of danger from him, it was true. He waited for me to answer, moving with the rhythm of the waves. In a way, he reminded me of the illuminated ice Frida had shown me that afternoon. He was that lovely, that unearthly.

"Hanna," I finally said.

Nothing happened except that Isolfr smiled again. "It was wonderful to meet you, Hanna. I look forward to working with you."

He dove down into the depths.

"Working with me?" I said.

I stayed up on deck as long as I could stand it, shivering in the cold as I waited for him to return, to explain himself, but he never did.

When I cleared breakfast the next morning, I pulled out the bones from the fish we'd eaten and scraped them as clean as I could. They were small, flimsy things, but combined with the bones from lunch and dinner, I should have enough to cast a fortune-telling charm of my own. I didn't expect them to tell me what Isolfr was or what he wanted—a creature like that had surely protected himself with magic—but I did plan on asking where Kolur was sailing us to. Just because he wouldn't answer my questions didn't mean I couldn't get answers.

I wrapped the bones up in a handkerchief and slipped them under the blanket on my cot. Then I went back on deck, where Kolur and Frida had started up their duties for the day. A week in and we'd established a routine, one that hardly involved me. If Kolur was too lazy to return me and so had to force me to accompany him on his errand—I certainly wasn't going to call this an adventure, because it was far too dull—he could at least have found something for me to do.

The sails curved outward under the force of the brisk, strong wind, looking like fluffy white clouds against the cold steely sky. The air smelled sweet. I pulled myself up from the ladder and closed my eyes and concentrated, trying to feel for that presence I'd felt earlier—

But there was nothing there.

"What the hell are you doing?" Kolur's voice interrupted my concentration. I opened my eyes.

"Nothing," I called back. "Just like you want."

He shook his head and kicked at the boards. "Looked like you were in a damn trance. Don't get like that out here, girl. It could mean something dangerous."

"It wasn't anything dangerous. I knew what I was doing." I walked over to him. Frida was hunched over the map, as always, tracing a path with her finger. Yesterday, I'd tried to slide up beside her and peek at our navigation plans, but she'd slammed the lid shut with a gust of wind before I could see anything.

"Fine. But I don't know that." Kolur glanced down at me. "You know it's not just icebergs we have to worry about out here."

He was talking about the Mists. I suppressed a shiver.

"Funny," I said. "Frida told me the exact opposite."

Kolur rolled his eyes, but Frida smiled at us from across the boat.

"Frida's a troublemaker." Kolur paused. "You want to take the wheel for a little while? Should be fine, what with her melting charm going."

"Sure." It was something to do, and when I took the wheel from him, I felt the strength of the ship beneath my hands as it cut through the water. Kolur slouched beside me, his arms crossed over his chest—waiting for me to mess up, no doubt.

"Is it just killing you?" I said. "Letting me do some work for once?"

"Focus on the seas, girl."

We sailed on. The ocean glittered around us; the wind flapped at the sails and brought that scent of cold, frozen flowers. I thought about Isolfr emerging from under the sea, claiming we were going to work together.

"Kolur?" I said, still looking out at the horizon.

"Tired already?"

"No." I chewed on my bottom lip, trying to figure out what to say. As angry as I was with him, he needed to know about Isolfr. He was right—we were far north, and the waters were dangerous. Keeping Isolfr a secret meant putting the *Penelope* in danger.

"Well? Spit it out, girl."

"Last night, I saw a boy swimming in the water beside the boat. I spoke to him, and he said his—" I stopped. Kolur had wandered over to Frida, and they stood side by side, staring down at the navigation table.

Ice welled up in my stomach.

"Kolur!" I shouted. "I was talking to you."

He lifted his head. "What's that? You tired already?"

My hands trembled, my head spun, and anger flushed hot in my cheeks. The *Penelope* veered off to the port side, and Kolur gave a shout and came running up to me. He yanked the wheel out of my hands and righted our path. The sails snapped. Dots of sunlight scattered across the deck.

"Are you sure you're okay?"

"I'm fine. You're the one who keeps ignoring—"

He turned away from me and stared out at the water. The wind ruffled his hair. "Maybe we can have you send a note down to your mother next time we dock. Think she'd like to hear from you."

For a moment, I was struck by this new piece of information—the next time we dock? Where was it? Someplace with messengers, if we'd be able to send a note.

But then the implication of his promise struck me heard. He'd talked about docking, but not about Isolfr. He didn't hear me. I brought up Isolfr and he didn't hear me.

I stumbled away from him without answering. The wind roared in my ears.

Magic could do that. Magic, and not much else.

●   ●   ●

That night, I crept up on deck, the way I'd done every night since we left Skalir. But tonight was different. Tonight, the air itself felt sinister, like the wind was laced with poison instead of enchantment. I had my bones with me, still wrapped up in their handkerchief. And I intended to get some answers.

Kolur was sleeping at the helm, the steering charm glowing in the darkness. I crept up to the bow, where the wind was strongest, and closed my eyes to get a feel for its magic. It was strong tonight, a glimmer behind my closed eyelids, a tremor in my muscles. I pulled the wind's strength into me so that it was racing through my blood, sparking and shining. I opened my eyes and dumped the fish bones into my palm. They jumped with enchantment. My whole body thrummed, the magic rising and falling with the swell of wind.

I murmured the incantation and scattered the bones across the deck. Kolur snored in the distance. The bones arranged into their patterns. At first I thought it was a scatter of islands, some archipelago in the north that I didn't recognize, and my heart leaped— was this where we were going? Jandanvar wasn't an island chain, I knew that much. But then I looked closer and saw that the bones had fallen into bland nonsense: Friendship. A long journey. Magic.

"Worthless," I muttered. I gathered them up and tossed them again, this time trying to concentrate on a specific question: *Where are we going?*

The bones clacked across the deck. They had fallen into the exact same formation as before.

I batted them away in frustration, sending them scattering toward the mast. Kolur slept through it all. I stood up and shivered in the cold. Water splashed around the *Penelope*'s prow, spraying me with a frozen mist. Moonlight bounced off the water.

"Hanna."

I jumped. The voice was melodious and soft. Inhuman.

"You!" I grabbed the railing and leaned over the side. Isolfr floated in the water, his eyes wide and shining, gazing up at me. "Did you put a spell on Kolur and Frida?"

He slid into the water so that his shoulders and neck and most of his chin were submerged.

"You *did*." I clung to the railing like it could save me. "Kolur!" I shouted. "Kolur, wake up."

"He won't." Isolfr's voice was quiet, a rush of whispers to blend in with the roar of the sea. "He won't wake up."

I stared down at him. Cold horror crawled up the inside of my stomach. "What did you do to him?"

"Made sure he slept through the night." Isolfr rose out of the waves, looking indignant. "Maybe I was helping him. Frida Kuhn, too." He wore a dark tunic and his pale skin gleamed in the moonlight. "I just want them to sleep."

"No, you don't." I wished now I hadn't kicked my bones across the deck, since I would have liked something to throw at him. "What are you doing? What do you want?" I paused. "What *are* you?"

His eyes went wide again. If I hadn't known better, I'd have thought him scared.

"Well?" I said.

He dove under the water.

I cursed and screeched in vexation. Across the boat, Kolur snorted but didn't wake up.

"Answer me!" I shouted into the water. Isolfr was down there, a dark shadow moving beneath the waves. "Tell me what the hell is going on. What do you want?"

The shadow moved back and forth. I was certain it would disappear. But then Isolfr's head crept up, water streaming through his hair. He looked like silver.

"Am I going to get an answer out of you?" I demanded.

"Only if you ask the right question." His lifted his chin, almost like he was trying to be brave. My heart slowed. Maybe he really was scared. Now, there was a thought. That this strange shimmering magical creature was afraid of *me*.

"What are you?"

He shook his head.

"What do you want?"

He paused. Opened his mouth. Closed it. The water sloshed around him. Finally he said, "To help."

"Help with what?"

"I can't tell you yet." He paused. "There are—factors."

I sighed. "Fine. Why did you enchant Kolur and Frida? They ignore me if I try to tell them about you."

"They can't know about me." His eyes flicked back and forth. "It would be—dangerous right now. I can't reveal my identity to them. But I can reveal it to you."

"I don't know your identity."

"I told you my name."

I sighed and leaned my elbows against the railing. Even with my coat, I was getting cold out here. I rubbed my arms. It didn't do much.

"Are you cold?" Isolfr rose farther out of the water. "I can show you how to create a heat charm."

I looked at him, considering. The wind blew straight through me. But I shook my head. "It'd be easier if you just gave me some answers."

"I've given you what I can."

I sighed. "Why is it dangerous for you to tell Frida and Kolur who you are?"

He hesitated. "It's quite complicated," he finally said. "But

Frida Kuhn has—a history. She's known to be unstable."

I glanced over my shoulder, at the open hatch leading down below, where Frida slept. Kolur had said Frida was a trouble-maker—

"Don't lie to me," I said.

"I'm not." Isolfr shook his head, throwing off dewy droplets of ocean water. "I'm just saying she's a powerful woman."

I laughed. "Sea and sky, are you scared of her?"

Isolfr floated in the water and didn't answer me.

"What did she do?" I hesitated. "Am I in danger?"

"Not from her." Isolfr bobbed with the swell of a wave. "She wouldn't hurt you. But she did some magic, back when she was training in Jandanvar, that harmed my brother."

"She trained in Jandanvar?" I was startled and the question came out too loudly, my voice echoing out across the night. Isolfr dove below the water.

"Oh, for—" I rubbed my forehead. This was starting to get tiresome. "Come back up!" I shouted. "I'm sorry I startled you."

His eyes appeared. His nose. His mouth. He really did have a lovely face.

"So she trained in Jandanvar and hurt your brother." I sighed. "And you don't want her to know you're here."

He nodded. "She's frightening."

"Fair enough." I didn't add that he seemed a bit skittish in general. "All right, one more question. Do you know where we're going?"

He nodded. The sea foam shone around him. "You're going to a place in the north. But I can't say more than that yet."

"Jandanvar?" I leaned over the railing, far enough that my coat was dampened with sea spray. "It's Jandanvar, isn't it?" Anger swelled inside my chest. "That place is halfway to the Mists! They let people from the Mists wander their streets. What's wrong with Kolur?"

Isolfr didn't say anything.

I sighed and stepped away from the railing. The wind played with my hair. Clearly no one was interested in giving me a straight answer.

"So, why will you talk to me?" I said. "Am I not as frightening as Frida?"

"No, of course not." Isolfr gave a disarmingly handsome smile. "I am to help you, like I said, to work with you. What you said about Jandanvar isn't entirely true, by the way."

"What?"

"That it's halfway to the Mists. It's in this world."

"I know that," I said. "But they still let the Mists through there. And it's a place of dangerous magic; that's what everyone says." It had never occurred to me that witches trained in those cold, frozen lands, casting spells up to the swirl of Jandanvar's lights.

"People live there," Isolfr said.

"Not human people."

"Frida is human, and she lived there."

I scowled at him.

"You are right to fear the Mists, though. Those who mean us no harm never leave Jandanvar." He lifted his chest out of the water and looked me straight in the eye. I trembled from the cold. Still, I didn't dare leave him to slink down below where I could crawl into my bed sheets until I found warmth. He was giving me answers.

"You should watch for mist on the water," he said. "A certain type. Very thick."

"Oh, I know," I said. "What do you think I'm wearing this bracelet for?" I lifted my wrist up and shook the bracelet for him to see. It glowed in the moonlight.

Isolfr frowned. "That's weak magic."

"It's better than nothing." I folded my arms over the railing, and my breath puffed out as I spoke. "Besides, any child of the north has been trained to look out for the Mists since we were babies." I counted off with my fingers. "Unnatural gray mist. Folk with flat gray eyes. Unusual star patterns. We learn the constellations just so we can tell if the Mists have been changing the night sky."

Isolfr almost looked disappointed. I figured he had his whole speech worked up, trying to warn me about the Mists. "But many humans have gray eyes."

I shrugged. "Mama told me you'll know the difference when it's the Mists and when it's just a human."

His shoulders sagged and he shook his head, flinging dots of water across the ocean's surface. "It's not enough. You need to learn to recognize those creatures that are particular to the Mists. The ones that the people of the Mists control." He looked at me. "Here on the open sea, they'll fly or they'll swim."

"So does everything else."

He gave me an annoyed look. "Yes, but these will be creatures unlike any you've seen before. They communicate on the veins of magic running through our world, so you'll *feel* them coming, a tremor on the air."

I looked away from him, out to the wind-beaten ocean, and shivered.

"They often blend in with the light and shadow, reflecting their surroundings like mirrors. You have to look for disturbances just out of the corner of your eye." He paused, treading water and gazing up at me. "Has that ever happened to you? Have you ever seen something move just on the edge of your vision, but when you look over, nothing's there?"

I toyed with my bracelet, spinning it around my wrist. "Sure. Happens to everyone, doesn't it?"

"*That's* the Mists," he said, "moving along the roads between worlds. Be careful if you see it."

I nodded. The cold was working its way through my coat. I couldn't stay out here much longer.

"Be careful," Isolfr said, and then he dove back into the water.

This time, he didn't emerge again.

CHAPTER FIVE

We continued on our journey to the north, and I continued my nighttime visits with Isolfr. Talking with him was like trying to figure out a puzzle: I'd ask him questions, he'd give me vague answers, but only if he was of a mind to. Frustrating, to be sure, but exciting, too. Something to distract me from the boredom of life at sea.

"So, if you won't tell me what you are," I said, leaning up against the railing, a blanket pulled around my shoulders, on top of my coat, "can you at least tell me where you're from?"

Isolfr bobbed in the water. He looked like a patch of moonlight.

"I'm from up there," he said, and pointed straight to the stars.

"The sky?" I said. "You're from the sky?"

He nodded. "I miss it too. My family has a palace in the air, and it's quite a thing to see."

"I'd imagine so." I'd no idea if he was joking, if this was in any way an honest answer. I'd never heard of creatures living up among the clouds, but then, neither Mama nor Papa knew about much in the way of spirits.

Whatever Isolfr was doing down here, I suspected it was more involved than protecting the *Penelope* from the Mists. I also suspected he didn't want to do it. Now, he never came right out and said that, because Isolfr never came out and said anything, at least not anything useful, but I got the sense of it anyway from how wistful he'd look when he talked about his home up in the clouds.

And then one night, when we'd been talking for a week or

so, he startled me with a sudden burst of straightforwardness.

"Do you trust me?" he said.

I blinked at him in surprise. I was out at the bow, our usual spot. The nights kept getting colder and colder, and the stars were sharper now, like flecks of diamonds up in the sky.

"What?" I said.

"Do you trust me?" He sounded out of breath, like he was nervous. He lifted himself up out of the water, his eyes fixed on me.

"Truthfully?" I hesitated. Isolfr looked so hopeful I didn't want to tell him no. "I'm not sure."

He furrowed his brow and dropped low into the water. Even in the darkness, I could tell my answer saddened him.

"Wait," I said. "It's not—please don't take it personally."

He lifted his eyes, and that wounded expression made his features even more unearthly.

"You have to admit you're a little hard to trust," I said. "Since you can swim in freezing water and claim you live in the clouds." I paused. "And you keep warning me about the Mists."

"That's to help you." He pushed himself up. "I want you to trust me," he said. "I have to show you something and I don't want you to be afraid."

A chill went through me, and I wrapped my arms around my chest to keep warm. "This is new," I said.

"I've been delaying it." Isolfr looked down at the water. "Kolur is a fool, you know, and he's on a fool's errand."

"I'll have to take your word for it, because I certainly have no idea what he's doing. I keep pressing both of them, but they never give anything away. I'm not even sure when we'll be making port next." I clung to the railing and pressed myself over the side of the boat. The sea spray stung my face and made my eyes water. Clouds drifted over the moon, turning everything dark. "What do you want to show me? Is it related to where we're going?" I felt a little thrill of curiosity—maybe I'd finally found a way to get Isolfr to tell me what was going on.

"No." He hesitated. "It's related to—it's from—the Mists, actually."

"The what?" I jumped away from the railing. The open ocean was too open, and I felt exposed. "No. Absolutely not. You won't even tell me what you are, and now you—"

"I'm not from the Mists!" He drew himself up and his skin gleamed and his eyes flashed with a ferocity I would never have expected from him. "I'm trying to *protect* you from the Mists. And that's why I need to show this to you. *Please*." A wave swelled and almost swallowed him up. He looked deflated after his outburst, a piece of silk caught on the current.

"I was tasked with warning the *Penelope* of the danger she's sailing into." Isolfr's voice was quiet. I had to strain to hear it over my racing heart. "I was asked to show you the threat you've been facing. I've put it off, because—" The waves surged again. "Because I was afraid. But I can't delay any longer. So even if you don't trust me— you'll have to trust me."

He smiled then, that charming bright smile, but I could see through it. And what I saw was fear.

I thought about my family's stone cottage on the road to the sea. I thought about Mama's garden, the way it looked in the summer, when all the herbs were blossoming and the vegetables were growing. I thought about Henrik playing in front of the fire, about Papa coming home from his fishing trips smelling of the ocean, about Mama singing pirate songs as she swept dirt out the back door.

I wondered if I'd experience any of it again.

I looked down at Isolfr floating there in the dark ocean. His eyes reflected the starlight. In the last week, I'd begun to set aside the reality that he wasn't human. I hadn't even realized I'd been doing it until now.

"Please," he said.

"What are we sailing into that's so dangerous?" My voice wavered. "Just tell me. I've thrown the fortunes, and I didn't see anything—"

"Because this part of your future is blocked. But you're traveling north, to the far north, the top of the world." Isolfr swam up to the *Penelope* and touched his hands to her side, the first time I'd ever seen him do so. Nothing happened. The boat kept moving through the water. The protection charms didn't even ripple.

That, more than anything, convinced me.

"Jandanvar?" I said.

He didn't answer.

I threw my hands up in frustration. "I still don't understand why you won't just tell Kolur, if this is so dangerous. I don't have any control over what he does."

Isolfr's face darkened. "I can't tell him. I'm sorry."

I shook my head and the freezing wind blew my hair into my face. "This is pointless, Isolfr. Fine. Whatever you need to show me, show me."

There was a long pause. The wind picked up, blowing in from the north. I wrapped my arms around myself, trying to keep warm. One hand brushed against my bracelet, and the magic in it hummed, telling me everything was all right.

Isolfr climbed over the railing.

Out of the water, he moved like a dancer, graceful and serpentine. When both feet were on deck, he looked at me shyly. His hair clung to his cheek. Water pooled at his feet and shone on his skin. That dark tunic was plastered against him.

"Hello," he said, like we hadn't just been speaking.

"Hello yourself. Are you sure you're not cold?" I nodded at his soaking tunic.

He shook his head. The *Penelope* rocked in the frigid wind.

"Well?" I said. "What is it you want to show me?" My heart started beating fast when I asked the question. And the boat's rocking made my head spin.

Instead of answering, Isolfr began to sing.

I was startled to hear which song: it was one in the old language that I knew well, about an ancient queen who was the first to sail between the islands. A wizard's song. The words were carefully chosen, the sort of words with magic in them that would weave in with the invisible veins of magic flowing all around us.

As Isolfr sang, he knelt down on the deck, his eyes closed. He lifted his left hand in an arc, palm flat, and his right hand thumped out a beat on the deck. The wind roared, bringing snow and chips of ice and a faint sparkle that looked like stardust. I was too astonished to be afraid.

My eyes itched and watered, and I rubbed at them. Splotches of light appeared on my closed eyelids.

When I opened my eyes again, I was no longer standing on board the *Penelope*.

I screamed and whirled around. We weren't even at sea anymore. The sky overhead was the thick golden color of autumn sunlight. The ground beneath us was flat and reflective, like a mirror. When I looked down, I saw myself staring back at me.

My chest hurt, and I took deep breaths, trying to capture air. "Isolfr!" I shouted. "What the hell did you do to me?"

Someone grabbed my hand, a touch gentle and cold. Isolfr. I shrieked and pulled away from him, terror vibrating inside me. He let me go, saying, "Wait. Hanna."

"Where are we?" My voice bounced around in a tinny, haunting way. "What did you do? Sea and sky, I should never have trusted you! You're a monster, aren't you? You—"

He grabbed my hand again and squeezed. "You're safe," he said. "I swear it."

I shook my head, but my panic was ebbing in spite of myself. The golden light cast a sense of calm over everything. It was obviously enchanted, but it didn't strike any warnings with the magic residing inside me, or the magic residing inside my bracelet.

"We're in a liminal space," Isolfr said. "The place between worlds. No one can hurt us here. Feel." He squeezed my hand tighter. "Concentrate. You're a witch; you can feel it. We're safe."

His hand was as cold as the night air aboard the *Penelope*, but it was pleasant, like the day after the year's first snowfall. I concentrated, steadying my breath. He was right. That sense of calm came from a protection spell, a sort not so different from the one Frida had cast over the *Penelope*. Only it was deeper, and older, and stronger.

I'd never felt magic like it.

"We'll only be here a few minutes. I want you to meet someone, but we have to do it someplace safe." Isolfr let go of my hand and raised his own hands up over his head as mirrors of each other. "Gillean of the Foxfollow, I call you!"

His voice rang out, sonorous and rich. It didn't echo emptily the way mine had. I stared where Isolfr stared. I had no idea what I was going to see.

Shadows appeared, moving together into vague shapes. They lightened; they distorted. It was a man. A skinny man, with a mop of tousled gray hair and a shuffling, awkward walk. When he saw Isolfr, he let out a sigh.

"Mr. Witherjoy!" he exclaimed, clutching at his chest. "Oh, you had me for a fright."

"I'm sorry, Gillean, I couldn't warn you."

"Your name's Isolfr Witherjoy?" I said.

Isolfr tilted his head. "It's both. Hanna, I'd like you to meet Gillean of the Foxfollow."

Of course it was both. I'd just said that. I was about to protest when Gillean turned toward me, and my body froze.

His eyes were gray.

Matte gray, like stones.

He was from the Mists.

He gave me a bow, practiced and easy. I stared at him in horror.

"You lied," I said to Isolfr, my voice deep in my throat. "You are from the Mists."

Gillean laughed.

I turned sharply to him, wishing I had a weapon beyond my bracelet. I didn't keep a knife on me, not when we weren't bringing up the nets. There was no reason.

"Forgive me," he said, and he smoothed down his dusty old jacket. "The notion that Mr. Witherjoy would be from the Mists—" He chuckled again and shook his head. "I assure you, he's quite of your world." Gillean's expression softened slightly, and he said, "And I don't mean to harm you. I can't harm you, in fact, even if I wanted to."

The golden light brightened, and my thoughts were suffused with peace. A world built of a protection charm. This would be a place to live.

"Why did you bring me here?" I asked.

"I was wondering the same thing myself," Gillean said. He looked at Isolfr. "You said you wouldn't need to speak with me again, after the last time."

"I know. I'm sorry. My orders changed."

Orders? Who was he working for?

"I need you to tell her about Lord Foxfollow," Isolfr said.

"Who?" I said.

Gillean's face went pale. He trembled and rubbed at his shoulder distractedly. For all the stories I'd heard about the Mists, my first encounter with a man from those lands wasn't particularly frightening. And yet not even that golden light could melt away the tiny chill of fear still crawling under my skin.

"It's all right," Isolfr said gently. "It'll be just like before. I need her to hear, though, from you. If I could have found another way to do this, I would have."

Gillean hesitated. "And you're sure I'm protected?"

Isolfr paused, just for a fraction of a second, before answering yes. It left an uneasy feeling in my belly, that pause.

"I was valet to Lord Foxfollow," Gillean told me. "He is a dangerous man, my dear. He has tired of all the power in our world, and so he wants to go after yours."

"Is that where Kolur's going?" I said. "To meet with this lord?"

Gillean didn't answer. He had a glazed look, like the past had entangled him completely.

"I served as valet to his father, too," Gillean said. "That had been pleasant enough. But when he died, and this Lord Foxfollow assumed his title—" He closed his eyes. Isolfr moved forward by a step, one hand held out as if to catch Gillean before he fell.

Gillean took a deep, shuddery breath and regained his composure. Isolfr stepped back. "Oh, it was awful, my dear. He's an awful man. You wouldn't know it speaking to him, not at first, because he's quite charming. He always knows what you want to hear. It was through pure manipulation that he gained all the lands in the Mists. But I don't imagine your world will go so easily. You humans have always put up a fight."

I was at once horrified and bewildered. Of course the Mists

had tried to gain access to our world before—Ananna had stopped one such man, and her lover Naji had done the same long before he met her. But Ananna was a pirate queen and Naji was one of the Jadorr'a, and it made no sense to me that Kolur would be swept up in that sort of destiny. He was a fisherman. And not even a very good one.

"But the worst is when Lord Foxfollow's charm fails him." Gillean let out a ragged breath, and Isolfr moved close to him and put his hand on his arm. Gillean nodded. "When he can't manipulate you into doing what he wants, he sends out his horrors. They were formed out of the magic of our world, a dark spell banned many decades ago. Lord Foxfollow pays no attention to such rules. His horrors take no solid form. They're constantly shifting, constantly *changing*. I can't imagine the havoc they would do here if they were released. I remember when he sent them after his cousin Rothe, when he learned that Rothe had been meeting with one of Foxfollow's rivals. It wa—"

Another ragged breath. Tears shimmered on his cheeks. Isolfr wrapped his arm around his shoulder with a gentleness I didn't expect.

"It's all right," he said. "You don't need to go on if you don't wish to."

Gillean sighed, a shuddery, start-and-stop noise. "Thank you." He looked up at me. "Forgive me, Miss Hanna. I wanted to be more helpful to you."

He seemed so small and frightened, standing there in the golden light. He wasn't what I imagined the Mists to be at all.

"It's all right," I said. "I think you have—helped me." That wasn't true; I still didn't understand why Isolfr had brought me here, or what Lord Foxfollow had to do with Kolur. But Gillean looked so shaky and awful that I couldn't express my confusion out loud. I didn't want him to feel his pain had been for no reason.

"Give me a moment," Isolfr said. "I want to see him back to his home safely." He and Gillean walked several paces away from me. I fiddled with my coat and watched as Isolfr conducted a simple protection ritual. Wizard's magic; human magic.

Cold swirled through the liminal space, the first wind since we had arrived. I could tell that it came from somewhere else.

Isolfr kissed Gillean on the forehead, and then Gillean evaporated on the wind.

Everything stilled.

Isolfr turned back to me. I straightened up, ready to demand answers. Before I could, though, Isolfr said, "Blink."

"What?" I willed my eyes to stay open.

"Blink."

"No. Tell me what's going on." I opened my eyes a fraction wider. "You warn me about all this danger, and then when I ask where you're going, you just say *north*?" My eyes were dry and itchy. "You tell me to watch for the Mists, and then you bring me here and show me this poor terrified man who tells me that a man is after us, a man who's a terror in a land of terrors."

"It's not a land of terrors," he said quietly.

"Shut up!" My eyes burned. "He's going to send horrors after us? *Why?* What did Kolur do? Just tell me wha—"

We were standing aboard the *Penelope*. The wind rattled the sails. Kolur snored over by the helm. Everything was dark.

Gods damn him. I'd blinked.

"Thank you." Isolfr materialized at my side, his skin glowing silver like magic. It made him lovely to look at, but I shoved him away, furious.

"Tell me what's going on!" I shouted.

"I am!" Isolfr twisted his pretty features into a scowl. "Lord

Foxfollow knows that Kolur is coming. I can't warn Kolur myself, because it will only make matters worse. Kolur doesn't like me. So I'm warning you."

"What? Kolur doesn't like you?"

Isolfr pointed out at the sea. "Those terrors that Gillean spoke of are tangible. Real. Lord Foxfollow will find a way to send them through the gaps between the two worlds. I can't tell you what they'll look like, because they'll adjust to whatever veins of magic they came riding in on. They may be beautiful; they may be ugly. I hope they won't look like any creature you've ever seen before, but I'm not sure I can guarantee that either."

He took a deep breath. I gaped at him and shivered in the cold.

"I'm trying to keep you safe," Isolfr said. "It's my duty. I don't have any say in the matter. I can't explain further, not right now. But I won't let Lord Foxfollow hurt you. Any of you."

He stopped, his chest heaving. I'd never seen him so sure of himself, and it disoriented me, to see him standing on the deck instead of swimming in the sea, his expression burning and intense.

"I'm sorry," I said. "I just don't understand."

Isolfr's shoulders slumped. He looked sad. "You will, eventually. I promise." He put one hand on the ship's railing. "But you can understand this: feel the magic." He looked me right in the eye, and for a moment I was mesmerized. "Feel the wind. Don't worry about the direction. You're a strong enough witch that when the horrors come, you'll feel a shift, like the whole world's gone dark."

My heart fluttered at the thought that I was a strong enough witch, and so I nodded even though it wasn't much to go on. But before I could ask him to clarify, he vaulted over the side of the boat with a splash.

When I rushed up to the railing, the water was empty.

CHAPTER SIX

I didn't see Isolfr for four days.

It wasn't for lack of trying. I went up on deck at night, standing in the sweet-scented wind while Kolur snored on unawares. But the water stayed dark and empty, and I felt a dull ache inside my chest. Maybe I'd been wrong to trust him—he'd toyed with me, then left me alone without any real answers.

One night, I felt a presence on the wind, a sense of intelligence swirling around me. I tensed and grabbed for my bracelet, thinking back on the warning Isolfr'd given me about sensing the Mists' horrors. But this presence wasn't a horror. It was simply there, surrounding me and the boat and the ocean itself, like it belonged in this place.

During the days, I spent most of my time hanging around Frida, studying her hand movements as she called down the winds. Papa could do a bit of wind-magic, and he'd taught me what he knew, but it wasn't much. Frida was a real witch. Sometimes when she was tracking our path on the carved map, I stood a few paces away, behind the mast where she couldn't see me, shadowing her movements with my own hands. I wasn't trying to cast her spells. I just wanted to understand how the movements felt. She moved more like a dancer than a witch. Maybe that was the trick.

The day after Isolfr took me to the in-between place, I spent the morning watching Frida throw new protection spells over the boat.

"They wore out more quickly than I expected," she told me, rubbing the bannisters with sparkling ground conch shell. "The north is tricky."

My stomach tightened up. "Maybe it's not the north," I said.

She looked at me, her eyes clear. "Did something happen?"

I hesitated. Kolur still wouldn't listen if I tried to mention Isolfr, but Frida was a *witch*. She had trained in Jandanvar.

"This boy, Isolfr," I said. "He's been swimming alongside the boat. I let him aboard last night and he didn't hurt me at all, and I'm sorry if—"

But Frida had moved down the railing. The wind whipped her braid around, and she lifted her head and squinted at me. "You have to do much more spell repair once you pass Skalir. Everything's thinner here."

I sighed and dropped my head back. The sky was empty, a flat grayish blue that reminded me of the Empire mirror Bryn's mother kept in her bedroom. So Frida wouldn't listen when I said Isolfr's name either.

In those four days, we never saw any land, only hunks of icebergs that Frida or I melted or moved with wind magic. They made me feel lonely, those icebergs, drifting out here in this emptiness on their own.

One day at lunch, we all sat huddled around a heat charm, eating the dried salted fish from our stores. We still had enough for a couple of days of normal eating, plus more if we skimped. Neither Frida nor Kolur had said anything about it, though.

"How long till your errand's done?" I said, breaking the silence.

Kolur glared at me.

"I didn't ask when we'd be back home." The sails creaked overhead. "Just about your errand."

Frida sipped from her water skin, silent.

"I told you, girl, it'll only be a couple of weeks, and then I'll have you safely back on Kjora."

"It's been a couple of weeks." I pointed at the remains of our meal. "Are you planning to stop anywhere soon to restock? We're going to have to start taking rations, you know."

Kolur gave me a cool look and then turned to Frida. "How close are we to Juldan? I imagine we could stock up on supplies there."

"Oh, not far. A day's sail. Half a day if I can get the winds to behave. It's a bit out of our way, but nothing too terrible."

Juldan. I thought about Papa's carved map. Isolfr had told me the truth, then; we were far north, although not as far as Jandanvar.

But Juldan wasn't our destination. We were just resupplying.

I frowned across the meal at Kolur, wondering how much longer until I'd get to go home. I'd be much more excited about this adventure if we were actually doing something.

Kolur seemed to make sure he looked everywhere but at me.

I lay in bed that night, unable to sleep. Frida had done up the navigation calculations and announced that we'd be sailing into the Juldan port late tomorrow morning. My mind spun with plots to keep Frida and Kolur on land, to convince them to forget their madness and sail back to Kjora. Passage on a ship back to Kjora would be too expensive for a fisherman, and passenger ships were rare besides, so I figured I wouldn't be getting home otherwise. But maybe I could try to convince a crew into letting me join them. Ananna had done that. She'd spun a good yarn about betrayal and set sail that very evening. Maybe I could manage the same when we were in Juldan. I could call down the winds, after all, and it wasn't like Kolur needed me, what with Frida on board. Besides, if I joined with a crew, maybe I'd have a chance for a proper adventure, like the kind in stories.

But then my thoughts wandered away from the north. What if

sailing home to Kjora meant that this Lord Foxfollow would follow us there? What if going home meant bringing horrors back to my parents and Henrik and Bryn?

I wondered if that meant I believed Isolfr. If I trusted him.

Things didn't make sense.

I stayed awake through the night, staring up at the lantern's light sliding back and forth across the ceiling. The air crackled like a storm was coming. My body buzzed. I rolled over onto my side and slid my hand under the knot of fabric I used for a pillow.

Sparks shot up my arm, radiating out from my bracelet.

I shrieked and yanked off the bracelet and stumbled away from the cot, dragging blankets and my makeshift pillow with me. The bracelet glowed.

I knelt down beside the cot, my breath caught in my throat. The air around the bracelet throbbed, humming with enchantment. Slowly, I reached out with one finger and poked it, this time prepared for the spark. It trilled up my arm, igniting all the residual magic inside me. I closed my eyes and grabbed the bracelet in my fist and concentrated—

Gray mist. Sharp, curving claws. Black ocean water. Light. Light. Light dripping like blood. Mist.

A scream.

I dropped the bracelet and jumped back. The air was still crackling around me. I leaned up against the wall and took deep breaths and tried to decide what to do. Kolur, I had to warn Kolur. Or Frida. No, she would have sensed the magic before I did, she should already know—

I heard a noise.

It came from up on deck: a slurred thump, a muffled shout. I cried out and then slapped one hand over my mouth. I was so scared that I started to cry.

Footsteps bounded past the cabin door, coming from the direction of the storeroom. They disappeared and reappeared overhead.

I was too frightened to move. I closed my eyes and strained to listen. The wind whistled around the *Penelope*, and it sounded as if it were weeping, too.

I thought I heard voices, droning with a low murmuring panic. Sweat prickled over my skin.

Someone shouted.

I couldn't stay here. Isolfr had warned me about this. He had chosen me for whatever stupid reason, and now that the time had come, I just stood in my room and cried.

Kolur and Frida were hurt or dead, and I was left alone on the *Penelope* to die, too.

I snatched up the bracelet. It was cold, but it didn't make me see anything, thank the ancestors. I took a deep breath and eased open the cabin door. I leaned against the frame. I listened.

Voices.

As quick as I could, I darted into the storeroom and grabbed the big straight knife we used to clean fish. It still glittered with scales from the last time I'd needed it. I held the knife close to my chest. My bracelet burned me, it was so cold.

I slid forward, cautious, terrified.

The boat rocked with the weeping wind.

I finally reached the ladder, but my fear had me paralyzed. Voices drifted down from the deck, fevered and distorted from the wind. One of them sounded like a woman's. Frida. Maybe she was hurt. Maybe I could save her. I'd never saved anybody. But Mama had. And Papa, too. Maybe there was a first time for everything.

I clutched the ladder and heaved myself up, the knife sticking out at an awkward angle from my right hand. The cold wind blew over me. It smelled of the sea, and it smelled of blood.

I peeked my head up out of the hatch. All the lanterns had burned out and everything was cast in silver from the moonlight. Two figures were hunched over at the bow of the ship. A woman, a man: Frida and Kolur.

Frida's long, dark braid swung back and forth in the wind.

"Kolur?" I gripped the knife more tightly.

Kolur turned toward me. Something lay at his feet. "Hanna, get down below."

"No! What's going on?" I scrambled the rest of the way up on deck. Frida looked at me as well, her expression unreadable. "What is that?" I pointed with the knife at the lump at their feet. It didn't move.

The deck was smeared with brightness.

"Well?" I moved forward, faking a bravery I did not feel. "What is it? What's going on——"

I froze. The sails snapped in the wind.

The thing at their feet was a body.

A body on the deck. A body that bled light.

Isolfr. In the moonlight, his body shone like alabaster. I shook and trembled and a bile rose up in my stomach. The boat seemed to tilt on the waves.

But then Kolur moved toward me and no longer blocked the body's face, and I saw its features twisted up in an expression of fear.

It was Gillean.

Gillean of the Foxfollow.

The knife clattered to the deck. I stumbled backward. My foot caught on the edge of the hatch. Kolur grabbed me and pulled me forward. The sudden movement made my head spin.

"I don't know what's going on," Kolur said in a low voice. "I woke up, and I found——" He nodded his head in Gillean's direction. "You probably shouldn't see it."

I yanked away from him. The world seemed to have less air in it, like we were all underwater. Gillean stared blankly at me in the moonlight. Light smeared on his face, and there were ragged tears in his jacket, all soaked with that same bright blood. Bite marks. Slash marks.

From sharp, curving claws.

Frida put her hand on my shoulder. "Kolur's right," she said. "You should go down below. It's safer. We don't know how this man got here, but he's from—" She hesitated. "He's from the Mists. You can tell from the way he bled."

"I do." The confession erupted out of me. "I know how he got here." A tear streaked down my face. Another. Another.

"You what?" Kolur stomped up at me and looked me hard in the face. "What? How could you possibly know—"

"I told you!" I shouted. "Isolfr, the boy in the water! He introduced me to—to—" I couldn't say Gillean's name. My voice trembled. "It's Lord Foxfollow. He has horrors."

I could tell they didn't remember anything about Isolfr. And why would they? They were enchanted.

I grabbed my knife again and tore away from them, my tears hot and frustrated, and ran to the railing. The water was dark and still. No Isolfr.

"Where are you?" I whispered. I could feel Kolur and Frida staring at me. The horrors traveled on veins of magic, that was what Isolfr had said, and I had felt it earlier, the magic harnessed by my cheap protection charm from Beshel-by-the-Sea.

I grabbed the railing tight and closed my eyes and tried to feel the magic on the air. It hummed around me. Normal.

"What are you doing?" Frida's voice was too close. My eyes flew open. She stood beside me, the wind tossing her braid out over the water.

"I'm feeling for disruptions in the magic." I managed to keep my voice calm. "Lord Foxfollow killed Gillean—that man—and brought him here. Because he was—" I couldn't keep my voice calm for long. "Because he was trying to help me." The tears came again, this time so many that I could no longer see anything but smears of light. Frida drew me in close to her, and I buried my face in her shoulder. She smelled of life on the sea.

That kindness surprised me.

"The magic's fine," she said. "I felt the disruptions, too. That's why I ran on deck. But I assure you that whoever was here is gone now."

I pulled away from her and wiped my eyes.

"I didn't see anything," Kolur said. "Didn't hear anything, either." We all looked at each other. Not at Gillean. "I woke up when Frida came on deck." Kolur was pale in the moonlight. "Whoever it was didn't seem interested in hurting me, at least."

"We're under a spell," Frida said. "That's the only explanation. But I can't feel it."

"It's Isolfr!" I said. "Kolur never wakes up when I talk to him."

But they both ignored me. I couldn't feel Isolfr's magic either, only the wind, cold and sharp and steady. I looked out at the water. There was still a chance that Isolfr was responsible for all of this, that Lord Foxfollow was a fiction he'd created. He'd put Kolur and Frida under a spell, after all. Maybe I only trusted him because he was so disarming, so shy, so beautiful.

And yet my bracelet never burned when he was near.

"We ought to give him a funeral," Kolur said, interrupting my worry. "Some kind of ritual. Get him off the boat, at least."

Frida didn't say anything.

"Bad luck to toss a man unceremoniously into the ocean," Kolur said. "Creates ghosts, and you don't want them hanging around a boat."

"He's from the Mists." Frida's voice rang out. "Even you aren't that softhearted, Kolur."

Kolur frowned at her. "Ain't about being softhearted. You know that. You've seen it."

There it was, some hint at their history. But I wanted a funeral for Gillean too, and it wasn't because of ghosts.

"No," I said, and sniffled. "No, he needs a funeral. He wasn't a bad person. He tried to help us."

"What are you talking about? You've never seen him before."

I sighed with frustration. Isolfr claimed he wanted me to trust him, but he also made me keep his warnings from Kolur. His logic was incomprehensible.

Frida smoothed down her shirt with her hands, a nervous gesture. "In all likelihood, this is a Mists trap."

"It's not." Kolur turned away from her. "If it was a Mists trap, we'd be trapped."

I shivered.

"Hanna, come help me." Kolur dragged the chest containing our spare sails out from its place beside the masts. I glanced at Frida one last time, but she was gazing out at the ocean. She didn't look happy. I left her there and went over next to Kolur. He pulled out a stretch of fabric.

"Oh, drop the damn knife, girl. Frida'll watch out for us."

"She doesn't seem happy about us doing this."

"She hasn't had the run-in with ghosts that I have. I don't want to risk it." He nodded at me. "Help me with this sail. We'll wrap the poor boy up nice and neat."

I jammed the knife into the belt of my coat so I wouldn't have to set it down. Then I grabbed the rest of the sail and hauled it out of the chest. "Do you know any rituals?" I said. "Funeral rituals? For the Mists?"

Kolur stopped and squinted up at the moon. "What makes you think I know rituals for the Mists?"

"You've been keeping a lot of secrets lately."

Kolur looked at me. "My history ain't *that* interesting," he said. "And anyway it'd be dangerous to get involved with Mists magic. Northern rituals are fine. Just trying to keep the ghosts away."

"Are you sure?"

"Know more about it than you do."

I rolled my eyes. He glanced over at Frida, who was watching us with her arms crossed over her chest. "You ever think that maybe this doesn't have anything to do with us?"

She glared at him darkly and didn't respond.

It's a threat, I thought, but I didn't bother saying it aloud. Isolfr's spell would guarantee they forgot it as soon as the words left my mouth.

"We need your help," Kolur said to Frida. "You can keep watch over here."

Frida sighed and walked over to us.

"This is dangerous," she said, looking at the sail I cradled in my arms.

"You think I don't know that?" Kolur gestured at me to hand him the sail, but I hesitated.

"How dangerous?" I said.

Frida swept her loose hair away from her face and looked at me. "We don't always know what the effect of using our rituals on someone from the Mists will be," she said. "Our rituals might attract Mist attention."

"But I know damn well what's going to happen if we just toss him in the water," Kolur snapped. "The spirits'll be on us before morning. You know it too." He jerked his chin at Frida. She looked away, scowling.

"We're not in a good position," Kolur told me. "But I'm willing to risk it."

I nodded. I didn't want to toss Gillean into the ocean without a funeral either. He had tried to help me. He had been kind. Maybe our magic wouldn't mix badly with his. Maybe the Mists had left our world and wouldn't see what we had done. Maybe some things are just worth the risk.

"Now let's see that sail," Kolur said.

This time, I offered it to him. He grabbed one end and walked across the deck, spreading it out flat.

We worked in silence until Frida said, "I assume you keep a jar of anointing oil on board?"

"Bad luck not to." There was no gloating about Frida giving in. Everything was quiet and somber.

Frida nodded and went down below. Kolur and I stood side by side next to Gillean. The sail we'd draped over the deck lifted up on the wind.

I shivered.

"You cold?" Kolur glanced at me. "I'll tell Frida to charm one of her heat globes."

"No," I said. "I'm not cold."

The night seemed endless, swarming around us, trapping us. When I looked over the railing, I couldn't tell where the ocean ended and the sky began.

"Probably some victim from one of their squabbles," Kolur said. He shifted awkwardly, and I knew he was trying as best he could to be a comfort. "They'll send 'em through sometimes. Way of getting rid of the bodies."

There was no point in correcting him, so I just said, "All right."

Frida climbed back on deck. She had the little stone jar of anointing oil—it was whale fat, really, that had been infused with herbs and blessed in a ceremony out on the wilds of the tundra. All sailors kept a jar on board, in case of death. Without the ritual, a soul would be trapped in our world as a ghost, one of the legion of the dead who haunt the living. And you didn't want a ghost aboard a boat.

I thought about that time when I was a little girl and Papa made us all go inside and bar the doors. "They didn't do the ritual," he'd said, and all night we heard the shrieking and howling of that lost soul weaving its way through the village. So while I wasn't sure if the anointing oil would work on Gillean either, I didn't want to risk hearing those awful cries again. A cold wisp of dread twisted inside me and whispered that Gillean's death was my fault, that it was *Isolfr's* fault. He'd made Gillean speak. But Isolfr wasn't here to do his duty and bless the deceased. It fell to me.

"I'll do it," I said. "I'll bless him."

Kolur looked up. He'd already opened the jar. "You sure?"

At his side, Frida frowned.

"Yes. It's supposed to be a woman, anyway."

"It's supposed to be an acolyte of Kjorana," he said. "Which you are not."

I scowled. "I can stand in her place. Let me do it."

Kolur glanced at Frida, who remained stone-faced. But he handed me the jar without more fuss. It was heavier than I expected and warm from where he'd been holding it. I knelt down beside Gillean. His blood glowed all around me. Up close, his face seemed—surprised more than scared. I'd never seen someone die before. Maybe it was a surprise for your life to be snuffed out of you.

I dipped my thumb into the oil and took a deep breath. There were tears in my eyes. He'd been kind to me. He'd tried to help me, best he could. He wasn't the way the people of the Mists were supposed to be at all.

He'd been kind, and now he was dead.

I turned my face away from Frida and Kolur so they wouldn't see me crying. I pressed my anointed thumb against his forehead. His skin was warm like he was still alive. Startled, I snatched my hand away, expecting him to move. But he didn't.

In a blur, the incantation came to me—I'd learned it as a child, like all children of Kjora. "Release his soul to the great sea," I whispered. "Let him find his way home." I touched my thumb to both of his cheeks, then to his mouth.

A sighing filled the air, like a hundred birds taking flight at once. But there were no birds here. As quickly as it came, the rustling was gone, and I was certain I had imagined it. For a moment, I thought I saw a shimmer floating above Gillean's brow, like a slick of oil across the surface of water, but then that was gone too.

I straightened up and wiped my eyes as discreetly as I could.

"We'll need to wrap his body," Kolur said softly.

I nodded and set the jar aside. Frida moved to help us, all three of us kneeling alongside Gillean and then pushing him at the count, one two three, onto the sail. Now that he was facedown, I could see the huge, jagged tears in his back, all glimmering silver.

"Something bad happened to him," Kolur said, looking sideways at Frida. "Something very bad."

"I can see that," she said.

I didn't want to think about Gillean's wounds.

Together, the three of us wound Gillean up in the sail. His blood glowed dully through the fabric, like burnished moonlight. Kolur nodded at me, and he and I picked him up, end to end. It felt like casting a fishing net into the water. But this was all we had.

I reminded myself that Gillean's body was just a shell, that with the anointment Gillean himself had fled to the great sea, where he'd swim among the souls of ancient fishes. It was only his body going into the northern waters.

Only his body, torn to shreds.

Gillean's body landed with a splash and bobbed up and down with the waves. Kolur muttered a prayer to the ancestors and then turned away, but I stayed in my place, expecting Isolfr to appear.

He didn't.

The swath of fabric drifted off into the moonlight.

When I turned around, Kolur and Frida were huddled close to each other, not speaking. I watched them across the deck. Frida was the first to break the silence.

"I'll cast another protection charm," she said. "You likely just sent out a beacon for the Mists."

Kolur grunted. "You'd rather we keep the body on board, let him be a beacon for ghosts?"

She didn't answer, only looked at me one last time. I stared back at her, and I got the sense she was studying me, trying to make sense of what had happened. I tensed and waited for her to say something. But she didn't.

Frida faced the north and lifted one hand against the wind. The sails groaned as the wind shifted. I walked over beside Kolur, my arms wrapped around my stomach. I wanted to draw into myself and disappear.

"Don't worry, girl," he said. "I'm sure it was just bad luck."

I wondered how many times he was going to repeat that. I hated hearing it. I hated that I couldn't correct him.

"Still, I gotta admit, I'm not looking forward to sleeping up here alone." He looked over at Frida. The wind blew her hair straight back away from her face, and her magic settled over us, prickling and almost warm. "It's gonna be a long night till morning."

"I'll stay up here with you," I told him. "To keep you company." I smiled a little. It was the right thing to do, just like anointing Gillean and sending him out to sea despite the danger, even if Frida didn't see it that way. "I don't imagine I'll be getting much sleep tonight."

He laughed, although the laugh was thin and nervous. Frida's protection charm pulsed through the wood of the *Penelope*. She dropped her hand and the sails swung back to accommodate the northern wind.

She walked over and stood beside us. "I'll stay on deck tonight, too," she said. "It's not a night to be alone."

I wasn't going to argue that point, and I wasn't going to deny the protection of Frida's magic, either. Better to have it there than nothing at all.

Dawn broke after an uneasy night. I only realized I'd fallen asleep when I awoke to a beam of pink sunlight settling across my face. I was curled up beneath a pile of seal furs, sleeping on a hammock I'd tied between the foremast and the mainmast. Frida slept on beside me. Kolur was up at his usual place at the wheel, sleeping too.

Everything was calm.

I crawled out of the hammock and stretched. My head was fuzzy. In the soft light of morning, it was hard to believe that last night a man, a man who'd been trying to help me, had died. Except I didn't have to believe it. I knew it had happened, and the pale stains soaking into the wood of the deck were just more proof.

I wanted to distract myself, so I set about checking the rope and the enchantment on the sails. I made sure that all the other magic running the boat was in order. Frida's charm was still in place, strong and steady. All of Frida's navigation notes were locked away, but I checked the carved map, placing my finger on the spot of ocean where I thought we were. Juldan was only a few finger widths away.

The *Penelope* glided slowly through calm waters. I wandered over to the bow and cast the charm to look for ice, just to have something to do. But I didn't find any; the water stayed dark and murky as always. In truth, I was as much watching for Isolfr as I was for ice. But I wasn't sure what I'd say, what I'd do, if I found him.

He'd put Kolur and Frida under a spell. Maybe he'd done the same to me.

I leaned against the railing, breathing in the cold scent of the sea. I wondered if Gillean's soul had found its way. Even in the calm, lovely morning, remembering his face made my stomach flop around.

I was still staring out at the water when I noticed something flicker beneath the surface.

"Isolfr?" I whispered. "Is that you?"

No answer.

"If it is, you better get up here. Something terrible has happened, and——"

The flicker beneath the surface skipped away. Probably just a fish. I leaned back.

The flicker returned.

It was stronger this time. Brighter. It didn't move like a fish. *Flicker* wasn't really the right word—*swirl*, maybe. Like cream dropped into the hot black coffee Mama fixed sometimes.

Only this felt—sinister.

And my bracelet was growing cold.

I didn't move from my spot, only kept my gaze on the place where the brightness swirled around in the water. Maybe it was magic left over from the ice-finding spell. But if that was the case, I knew, then my bracelet wouldn't be burning into my arm.

The swirl thickened, became solid. It rose out of the water, a thick gray mist.

"Kolur!" I screamed. "Frida!"

The mist rose and rose until it formed the shape of a person. Two bright eyes appeared. They blinked once.

The magic inside of me rioted.

The mist-man disappeared.

"Hanna!" Kolur pulled me away from the railing. "Don't let them see you."

I was dizzy. Frida was already at the railing, drawing up the wind. I closed my eyes and concentrated, trying to feel for abnormalities. But my heart was racing too fast. I couldn't get a hold of anything.

"They're close by." Frida turned toward us. "That was a scout. We need to get down below, into the cabin. Hanna and I—" She hesitated, just for a second, her eyes flicking over to Kolur. He stared blankly back at her. "Hanna and I will have to use what magic we can down there. It'll be easier to protect a smaller area."

Kolur nodded. "Hanna, do as she says. Gather up your strength, girl."

I wasn't sure that was possible right now. "This is because of us," I said. "Because of the body. They followed it—" I felt sick. The funeral rituals. All I'd wanted was to honor Gillean, and now look what had happened.

"Don't think about that," Frida said. "Come." She put her hand on my back and turned me toward the hatch leading down below.

And then we both stopped.

I was certain we saw it at the same time.

A warship, towering toward the sky, big enough to cast a shadow over the *Penelope*. It looked carved out of gray stone, and towers rose up from its deck instead of masts, all of them billowing mist.

It was sailing right toward us.

I froze in place, trapped by the warship's shadow. Beside me, Frida cursed, then shouted Kolur's name.

"I see it!" he called out, his voice strained and small.

The ocean churned around the warship's prow, frothy and grayish white. I couldn't see anyone moving on its deck. It was a hollow, empty ghost.

"It's the Mists, isn't it?" I asked.

Frida hesitated for a moment. Then she said, "Yes. I think so."

After we had cast Gillean into the sea, he had drifted toward the west, sinking as he went. Trailing light. And now this ship, huge and monstrous and run by magic, was sailing toward us. From the west.

I thought it was the right thing to do, casting the rites. He died because of me. But now we were going to die too.

Kolur shouted behind me. I couldn't make out what he said, his words distorted by my panic. But Frida called out, "Right away!" and bounded off.

I still couldn't move.

"Hanna!" My name rose out of Kolur's shouting. "Hanna, get the hell away from the railing!"

An enormous dark wave, rising from the warship's path through the water, swelled underneath us. The *Penelope* rocked back and I went skittering across the deck, landing hard on my back next to the masts. For a moment I stared, dazed, at the pale blue sky.

"Hanna!"

The boat lurched.

That broke me out of my spell. I scrambled to my feet, clinging to the mast for support. Kolur glared at me over at the helm, where he was fighting the wheel for control of the *Penelope*.

"Turn the sails!" he roared. "That ship's not turning away."

I nodded.

"Don't use magic. It's too dangerous right now." The wheel

whipped out of his grip and went spinning, and the boat spun with it. Everything tilted to starboard. I toppled sideways, grabbing on to a loose rope before I tumbled over the railing. As soon as we righted again, I went to work, loosening the knots and dropping the sails. Kolur's words echoed in my head—*don't use magic*. I listened to him. Now was not the time to be contrary.

We rocked back up. I stopped thinking about Kolur's orders and just acted on them. I'd shifted the sails plenty of times without magic, but always on calm seas, and never when the situation was so dire.

The boat tilted again. Freezing seawater splashed over me, so cold I gasped and nearly dropped the rope. Shivering, I drew the rope tight and tied it off in its new position, although my hands trembled so badly, I was afraid I wouldn't be able to make the knot.

I tied off the second rope just as the boat lifted up on a great wave. For a moment, we stayed there, at its peak, higher than a fishing boat should be. The air sighed around us. The warship was close and so tall that it blocked out the sun, and I clung to the mast and stared up at it. Figures stood up on deck now. Men with no faces, lined up in rows, watching us.

It was the longest second I'd ever known.

And then we plunged back down. Seawater poured over the deck, burning with cold.

In the shock of that freezing water, magic stirred. Wild magic, tumultuous and deep and unfathomable. I held on and stared at the dark gray side of the warship, and I knew I was going to die.

Water rose up around us, glittering in the sun.

The magic tasted like salt on my tongue.

And then the ocean crashed down on the *Penelope*, and for a moment, all I saw was light splitting through the murk, and all I felt was a cold so deep, it sank straight to the marrow of my bones.

Then darkness.

CHAPTER SEVEN

In my dreams, I heard the sharp cry of a seabird.

My dreams were unclear, nothing but murky shapes in the dark, momentary dots of brightness, a sense of floating in thick air. That bird cry was the only moment of lucidity.

It happened again, louder.

Again.

The murk brightened and cleared away. I felt the ground beneath me, rough and cold, and I smelled pine. In the distance, someone sighed, over and over.

I pushed myself up to sitting and blinked, trying to clear out the shadows. Slowly, shapes formed: a march of trees in the distance, smooth gray pebbles underneath me, the ocean. That was the sighing, I realized. The ocean, rolling in along a shore.

I was on a shore. I was dry, by some gift of my ancestors, and I was alive.

I stood up, my legs shaking. The tide was out and dark seaweed dotted the beach in clumps.

There was no warship anywhere.

Relief flooded through me and turned to hysterical laughter that echoed up and down the beach, blending with the rush of the waves. I turned in place, taking in my surroundings. I didn't see the warship, didn't see any hint of the Mists at all—but I didn't see Kolur either. Or Frida. Or the *Penelope*.

"Shit," I whispered. A wind blew in from the north, tousling my hair. I turned left and right, trying to decide which direction to go first. We must have washed ashore Juldan, protected and unharmed—there had been that surge of magic before the world went dark. It wasn't borne by the wind, so it wasn't Frida's. It had been borne by the sea. Kolur? I couldn't imagine it. Of all the explanations of his behavior, the idea that he was a powerful wizard was the most absurd. I just couldn't accept it.

Following some instinct burning inside of me, I went left. The wind pushed me along. I still wasn't entirely in my right mind; everything was trapped in a pale haze, and I stumbled over the unfamiliar beach, afraid of what I would find. Or of what I wouldn't.

I didn't know how long I walked. Everything on the beach looked the same—the trees, the seaweed, the stones. Despair crept up on me, worse than the cold.

Maybe I wasn't alive at all. Maybe that's why I was dry. This wasn't a blessing from my ancestors at all. I stopped walking and stared down at the ground, and tears welled up in my eyes. I'd never felt so empty, so alone.

And then I saw it. A piece of broken board. Smooth, polished birchwood.

The same as the *Penelope*.

I bent down and picked it up. It was damp with seawater, but other than that, it was just a broken splinter of wood. Seeing it gave me a shuddery feeling like I was too cold.

I tucked it under my arm and kept walking.

As I walked, I found more hunks of wood, all that same polished birchwood as the *Penelope*. That shuddering turned heavy and settled in my stomach, and I walked as quickly as I could. It didn't take long before I saw a dark lump farther down the beach. It didn't look like a ship, even a wrecked one. I stopped and stared at it, still holding that first piece of wood close to my heart. The lump looked like a much larger version of the clumps of seaweed that had washed ashore.

The north wind blew. I moved forward.

The lump was a towering mass of seaweed, dark and stringy and swaying back and forth from the wind. It was taller than me. As tall as a fishing boat.

The sick feeling intensified.

"Hello?" My voice sounded small. "Kolur? Frida?"

I edged closer to the mound of seaweed. The air crackled with leftover sparks of magic. This was the *Penelope*, I was certain of it, but she'd been transformed. Magic can do that, when you use too much at once. It changes the ordinary into the extraordinary.

I reached out my hand, the hand wearing my bracelet, and ran my fingers over the seaweed. It made a chiming noise, and the blood in my hand jolted. Beneath the sweep of seaweed, I could make out the dark wood skeleton of the *Penelope*.

A boat was one thing. But if Frida and Kolur had still been aboard when this happened—

"Kolur!" I shouted, louder this time. My voice carried on the wind. "Where the hell are you?" I whirled in place, feeling wild and out of control and alone. The whole world was empty. "Kolur!" I screamed. *"Kolur!"*

"Quiet, girl. You make enough noise to wake the dead."

I thought I imagined his voice at first. It seemed to come from everywhere. But I realized that was just the wind, and when I whirled around, kicking up sand, I saw him shambling toward me. He was pale and his face was ragged, but he didn't seem hurt.

"Oh, sea and sky, you're alive." I slumped with relief. "I thought I was alone here. I thought I was *dead*—"

"Not so lucky, I'm afraid."

I scowled at him for making such an awful joke. But he only

squinted up at the *Penelope*. "Shit," he said matter-of-factly.

"Will Frida be able to fix her?" *Was Frida even alive?* "Or are there wizards in Juldan——"

Kolur glanced at me, frowning. "I don't know. Probably have to get a new one."

"A new——" The air escaped me. A new *boat*? "We can't afford that, can we?" Did Kolur have money? Why hadn't he sent me home in Skalir?

Kolur shrugged. "Depends on where we are. Not every transaction requires money."

"Depends on where we are?" I blinked and looked around, at the sea and the trees. "Aren't we in Juldan?"

Kolur looked over at me. "There was magic involved in setting us free," he said after a moment. "Surely you felt that. We could be anywhere."

Frida. Or maybe Isolfr. He could swim in the frozen ocean; perhaps he could channel enchantment through it as well.

"We need to find Frida," Kolur said. "I take it you haven't seen her."

"You mean you haven't?" My sick feeling returned, stronger than before. Isolfr might have sent us here, but Frida would be the one to get us home. That was the whole reason Kolur had brought her aboard.

"She'll be around her somewhere." He walked out past the remains of the *Penelope* and gazed down the shoreline. "This way." He pointed to the left.

"How do you know?"

"Just a feeling. Come on."

I joined him, and we walked down the beach in silence. The old magic radiating off the boat muffled the air around us, muting everything. I hadn't noticed how drained the colors were until I saw the *Penelope*. Now I couldn't not notice.

We hadn't been walking long when I spotted a streak of brown against the gray expanse of the rocks. "Look, there." I pointed. The streak wasn't moving. "You think that's her?"

"Might be. Too far off to tell." But Kolur broke into a jog and I followed along behind him, cold air burning in my lungs. When I was close enough to see it was Frida, I began to run.

She didn't move.

I knelt down beside her and pressed my fingers under her nose. Still breathing. Kolur's footsteps crunched over the stones. He wasn't in much of a hurry.

"Frida!" I shook her arm. She had all the magic; she would be able to get us to safety. "Frida, wake up."

Her eyelashes fluttered. I shook her harder. By now Kolur had joined us, and he said, "Frida, open your damn eyes."

She did.

"Well, that was exciting," she said. "You know I hate the water, Kolur."

Kolur laughed. "We do what we have to do."

"What?" I said.

They both ignored me. Frida sat up and shook out her hair. Then she patted it with one hand. "Dry," she said. "Thank you."

I swiveled to look at Kolur. There was no way he'd done this. Kolur bought his charms from shops in the capital. He made me do all the magic on board the *Penelope*. He was a fisherman, not a wizard.

But Kolur didn't respond to Frida's thanks, just stuck out one hand to help her to her feet. She accepted it and, once standing, put her hands on her hips and glanced around.

"Where are we?"

"Don't know," Kolur said.

"The *Penelope*?"

"Damaged," I said. "Magic-sickness."

"Figures." She took a deep breath, clearly less upset by this situation than I was. Both of them were, but Frida's nonchalance was more frustrating. Kolur never told me anything. But Frida was a witch, a real witch. She had been to Jandanvar; she had seen the magic at the top of the world. And all the little charms she'd taught me aboard the *Penelope* didn't make up for the fact that she kept Kolur's secrets for him.

I was worked up enough to demand an explanation when Kolur said, "I figure we should keep walking west. Bound to run into someone sooner or later."

"How do you know that?" I said. "How did any of this happen? How are we all still alive?" Questions tumbled out of me, one after another. "And that warship! What happened to it? Is it going to come after us?"

"Oh, it's still out there," Kolur said. "But we got some time before it comes after us again."

"How do you *know* that?" I shrieked, but I knew I wasn't getting answers from either of them. They were already walking down along the waterline, heading to the west.

I hated them both. I was glad they were alive, but I hated them more than I ever hated anyone. Even Isolfr. He had at least *warned* me about the Mists. Not that I'd been able to do anything about it.

I ran after Kolur and Frida, stumbling over the stones. They both trudged along in silence. We followed the gentle curve of the beach, not passing any houses or boats or people or animals. No signs of civilization. Uneasiness peeked through my anger, and I thought about the chains of uninhabited islands, places where no creatures could survive.

"How do you know we're going in the right direction?" I asked when I couldn't stand the silence anymore. "There's nothing here but trees."

Kolur glared at me. "I know, girl." He jerked his head off to the west. "We landed a bit farther off than I expected." He turned away and took to walking again. Frida did her best to ignore both of us.

"Than you expected?" I caught up with him. "So you can do that kind of magic, then?"

Kolur grunted. "Plenty of people can do that kind of magic."

"Sea and sky, I am so sick of you not answering my questions."

"Stop, both of you." Frida stood a few paces ahead of us, pointing at the sky. "There's smoke."

She was right; a thin gray twist curled against the sky.

"Ah, finally." Kolur took off again. I glowered after him. I'd every intention of returning to that conversation, even if I had to make him listen to me.

Seeing the smoke did give me hope, though. There were others here. We weren't stranded on one of the empty islands.

It didn't take long before we had circled around the bend and come across a round fabric tent. Smoke drifted out of a hole at the top of the roof. There was no garden, only hard frozen soil, but the rocks had been arranged like a path leading to the tent's opening, and that gave it a feeling of permanence.

"Huh," Kolur said. "Don't look Juldani, does it?" He glanced at Frida, but she only shrugged.

I had no idea what a Juldani tent looked like. My anger with Kolur flared again, that he'd lived the sort of life where he would know that, and he chose to keep it a secret.

Kolur walked up to the door and tugged a rope attached to a metal bell. A few moments later, an old woman answered. Her hair was knotted up in a brightly embroidered scarf that made her face look perfectly round.

"Excuse me, ma'am," Kolur said, speaking with a sharp, prickly dialect I didn't recognize, "but would you mind telling us what island we're currently on?"

The woman scowled at him. "Lost your way, did you?" Her dialect wasn't the same as the one Kolur spoke, but it wasn't much closer to the Kjoran way of speaking I was used to.

"I imagine this must happen to you frequently," Kolur said. "Weary, confused sailors finding their way to your door."

This didn't sound like him in the slightest. He was being polite, for one. I didn't like it. I snuck a glance at Frida, but she had her arms crossed over her chest, looking bored.

"No," the old woman said, "it doesn't. Because most sailors aren't so stupid as to get blown off course." She poked her head farther out the door and looked at each of us in turn. "Not much of a crew."

"They're better than they seem," Kolur said.

That *really* didn't sound like him.

The woman made a scoffing noise. "You're in Tulja," she said.

Tulja. The name was foreign and unfamiliar, and I was struck with a flurry of panic that it wasn't Juldan, or even Jolal, which was only a day or so farther north. Tulja? I couldn't even remember it on Papa's carved map.

"Rilil is up the road there, if you're looking for sailing work." The woman scowled at us again. "Now, if you'll excuse me, I have business to attend to."

She yanked the curtain shut. Kolur turned to face us, and before I could start in on him, Frida did it for me.

"Tulja!" she said. "You brought us to Tulja?"

There it was again, the idea that Kolur had done magic.

"Didn't mean to. It's farther north than we were, though." Kolur grinned. "Let's see what we can find in Rilil, shall we? I hope someone's selling a boat." He breezed past us and made his way to the frozen dirt road the woman had pointed to. I hung back with Frida.

"How did he bring us here?" I asked her.

She sighed and ran her fingers through her hair. "I'm not the one to answer that, I'm afraid."

"Gods! No one will tell me anything."

"Because you're young and ignorance will better serve you. Come, before Kolur leaves us behind."

I couldn't believe she'd said that to me. I stood in front of the old woman's tent, watching Frida hurry to catch up with Kolur. Ignorance would better serve me?

I thought of Isolfr then, and Gillean. Isolfr had tried to tell me about Lord Foxfollow, and Gillean had died for it. And look at all the good it had done. The warship still attacked us. We were still trapped here on Tulja—wherever Tulja was.

I realized Kolur and Frida seemed in a mind to leave me. "Wait up!" I shouted, and ran up the road to catch up with them. Panting, I said, "So where is Tulja, exactly?"

"North," Kolur said. "A bit longer of a sail than I expected."

"How long?"

He didn't answer.

"How long, Kolur?"

"Nothing you need to worry about. We'll be in the town soon."

I fumed. My anger was like magic, propelling me along the slippery, miserable road. I gave up trying to ask questions, because I knew it would just leave me angrier than I had started. My mood did not make for a pleasant walk.

After a while, we began to pass more signs of life. There were round white tents, and a handful of little stone huts, and fences that held in great shaggy horned creatures that stared at us with the doleful eyes of deer and caribou. Every now and then, we'd pass someone standing outside one of those houses, and they studied us like we were a danger. That sense of hope I'd got from the smoke seemed ridiculous now. So there were people. What if they refused to help us? Or mistrusted us enough to attack us?

Civilization suddenly seemed more dangerous than the wild.

The ground was patched with snow, and ice daggers still hung from some of the fences. We were much farther north than we should be.

Eventually, the tents and grassland gave way to something like a proper town, although the buildings were really just mounds dug out of the earth, some of them augmented with stone or grass roofs or scraps of that same thick fabric that had made up the old woman's tent. Everything was crammed in close together. The roads remained unpaved, and the signs hanging next to the doors were painted with unfamiliar letters. Pictures, really. I squinted at them as we went past, but I couldn't read them.

Kolur could, however, because he stopped in front of a sign jammed into the ground next to one of the larger mound-buildings and said, "We need to eat. Get up our strength."

I wasn't hungry. But Kolur and Frida both ducked inside, and I wasn't about to let them leave me alone.

It was a mead hall—the sort of thing, in Kjora, you'd find standing alone in the wilderness. It was odd to see one in a town, even as small and semi-permanent a town as this one. Faces turned toward us as we walked in. Mostly men, their hair long and plaited. They turned away from us just as quickly. It was a relief to know we weren't of interest.

Kolur led us to a table in the back, one that was shoved up against a stone-lined wall, underneath a sprawling set of antlers. "Sit here," he said. "I'll tell the mead master we'll be wanting some food."

I hadn't realized how exhausted I was until I sank onto the hard, rough-hewn wood of the bench. My legs seemed to dissolve away from me, and every joint in my body was filled with a dull, distant ache.

"He's right, you know." Frida peered at me in the smoky candle-light. "We need to rest. Gather our strength. That magic took a lot out of us."

"The magic," I said. "It wasn't yours."

"I won't give you your answers." She tilted her head. "Ask Kolur."

"Kolur won't tell me anything." I glared down at the table. Voices rose up in waves, laughing, shouting lewd remarks at one another. It was the sort of place Mama would love but wouldn't let me go; the sort of place Papa would hate, and not on my behalf, either.

I missed them.

"They've got eel pie on the menu today." Kolur's voice boomed out behind me, and he slid into place on the bench, depositing a trio of mugs filled with frothy dark ale. "Drink up. You too, Hanna." He nudged the mug toward me. I just stared down at it balefully.

"How did we get here?" I asked.

"We walked."

I lifted my face to him, my cheeks hot with anger. My hands shook. "You know that's not what I meant."

"For the grace of the ancestors," Frida said, "just tell her." She sipped at her ale. "This whole thing hasn't exactly been the quick errand you promised me, either."

"What is going on?" I shouted, loud enough that it caused a momentary pause in the surrounding chatter. Kolur ducked his head and looked down at his ale. I was too angry to care. "An errand?" I snarled at him. "And the Mists are after us—I know who was behind that warship. Lord Foxfollow."

I was hoping Isolfr's spell wouldn't work when we were on land, hoping that it was tied in some way to the *Penelope*. And for a moment, it looked like my hopes might pay off—Kolur's eyes flickered with confusion. "How did you—" He stopped himself. "Drink your ale, Hanna. Food will be here soon."

He was still blocked. I slumped down and took a long drink in frustration. The ale was bitter and thick, like soil. Drinking it made my stomach woozy.

How did you, Kolur had said. How did I what? How did I know? Was he familiar with Lord Foxfollow?

"The Mists," I said. "Lord Foxfollow. Why are they after us?"

Kolur and Frida stared at each other across the table, Frida glowering at him like she wanted to scold him.

"We'll be gone months," she said.

"Months?" I squeaked.

Kolur looked at me then. He swirled his ale around in his cup. "She's right," he said. "I should tell you."

I didn't believe he would. This whole conversation was piecemeal anyway, what with how he couldn't hear half the things I had to say.

"The Mists are after us," he said.

"I know!" I slammed my cup down. "I've been saying—"

"Specifically, they're after me. I thought I'd be able to avoid them while I took care of things, but—" Kolur scratched at his head. "I haven't been entirely honest with you."

Frida gave a snort of laughter, but I just glared at him. "I noticed."

"I don't mean just in the last few weeks. I mean—well, pretty much since I met you. Since I met your mother." Kolur drained the last of his ale and wiped his upper lip dry. "I ain't a fisherman. At least, not by training. I'm a wizard. A waterwizard. I learned my trade on the seas of Undim, in the far north—"

"Almost to the top of the world." I was suddenly too dazed to be angry. The magic during the battle had belonged to him. And if he trained on the Undimian sea, that put him in a very special class of wizards indeed. Most people do magic. But only some people can *do* magic, can do it well enough to make it their calling. Those people learned at the Undim citadels. That was where I'd always wanted to learn.

"Then why—"

"It's a stupid story." Kolur laughed a little. "There was a woman. A, well, a queen. The queen of Jandanvar."

"The *what?*" I squawked, loud enough to draw stares.

"I met her shortly after I finished my training. She came out to see all the new wizards, in this big glass boat, the sunlight sparkling everywhere—"

"Get on with it," Frida said.

Kolur shot her a dark look. "Fine. We met. Fell in love. You know how it is."

I didn't really, but I didn't say anything.

"But the problem with falling in love with a queen is there's a certain expectation that you'll be king." He grunted and turned toward the center of the hall, where a big clump of sailors was singing old drinking songs. "I didn't want that. I didn't even want to live in Jandanvar, much less rule it. I tried to convince her to run away with me, down to the south, the far south, to the Empire. But she wasn't going to do that. We were at a bit of a stalemate."

"A stalemate," Frida said. "You're both stubborn asses; that's the problem."

"What does this have to do with anything?" I said. "You're this great wizard and you've been living as a fisherman for the last ten years? All because you didn't want to be king? Who doesn't want to be king?"

"Anyone with half a thought in his head." Kolur leaned back. "I went to the citadels because they recruited me. I had the touch, they said." He wriggled his fingers. "But I'd always wanted a simple life."

I rolled my eyes.

"I was a fool," he said, "to leave her the way I did. I got scared. But that's why we're out here, to set things right." He glanced at Frida, glanced back at me. "We're going to Jandanvar."

I stared at him. His admission rang in my ears. I knew it.

"When I called on the favor of the sea, I asked her to take us as far north as she could. That brought us here, to Tulja." He coughed. "We're about three months' sail from Juldan."

All the sound went out of the room. My ears buzzed, my heart raced. Three months away. "Were we—have we been *out* for three months—"

"Oh no," Frida said quickly. "Only about a day or so. We traveled on the magic."

I looked at her, and then I looked at Kolur, and then I took a drink. It burned the back of my throat.

"It was quite safe," Kolur said. "No need to worry."

I glared at him. "I didn't even know you could do that sort of magic until just now. Don't tell me it was *quite sa*—"

"Three eel pies." It was the server, a girl in a long brown dress. She dropped the pies on the table along with a trio of dinner knives. The pies smelled salty and rich, and my stomach flipped over a couple of times.

"Ah, that's better." When Kolur cut into his pie, steam billowed up into the air, and the smell of cooked eel was even stronger.

"You really ought to eat," Frida said. "It can make you sick if you don't."

I glared at her, but I knew she was right. If we'd been traveling along veins of enchantment, my body would need to fight off that desire for transformation that occurs whenever too much magic gathers at once. I cut off a tiny slice of pie. It was better than I expected, the wild taste of eel tempered by some pungent, savory herb I couldn't identify. With that one bite, I realized just how hungry I was, and I ate the rest of the pie quickly, hardly stopping to taste. Having a full belly renewed my strength. And renewing my strength gave me even more incentive to get answers out of Kolur.

"So why are we sailing to Jandanvar?" I demanded. Kolur was only half finished with his pie, and he glanced up at me, amused. "What does all of this nonsense you've told me have to do with the Mists?"

"Done already? And you're the one who said you didn't need to eat."

"Kolur," Frida said, making his name into an admonishment.

I pushed my plate aside and leaned over the table, still glaring at him. He sighed and set his knife down.

"It's not nonsense," he said.

I waited for him to explain.

"It's my life." He laughed, bitterly. "My whole life, that I threw away. The Mists are after us because the queen is set to marry one of them."

"What?" I said. "Why would she do that?"

"The boundaries are thinner at the top of the world. The Jandanvari have more connections with the Mists." He shook his head. "She's the first to marry one of them, though. I don't know what's she's thinking, agreeing to that damn Lord Foxfollow."

When he said the name, he seemed to speak into a vacuum. There was a dullness to his words.

"Yeah," I said. "I know who Lord Foxfollow is."

But Kolur ignored me, as I expected. "I don't know much

about him. He's powerful, from what I understand. I don't know why she agreed—" He stopped, and I couldn't tell what emotion was trying to work its way out. "We're sailing to Jandanvar to stop the wedding."

I stared at him. He wouldn't look at me, only picked up his knife and cut off another hunk of pie.

"We're what?" I said.

"Going to stop the wedding."

My ears were buzzing again. My whole body felt hot.

"We were almost killed by the Mists," I said, quietly and evenly. "A man, an innocent man, was killed for trying to warn us. We risked our lives on the magic."

Kolur was making every effort not to look at me.

"All so you could win back some queen!" The words erupted. "A woman *you* abandoned. You had your chance, Kolur. And now you're bringing the Mists down on me and on Frida and on *every-one*—just because she's marrying someone who *isn't you*?"

Kolur stared down at his pie. Frida sat off to the side, staying still, staying quiet.

"Well?" I asked.

Kolur lifted his head. "Yeah," he said, "that's about the whole of it."

I screeched in anger and shoved away from the table. The plates and cups rattled. "That's stupid!" I said. "And dangerous! Why didn't you just sail off on your own? Why'd you have to bring me with you?"

"I told you." Kolur's voice was firm. "I had no idea until we were out on the water. When I threw the bones, trying to find the skrei, that's when I saw that I was going to lose her if I didn't—"

"I don't care." I curled my hands into fists. "I don't care about your stupid queen, Kolur. Do you have any idea what you've gotten us into?"

"More than you," he snapped.

I screeched again and stood up. I knew plenty. I knew more about Lord Foxfollow than he did. More about how dangerous he was, more about the sort of weapons he used. And if I said anything about it to Kolur, my words would slip out unnoticed, all because Isolfr had cast some idiot's spell on him.

It was starting to make sense to me, in the senseless way that magic often goes. Isolfr was probably a subject of Jandanvar. They weren't quite human; everyone knew that. It seemed odd that the rest of Jandanvar wasn't protesting this marriage, but perhaps they weren't aware of the extent of Lord Foxfollow's cruelty. Or perhaps he had most of Jandanvar under some sort of Mists spell. And if Isolfr knew Kolur was coming, through magic or divination, he saw some possible hero. And so he intercepted us, gave me the warnings . . . I still didn't understand why he was keeping it all secret from Kolur, or why he was forcing me to keep it secret. What had he said—he wanted Frida's help but he was *frightened* of her? Sea and sky and the ancestors.

No one would tell me the truth. And I was sick of it, sick of being a puppet they pushed around whenever they needed.

I slammed out of the mead hall and into the freezing sweep of the town, ignoring Kolur as he called out my name. The sky was starting to darken, later than it had in Kjora. Now that I was out of the smoky, rowdy mead hall, my thoughts settled a little. I was three months away from home, and adventuring wasn't remotely like it had been in the stories about Ananna. I might as well be home in Kjora for all the excitement I was having here in Tulja, and I realized, stalking through the freezing wind, that Kjora was exactly where I wanted to be. Kjora, where spring brought warmth and our houses weren't mounds in the dirt. But I had no money, no boat. I refused to stay with Kolur, and I refused to help Isolfr at whatever he was trying to do. That did not leave me with many options—the only thing I had to trade was my half-formed magic and my skills aboard a boat.

A boat.

The old woman had said the docks were here, and we were close to the sea besides, having followed the shore to get here. I walked up to a woman sweeping out her shop with a straw broom, the handle wound up in blue ribbon.

"Excuse me," I said. "Excuse me, how do I get to the docks?"

She squinted at me. "Come again?" Then she frowned. "Empire?"

Her accent was thick. I shook my head. "Not Empire. Kjoran."

"Oh. Yes." That seemed enough for her. Kjora was a long way away, and maybe she thought of it as part of the south. "Where would you go?"

"The docks."

"Oh! The docks. Yes." She pointed to the west. "That way. Follow the signs."

"I can't read the signs."

She frowned again, like she was puzzling through what I'd said. "Oh, I see. Kjoran. First street on the right will take you there." She gave a satisfied nod rather than a smile.

I thanked her, hoping that was enough to find my way. I pulled my coat tighter around my chest and walked until I came to the first crossroads. A sign hung from a pole jutting sideways out of the ground, painted with those same unfamiliar letters I'd seen everywhere. I studied them for a moment, but it wasn't any use. I was too far from home.

For a moment, I was almost knocked out by a dizzying wave of fear. I couldn't even read the signs. I'd never been on my own before, not even in Kjora.

This was a specific kind of loneliness, I realized. One that was born out of fear.

Then the wind shifted, and I got a whiff of the sea, briny and comforting in the way that it smelled just like the sea at home. I decided to take it as a sign from the ancestors that I had made the right decision. I walked the rest of the way down the road. All the flapping tent-buildings of the village disappeared, replaced with rocky soil and smatterings of pine trees. My fear returned, sharp and sudden as a blade. I wondered if the woman had steered me wrong, if she'd sent me into some sort of trap just because she took me for Empire.

I wished I had a knife, at the very least.

But then I heard shouts, men's voices calling out fishermen's cues. I recognized most of them—some things are standard across the islands, I supposed.

I went around a bend in the road, my heart pounding, and came to the docks.

There wasn't much to them. Not like the docks at Skalir or even back home in the village. Just long slabs of barnacle-encrusted wood jutting out into the choppy water and a handful of rickety boats bobbing in the waves.

My spirits sank at the sight of it.

I'd been hoping for sailing ships big enough to make the journey south, but I knew immediately there was nothing but fishing boats here, most of them smaller even than the *Penelope*. If I wanted to sail home, or even to the closest island, I wouldn't be doing it today. Or any time soon, most like.

I didn't see anyone who looked like they might be a dockmaster—figured, in a place this small. So I straightened my shoulders and walked over to a trio of fishermen standing next to a worn-out old cog, the same sort as the *Penelope* and thus practical for longer trips. They fell silent as I approached, staring at me like I was a ghost.

"Excuse me," I called out, conjuring up my bravery. "I'm looking for work."

The fishermen blinked at me. For a blinding moment, I was afraid they didn't understand me. But then one, the youngest of the three, spoke up.

"Most men around here won't hire an Empire sailor."

"I'm not Empire; I'm Kjoran."

The fishermen conferred among themselves, muttering and grunting, the way men do. I shifted my weight, embarrassed at the thought of them talking about me.

The younger sailor turned to me. "You sound Kjoran."

"That's what I just told you. I've never been farther south than the Sunbreak Sea."

He laughed. He wasn't handsome, exactly, not like the suitors Bryn was always entertaining—too weatherworn, his skin patchy and red from all that time spent out at sea. But his face was friendly, despite him thinking I was some Empire spy.

"There's not a lot of work around here." His accent wasn't as thick as the shopwoman's, which I was grateful for. "Not a lot of fishermen on this island. Just Geir, who works alone, and Baltasar's boat, which is the biggest around." He jutted his chin inland. "Most of Tulja raises yaks. You got any experience with yaks?"

I shook my head. "I can do magic."

The fisherman turned back to the others and took to muttering again. I strained to listen to what they were saying, but their accents were too thick and their voices too low.

He turned back to me again. "What sort? Sea-magic?"

"Wind." I held up my hand. "You want to see? I know plenty of protection charms, and I can set the sails so you won't have to mess with them when we're out on the water."

The young fisherman turned to one of the elder ones, a fellow with a bushy yellow beard and rheumy eyes. He nodded, once, and I took a deep breath and concentrated, pushing aside all the turmoil from earlier. The wind was gentle, but it was blowing in from the southeast. Made my job easy.

I closed my eyes and hummed to myself, and the strength of my ancestors rose up inside me, drawing forth the magic inherent on the air. The wind shifted so that it was blowing straight from the south, and it brought with it the scents of home—Mama's ice-berry pie, the soap for bathing we kept in a little ornamented box, the herbs growing in the garden next to the front door. My hair whipped around my face and my coat whipped around my legs and I opened my eyes and the three fishermen were all staring at me in wonder. Behind them, the sails of the fishing boat rattled and flapped; I couldn't do anything with them if she wasn't moving. But I could sculpt a protection spell, and I did, weaving the wind into a blanket that settled over all of us, me and the fishermen. It was thick as smoke.

"Good enough for you?" I asked, out of breath from holding the magic.

The younger fisherman laughed. "C'mon, Baltasar, that's better than anything Reynir's ever conjured up."

The man with the yellow beard harrumphed. "Don't take much to beat out Reynir. You can stop, Empire girl; I've seen enough."

I let the magic drop. The protection shimmered away; the wind settled and shifted out of the southeast again.

"I'm not Empire," I said. "My mama was, technically, but she was a pirate, so she never pledged allegiance to the emperor. And my papa's family has lived in the north all the way back to the time of Helgi."

The younger fisherman grinned at me. After a moment's hesitation, I smiled back.

"Please," I said, and I addressed Baltasar, speaking as formally as I could. "I was washed ashore when my boat was attacked. My captain"—I figured that was better than saying "apprentice master"—"led me astray about why we were going north. I'm just looking for a way to earn money to support myself."

Baltasar studied me. He tugged at his beard. I held my breath like I was about to drop underwater.

"Fine," he said. "I'll take you on. Be here tomorrow at dawn. We'll be catching lisilfish."

I didn't know what lisilfish were, but at least I wouldn't starve here in the north. And maybe, eventually, I'd find a way home.

CHAPTER EIGHT

My new fishing boat was called the *Annika* and it was a good sight larger than the *Penelope*, despite being moored here at these sad little docks, on an island more known for raising yaks than catching fish. The fisherman who got me hired, Finnur, told me that the crew was pretty sizable, about ten men all told. Well, eight men and two women, me included.

After Baltasar hired me, I wandered back into Rilil to try and find a place to sleep for the night. We had a three-day run out to the Blackened Sea tomorrow, so at least I'd only have to spend one night in an inn. However, I was wary of coming across Kolur and Frida. I'd run straight from the mead hall to the docks without giving much thought to either of them, and I was still angry at the way they'd dragged me north and kept secrets from me and put me in danger of the Mists.

I asked directions to the closest inn from a woman selling hunks of charred meat from a cart, right at the edge of the docks. She frowned at me, made me repeat myself a couple of times, then pointed me off to the west. The inn proved easy to find, since beneath the picture-letters was the word "inn" itself, spelled out for travelers, I guess.

It was one of the more permanent buildings, with actual stones stacked up around the mound, and a real wooden door. I went in. The room was dark and smoky from the fire burning in the hearth, but an old man was behind the counter, cleaning out ale mugs.

"Can I help you?" he asked without looking up.

"I need a room. Just for one night."

"Very well. Fifteen stones."

I stopped. "Stones?"

"Aye, what we pay with up here." He squinted up at me and set the mug aside. "You don't got none, do you?"

I pulled out my pouch of gold discs and counted out fifteen of them. Then I laid them on the counter. "I've got these."

The man stared down at them. They looked flat and dull in the lantern light.

"No good here," he said, and chuckled. "Haven't seen discs in a while, though." He pinched one between his thumb and forefinger and held it up. My stomach felt heavy.

"What do you mean, they aren't good here?" I asked. The man looked at me. "I mean, they're gold. That's good everywhere."

"Good in the southerly islands, not the northerly ones. If you want to stay at my inn, you got to round up fifteen stones." He tossed my disc back on the pile. It hit the others with a flat metallic ring. "Not going to steal it, girl. I told you, they're worthless."

I swept the discs back into my pouch, keeping my head low because I was afraid I might start crying and I didn't want him to see. Kolur had betrayed me, and here I was trapped in a land where I barely understood the language and my discs didn't have any value and so I couldn't even buy a room at the inn. I bet Kolur knew about Tuljan stones. I bet he had whole piles of them sewn into his boots.

All I had was the *Annika*.

I mumbled a thank-you to the innkeeper and walked back down to the docks. My limbs were heavy and the air seemed colder than it had before I left. I wrapped my arms around myself, trying to warm up. It didn't work.

The *Annika* sat where I'd left her, tall and majestic in the thin sunlight. Baltasar and Finnur and the others weren't standing on the dock anymore, but the gangplank was down and I figured since I was technically an *Annika* fisherwoman, I had permission to climb aboard. So I did.

The deck had that eerie empty quality ships get when they're moored on land and aren't ready to sail yet. Except it wasn't truly empty. Baltasar was up at the masts, tugging on the ropes and fooling with the sails, with the help of a spidery, gray-haired man I hadn't seen before.

"Excuse me," I called out.

Baltasar glanced up at me. "Don't need you till tomorrow, sweetheart."

I walked up to him anyway. "I'm in a bit of a predicament," I said.

Baltasar laughed, his attention back at the ropes. The other man, though, kept sneaking glares at me, his brow furrowed. I tried my best to put him out of my mind.

"It turns out I can't pay for a room at the inn with my gold discs," I said.

The wind picked up and one of the sails yanked out of the spidery man's hand. He cursed and went chasing after it, shouting something back at Baltasar. His accent was so thick that I didn't catch it except the words "witch" and "what she's done" and "don't trust."

"You hush up, Reynir!" Baltasar snapped. He turned to me. "Don't mind him. He's angry we're replacing him on the masts. But he's a seawizard, and he's never been able to control the wind."

The loose sail flapped out over the edge of the boat, and Reynir jumped up to try and grab it. He wasn't having much luck.

"See what I mean?" Baltasar laughed again. "Now, what's your worry? Something about gold?"

"I can't pay for a room at the inn," I said.

Baltasar nodded.

"And I can't stay with my old captain, since we had a—a falling-out, and it'll be too cold for me to sleep out in the open, and—" I stared at him pleadingly. "This is an overnight boat, isn't it, sir? Please, you can take it out of my pay, but I've got nowhere else—"

Over on the starboard side, Reynir managed to wrestle the sail away from its freedom. Baltasar held up one hand.

"You can sleep aboard tonight if you want. Down in the crew quarters. Nothing fancy. I'll be here myself." He shrugged. "Might do you well to get used to the boat and her sails." He nodded over at Reynir, who was pulling the loose sail back into place, scowling all the while. "No way you can do any worse than Reynir."

"I heard that!" Reynir shouted back, and he glared at me one last time. Baltasar just found it funny.

"Oh, thank you," I said. "I promise you, you won't be disappointed in me."

I didn't sleep well that night. The crew's quarters were cold, even with the heat globes Reynir produced for me and Baltasar—I suspected he'd made mine weaker than he ought to. Plus, I was fretting about my future, which never makes for a restful sleep. In the end, I wrapped a warm sealskin blanket around my shoulders and went up on deck. Better than hanging in that uncomfortable hammock, waiting for sleep to overtake me.

The docks were quiet and dark. I walked up to the railing and looked down in the water, but Isolfr wasn't there.

Good. I think I wanted to see him less than I did Kolur. The wind blew over me and the magic sank into my skin. Everything felt as it should: no disruptions, no sense of darkness on the horizon. No Mists.

For a moment, a small and shivering moment, I let myself

think that it was over, and that was enough for me to go back down to my hammock and finally fall asleep.

Not that my sleep was restful. I was jarred awake the next morning by Reynir, his thin, pointed face like a remnant of a nightmare. "About to make sail," he snapped. "Better go out there and prove what you can do with the winds."

The morning was a blur after that. The sun was just starting to rise as the crew stormed aboard, and their laughter and groans and roughhousing finally woke me up completely. Reynir, who turned out to be the boat's fortuneer, gave me the directions to the Blackened Sea with a scowl, and I called down the winds and the *Annika* sailed off to the west.

Since I wasn't a strong witch like Frida, I had to stay up on deck the whole time, in case the winds shifted directions or there were other unforeseen problems. It was dull work and cold, but fairly mindless, and I was able to watch the crew ready the nets and prepare the preservation charms. I wasn't a part of a crew at all. Sometimes it felt like watching a play.

At lunchtime, Finnur brought me a jar of dried and salted meat. He said it was yak's meat.

"Thought you might be hungry," he said.

I was, and I smiled at him in gratitude. "Thank you," I said.

"You got to soften it in your mouth first," Finnur said, pointing at the jar. "Like this." He pulled out a strip and tossed it into his mouth, and his jaw worked around a bit. "Don't try to chew till you can." He spoke around the hunk of yak's meat. "Not the best meal out there, but better than nothing."

I nodded, grateful for his kindness. I pulled out a strip of my own, studied it for a moment, and then slid it into my mouth. Finnur was right; it was tough as tree bark. I let it sit under my tongue, tasting the salt.

"So do you know what kind of fish we're after?" Finnur asked.

"Baltasar told me." I paused, trying to remember. "Lisilfish, wasn't it? I don't know them."

"Wouldn't imagine so. They ain't much in the way of southern fish." Finnur leaned up against the mast. "Trickier than skrei or ling. With normal fish, you can just drag 'em up on deck and let 'em suffocate. Not so with these buggers." He pulled away from the mast and walked over to the railing, gesturing for me to join him. I did. The fishing net trailed out behind us, glimmering in the pale northern sunlight. Light flashed beneath the water, and my heart jumped with it, but Finnur said, "That's the lisilfish there. You can see 'em flickering."

"Is that what makes them trickier?" I leaned farther over the railing. I couldn't get a good glimpse of them, but they seemed to be swimming among the nets like any other fish.

Finnur laughed. "No. You'll see when we drag 'em aboard." He stared thoughtfully out at the water. Baltasar says it's cause they swam south from Jandanvari waters, and that makes them smarter than most fish."

Hearing the name *Jandanvar* made me dizzy. I thought of Kolur the last time I'd seen him, his face illuminated by the murky light of the mead hall. Then I thought about Gillean. I pulled away from the railing and pretended to test the wind, just in case Finnur was of a mind to keep talking about Jandanvar. But one of the crewmen called him over to help with a tangled net.

We dragged the nets in late in the afternoon. Baltasar rang the big brass bell that hung from the highest mast and shouted, "Net time! Net time!" He handed the wheel off to one of the younger boys and jumped down from the helm. "You," he said, "Empire girl. Stand off to the side. You'll just want to watch the first time."

"I've brought in fish before," I said.

"Not like this, you haven't. Stand off to the side."

I did as he asked. He wasn't Kolur; I couldn't sass him and expect to have a job the next time the boat went out to sea.

He wasn't like Kolur. Definitely a good thing in my mind.

I took a place over on the port side, close to the masts in case trouble stirred up with the wind, but still in good view of the net. Half the crew crowded around. I frowned. Seemed a lot of men to bring in just one net.

"Grab the net!" Baltasar called out. Everyone did as he asked, winding their fingers up in the ropes and bracing themselves against the deck. "Hold!"

They held. The boat rocked back and forth; the wind rippled through the sails. The tip of my nose burned from the cold.

Everyone seemed to be holding his breath.

"Draw!" Baltasar shouted, and in one great gasp of effort, every single one of those fishermen heaved at the net. Water splashed up along the side of the boat and the net erupted into the air. It was full of tiny silver sparks that threw bits of light all around the deck.

It went up into the air.

And it *stayed* in the air.

I'd never seen anything like it, this net of fish floating over a boat like those brightly colored kites children play with during the windy months. It swayed back and forth, showering water over the fishermen, who grimaced and grunted and chanted something in a language I didn't recognize. I felt like I needed to dart forward and help, but whatever magic this was, I didn't know it.

"Drop!" Baltasar shouted.

The chanting swelled. The air rippled. And then, with a rush of coordinated movement, the net slammed against the deck.

It stayed there.

The crew burst into shouts of joy, laughing and slapping at one another's backs. Finnur made his way over to where I stood watching. He was soaked with seawater, his hair plastered in dark ribbons against the side of his face.

"See what I told you?" he said. "Tricky."

I looked over at the net. Someone had already cast the preservation charm, and one of the crew, the other woman, was loosening the net so she and another crewman could dump the fish out properly. I wondered why they cast the preservation charm first, but then I saw that the fish were still moving, swimming around the air like it was water, hemmed in by the shimmer of the preservation charm.

"They aren't dying," I said.

Finnur shrugged. "They don't die easily, no. Natan puts a poison in the preservation charm to slow their hearts. It takes a minute to work. Says it's not painful."

"And people want to *eat* these?"

Finnur laughed. "It's a Tuljan delicacy, actually. Lisila. I'll have Asbera make it for you sometime. The poison can't hurt humans."

I looked at him. He seemed serious, not like he was going to make fun of my supposed Empire ways.

"Really?" I said.

He nodded. "Asbera makes some of the best on the island. That's why I married her." And he pointed to the fisherwoman, who was standing with the other crew and laughing now that the lisilfish were all out of the nets.

The rest of the trip continued much like that first day. We caught seven more nets' worth of lisilfish, moving from place to place according to Reynir's calculations. I controlled the wind the whole time and never once let us blow off course, but Baltasar wouldn't let me help draw in the nets.

"Maybe next time," he grunted when I asked him about it. "You need to learn the spells first."

We arrived back at the Rilil docks midafternoon during the third day, exactly when Baltasar promised we would. That level of honesty was a refreshing change of pace. The stores of lisilfish weighed down the *Annika*, and it took the entire crew to bring them to the market, where Baltasar sold them to a tight-faced, thin-lipped young man who tutted over the size of the fish. Still, Baltasar haggled him to a price of nearly four hundred stones, and I could tell by the whoops of excitement from the crew that it must be a good deal. We each got an equal share. When Baltasar handed me my pouch, the stones clacking together, I felt a surge of pride. With Kolur, I'd only been an apprentice, and so my share was always small and went straight to Mama besides.

"A job well done," Baltasar said. "Next trip planned is two days from now. You'll be there."

I nodded, pleased. I shook the bag of stones and opened it up. They actually were rocks, sea stones that had been polished down into evenly sized discs about the same size as my gold ones. What a difference materials make.

A couple of crewmen muttered cold words to each other, and I had a creeping feeling that they were about me. But I told myself not to be bothered. The captain appreciated my work, and I was paid, and if I could put up with that islanders' paranoia that is the trademark of the north, I'd get home for certain.

"Good haul this trip." Finnur sidled up alongside me, Asbera at his side. "And two days without sail. A nice break."

I nodded, but his comment struck me in a cold place. I still didn't have anywhere to go. I tightened my grip on my wages. Finnur and Asbera both stared at me. Then Asbera frowned.

"You don't have a place to stay," she said in a soft, whispery voice I would not have expected to belong to a fisherwoman.

I considered lying, but Finnur had been so kind to me that I didn't want to. I shook my head. "I can find something," I said. "I know there's an inn——" But it would cost fifteen stones a night. With two nights, I'd have spent almost all of my wages. I wouldn't be able to save anything. And even though sailing aboard the *Annika* had been a fine experience the last three days, I still didn't want to spend the rest of my life in the little earth-mounds of Tulja. I wanted a way home.

"Oh, don't stay at the inn," said Finnur. "It's filthy. The old man who runs it never airs out the beds." He nodded down at my wages. "With all we got today, you'd have enough to put in for a room at the boarding boats down on the docks' edge. You won't save much from today's payment, but you'll have plenty once we get back from our next trip."

My heart sank. I looked back and forth between Finnur and Asbera, who stared at me with identical expressions, calm and sympathetic. I looked down at my wages.

"What about food?" I muttered.

"Oh, don't you worry about that," Finnur said. "We'll cook for you." He grinned. "I promised you I'd have Asbera make lisila."

"You didn't tell *me*," Asbera said, but she laughed. "Yes, we don't mind. We've plenty to share."

I hesitated. I wanted to trust them, but I'd trusted so many people since I'd left Kjora, and none of that trust had worked out. Kolur and his lies. Isolfr and his—I still didn't know what. Because of him, I'd seen a dead man, and I'd almost died myself.

"We really don't mind," Asbera said. She leaned in close to me and lowered her voice. "And we're not frightened of the Empire like the rest of these louts."

I scowled. "I'm not from the Empire. My mama was born there, that's all."

Asbera brightened. "Well, then, we really have nothing to fear. Come, let's take you to the boarding boats."

And against my better judgment, I relented. I was tired and sore from the last three days of work, and I knew I needed to think in the long term if I was to ever leave.

"The boarding boats," I said. "All right."

Finnur laughed and slapped me on the back. We left the merchant. The rest of the crew had dispersed, and the docks were more bustling than I'd seen them before, what with all those one-man sailing boats coming in from the sea. Asbera and Finnur led me past the crowd to a collection of ramshackle, sailless boats roped and moored together. A wooden sign flapped from a pole jutting sideways out of the ground, but like all the signs here, I couldn't read it.

"Here we are," Finnur said. "Let me take you to see Rudolf. We can get you set up while Asbera cooks."

Everything was happening so quickly. I nodded, and Asbera trotted off to a narrow dinghy that bumped up against the pier.

"So you just live here?" I asked. "On the water?"

"Yes. Most of the crew does." Finnur shrugged. "It's cheap. And we don't have to maintain anything while we're gone." He led me down a rickety wooden walkway to a junk painted with more unfamiliar letters. Finnur banged on the side of the boat and shouted, "Rudolf! Got someone who needs a place to live!"

There was a pause. The boats knocked against each other, a pleasant, hollow sound. Then footsteps echoed from the deck of the junk and a man's face appeared over the railing. He was even more weatherworn than Kolur. He scowled at me.

"Empire?" he barked.

Before I could explain, Finnur said, "No, she's from Kjora."

"Southerly." The man—Rudolf—made a coughing noise. "Well, as long as you can pay, you can stay here." He rapped his fingers against the railing. "Fifty stones a month."

I felt like I'd been stabbed through the stomach.

"Don't be an ass," Finnur said. "Me and Asbera pay thirty."

Rudolf scowled. "I don't know this girl."

"She works aboard the *Annika*. Baltasar's word ought to be good enough for you."

Rudolf paused. I reached into my coat pocket and rubbed my fingers against my wages. Thirty a month was a good sight cheaper than thirty for two days.

"Fine," Rudolf said. "Thirty stones, once a month. That don't cover food, girl. This ain't an inn."

"I know it's not, sir." I counted the stones out into my palm, dismayed to see almost all of my wages disappear. Rudolf dropped away from the boat's railing, and I stood waiting for him with the stones piled high in my hand. A few moments later, he reappeared at the top of the gangplank. I handed him his payment and he counted it out and nodded once, satisfied.

"You've got the *Cornflower*." He deposited the stones into a worn, velvet sack that he tucked away inside his coat. Then he pulled out an enormous metal ring, jangling with keys of all cuts and sizes.

"Can't do much with the deck," he said. "I keep an eye out, got a couple of charms up. May or may not keep someone off. But you can lock up the captain's quarters and the storage room well enough. Recommend you keep your valuables in there. Ain't responsible if they get stolen."

"Of course. I understand."

Rudolf pulled off a long, slender key from the ring and handed it to me. "Finnur can show you where it is. Ain't that right, Finnur?"

"Sure thing. It's right next door to us." He grinned at Rudolf. Rudolf scowled in return.

"I don't get payment on the first of the month," he said, "I'll send my dogs after you."

And with that, Rudolf hauled himself back up his ladder and disappeared over the railing.

"Don't worry about the dogs," Finnur said. "All you have to do is feed them sausages and they'll be rolling around on their backs, waiting for you to play with them." He laughed. "Come on, I'll show you the *Cornflower*."

We walked down to the edge of the pier. I still had this dazed, edgy feeling, like it was a huge mistake giving my money to that man. Of course, I hadn't had that feeling in all the time we were sailing north from Kjora, so maybe my intuition wasn't what it should be.

Finnur reached down in the water and picked up a thick salt-encrusted rope that was tied to the pole jutting off the pier. He tugged on it, and the dinghy drifted toward us, bobbing on the water.

"Unfortunately, we're not pierside," he said. "But it's not a big deal, taking the dinghy."

He let me step on first. It sank a little beneath my weight, but it was dry and solidly built. Finnur rowed us around the tangle of moored boats. The rope attached to the rowboat was long enough that it uncoiled out behind us, disappearing beneath the water's surface. When we came to another junk with *Crocus* painted across the side, he jabbed the oar straight down into the water, locking us into place.

"That's where Asbera and I live," he said, pointing at the *Crocus*. "The *Cornflower*'s right there, just down that gap. We should be able to climb over from the *Crocus*."

I nodded dumbly and watched as he crawled up the ladder onto the deck of his boat—of his home, I reminded myself. And I thought then of my own home, my real home, landlocked and built of gray stones. I couldn't see much of the *Cornflower* from here, only a strip of peeling gray wood rising out of the water and some sailless masts, part of the forest of masts that made up the boarding boats.

"You coming?" Finnur was aboard the *Crocus* now, standing beside the ladder, waiting.

"Yeah, sure." I made my way up the ladder, looking over at the *Cornflower*. I saw more of it the higher I climbed, but there wasn't much to see. Just a moored cog. It was hard to think of it as a home.

Like a gentleman, Finnur helped me over the railing. The deck of the *Crocus* didn't look like any boat I'd been on. No sails, and the wheel had been removed at the helm. There were pots filled with lichen and little blue flowers and shrubby, tough-looking herbs. Tall glass jars sat at random intervals, half full with gray water. Ropes of dried vines hung from the masts, twisted together into figures that looked human and animal at the same time. Protective charms, most like.

"You can see the *Cornflower* from the starboard side." Finnur pointed. "No one's lived there for a while, but Rudolf usually keeps the empty boats clean."

I nodded and walked over to the side of the boat. The *Cornflower*'s deck was empty except for a pot of its own, lichen dangling over the sides like a waterfall.

"It's warmer down below," Finnur said. "We can see about looking for a plank to get you across the way. But it'll be nice to have a rest first, don't you think?"

"Sure." I looked away from my new home and followed Finnur down belowdecks. I expected it to look like the *Penelope*, may the gods take her: sparse and empty save for stores and fishing supplies. But it didn't. It was hung with brightly colored tapestries and stuffed with carved wooden furniture. There was a hearth, just like in a house, filled with hot, glowing logs. Asbera was there, her hair tied back, stirring a great cauldron of something that smelled like fish and spices and made my stomach grumble.

"Hello, Hanna." She glanced at me over her shoulder and smiled shyly. "Did Rudolf give you a fair price?"

"I guess," I said. "I don't know."

"Thirty stones," Finnur said. "What we're paying."

"Oh good." She gestured at the table. "Please, have a seat. I'm afraid the lisila isn't quite ready yet. We still have tulra ale, don't we, Finnur?"

"We do." Finnur ducked out into the corridor, his footsteps echoing around the room. I sank into one of the chairs, exhausted. I hadn't realized just how much so until now, after three days on the *Annika* so soon after being washed ashore by magic. Really, I just wanted to sleep.

Finnur returned with a mug of some frothy amber liquid that I assumed was ordinary ale until I sipped it and found that it was sweet and buttery and not at all fermented.

"Tuljan specialty," she said. "We make it out of the tulra flower, from the far north."

She smiled, but I stared down at the foam in my drink. The far north. It seemed that even when I left Kolur, the top of the world was still haunting me.

Asbera sat down across from me with her own mug, and Finnur sat beside her and rested his hand on her arm.

"Everyone wants to know what brought you to Tulja," Finnur said.

Asbera sighed and slapped at him. "That's rude."

"Well, it's true!"

"It's fine." I stared down at my mug again. I didn't want to tell the truth, at least not the whole truth. "My ship wrecked here, like I said. Had a falling-out with my captain." I shrugged. "We weren't supposed to go this far north."

Finnur gave a nod like he understood everything. Asbera stood up and checked the cauldron bubbling on the stove.

"I'm grateful for the work." I paused, still not sure how much I should tell them. "But I'd like to try and sail home to Kjora if I can. I miss my parents."

"Ah yes, I miss mine, too," Asbera said from the stove. "They're yak tenders, you know, out near the base of the mountains." She grinned at Finnur. "This one came by looking to trade pelts for Baltasar. He'd only just been taken on as an apprentice. He wound up living in an old yurt for the better part of the winter." She laughed, and Finnur gazed up at her the way Papa would gaze at Mama sometimes.

"That's a nice story," I said, and then, because I felt a need to fill the silence in a way that wouldn't involve explaining why my captain had been sailing us north in the first place, I told them about Mama and Papa, and how Mama'd served aboard the *Nadir* and decided she loved the north more than she loved the south. That drew smiles out of Finnur and Asbera both.

"That's why the Empire's always trying to claim our islands," Asbera said. "Because they all know deep down it's better here."

I laughed at that, even if I didn't know myself one way or the other. I'd only ever belonged to the north, even if Mama's ancestors, warm and smelling like honey and spices, spoke to me sometimes through the winds.

Asbera checked the cauldron again, and this time she clapped her hands together and said, "Oh, praise joy, it's ready. I'm *starving*. Aren't you, Hanna?"

I nodded. "Three days with nothing but salted fish—"

"Oh, don't even say the words." Finnur slapped his hands on the table. "Here, Asbera, let me help. Hanna, you stay. You're our guest." He got to his feet and pulled carved wooden bowls out of the cupboards next to the hearth. Asbera spooned the bowls full of lisila and then delivered the bowls to the table. The lisila was a sort of stew, with a creamy white broth that shimmered like moonlight. It smelled of herbs, fragrant and grassy like summer.

"Once you've had a taste of this, you'll wish everything else you ever eat is lisila," Asbera said.

I assumed she was joking, or boasting, as cooks do. But when I sipped from the rim of my bowl, I could hardly believe that what I tasted was real. The flavor was savory and so complex I couldn't quite define it, but as soon as I tasted the lisila, I wanted more. It didn't help that I was so hungry. I'd slurped down half my bowl when I glanced up and found Asbera and Finnur laughing at me.

"Told you," Asbera said. She sipped at her own bowl and closed her eyes. "As good as I remembered."

"It's the lisilfish," Finnur said. "They cook down and create—*this*." He gestured at the bowls.

"Shame they're so expensive."

"Oh," I said, cheeks warming. "I didn't know. I'll be happy to help pay—"

"Nonsense." Asbera shook her head. "You need to save your money, like you said." She smiled and took another sip from her bowl. "I'm sure you'll find some way to repay us in the future."

I nodded. I certainly hoped so.

But more than that, I hoped that Asbera and Finnur were as normal as they seemed, and that the rest of my time in Tulja would be as simple and satisfying as my evening aboard the *Crocus*.

CHAPTER NINE

After dinner, Finnur helped me get settled aboard the *Cornflower*. It was a much smaller boat than the *Crocus*, but belowdecks was well cared for: the holes in the ceiling patched, the floor dry. The hearth had been cleaned of old ashes, and there was an actual bed in the captain's cabin, with a small, hay-stuffed mattress. After weeks of sleeping on cots and hammocks, I found it an unimaginable luxury.

I slept easily that first night, deep and steady, although I dreamed, something I hadn't done aboard the *Annika*. My dreams were strange but not unsettling: I was at the base of a tall, rocky mountain, surrounded by yaks that snuffled and pawed at the frozen ground. Wind roared over the mountains, coming from the north. It smelled of tulra ale and seemed to have a voice of its own, whispering my name, telling me I was safe. I believed it. I was certain it came from Finnur and Asbera.

When I woke, sunlight was spilling in through the doorway. I'd left it open in the night. I got up and stretched, feeling refreshed for the first time in weeks. A cask of lisila sat on my bedside table, left over from left night—Asbera had given it to me when I left the *Crocus*. I ate it quickly, and it was just as delicious for breakfast as it had been for dinner. Finnur had told me there was a shared well in the center of the town, so I dug around in the storage room until I found some empty skins. Then I went up on deck.

The air was cold and bright and still. The deck of the *Cornflower* was bare in comparison to the deck of the *Crocus*, but I had no intention of draping it with plants and charms. That would suggest I planned on staying here for a long time, and I didn't. My bracelet could protect me for the time being.

The dinghy was still where we had left it the night before, lodged in the space between the *Cornflower* and the *Crocus*. I lowered myself down and rowed to the pier. The docks were mostly empty, just a pair of fish-boys running errands back and forth between the boats and the shops in the village.

Everything felt as much like a dream as the base of the mountain had.

I followed Finnur's directions to the well. To my relief, no one was there, and I filled up the skins and dropped them into my bag. I realized I didn't want to go back to the *Cornflower* yet. There wouldn't be much to do besides sit on my cot and count down the days until we made sail again.

So I walked through the streets of Rilil, weaving through the mounds of earth and piles of stone. Most of the doorways were graced with twists of vine, simpler, more decorative versions of the charms Asbera and Finnur kept on their upper deck. I hadn't taken those vines for charms when I'd been walking through the town with Kolur and Frida; in fact, I'd hardly noticed them at all.

Thinking on Kolur and Frida made me feel all twisted up. It had been easy to forget about them those three days at sea, but now that I was back in Tulja, I knew there was a chance I'd run into them. And I didn't want that.

I passed the last semi-permanent building, and the road opened up into a huge field dotted not with yaks like I expected but with the same round, leathery tents that the old woman had lived in. They were clustered like people drawing together for warmth, and smoke drifted out of the tops of most of them. Far off in the distance rose a mountain, purplish gray in the misty air. It looked like the mountain from my dream—but then, all mountains tend to look the same.

I turned and walked in the opposite direction. The water skins were starting to get heavy, but I still wasn't in a mind to go back to my boat. Too dull and lonely, sitting down below by myself.

Eventually, I came to the other end of the village, to the road leading down to the ocean. I dusted some old snow off a nearby stone and sat down and took a drink of water. Birds circled overhead, crying out to one another. I smelled salt and fish. It was peaceful, in its way. Peaceful and lonely.

And then I heard singing.

It was distant, coming from the direction of the beach. I couldn't make out the words, but as I listened, music joined up with the singers' voices, a jangly, rhythmic instrument that I didn't recognize. Part of me thought that maybe I should leave, that I was hearing something I wasn't meant to as a daughter of the Empire and the southerly islands both, but I stayed put. The music grew louder. I realized they were singing in the language of the ancients.

Figures appeared on the bend in the road, moving in a procession through the cold, gray air. And they weren't human. They were monsters.

All sorts of monsters, some with great shaggy coats and others with sharp, needly beaks and still others like men built of straw. My fear paralyzed me in place. I thought of the warship slicing toward the *Penelope*, thought of Gillean's dead body. I thought of the Mists.

The monsters moved closer. One of them, a creature with a bulbous, oversized boar's head, shook a ring of metal that flashed in the thin sunlight. Another carried a torch that guttered and sparked an unnatural orangey gold.

They come on the veins of magic—

Isolfr's words appeared unbidden in my head, and without

thinking, I reached out to the magic on the wind, testing, trying to find that sense of *wrongness*—

There was none. The magic was calm, peaceful. Nothing wrong, nothing dangerous.

The figures drew closer. I scrambled off my rock and crouched half behind it, clutching my bag tight, too afraid to take my eyes off these monsters. The singing poured over me.

Not a single one of the creatures' mouths moved.

I frowned. That didn't make sense.

As they passed, the straw-man turned his head, pale gold shedding off him. His eyes peered out of the mound of straw. They were dark and benevolent—human.

They were human.

The monsters sang, but their mouths didn't move.

Masks, I thought, and I straightened up, still trembling. None of the other costumed men looked at me; they just continued their procession into the village. The torch sent sparks and smoke up into the sky, and I felt the shudder of its enchantment, a warmth and protection I hadn't expected.

At the first shop, a family stepped through the curtain in the doorway, a man and his wife, their little girl. The girl tossed something at the procession—it looked like dried flowers. She didn't seem scared, only grateful.

I slumped down on the rock, sighing, and watched the procession make its way through Rilil. Magic trailed in its wake, settling over the village like a balm. Magic, it was just magic. Protection.

It just didn't look like any protection I had ever known.

The *Annika* left for another trip two days later. Couldn't come soon enough. I'd spent the rest of my money on food and wasn't able to save anything for the trip home. I hoped this payment would be as large as my first, since I wouldn't have to worry about doling out most of it for a place to stay.

Asbera and Finnur were already aboard when I climbed onto the deck in the pale early morning hours. Asbera smiled like she was glad to see me.

"Hanna!" she said. "I hope you're settling in all right." I hadn't seen either of them for those two days, since I didn't want to come across as a burden. I was glad to see her, though, since I had questions, mostly about those costumed men and their magic.

"I am." But I didn't have time to say more than that, since Baltasar blundered up on deck. Reynir stumbled behind him, reading fortunes from a little scrap of scroll. He glared at me when he saw I was back.

"Gather round!" Baltasar shouted. "We're going southeast today, looking for lampreys. Reynir here says we can make the catch of the season if we can get there before those damned Kjiljans."

The crew applauded and stomped their feet against the deck. A little thrill of excitement worked through me too. Maybe the catch of the season would be enough to get me home.

"Well, what are you waiting for?" Baltasar cried. "Get on with it!"

The crew erupted into action. So much was happening, I didn't have time to think—and I was grateful for that after spending the last few days doing nothing but thinking. I called the wind into the sails while a couple of crewmen aligned the spars. The *Annika* pulled out into the water and swung around, moving parallel to the shore, heading west. The land was dotted with those little round tents, gray smoke twisting into the air.

We sailed.

It took most of the day to get to the southern point where Reynir claimed we'd find fish. Most of the crew spent the time lolling around the fires, throwing dice and playing Hangman's Gambit, another gambling game Papa had taught me to play last year. No one asked me to join them. Which was fine, seeing as how I didn't have any money to gamble.

Still, I felt isolated standing there among the masts, watching the men throw dice and count out stones. They got to wait out the trip, but I had to control the winds. I'd never thought of it as especially tiring magic, but the *Annika* was much bigger than the *Penelope* and it proved to be more work than I was used to.

The sun finally started to sink into the horizon. The winds shifted to the northeast, and so I didn't have to control them as much. I was grateful for the break. But then I took one look around the deck, at the fires glowing in the darkness, and suddenly felt very lonely.

"Are you hungry?"

It was Asbera. She'd been scrambling up on the masts all day, where the men were afraid to climb, and so I hadn't seen much of her.

"Yeah," I said, grateful to have someone to talk to. "It takes a lot out, controlling the winds."

She grinned. "I bet." Then she handed me a fish that had been grilled by the fires. "Finnur caught them earlier. Fishing off the side like a child. No one believed he'd actually get something." She laughed.

"Thank you." I stared down at the fish, its scales blackened by the smoke. My stomach grumbled, and I peeled the flesh away from the bones and nibbled at it. Skrei. Nice to eat something familiar. It reminded me of Kjora.

I expected Asbera to leave me and go back with the others, but she stayed by my side.

"The wind's shifted," she said. "You don't have to keep controlling it, do you?"

I shrugged. "I don't mind." I took a bite of fish to keep from saying anything more.

"You shouldn't let the crew get to you," she said.

"I'm not."

She smiled and the skin crinkled around her eyes. "They'll exclude you until they don't anymore. It's our way here in Tulja. We can't help it."

Part of me wanted to believe her and part of me didn't care because I just wanted to go home.

I finished the fish and tossed the bones overboard. I checked the water, the way I did whenever I was at the railing, looking for a shadow beneath the waves, a glimmer like moonlight. But there was nothing there. Isolfr had dragged us into danger and then he'd abandoned us.

"How do you like Tulja so far?" Asbera asked. "Aside from"— she waved at the crew—"all that. I really do promise it'll get better. They just have to get accustomed to you."

I hesitated, trying to think of a diplomatic response. "It's different," I finally said. "Different from what I'm used to."

"I'm sure I'd feel the same way if I ever visited Kjora."

She laughed, and after a moment, I joined in with her. I'd let my magic die away a little as we spoke as a way of alleviating my exhaustion, and only just now realized it. The boat rocked along with the wind, moving us to the southwest. I sighed, my limbs loose with freedom.

"It's strange," I said. "Certain things are the same, and certain things are different. I can't read your alphabet, but most of the food is the same, assuming it's not a dish from—from the north." I hesitated. "And the other day, I saw a parade, all these people in costumes—we don't have anything like that in Kjora."

"Oh, the Nalendan." Asbera smiled. "Did they give you a fright?"

"A little. I felt the magic and realized they weren't dangerous." I shrugged, trying to be nonchalant.

"Oh, you poor thing. I didn't realize they were going to be parading while you were out, otherwise I would have made sure to mention them to you."

"It's fine, really."

"I've heard they're another tradition we borrowed from Jandanvar, but us Tuljans like to claim we invented their magic whenever we can." She laughed. "They're a means of protecting us from the Mists. Do you know of the Mists as far south as Kjora?"

I nodded. I couldn't bear to say anything more.

Fortunately, Asbera didn't seem so keen on talking about them, either. "There is a group of priests who live out on the plains whose entire job is to watch out for the Mists. Whenever they feel them encroaching, they call for the Nalendan to protect our village."

I shivered. I wondered if this was our fault, if Kolur had brought the Mists here.

"How often do the Nalendan cast their charm?" I asked. "I mean, how often do the priests feel—"

"Oh, pretty often. Twice a month or so." Asbera interrupted me before I could say the word *Mists*, her expression uncomfortable. But she must have seen something in my own expression, fear or something worse, because she smiled and laughed. "My father used to say the priests can't actually see anything at all, and they just call down the Nalendan to amuse themselves."

But her words did nothing to console me.

I wound up with wages of thirty-five stones after we returned from that trip—it turned out lamprey was a favorite among the Tuljans. I ate dinner with Asbera and Finnur that evening, just as we had after the first trip. No lisila, but Asbera did bake the lamprey with wild roots and strips of dried yak meat. It was delicious.

After dinner, Asbera walked me up to the deck of the *Crocus.*
Night was just starting to fall, streaks of gold sinking into the water.
The north wind blew strong and sweet-scented, and it knocked the
vines and charms around, stirring up their magic.

"I have a gift for you," Asbera said.

"Oh, that's—you don't have to do that." I shook my head.
"You've given me enough already—"

"It's nothing," she said. "Just a little thing." And she pulled a
stonework jar out of her dress pocket. "I used to keep meal in it,
but the side cracked." She handed it to me. "It'd be perfect for saving stones."

I took the jar and turned it over in my hands. I almost wanted
to cry.

"Just make sure you keep it locked up in the captain's quarters." She laughed. "I'd hate to see your savings get whisked away."

"Thank you," I said. "This was very thoughtful."

We looked at each other in the long violet shadows. It felt good
to have a friend.

And so the days went by. They turned into one week, into two
weeks. Our wages at the end of each fishing trip were good and
steady, and with each payment, I made sure to drop a few stones
into my jar. Sometimes at night, I'd lift the jar and shake it next to
my ear, listening to the stones banging around. It was reassuring, a
reminder that I was *doing* something to get home. Better than waiting for Kolur or anyone else to take care of my problems for me.

One afternoon, I shook out a handful of my saved stones and
went into the village to find a wizard. It took a long time, in between
my trouble understanding the Tuljan accent and something about
the way I was asking, but eventually an old man pointed me to a
tent on the outskirts of the village. I couldn't read the sign jutting

out of the frozen earth, but I pulled on the bell and the man who answered wore faded, tattered blue robes beneath his coat.

"Yes?" he said, peering at me suspiciously.

"Are you a wizard?"

"Of a sort." He stepped out of the tent and studied my face closely. "How'd you get so far north, Empire girl?"

I sighed. "I'm from Kjora. Can you send messages across the islands?"

His eyes narrowed at that. "Across the islands? Why would you want to do such a thing? Surely if you're *here*, you can travel south on your own."

His words made my cheeks burn. "No," I said. "I can't. Can you send the message or not?"

"Can you pay?"

I held up my stones.

That was all it took. The wizard was worse even than Larus, but at least he could send a messaging spell. I wrote a note to my family. I'd been wanting to do it since I left Kolur, but I didn't know what to say, if I should tell Mama the whole truth about him or not. I spent a good amount of time with the quill in one hand, staring down at the parchment while the wizard tapped his fingers and sighed impatiently.

Dear Mama and Papa, I eventually wrote, *I want you to know I'm safe. I'm just out having an adventure, like Ananna of the Nadir. You don't need to worry.*

I wasn't sure how true that last part was, but I knew I didn't want them to worry, even if they did need to.

I stood with my arms wrapped around my chest as he enchanted the parchment and turned it to sparkles of magic that floated on the air.

"How will I know they get it?" I said.

He shrugged. "You won't. Takes a long time for messages to travel across the islands."

And that was that. I hoped by the time the wizard received a reply from them, I'd be on my way home.

After that, my time aboard the *Annika* smoothed out, but I never truly felt like I belonged. I took my meals with Asbera and Finnur and hung my hammock up alongside theirs, and that was enough to quiet the whispers and stop the curious looks. It wasn't ideal, but it wasn't terrible, and that was good enough for me.

When the ocean wasn't safe or when Reynir couldn't find any worthwhile catches, we'd have a day or two off. Asbera showed me around Rilil, pointing out the different shops, the grocer and the magic-dealer, the moneylender and the ship repair. Other days I spent alone, when I needed to be with my thoughts. I walked down to the beach, following the road that had brought me here, and fed scraps to the sea birds. I said a prayer at the circle on the edge of town, listening for the voices of my ancestors.

I never heard anything.

I also never heard anything about Frida and Kolur. Asbera didn't go in much for rumors, and the rest of the crew wasn't friendly enough to share what they'd heard. Still, I wondered. If they were still in Tulja, if it had been the right thing, leaving them and coming to work for Baltasar.

One day, we had a short run out to the Brightly Sea. We took only half the crew and were back by lunchtime with a big catch of skrei, and I was grateful that Baltasar had asked me along, since it was easy work for quite a bit of pay.

I walked along the docks, a pouch of nearly fifty stones weighing down my pockets. I was in a good mood and didn't feel like eating salted fish back on the *Cornflower*. So, even though I knew it was wasteful, I walked down to the Yak's Horn, an alehouse Finnur had talked about. He said the ale was good and the food was better, and that sounded like a fine idea to me.

The Yak's Horn was located at the far end of the docks. I made my way along the damp stone path. Things were busier than usual—more boats in the water and more fishermen crowded around them. I paid careful attention to the voices, hoping to hear a southerly accent, someone who could take me back to Kjora.

And I heard one. A familiar one, shouting curses into the air.

I stopped. I was standing in front of a junk that was all carved up in the Jolali style with icons of the sea spirits. It didn't have sails yet, but the wood was freshly painted, and it was in better shape than most of the boats here. The name across the side read *Penelope II*.

"I told you, boy, I don't want the twisted, I want braided! Holds together better." Kolur stomped across the deck.

I almost walked away. I had nothing to say to him, and if he'd had the money to buy that gaudy new boat, he'd had the money to send me home back in Skalir. But before my anger could overtake me, a second figure joined him, not Frida but a young man. The spiky, elaborate icons shielded the young man at first, but as he darted back and forth, I saw his pale skin and pale hair, his graceful way of moving. He looked entirely human now, his ethereal beauty replaced by a bland, forgettable handsomeness. But I still recognized him immediately.

Isolfr.

I stared at him. He stammered out something to Kolur—"Yes, sir, I'll run to the supply shop now."—and then scurried over to the ladder. I was too bewildered to move. Kolur shouted something toward the bow of the ship, probably at Frida, and then walked out of my line of sight.

And then Isolfr dropped down to the dock, a loop of rope draped over his shoulder. He had his head down.

"What the hell are you doing?" I said.

He jumped, stopped, looked up at me. For a moment, his eyes glimmered like starlight, but then they returned to a normal, flat blue. It was my imagination, I told myself, a trick of the sunlight.

"Well?" I said.

"Please, miss," he said, "I'm going to the repair shop."

I scowled at him, not having the patience to deal with his tricks. But then he winked.

"The repair shop," he said again, and scrambled off.

I sighed. I did not want to get involved with him again. I wanted to eat my lunch and go back to the *Cornflower* and shake my jar of stones and think about home.

But I was also angry, angry that he had foisted upon me the warning about Lord Foxfollow and then disappeared, that he had transformed himself into a blind spot for Kolur and Frida and then wheedled his way aboard this new version of the *Penelope*.

So I followed after him. I figured it was the only way I'd get answers.

I waited for him outside the repair shop, leaning up against the post of a sign I still couldn't read. The repair shop was all above-ground, and every now and then, the wind would blow the curtain door aside and I'd see him studying the different loops of rope. When he came back outside, he lifted one hand in a wave.

"What in sea and sky is going on?" I said.

"I can explain." He smiled. "You're hungry, yes? Would you like to get something to eat?"

"No." I didn't like that he knew I was hungry. "I want you to explain what the hell you're doing." I leaned close to him, lowering my voice. "You wouldn't let me tell Kolur who you were, and now you're *working* for him?"

"Well, you ran off." Isolfr turned and headed down the path, over to an empty space where the shops ended. He tossed the rope to the ground and gestured for me to join to him. I did, stupid me wanting my answers, and he cast a spell that washed over us both like a sudden wind.

"What was *that?*"

"So no one can hear us." Isolfr sat down on the rope. "So yes, I'm working for Kolur, but he doesn't quite *know* that. He thinks I'm a Tuljan boy named Pjetur."

"You're insane," I said. "Why are you doing this to us? To him?" I pointed to the docks, in the direction of the *Penelope II*. "How'd he even afford that ship, anyway? Was it you? Do you have money? Could you have sent me home?"

"He didn't buy it with money." Isolfr ran his hands over the rope. "He got the boat in exchange for a spell he and Frida performed—Jandanvari magic, very dangerous." Isolfr looked up at me. "And the boat wasn't seaworthy. Still isn't. That's why we're still here, doing repairs."

"Doing repairs to go on a fool's errand, is that it? And now you're helping him? You aren't even human. Why do you *care?*"

Isolfr drew his knees up to his chest. "I'm helping him because you won't," he said quietly.

"Because I *won't?*" Anger flushed in my cheeks. "I tried! But I had no idea what to do. You just gave me all these warnings and then—then *Gillean* was on deck and he was *dead*—"

"That was Lord Foxfollow," Isolfr said. "He found out. I had to go into hiding."

I wanted to hit him. "I'm lucky Kolur turned out to have magic. All you did was tell me what was coming and give me no way to fight it, and then you wouldn't even let me warn Kolur."

Isolfr's cheeks colored, twin spots of pink like on a doll. "I admit that clouding his memory may not have been the best course of action."

"They why did you do it?" I glowered at him. "Why are you *still* doing it?"

The color on Isolfr's cheek deepened. "You wouldn't understand."

"I think I have a right to know." I crossed my arms over my chest. "You're the reason I'm stranded here, after all. If you hadn't gotten involved—"

"You and Kolur and Frida would be dead," he interrupted. "Lord Foxfollow would have hunted you down."

"He only found us because we gave Gillean a funeral." I threw my hands in the air. "And we only had to give Gillean a funeral because his body dropped on our boat. Don't try and lay the blame on me, Isolfr. Don't you dare."

Isolfr shrank back. The magic of his spell shimmered around us, sweet and bright like honeycomb candy. "He would have found you anyway," he said. "Maybe you would have gotten all the way to Jandanvar first. But he would have killed you eventually."

There was an intensity in his voice I didn't expect. It shuddered through me and left me cold. But I wasn't going to back down.

"I still wouldn't say that anything you've done has helped us." I peered at him, trying to find some clue in those washed-out human features. "Why are you keeping Frida's and Kolur's minds clouded? At least tell me that much."

Isolfr looked down at his hands. "Fine, I'll tell you," he said.

I preened, hearing that. But it wasn't enough to quell my anger with him.

"Well?" I said.

"I'm getting to it." He looked up at me. "It's Frida. She's terrifying. When she was training in Jandanvar, she called down one of my brothers and she—she *bound* him to leach out his strength for her spell. My sister had to save him. He almost died."

"*Can* you even die?" I snapped. But Isolfr's eyes widened and I felt a pang of guilt. "Sorry," I said. "That wasn't—"

"Yes, I can die," he said. "Just not like you."

"What are you?"

He ignored my question. "Kolur was helping her. If either he or Frida saw me in my true form, they'd know what I am. They'd—recognize me. And I—I didn't want that."

"You're scared of them." It was a strange thought, and an unsettling one. A month ago, I would have found it laughable that anyone could be scared of Kolur, but now I wasn't so sure. He'd pretended to be a fisherman when he could have been a wizard. Maybe there was some wicked explanation. I shivered.

Isolfr looked away. The magic around us rippled and flickered. For a moment, I thought it was going to disappear completely.

"I was sent to warn them." He spoke down into the grass. "To give them aid. But I couldn't do it." His shoulders hitched, and I felt a twinge of pity for him that turned to irritation quickly enough.

"Who sent you?"

"My superiors. Their names are cloaked, so there's no point in me even saying them." He almost sounded miserable. "I don't know why they sent me. I told them what Frida and Kolur had done—"

"They wouldn't have hurt you," I said. "If you really are trying to help."

"I am!" He leaped to his feet and grabbed the rope. "And anyway, I'm working with them now, aren't I?"

"In disguise! You could have just done that from the beginning."

Once again, I'd said something he didn't want to hear, so he ignored me.

"This is pointless. I hope Kolur makes you empty their chamber pots." I stalked away from him and straight into the spell. At first I thought it was going to hold me in place, but the air yielded when I passed through. My ears rang, and my skin prickled. When I turned around, Isolfr was gone. No, not gone, just invisible. The way I'd been a few seconds previous.

"Don't come looking for me!" I shouted into the empty field. Then I stormed back down to the road. Isolfr didn't follow me, thank the gods. It figured that not only did I have to get saddled with some magical do-gooder, I had to get saddled with a cowardly, incompetent one.

The wind picked up, northerly and sweet-smelling. I shivered and drew my coat closer around my chest. And for a moment, I worried. Not about Isolfr—he wasn't human; he could take care of himself. But Kolur. Kolur and Frida, too, both sailing into the trap of Lord Foxfollow with only Isolfr to help them.

I shook my head. No. Kolur had lied to me. About where he was taking me, about his past. His business wasn't mine any longer. Lord Foxfollow cared not for me; I didn't want to steal away his bride. All I had to think about was earning enough money to get home.

The wind continued to blow, and I continued to shiver beneath my coat.

CHAPTER TEN

I hoped that would be the end of it. I hoped Isolfr would slink back to the *Penelope II* and do whatever weaselly things he could to keep Kolur and Frida out of trouble. Meanwhile, I'd continue to sail out with the *Annika* and we'd all go our separate ways. That's what I hoped life would be like.

And for a while, it was.

The jar in my captain's quarters grew heavier with stones, even though I had to dump out a handful to pay Rudolf the rent for my little moored *Cornflower*. I drew down the winds as the *Annika* sailed up and down the Tuljan coat, I ate meals with Asbera and Finnur, I fetched water from the well, and I bought food from the grocer.

It should have been peaceful, if not satisfying. But it wasn't. Something always niggled at the back of my head, a note of discomfort that made me toss and turn at night as the waves slapped against the walls of the boat. Whenever I was in town, I found myself looking over my shoulder, watching for the Mists.

I wanted to blame my encounter with Isolfr, thinking he must have planted ideas in my head. But deep down, I knew that wasn't it.

After a particularly long trip aboard the *Annika*, I went over to the *Crocus* for the usual dinner with Asbera and Finnur. I climbed over the railing, like always, but this time I saw something that made my heart pound: they had switched out the twisted-up vine charms, swapping the old for the new, and added at least twice as many as before. The charms hung from the masts like sails, dropping small oval leaves across the deck.

Seeing them stirred up a whisper of fear.

"Hanna! I thought I heard your feet on the ceiling." Asbera's head appeared in the hatch. "Dinner's almost ready." She stopped and set her hands on the deck and stared at me. "What's wrong?"

"You changed the vines," I said.

Her expression flickered. "Yes," she said. "I brought in some new charms. For protection."

"Were you robbed?" The question sounded naive, even to me.

Asbera shook her head. She shifted her weight like she was uncomfortable. "It's nothing, Hanna, it really isn't. You just have to be careful this far north."

"We know what the Mists are in Kjora."

"I know you do." She smiled. "Nothing's happened, you understand. It's just—a need for precaution."

I went down to dinner feeling uneasy.

The next day, I went into Rilil for the first time in nearly a week, and I saw that the charms hanging above the shop doors had gotten bigger too, plumped out with gray moss and dried flowers and wrapped in red ribbons. Tuljan characters were scratched in the soil and stained with red dye. I didn't have to read them to know that they were protection spells.

Compared to the elaborate earth-magic charms of the Tuljans, my bracelet from the Skalirin magic shop seemed paltry and weak, but I knew it was better than nothing. To calm myself at night, I practiced the protective wind charms I knew, standing up on the stern of the *Cornflower*, facing out to sea. I called the south wind, and its magic washed over the boat, settling in all the nooks and crannies. I hoped it would bring me the protection I needed.

One evening, everything still bright with the late spring sun,

I went for a walk along the docks, my hands tucked tight into my pockets to protect against the chill. I stopped when I spotted the *Penelope II* against the horizon, her Jolali carvings cast in silhouette against the white sky. At that point, I turned around and went back home.

I'd just wanted to know if Kolur had finished the repairs or not. I'd just wanted to know if she was still in port.

The *Annika* crew wasn't an exception to all this new paranoia, either. They took to muttering prayers whenever we left the docks and before we returned, whispering to themselves in a thicker-than-usual Tuljan dialect, the words guttural and unfamiliar. Finnur, seeing me listen in one morning, grabbed me by the hand and said the prayer over me, flashing a bright smile when he finished. "Now you're just like the rest of us," he said. It was from him that I learned the words were a prayer at all—an ancient one to guard against the Mists.

And then there were the Nalendan.

We saw them one morning as we dragged the night's catch to the market. The jangling, pounding music drifted down the street, and everyone in the crew stopped and set their loads down, even Baltasar. I followed their lead and rested my package of ling at my feet and stood straight and unmoving. The music set me on edge, even if it was a protection spell.

The costumed men approached, chanting the same song as before. Magic shimmered around them. The shopkeeper across the way tossed flowers and the man dressed as a pine tree bowed to her, the pines needles of his costume shining in the light.

Magic settled around us like a blanket.

The costumed men passed, and the air sighed with relief. The crew gathered up their packages, but the high spirits from our successful catch had disappeared. Asbera was frowning.

"What's wrong?" I whispered to her as we made our way down the street.

"The Nalendan," she said. "They were just here, remember? And to see them again, so soon—" She shook her head. "No matter. We should be grateful for the catch, don't you think?"

I nodded, although her words kept me on edge. We didn't speak the rest of the way to the market.

The costumed men disappeared around a curve in the road, but I could still hear their music on the wind.

A week later, Asbera and Finnur and I went out for drinks. We'd gotten back from a four-day trip and had the next few days off, so it seemed a fine idea to go down to the mead hall for a round or two. I knew we hoped the drinks would help dull the fear that had been cutting through Rilil lately. Not that any of us admitted that out loud.

The mead hall was crowded when we arrived, the lighting dim and smoky. I looked over the mass of faces, scanning for Kolur. I was about as keen on seeing him again as I was on seeing Isolfr. But in the dark light, it was too difficult to make anyone out. All the men looked the same, with their long hair and their thick northern beards.

"In the back," Finnur said to me. "There's always a place there."

We pushed through the crowd to a table in the corner. Asbera ordered ale for all three of us. "I'm looking forward to the next few days," she said when the serving girl had left. "Some of my herbs need tending to." She paused. "Maybe you'd like some, Hanna?"

I looked down at the table and twisted my bracelet around my wrist. The herbs, like the pieces of vine, were enchanted to protect the *Crocus* from the Mists. Everyone was protecting themselves from the Mists, but not a single damn person would admit to it outright. That probably explained why the mead hall was so crowded tonight. All that fear.

"I don't want to be a bother." I'd learned not to bring up the Mists myself. It worked out better that way, to keep my head down. "I'm sure you need them."

"I can spare a few." She smiled, and Finnur looked at her and then looked at me and grinned.

"Yeah, it's a right jungle on deck," he said. "Just like Jokja. You ever hear the stories about Jokja?"

"My mother sailed there," I said. "Her captain was friends with the queen's consort."

Asbera's eyes lit up. "Really? I hear the Jokja royalty is *grand*, that the palace is made entirely out of jewels. Is that true?"

Off to my side, Finnur scoffed, but I shook my head. "Not really. But Mama said you could feel the jungle's magic if you went too close."

Asbera's eyes glittered. Our drinks arrived, and the serving girl slammed them down on the table without saying a word. Finnur lifted his up in the air and said, "To two days of freedom."

"Freedom!" Asbera and I called out, laughing. We clicked our drinks together, ale sloshing over the sides, and drank. I didn't feel free. Every day away from the boat was a day I wasn't earning money to return back home.

"Hanna?"

The voice came from behind me. It was soft and silvery like moonlight. My stomach dropped out at the bottom.

"Who's this?" Asbera grinned. "Should we know him?"

"I'm Pjetur." Isolfr sat down in the seat beside me. I didn't bother to correct him; something told me Asbera and Finnur wouldn't hear me if I did. "I work for Hanna's old captain."

"Ah," Finnur said. "So you can shed some light on Hanna's mysterious past."

Asbera smacked him on the arm.

"Afraid not. I know as little as you do."

I ignored him and scanned the faces of the mead hall again. This time I did find Kolur, sitting over in the corner with Frida. He was staring at me, scowling, but when he saw me looking, he lifted one hand in greeting.

I turned away from him.

"Kolur asked me to check on you," Isolfr said. "He wants to make sure you're all right, that you have everything you need."

"Is that so?" I stared down at the foam of my ale, looking for patterns the way you do in tea leaves and coffee dregs. I didn't see anything.

"Yes. Things have been—" Isolfr stopped when he saw Asbera and Finnur staring at him with unease. "Stormy."

"Been clear skies for me." I took a long drink of ale. "And they'll be clearer once Kolur leaves."

"Is that true?" Finnur asked. "About Kolur bringing—"

Asbera looked at him sharply, and he didn't finish his question. But I knew he was asking if Kolur brought the Mists here.

"Yes," I said. "That's why I left him."

"You poor dear," Asbera said. "No wonder you want to get away."

"You can't lay the blame entirely on Kolur." Isolfr looked shyly over at Asbera. "Hanna has a tendency to exaggerate."

I glared at him.

Asbera laughed. "Not from what I've seen."

"Not from what he's seen, either." I turned to Isolfr. "Are you finished here? *Pjetur?*"

He recoiled a little at the snap in my voice, but he did answer with "I am." He didn't move away from the table, though, only stared at me with his flat pale eyes. "You could do a great deal of good aboard the *Penelope II*, and if nothing else, it would be a free place to sleep." He paused. "I'm sorry I didn't help you enough before."

"Not interested," I said. "Like fishing better."

Isolfr granted me one last hopeless look. Then he stood and gave a weird, formal bow to Asbera and Finnur both before scuttling to Kolur's table.

"My," said Asbera. "I bet that's an interesting story."

I swirled my ale around. "It's not."

"Prettiest fisherman I've ever seen," said Finnur.

Asbera laughed. "I was thinking the same thing. You sure you don't want to go back to the *Penelope II*? Might be worth the——" Her voice hitched. "The danger."

I knocked back a swig of ale. "Hardly." I didn't want to talk about this, didn't want to talk about Isolfr, or Pjetur, or his unsettling beauty. They hadn't even seen him in the moonlight and the ocean, the way I had. They'd only seen this watered-down version of him, his beauty faded into handsome blandness.

"You sure about that?" Finnur said. "I feel like Asbera's about to go in your place."

Asbera shrieked and shoved him, a blush creeping along her cheeks.

"She likes her fishermen pretty," Finnur said, and Asbera grew redder and redder. I watched them laugh and flirt with each other, and I didn't bother to correct Finnur. Isolfr wasn't a fisherman. Isolfr wasn't even human.

Hard to fall in love with something like that.

We wound up staying late at the mead hall, later than most of the folks there. We certainly stayed later than Kolur and Frida and Isolfr—I saw them gather up their things and leave while Finnur was in the middle of a dirty joke. When they walked away, I was finally able to relax.

By the time we left, I'd drunk much more mead than I was used to. The candles lighting the hall were as bright and golden as summer suns, and Finnur and Asbera seemed to glow, especially when they looked at each other. It was nice, all that warmth drawing us together. Stumbling out into the cold, empty street was a shock.

"Everyone's gone hooome!" Finnur sang out, throwing his hands wide. Asbera and I laughed at him, and our voices echoed up into the night air.

"Look at the stars," Asbera said, leaning back. She grabbed my arm and pointed. "Look!"

I looked. Like the mead hall candles, they were bright, a brilliant spiral of light spilling across the black sky. For a moment, Asbera and I stood very still, clutching at each other's arms and looking up at the stars. Our breath crystallized on the air in great white puffs.

"Beautiful," I finally said.

"You act like you've never seen stars before," Finnur shouted, and he smacked me on the back, startling me out of my daze. I looked over at him and grinned. He had his arms slung around both our shoulders. "Asbera and Hanna," he slurred. "Never seen the stars."

Asbera tickled his ribcage, and he crumpled into laughter that sounded hollow in the empty street. Even after he stopped laughing, I could hear it still, bouncing off the music.

Music.

Finnur's laughter—and music.

Jangling, pounding music.

"Shhhh," I hissed. They were all wrapped up in each other's arms. "Do you hear that?"

"No," Finnur said, but Asbera tilted her head like she was listening.

"Yeah," she said. "I hear it." She pulled away from Finnur. "The Nalendan."

The name sent a chill down my spine.

"Protecting us from the—you know." Her face was pale in the starlight. "They never march this late, do they, Finnur?"

"We don't usually have this much to worry about." Finnur's voice was throaty, bitter. He must have had a lot to drink, if he was acknowledging the threat outright. I shivered. "Thank your captain for us."

"Shush," said Asbera.

We pressed together, swaying in the middle of the road. A pinpoint of blue light appeared in the distance. The music rose and fell with the wind.

Coldness prickled at the back of my throat.

"Maybe we aren't supposed to be here," I said.

"Nonsense," said Asbera. "We just need to find some snowflowers to throw at them." She pulled away from Finnur and me and stumbled over to the grocer's across from the mead hall. It was closed for the night, the curtain pinned shut, no light spilling out around it. She rang the bell.

"They're closed." Finnur chased after her. The light at the end of the road grew bigger, wreathed in a shimmering halo of magic.

"I really don't think we're supposed to be here," I whispered.

I glanced over at Finnur and Asbera and found them kissing each other, like they'd forgotten where we were. "Hey!" I shouted. "Pay attention! We need to go home."

They pulled apart and both turned to me, their faces pale in the moonlight. "Don't be silly," said Asbera. "It's good luck to see the Nalendan."

It didn't feel like good luck, being out here alone in the dark. I looked back at the light. The Nalendan grew closer. Their singing was stronger, louder. I ran over to Finnur and Asbera and we stood in a line, waiting. My heart pounded in my chest. My thoughts were dizzy with drink. I didn't feel like I was part of this world.

My bracelet. I'd forgotten I was wearing my bracelet.

I touched it and the vines were cold. My heart skipped a beat. *No*, I told myself. *Of course they're cold, it's cold out here.*

The singing was louder now, louder than it ought to be. Finnur and Asbera both grinned wildly, like children waiting for gifts on midsummer. I pressed closer to them, still touching my bracelet. The wind lifted, rustled my hair. It blew in from the north and smelled of flowers. It was so soft against my skin it almost felt like protective magic.

For a split second I felt that presence I had known when I was aboard the *Penelope*. But then it was gone.

"Here they coooome," Finnur said, under his breath.

In the dark, all I could see were shadows: the silhouette of a man-sized pine, the shaggy hulk of a yak's-head mask, the twist of goat's horns, the straw-man shaped like a star. I trembled. I held my breath. Closer. Closer.

The music buzzed. It didn't sound right. I told myself it sounded that way because of the drink, that the ale had made me paranoid. I gripped my bracelet tighter, and it was so cold that it seared into my fingers.

"Something's *wrong*," I whispered. Finnur and Asbera didn't hear me; they stood transfixed, staring at the costumed men. "The music—that isn't right—"

"It's the Tuljan dialect," Asbera said, but her voice was slurred, and she sounded distant, not part of herself.

"No, that isn't it." The wind blew harder and amplified the

singing. Clarified it. The words were sharp and unfamiliar. "I don't think that's the ancient language at all."

But Finnur and Asbera weren't paying any attention to me. They moved forward, toward the costumed men, drawn on some invisible wire.

"Stop!" I shrieked. "This isn't supposed to happen." I grabbed at both of their arms, yanking them back.

The costumed men halted. They'd never done that before. Their singing died away and their heads turned, in unison, and they bore down on the three of us.

A tree, a goat, a straw-man, a yak. I felt suddenly diminished.

Asbera and Finnur pulled away from my grip and moved toward the costumed men. The tree smiled, his teeth bright in the moonlight.

"No!" I screamed, and I tackled Asbera and dragged her to the ground.

"What are you doing?" she asked, spitting out muddy snow. Her voice didn't sound so curiously flat. "What's wrong with you—"

She stopped. Finnur was almost to the costumed men. The goat lifted his great shaggy arms as if to envelop him.

"This isn't right," Asbera said.

"I've been saying that!" I scrambled to my feet. The goat drew Finnur into an embrace. His eyes glittered behind his mask. Gray. His eyes were gray.

All of them, their eyes—they were all gray.

The Mists.

The air slammed out of me.

"No," Asbera whispered, low and fluttery. "No, no, no, no."

The yak stepped forward. The mask was carved from wood and painted in dull brownish-gray. The mouth was fixed in a permanent snarl.

"Friend of Kolur." Its mouth didn't move as it spoke. Asbera let out a strangled squawk and grabbed my hand. The goat pulled Finnur closer, wrapping its furred arm around Finnur's neck. Finnur was so pale, his skin looked like snow.

"Stop it!" I shouted. "Let him go!"

"*Friends* of Kolur," the monster said.

"No!" I cried. "Just me. They've never met him. Please, let Finnur go."

All the stories about the Mists flooded through my head. You couldn't outsmart them; you couldn't undo their magic. And that was terrifying, because dressed in the costume of the Nalendan, they had undone Tuljan magic. They had turned the protection spell into a weapon.

"Let him go!" I shrieked.

The straw man hissed.

I didn't stop to let myself think, because thinking only reminded me of all the horrors I could face. I just launched myself forward and grabbed Finnur's hand and tried to wrench him free from the goat. Asbera screamed behind me, but then she was at my side, pulling too. Finnur stared numbly at both of us.

The costumed men didn't do anything to stop us, although they didn't let go of Finnur either. The goat didn't struggle, just held him tight, and the other three stood in a circle, watching.

"Curious," said the straw man with a dry, crackling hiss.

"Yes," said the tree. "Most curious."

"Come back to me, Finnur!" Asbera cried. "Please. Remember. Our little sea-house. Come on, darling—"

We pulled harder, and then, without any warning at all, the goat let him go.

All three of us fell backward onto the cold, hard ground.

"Friend of Kolur," said the tree, and all four of the costumed men turned toward me. I froze in place while Asbera and Finnur crawled away.

"Friend of Isolfr," said the monster.

Asbera cried out, her voice strangled. I tried to twist around to look at her, but I couldn't move. I was bolted to the ground. The costumed men crowded in close.

"What do you want?" I screamed.

The wind gusted. Through the cloud of my fear, I thought I might be able to conjure the south wind, to pull out enough magic that Finnur and Asbera and I could escape. It probably wouldn't work, not against Mists magic. But I could try.

"Our lord does not appreciate what you've been doing," said the straw-man.

"No," said the goat. "Not at all."

"He's sent us to make you stop," said the tree.

"You and Kolur and Isolfr," said the yak.

"I don't even sail with Kolur anymore." I concentrated hard on the wind. It was cold and damp and blew my hair straight away from my face. The costumed men's gray eyes glittered at me from behind their masks. "I haven't seen him for days. I can't help you."

Magic coursed through the wind, fine and gossamer like lace. It tingled against my skin. *Concentrate. Concentrate.*

The costumed men looked at one another.

"Of course you can help us," said the goat.

"Friend of Kolur," said the tree.

"Friend of Isolfr," said the yak.

I started to cry. The wind pummeled against my body, and my hair blew straight out behind me—

And then my hair tumbled into my face.

The wind had shifted. I could taste the south on it, mangos and warmth and the distant brightness of spice. With the southerly wind, the magic didn't feel like lace; it felt like sunlight, like ocean water, like air. It was everywhere, and all I had to do was reach out and harvest it.

I squeezed my eyes shut. The magic flowed through me, changing inside my bloodstream. I whispered an incantation in the old tongue, and I told myself it would work, it would have to work—

The paralysis lifted.

My eyes flew open, and I jumped to my feet. The wind swirled around us, looping around the costumed men like a rope. I stumbled away from them, gasping with the effort. Asbera and Finnur lay tangled up against each other, their eyes closed.

The tree broke free of my chains.

"Friend of Kolur. You cannot stop us."

I strengthened the magic, and the wind knocked him away. He landed on his back, shedding pine needles in the moonlight. I knelt beside Asbera and Finnur and sent the magic flowing through them. Their veins glowed golden beneath their skin.

"Wake up," I whispered in the ancient tongue. "Wake up, wake up, wake up."

Asbera's eyes opened first. She stared at me like I was a wild animal.

"Hanna!" she gasped.

"You must move." I said this in the ancient tongue too. Asbera's eyes widened and her arms jerked and the wind dragged her body up until she was standing. Then it dragged Finnur up. His eyes fluttered.

"Run!" I screamed at them, still in the ancient tongue. "Run! Run home!"

The costumed men wailed over the roaring of the wind. I couldn't tell which direction it blew; it seemed to come from everywhere, north and south, east and west. Asbera and Finnur raced away, their movements jerky and awkward and not entirely their own.

I whirled around to face the costumed men. The thread of magic had tightened around them. I stared; I hadn't tightened it. I'd been tending to Finnur and Asbera, and doing so had sapped me of my strength.

The rioting wind howled and howled, drowning out the cries from the costumed men. It howled so much that it became a voice, sharp and shining and cold like ice. I wasn't sure if I imagined it or not.

It spoke the ancient tongue.

Run, it said. *Run. Run away.*

And I did.

CHAPTER ELEVEN

Somehow, I made it back to the boarding boats. The wind faded the farther I got from the costumed men, and by the time I was back on the docks, it was a gentle breeze, strong enough to rock the boarding boat sign back and forth on its post but nothing more. I leaned up against the signpost. My legs trembled and my lungs burned and every muscle in my body ached. I prayed to all the gods and ancestors I knew that the costumed men—the *Mists* men—wouldn't come for me. I had no more strength left to fight them.

"Hanna?"

Asbera's voice trembled from out of the thick night. It sounded small and afraid. She stood at the end of the dock, a magic-cast lantern hanging from one hand. "Hanna—what happened—"

She moved toward me, although her steps were slow and unsteady. She must have been weak too. The lantern swayed, the blue light gliding across the docks. As she drew closer, I saw the streaks of tears on her face.

"Finnur?" I asked.

"He's alive." She hung the lantern from a hook on the sign. For a moment, we stared at each other. Then she flung her arms around my shoulders and buried her face in my neck. "Oh, thank you, Hanna, we would've—I don't even want to think what would have happened if you hadn't been there."

I hugged back as best I could. My thoughts were clouded with exhaustion.

Asbera pulled away and smiled through her tears. "You were so brave. I can't believe they—that was the Mists, wasn't it? They *desecrated* the Nalendan." She looked ill. "How is that even possible?"

"I don't know." I stood there, wobbling in place.

"We have to tell the priests," Asbera babbled. "We have to warn them. I just don't know how this could have happened."

"They were trying to find me." I stared blankly ahead. "The Mists. It's my fault you were hurt."

"We weren't hurt." Asbera grabbed my hand. "We weren't hurt, because you saved us."

I shook my head. Asbera pulled me into a hug, almost knocking me off balance, and I could smell the smoky-sweet scent of magic on her, and the sharp tang of old fear.

"Thank you," she said when she let me go.

It felt wrong, taking her thanks. Humans weren't able to defeat Mists magic; everyone knew that. And certainly not humans like *me*, some fisherman's apprentice who could control the winds for ships and not much else. Someone must have helped me.

Kolur. Kolur had dragged us away from the Mists before. And that fierce northern wind—Frida, maybe, helping him.

"You can stay with us tonight," Asbera said. "I wouldn't feel comfortable letting you go back to the *Cornflower* alone."

I nodded, feeling numb. Asbera rowed us back to the *Crocus*, and the slap of the oars against the water kept time with the beat of my heart. She took me down below, past the rustling plants and dried-out vines. Finnur was stretched out on a cot beside the hearth, liquid bubbling in a cauldron on the fire. It released peppery-scented steam into the air, and the magic tingled across my skin like an ointment.

Asbera knelt beside him and pushed his hair off his forehead. Her eyes shimmered.

"Is he going to be all right?" I asked.

She didn't answer right away, just kept stroking his hair and staring down at him. "Yes. We got away just in time." She stood up and wiped at her eyes. "Can I get you something to drink? Or eat? You must be exhausted, all that magic—"

I nodded. Yes. Food. Food was necessary to rebuild your strength. I sat down at the table and watched Finnur as Asbera rummaged around in the storage barrels. He shifted, stirred, rolled over in his sleep. Seeing that movement gave me a rush of relief.

For the first time since we'd left the mead hall, my heart began to slow.

That night, I slept on a hammock in the corner of the *Crocus* hearth-room and woke to find Asbera feeding breakfast to Finnur.

"He's doing so much better," she said when I knelt down at her side.

"Thank you," Finnur added. His voice was scratchy and thin. "That was—well, I don't want to go through it again." He started to cough, and Asbera dropped his breakfast to the side and tilted a cup of water to his lips. "I'm fine," he said, batting her hand away. He did look better. There was more color in his skin, and his eyes were no longer glassy and blank.

"Would you like something to eat?" Asbera asked, turning to me.

"Thank you, and thank you for letting me sleep here, but I need to go—"

"Don't be ridiculous," Asbera said, and Finnur coughed in protest.

"It's fine, really," I said. "I need to speak with—with someone. My old captain. I'll be back aboard the *Cornflower*, so—"

"This is no time to be alone," Asbera said.

"I agree," Finnur said.

I forced myself to stay patient. I really was grateful that I didn't have to spend the night by myself. But I needed to speak with Kolur. He'd likely saved me last night, and Mama and Papa had taught me well enough that I knew I should thank him. But I also knew the only reason the Mists were still here was because the *Penelope II* hadn't moved on yet. I wanted to know what sort of repairs they were doing and how long those repairs would take.

Asbera sighed, her brow creased with concern. "At least stay for breakfast," she said. "Make sure you have all your strength."

I hesitated. As anxious as I was to get to the *Penelope II*, I had to admit that Finnur's breakfast porridge, flecked with sweet flowers and dried ice berries, looked nourishing and warm.

"Fine," I said. "But just breakfast."

Asbera scooped me up a bowl of porridge. I ate it mostly in silence, trying hard not to think of last night. When I finished, Asbera walked me up to the deck.

"Come back straight away," she said. "And take a bit of protection vine. It's good luck."

It was more than good luck, even I knew that, but in the morning's bright glare, Asbera wasn't willing to talk about the threat of the Mists outright.

So I snapped off a bit of vine. The magic shuddered through me at the moment of breakage, a magic far more powerful than any in my bracelet.

"Thank you," I told her. "I won't be gone long."

"Wait." She put one hand on my arm. "We have to report what happened to the priests. If the Nalendan can be violated—" She covered her heart like the thought pained her. "When you come back, we can make the trip together."

"Of course," I said.

And with that, I was on my way to the *Penelope II*.

The sun was out, and the air was cold and brittle. People milled around on the docks, hawking cheap, weak-looking protection charms along with the usual salted cod and fishing supplies. I shivered every time I passed one of the charm merchants.

As I walked, I thought about Kolur. That was powerful magic, to stop the Mists the way he did. I wondered what other secrets he'd kept from me and Mama and the rest of the village.

The *Penelope II* was moored in its usual place. The gangplank was down, so I climbed aboard as if we were back on Kjora. I peeked my head over the railing but didn't see anyone.

"Hello!" I shouted. "Kolur? I need to speak with you."

No answer but the rushing sea. I hoisted myself up on deck. The *Penelope II* was bigger, a proper frigate, with three masts instead of two, and a wider deck. It wasn't the sort of boat you used just for fishing.

"Kolur!" I shouted. "It's Hanna! I really need to—"

"Yeah, yeah, I heard you, girl."

Kolur's voice came from behind me, as gruff as ever. I whirled around and found him climbing out of the hatchway with a loop of rope draped over his left shoulder.

"What do you want? We're still heading north, so I don't got a job for you."

"All I wanted was to thank you for last night." I rushed over to him and helped pull him on deck. "I would never have gotten away—"

"The hell are you talking about?" Kolur dropped the rope on the deck. "I spent last night patching the hull. Took me hours, too. That good-for-nothing Pjetur fell asleep at sundown and couldn't be roused. Sleeps like a man damned, he does." Kolur kicked at the rope and squinted up at the masts. "Really don't feel like climbing up there this morning."

"You don't have to do this." I crossed my arms over my chest. "You already told me you were some great wizard. You don't have to pretend anymore."

"Ain't pretending." He looked over at me, frowning. "Did something happen to you?"

I felt cold. "Yes! I was attacked by the Mists. And I called up my magic but it wasn't enough, just me. Someone was helping—"

Kolur looked as confused as I felt. Not to mention horrified. "The Mists *attacked* you?" he said. "Sea and sky, girl, and you got *away*?"

"That's what I'm trying to tell you! Someone helped me." That cold feeling grew stronger. "It wasn't you. Frida, it must have been Frida—"

"Frida was helping me," Kolur said. "Patching the hull." He studied me, his eyes sharp and keen. "This some trick? To get back at me?"

That cold, creeping feeling turned my whole body to ice. "Not a trick," I said softly. "Someone helped me. It wasn't you. It wasn't Frida—"

Isolfr? Not that he'd done much to help me in all this time.

Kolur was still staring at me. "If you really did get attacked by the Mists," he said, "you need to talk to the Tuljan priests."

"When the Mists attacked," I said, "they called me friend of Kolur."

Kolur paused. Then he rubbed his forehead. "Shit. I'm sorry, girl. These repairs are taking longer than I expected, but they shouldn't be coming after you now that you're not a part of my crew. You really do need to go to the priests, tell 'em what happened. They'll get you protected."

I felt numb. The priests' magic had failed so spectacularly last night—not just failed, but been desecrated, like Asbera said. Corrupted.

"Thanks," I mumbled, and I turned and stumbled off the boat. Kolur called out my name, but I ignored him.

Asbera and I walked to the temple as soon as I got back to the boarding boats. We wrapped our arms in vines and carried moss in our pockets, Tuljan charms to keep the Mists away. Finnur was too weak to hike to the base of the mountain, so he stayed behind with Benedict and Harald, two friends from the *Annika*.

I was nervous and on edge. We took a long way through Rilil so as to avoid the place where the Mists had attacked us, walking with the yak herders back to the field of tents, the yaks grunting and shuffling over the hard soil.

"When we arrive at the temple," Asbera said as we left the edge of the village, "Let me speak to the priests. They'll recognize my dialect more easily. The priests have all the worst traits of us Tuljans, and they can be terribly distrustful of foreigners."

I nodded, grateful that I wouldn't have to say anything. I didn't have much practice dealing with the holy.

"I do hope they'll be able to help us," Asbera said after a pause.

"I'm sure they will," I told her, although I had my doubts. The Mists had used the Tuljans' own charms against them—what else could the priests possibly do?

We threaded through the field of tents. Children clumped together when they saw us coming, their eyes big and curious.

"You don't see fisherfolk so much, living out here," Asbera said softly. "I remember the first time I saw Finnur. I wasn't sure he was even human."

I smiled politely, but I thought of Isolfr.

It took the better part of a day to weave through the tents. The mountain loomed in the distance, its peak shrouded with thin white clouds. We took our lunch in the grass, crouching down and eating the salted fish and crackers that Asbera had prepared. The cold, biting wind whipped my hair into my face as I ate. I would have given anything for a glass of mulled wine, but we wouldn't be back in the village until nightfall.

After lunch, we continued to walk. We had run out of things to say—and we'd had little to say in the beginning, truth be told, as I fretted over the mystery of my aid last night. I assumed that Asbera was worried about Finnur.

Our thoughts were our true companions that trip.

The tents became more sporadic in the afternoon, and soon they disappeared completely, giving way to an ocean of yellow grass. The mountain didn't seem any closer.

"It just keeps pulling away from us!" I cried. "We're as far away as when we started."

"No, we're making progress." Asbera frowned up at the mountain. "It just always looks closer than it is."

We walked. My legs ached, and my lips cracked from the cold wind. I was ready to give up, to turn around and march back to the village and huddle up on the *Cornflower* with every protection charm I could buy or cast. But then I saw a curl of white smoke in the distance, drifting up from the rocks of the mountain.

"There." Asbera sounded relieved. "The temple."

"All I see are rocks."

"It's built into the mountain's base. You have to look *close*." She pointed, and I followed the arrow of her finger. I couldn't see anything. And then, with a blink, I could: a stone building jutting out of the ground, the smoke twisting around it like a wraith.

"From here, it's not much longer," Asbera said.

We waded through the grass. Now that I had seen the temple, I couldn't imagine ever not seeing it, and as we approached, the carvings in the stone grew more elaborate. Figures rose out of the rock, the faces of gods and ancestors I didn't recognize. The same moss that Asbera and I carried in our pockets grew in hollowed-out stones that created a path leading to the temple entrance. Candles flickered among the rocks, the flames golden with magic and ever burning.

Asbera stopped a few paces from the start of the path.

"There are certain rituals," she said. "Simple ones. Just watch me and you'll be fine."

"Understood," I said. There was a temple in Kjora, in the capital city, but I'd never been there. I'd no idea if it was like this one or not. It certainly wasn't built into a mountain.

Asbera stepped forward. She stooped and picked up two candles and handed one to me. It was cool to the touch, and no wax dripped down its side.

"Remember," Asbera whispered to me. "Stay silent. I'll speak."

I nodded. She stepped in front of me and we proceeded in single file through the entrance of the temple. It was dark on the other side of the doorway, darker than it ought to be with the wan sun still shining outside. Our candles cast small spheres of golden light, and I barely made out Asbera's outline ahead of me. She moved slowly, one hand outstretched to the cave's wall. I wasn't sure if that was a ritual or not, but I touched the wall just to be sure. It was cold and wet, the rock slimy beneath my fingers.

I couldn't say how long we walked in the dark. The moments seemed to stretch out and out until I could no longer count them. The only things that kept me from turning around were the sight of Asbera ahead and the sound of her shuffling footsteps.

A light appeared in the distance.

It was bluish white, like a star, not the eerie golden light of our candles. Asbera let out a breath. "We're here," she whispered. "Stay alert."

I nodded before remembering that she couldn't see me. "Yes, I will."

We edged forward. The bluish light grew brighter and brighter until it became a doorway, towering several heads above us and carved with the same faces as the exterior. The air smelled of burning cedar.

Asbera stopped in the doorway and spoke, her Tuljan dialect exaggerated. I gathered she was asking permission for us to enter.

When she finished speaking, the silence rang in my ears.

"Yes, Asbera Corra and the Kjoran Hanna Euli. You may enter."

The voice boomed like an echo. Asbera bowed her head as she walked through the entranceway, and I did the same, keeping my gaze on the back of her feet. She stopped. I stopped. I lifted my head just enough to see that she had lifted hers.

The room was enormous and carved out of rock that glittered and shone in the light of the lanterns drifting through the air, like leaves caught on a pond. Three priests stood in a row before us, wearing the same shaggy gray furs that the Nalendan goat-man wore. At least they didn't have on masks.

Hanna set her candle down in a grooved indentation in a nearby rock, and I shuffled up beside her to do the same. She bowed.

"Priest-lords of Tulja," she said, "we bring distressing news."

Her accent wasn't as strong now. The priests exchanged glances.

"Of what, child of Tulja?" asked the priest in the middle.

Asbera hesitated. She smoothed her hands along the fabric of her skirt.

"The Mists," she said. "The Mists perverted the magic of the Nalendan and attacked us two nights ago. They took on the form of the Nalendan and lured us into a false sense of safety by profaning the Nal ritual."

The priests turned to one another and murmured among themselves, too quiet for me to hear. In the blue light they looked like ghosts.

One of the priests stepped away from the others. His furs dragged along the damp cavern floor as he glided toward us. I shivered and then forced myself to stand still. Asbera kept her gaze on him.

"Yes, we know," the priest said.

"We sensed the magic crumble," said one of the others, his voice drifting out of the shadows. His accent was almost too thick for me to understand.

Asbera let out a muffled cry of fear.

"Don't worry, child of Tulja," said the priest closest to us. "We drove them out for the time being." He set one hand on her shoulder, although he looked uncomfortable with the gesture. "When they return, we'll be prepared."

Asbera nodded. "Thank you, priest-lords of Tulja." She bowed and reached out for her candle. But the priest covered her hand, stopping her.

"No. You mustn't leave yet."

Asbera froze, and a sharp blade of fear plunged into my belly.

"This one," the priest said, turning his gaze on me. I gasped at the sight of his eyes, for they had no whites, only a matte silvery blue surrounding a tiny dot of black pupil. "This one helped you escape."

Asbera blinked, looking confused. "Yes," she said. "Yes, she saved my life, and the life of my husband, Finnur Corra."

The priest smiled. It was not a warm smile.

"No," he said. "Not this one. The north wind." He pointed up at the ceiling and without thinking, I looked up. I saw nothing but pointed columns winding down from the rocks. "The north wind saved you. This one only helped."

Behind him, the other two priests murmured.

Asbera kept her back straight. I got the sense it would not be proper for her to turn around.

"Your friend is the reason they are here." The priest was speaking directly to me now, his cold metal eyes taking me in. "Your friend from Jandanvar."

I froze, too afraid to move.

"He seeks to destroy their schemes, and they shall stop him however they can."

The weight of the priest's gaze made my skin crawl.

"I'm—sorry?" I said.

"However, the north wind would destroy us all." With that, the priest whirled around and glided back to the others. They murmured to one another. Asbera glanced over at me, her face frightened and pale. She mouthed one word: *What?*

I shook my head. I knew then I would have to tell her all that I knew about Kolur, although I didn't understand what Kolur's choices had to do with me. I no longer served aboard the *Penelope*. I was just a fisherwoman saving money for the journey home. Even Isolfr had finally offered his aid to Kolur directly, more or less.

I had so many questions but I was too afraid of the priests to ask them.

"Go in peace, child of Tulja," the priest said. "You have nothing to fear. Our magic will protect you."

For a moment, I expected Asbera to protest, to demand an explanation. We had walked all this way for nothing.

Although he had mentioned the north wind—a presence on the north wind. I had felt it too. Maybe he was just referring to Frida—maybe that was the real reason why Isolfr was frightened of her.

Asbera picked up her candle and gestured for me to do the same. She bowed deeply in the direction of the priests, holding the candle level with her forehead, before leaving the chamber. I trailed behind her. Our candles guttered in the dark, and the movements cast long, eerie shadows along the wall. I thought I saw the shape of goats and trees and yaks.

When we finally stepped out of the cave, the sky was purple with twilight. Both candles were extinguished at once.

"What were they saying?" Asbera looked at me. "Someone helped you? You know someone from Jandanvar?"

I took a deep breath and set my candle down on a nearby rock. Asbera cursed and shook her head and snatched it up. "We have to drop them in the urn."

"Oh. Sorry."

"What was all that about?"

"I didn't understand all of it." We walked away from the cave, and when we passed an urn carved out of the rocks, Asbera tossed both our candles in. I never heard them hit the bottom. "Kolur, my old captain, trained as a wizard in Jandanvar. He's trying to win back the love of the Jandanvari queen. That's why I left him. I thought it was stupid, and I just want to go home." Tears edged at my eyes. "I don't have any ties to the Mists, I swear. They're trying to stop Kolur, and I'm entangled in it now—"

I collapsed on an outcropping of rocks, ignoring the patches of ice and frozen mud. My tears stung hot against my cheeks. "I didn't even know what he was doing until we landed in Tulja. And now I'm stranded here, and the Mists are attacking, and I don't know what to do. I keep feeling something in the north wind, and I don't know why. My magic comes from the *south*—"

"Oh, sweetheart." Asbera sat beside me and wrapped her arm around my shoulder and pulled me in for a hug. I wept out all my frustrations.

"It's not your fault," she said after a few moments had passed.

"I know, but it just—" I shook my head. "I don't know why all this is happening to me."

"Dumb luck." Asbera smiled. I wiped the last remaining tears away from my eyes. "And it was dumb luck that you happened to run into Finnur when Baltasar had been saying for weeks he was sick of Reynir messing up the winds. Dumb luck that we became friends."

I smiled at that. I knew we were friends, but it was another thing to hear her say it out loud.

"The priests will keep us safe," Asbera said. "They always have before. And sooner or later, this Kolur is going to leave for Jandanvar, right?"

"He says the repairs are taking longer than he expected."

"But all repairs end eventually. See? Soon everything will go back to normal." She grinned. "Maybe you'll even marry some Tuljan fisherman and stay here with us."

I laughed. "Maybe."

Asbera stood up and pulled me to my feet. The sun was liquid gold on the edge of the horizon.

"Time flows differently inside the temple," Asbera said. "How would you like to spend the night with the yak herders? I used to be one of them. I'm sure they'll extend their hospitality."

I didn't like the thought of walking through the night, and I suspected Asbera felt the same, even if she wouldn't say it directly.

"Yes," I said. "I think that would be lovely."

CHAPTER TWELVE

I was too accustomed to southerly ways, as well as life aboard a fishing boat, to appreciate spending the night in one of those round tents the way Asbera clearly did. I had some trouble sleeping that night, curled up on my bed of yakskin, listening to the wind howling outside. The north wind. I knew it because I felt flickers of that presence as the wind pressed against the white fabric of the tent. I shivered but I wasn't afraid—that presence had helped me against the Mists.

The next day, Asbera and I returned to Rilil without trouble, and the bright morning was still and cold.

Finnur healed from his exhaustion within a few days' time, although he didn't go out with us on the *Annika*'s next run. "Lazing his life away," Asbera told me as we drew up the sails together. She laughed, but I could tell she worried about him. Still, he was waiting for us when we returned three days later, stretched out on the deck of the *Crocus* in a patch of lemony sunlight, braiding vines together to make more charms.

The *Annika* went on two more short trips, leaving in the morning and returning in full dark of the same day. Finnur was well enough to sail on the second trip, and when he climbed aboard, the crew shouted boisterously for him. Even Baltasar looked pleased, and he slapped Finnur on the back as Finnur picked up a coil of rope and shouted, "Back to work!"

There were no more attacks from the Mists.

I didn't let my guard down, though. In those first few weeks after the attack, I wore my bracelet everywhere, even to bed, and the dried vines grew so brittle and worn that they finally frayed and fell apart. I was lucky it happened while I was aboard the *Cornflower* and I was able to find the bracelet lying unceremoniously on the middle of the deck. I repaired it with a bit of red yarn from the magic shop, murmuring Kjoran protection charms while the south wind swirled around me. When I slipped the bracelet back on, its magic was stronger than it had been before, and it pulsed with my heartbeat.

The magic around the village began to change after our visit to the priests—a gradual fortification that made the air taste of metal and incense smoke, like the air in the priests' temples. This new magic crackled against my own, particularly when I returned from sea and was weak from using it so much during the trip.

More charms appeared around the village, not just vines and moss, but also tiny figurines carved from mountain stone. They materialized in windows and at crossroads, always watchful. I didn't like them, because they bore the same shapes as the costumed men: a yak, a goat, a straw-man, a pine tree. Everywhere I went I felt a jolt of fear, seeing one of them lurking out of the corner of my eye.

It didn't help that I'd learned that the boats leaving Tulja rarely sailed as far south as Kjora. My jar of stones was almost half full, and I carted it down to the dock master, who lived and worked from a moored junk at the edge of the bay. He was kindly enough, his face wizened and bearded, and his eyes crinkled with a smile when I set the jar on his desk.

"I want to book passage to Kjora," I told him. "How much will it cost? These are all the stones I have saved up."

The dock master picked up my jar and gave a good hard shake. "You've saved quite a bit, Empire girl. I heard about you. Working aboard the *Annika*, yes?"

I shifted in my seat, impatient. "Yes. Is it enough to get me home? I'm from Kjora, not the Empire. And of course I'm willing to work while I'm on board the ship too."

The dock master set the jar back down. "If you're willing to work, you wouldn't need to pay for anything." Another smile. "But you'll have a good spot of trouble finding a boat that'll take you as far as Kjora. Best I can do is get you to Latul, and it might be months before another boat comes along. I'm sorry, my dear."

My lungs felt hollow. I thought of all those eerie figurines watching me from the shadows of Rilil. There was even one in the dock master's office, sitting next to a window covered by a scrap of hide. A yak-man.

But even I knew this wasn't the fault of the costumed men. It wasn't even the fault of the Mists.

"You save a bit more, you might be able to buy a boat." The dock master shrugged. "Don't know about a crew, though."

"How much more?"

The dock master hesitated. He looked down at his hands. "Quite a bit more, in truth. A lug or junk capable of that sort of journey—at least three thousand stones."

I stared at him. Three thousand stones. I hadn't counted the stones in my jar, but I doubted I'd earned three thousand stones in all the time I'd been working for Baltasar.

"I'm sorry, Empire child," the dock master said, not unkindly. But his words still struck me hard in the heart.

"I'm not from the Empire." I grabbed my jar and stalked out of his boat. Out on the dock, the air was clean and crisp, and the wind was blowing from the north. I drew my thoughts into myself. I had a feeling that presence would be there, lurking, and I didn't want to sense it right now.

I held my jar tight to my chest and went back to the *Cornflower*. It had been such a push and pull to save these stones, eating nothing but salted fish even on my days off, taking on every day trip out to sea that Baltasar would let me. And even then, I still had to pull stones from the jar to pay Rudolf another thirty so I could stay on the *Cornflower*.

By the time I made it back, my cheeks were streaked with tears. I stood next to the railing and gazed over the deck. The empty masts looked like dead trees. The whole thing felt like a prison. It wasn't home. No matter how kind Asbera and Finnur were, it would never be home.

And then I spotted a figurine of a straw-man.

It was set next to a piece of vine that Asbera had given me. I stared at it for a few moments, my heart pounding. My tears all evaporated with my fear.

"The Mists?" I whispered.

I crept closer, holding the stone-jar tight against my chest, squeezing it for support. When I was a few paces away, my head thrummed with magic. Good magic. Protective magic.

Tuljan magic.

I still wanted to throw it into the ocean, but I knew better than to disrespect a protective totem. So I let it be, and I went down below, where I set my jar back in its usual place and tried not to think about home.

That evening, when I went to the *Crocus* for dinner, I learned that Rudolf had installed figurines on all the boarding boats— Asbera and Finnur had discovered a miniature goat on their deck.

"It's true magic," Asbera told me as she poured another glass of ale.

"I know," I said. "I can feel it."

She smiled. "I told you the priests would help."

Still, I had my doubts.

That was the last day when anything new happened. The twin

emotions of disappointment and fear braided together into a sense of numbness that highlighted the drudgery of my routine. I'd been used to routines back on Kjora—the constant cycle of chores and tending to Henrik and sailing out to sea with Kolur—but here on Tulja, the repetition was endless and dull. Every few days, I went out with the *Annika* and received payment that I then spent on food and boarding and patching my coat and stockings. Despite having a new goal, vague and ill defined—*buy my own boat*—I felt like I saved less money than before. One morning, I pulled on my left boot, and my big toe peeked through the leather. I stared at that toe for a long time. It didn't feel like it belonged to me.

And then I counted out stones from my jar, my heart heavy. I couldn't go without boots, not if I'd any intention of living as a fisherwoman.

In all those weeks, I didn't allow myself to think on Kolur and Frida and Isolfr. They were still in Tulja—I saw the *Penelope II* whenever we sailed in and out of harbor, her carvings distinct and strange against the dull Tuljan boats. According to the rumors swirling around the docks, most folk didn't think they'd ever get through all the repairs.

I doubted that, though. I knew from experience how driven Kolur was when he wanted something. He'd kidnapped me away from Kjora just because his fish bones told him to go north.

On and on life went, until one day, while I sat up on the deck of the *Cornflower* mending sails for the *Annika*, I heard a bell.

It tinkled just off the starboard side, down by the water. I set the sail aside and walked over to the railing and looked down.

Isolfr.

He was in his human disguise, his Pjetur disguise, all bundled up like the cold affected him. He sat in the dinghy, one oar lying across his lap. He chimed the dinghy's bell again, then called, "Hanna!"

His voice was bright and sparkling like starlight. It set all my nerves on edge.

"What the hell are you doing here?"

"I need to speak with you."

I stared down at him, and he squinted up at me.

"You could have just climbed aboard," I snapped. "It's not like I pulled the gangplank up."

"I thought I needed your permission."

I sighed. He sounded so sweet and sincere, like he didn't fully understand the ways of humans. Probably he didn't.

"What do you need to talk to me about?" I asked.

He hesitated. That got my guard up. I pressed my hands tight against the railing and leaned out far over the water. The wind blowing off it was cold as death. "Well?" I said. "What is—"

"We're leaving."

All my words came up short. I pressed away from the railing. The sun seemed too bright and too cold all once.

"Fine," I said. My voice was weak but I knew the wind carried it. "You can come up."

I turned away from the railing without bothering to check if he'd heard. I knew that he had. He wasn't human. He didn't have a human's weaknesses.

A few moments later, his icy blond hair appeared beside the railing. I gathered up the half-mended sails like they were a protection shield. He looked like a flash of moonlight off the surface of the ocean.

We stared at each other.

"I'm sorry you were attacked," he said. "I never meant—"

"So you admit it's your fault."

"What? No, of course not—"

"Then don't say you're sorry, and don't say you *never meant* anything." I grabbed my mending needle and shoved it into the sail fabric. It was satisfying, feeling that give against the needle's sharpness. A good outlet for my anger.

"Hanna." I heard footsteps and when I looked up, he was kneeling beside me, staring at me with his huge, imploring eyes. "Are you sure you won't come with us?"

My arm froze mid-stitch. The air went still.

"The Mists attacked me," I said slowly. "Because of Kolur." I paused. "And because of you."

Isolfr opened his mouth to speak, but I interrupted him.

"They told me that," I said. "They called me 'Friend of Isolfr.'" Isolfr didn't look like himself, with his dull skin and human features and his brow knotted up with worry. "When you sail for the north, they'll follow you and leave me be."

My blood pounded in my ears. I turned back to my mending, but I couldn't concentrate, not with him crouched there beside me.

"Just go away," I muttered, not looking up. "Just leave me alone."

"I will." He touched my arm, lightly, with the tips of his fingers. Magic buzzed between us and I cried out like I'd been stung, even though it didn't exactly hurt. "But I just—we're leaving tomorrow, while you'll be out on your fishing trip—"

I looked up at him. "How the hell do you know that? About me being out fishing?"

"I hear people talking. I wanted to give you one last chance to come with us."

I glared at him. But he didn't turn away. In fact, he looked desperate.

"Your magic is so much stronger than you realize," he said. "So much stronger than *I* realized—"

"It's still not as strong as Frida's," I snapped. "Ask her."

He shivered. "You know I can't."

"I know you're a coward. She isn't going to hurt you, whatever the hell you are. At least not if the Mists are on their way."

He looked at me for a moment, and I could tell he knew I was right. But when he spoke, all he said was, "You would be such a help. Please."

He touched my arm again and leaned in close. Magic crackled. "It's going to be dangerous, what we're doing," he said. "And there's the fate of the whole world—"

"Oh, shut up!" I yanked away from him. "The fate of the whole world? Did Kolur tell you that? You've got a lot to learn about the world, if you think him winning back some queen puts the world in danger."

Isolfr frowned. "It's not just about the Jandanvari queen. I haven't explained it properly."

"Well, don't bother. I'm not going. I just want to get back home to Kjora and convince Mama to send me off to the capital to study to become a witch. Can you do that?"

He hesitated for a moment before shaking his head. "Then I'm staying here." I turned away from him, but I could still feel the prickle of his eyes on me, the lingering spark of our shared magic. "Please leave."

When I finally looked up, Isolfr was gone.

Our fishing trip out to the eastern side of Tulja was uneventful. The winds were in our favor, and there wasn't much for me to do beside tighten the ropes and prep the nets. It gave me a lot of time to think, mostly on Isolfr. I wished I hadn't lost my temper and sent him away. Now that he was gone, now that the *Penelope II* was likely cutting her way through the dark seas, it was easy to see that he might have been willing to answer my questions. Maybe.

But I hadn't wanted to go with them. That I knew for certain. It was unfair that Kolur was on his way to Jandanvar and his queen and I would need another three jars of stones to make it back to Kjora.

I tried to focus my attention on the *Annika*.

With the trip such an easy one, it wasn't long before the crew were all sitting around the deck, throwing dice. Baltasar didn't even complain about it from his place at the helm.

We were after capelins. They were a rarity this time of year, and Reynir seeing them when he threw the bones could mean a big payload for the rest of us, even though we had to do a day's sailing to get out to the patch of sea where the bones had spotted them. By the time we arrived, the stars had come out and the air was cold and windy. The crew was in a mood, too, after a day of easy sailing. Some of them had been drinking like pirates.

"Drop the nets!" Baltasar shouted from the helm. "We're here!"

We all shambled into action. It took the crew longer than usual to toss the nets over the side of the boat. They landed with a *slap*, and the ocean churned around us. Fish scales glinted in the moonlight.

"I remember the last time we got a load of capelin," Asbera said as we watched the starboard. "The yak herders use the oil for tanning, so they're willing to pay for it. Do you remember that haul, Finnur?"

He nodded, his eyes on the water. "Felt like enough to retire."

I laughed. "I doubt that."

He looked up at me. "Said it *felt* like it. Not that it was."

The nets filled quickly, which put us all in good spirits. As irritating as Reynir was, his bones rarely steered us wrong. Asbera and I worked together to drag our net on deck. Capelins spilled across our feet, like the stars themselves had fallen from the sky.

"It's gonna be a good trip," Asbera said.

I cast the preservation charm. All around us, the rest of the crew was doing the same, dragging the nets aboard and whooping and hollering when they saw what they'd caught. We dropped our own net back into the water. The *Annika* rocked against the waves.

"Wind's up!" Baltasar shouted. "Hanna, tend to the sails!"

Asbera nodded at me, a cue that she could watch the nets herself, with Finnur's help. The wind was shifting in an odd pattern, and it was hard even for me to tell which direction it blew from. I gathered up my strength, dragging the magic out of the air and into myself.

The wind swirled around us. The boat lurched, swung off to the port side.

"Hanna!" Baltasar shouted. "Tend to the sails!"

"I'm trying!" I pressed down the sudden surge of panic and tried to concentrate. The wind whistled in my ears and blew harder and harder. My hair whipped into my face. I had the magic fine, but this wind wasn't minding me.

The boat swung again, the bow plowing into an incoming wave. Freezing water crashed over the deck. All the heat globes blinked out. The magic-cast lanterns swung wildly from the masts, throwing disjointed shadows over everything.

"For the love of the ancestors!" Baltasar shouted. "Get ahold of the winds!"

"I'm trying!" And I was. I concentrated so hard that white spots appeared at the edge of my vision, that the magic stung as it crept through my blood. But the wind went through me like water sifting through fingers.

It wasn't—*right*.

The crew shouted around me, no longer joyful from the catch but full-on spooked. Benedict and Zakaria were already turning the sails, trying to catch the wind without enchantment. My knees buckled. Magic burned at my brain. I stumbled backward and would have fallen if strong arms hadn't caught me. Finnur.

"Something's wrong." His voice sounded far away. "It's a storm. It's—"

He was still talking, but I couldn't hear him. I twisted around to look at him. His mouth moved.

"I can't hear you!" I said. "What's going on?"

Another wave crashed over the side and knocked me flat on my back. The water was so cold, I thought I'd died. I blinked up at the sky, dazed. I heard shouting again, frantic, terrified voices.

"—na! Are you okay?"

Asbera this time. She helped me to my feet. The *Annika* swung in a wide arc, throwing off a spray of white-capped seawater.

"I'm sorry," I sputtered. "I couldn't—the wind—"

"That's because it's not wind," she said. "It's a denala."

I froze. A denala. I'd heard of such things, stories from Kolur and some of the sailors he'd drink with in the evenings, but I'd never seen one myself. They were storms of magic.

Papa had told me once they were tied to the Mists.

"No," I whispered.

"We need you to ignite more heat globes before we all freeze." Asbera dragged me a few paces across the deck before the boat tilted and we went sliding, slamming up against the masts. "This water's dangerous," she gasped out.

But I knew if this was a true denala, we'd have more to fear than just freezing.

It was already happening: when the water slid back across the boat, the surface shone like a mirror. The preservation spell that held our catches of capelin turned to saltwater, and the fish woke up again, their eyes shining like moonlight, and swam in circles through the air.

Screams of horror erupted on the deck. I knew I couldn't light any heat globes.

"Get 'em overboard!" Baltasar shouted, his voice roaring over the wind. "Before they contaminate the rest of the boat!"

I scrambled over to the nearest grouping of fish.

"Hanna!" Asbera shouted.

"You heard the captain!" I gestured for her to join me.

"Finnur!" she cried. "I have to get to Finnur!"

Sea and sky. In the panic I'd almost forgotten him—the magic-sickness would affect him the most if he was tainted with it, since he'd been struck the worst by our encounter with the Mists.

"Go!" I shouted. "I'll take care of this!"

Saltwater splashed across my face and into my mouth; I spat it out, afraid of tainting myself. Then I turned to the fish, bracing myself against the rocking of the boat. Reynir and Harald stood nearby, although they did nothing to throw the fish overboard. Of course. No one wanted to touch the globe of water they swam in.

"You," said Harald. The boat swung out again, almost flinging us all into the seething ocean. "You've got magic."

"No," I shouted back. "We can't use magic here."

"She's right," Reynir shouted over the storm. "Any magic will just make things worse."

"I ain't touching that," said Harald.

I looked at that globe of water floating a hand's width above the deck, a serene spot of calm in the midst of the storm raging around us. The denala's eye. Except there were three eyes to this storm, all hovering around the boat.

I didn't want to touch it either, but Baltasar was right; the longer we kept it aboard, the more harm it could do. So I took a deep breath and raced forward and shoved it with my gloved hands. It only moved a little, the way the preservation spells will do. "Help me!" I screamed.

Reynir and Harald hesitated. I shoved it again, and it edged closer to the side of the boat.

"I'll never get it off without your help."

The *Annika* tilted. Another wall of water crashed over us. I screamed at the cold and I was certain that my skin tingled, magic-sickness making its way through me.

I shoved the globe again. It slammed up against the side of the boat, and the water exploded everywhere and the fish slammed down on the deck, flopping and gasping. I shrieked and stumbled backward, trying to whisk that enchanted water off me. It steamed on my clothes with a sweet medicinal scent, and my head was suddenly crowded with strange images, castles in the mist and women with gray eyes.

I shrugged out of my jacket and tossed it overboard. My head cleared.

"You okay?" Reynir asked.

"No thanks to you." I whirled away from him, back toward the interior of the deck.

The *Annika* was in a shambles.

The deck gleamed silver. The masts had grown knobby and twisted, like trees, and the sails were tattered silk dresses snapping and fluttering in the freezing, choking winds. All results of the magic-sickness, the way too much magic will change things.

The crew stood in clumps, staring up at the sky. I followed their gaze.

Clouds swirled overhead like a cyclone.

"Down below!" Baltasar bellowed. "Everyone get down below!"

There was a pause, as if we'd all forgotten how to move.

And then the boat lifted up high on the crest of the wave, tall enough it seemed we'd be sucked into the spiral of clouds. Everyone erupted into movement. We raced to the hatch, shouting and shoving. I slid down the ladder and landed with a smack on the damp floor. Water dripped through the rafters. Seimur, one of the other fishermen, slid down and landed on top of me.

"Get out of the way, Empire girl!" he shouted.

I wormed out from under him.

"Get to the hold," someone shouted from the darkness. Seimur disappeared down the corridor. I followed, weaving back and forth to avoid the dripping water.

A light appeared at the end of the corridor, flickering and orange. Candle flame. Good.

The hold was crowded with crewmen. A handful of candles were dotted across the darkness. For all the shouting and cursing up on deck and in the corridor, the hold was hushed and silent. In the fluttering candlelight, I found Asbera sitting in the corner, next to a barrel of drinking water. Finnur leaned up against her, his face pale.

"Hanna!" she whispered, as if she didn't want to break the silence. "You're all right."

I nodded and slid into place beside her. Finnur stirred. He looked worn out.

"Where's your coat?" Asbera asked.

I shook my head. "Water got on it." I drew my legs up close. For the first time since the storm had hit, I realized how cold I was. My teeth chattered and my bones vibrated. The candle guttering next to Asbera did not give off enough heat.

The boat lifted, tilted. Everyone in the hold let out a long, terrified gasp. Hands snatched out to grab the candles—

We slammed back down, hard.

Voices filled up the darkness, whispered prayers and Tuljan lullabies. I squeezed myself tighter, trying to draw warmth out of myself. The walls rippled beneath my back and revulsion rose up in my throat but I fought it down, because our choices now were to stay aboard and face the magic-sickness, or jump into the ocean and freeze.

I closed my eyes and told myself I wasn't going to die.

CHAPTER THIRTEEN

Sunlight.

Pale and thin but certainly there, wavering through the cracks in the ceiling. The candles had burned out in the night and men were sleeping, sprawled out in piles on the floor of the hold. I sat up and stretched. Every muscle in my body ached. At least the boat was still a boat and the walls were still walls. And none of the sleeping crew seemed affected by the magic-sickness.

I stood up, my legs wobbling, and braced myself against the wall. I realized the entire crew wasn't down here—only about five men. Asbera and Finnur were gone.

Panic seized me, cold and violent. But then I heard voices coming from up above.

I picked my way over the sleeping crewmen and climbed up on deck. The sun was blinding; I hadn't seen it that bright since we'd left Kjora. It bounced off the water's surface, flinging light all over the boat. The air was calm and sharp with cold.

The *Annika* might still be above water, but she'd been half destroyed in the denala last night. Her deck gleamed silver in places, and the sails-turned-silk-dresses had no doubt been thrown overboard. A group of crewmen stood near the helm of the ship, bundled up in cloaks and shabby furs. They spoke in low voices.

"Hello," I called out.

They turned toward me. One of them was Asbera. My lingering panic dissipated.

"Hanna!" She rushed across the deck to my side. "I tried waking you, but you wouldn't stir. I was worried."

"I'm sore," I said, as if that offered any kind of explanation. "Where are we?"

"That's what we're trying to figure out." Asbera looped her arm in mine and led me across the boat.

"Finnur?" I asked. "Is he——"

"He's fine. Resting. See?" She pointed past the helm to the stern of the boat, where Finnur was stretched out on a hammock, covered in furs. "He wanted fresh air after spending the night down below."

We joined the rest of the crew. Baltasar was there, looking drawn and worn out, like he hadn't slept at all, and Reynir and Harald. They ringed the navigation table, staring down at a map pinned with rocks.

"Hanna," Baltasar said. "Am I glad to see you're all right."

"I'm glad to see it too." I smiled weakly at him, but he didn't return the gesture.

"Had to ditch the sails," he said. "Tainted with the sickness. We've got some old ones down below. Need patching, but they should be enough to get us home. You well enough to call the winds?"

I hesitated. "I'm——not sure," I finally answered. "And I'm not certain it's safe——"

"Oh, it's definitely not safe," Reynir said. "We'll have to wait at least a day before we do any sort of magic."

Baltasar grunted. "So we're just sitting in the water till then? Air's still as death."

"That's what I told you."

"Boys," Asbera said. "We shouldn't fight. We have to wait until nightfall to find out where we are. Not unless someone passes us by."

The rest of the crew grumbled. She was right; without the stars or a strong spell, we'd no way of locating ourselves. Standing around the navigation map was just wishful thinking.

"I hope we haven't crossed over."

Everyone stopped talking. It was Finnur who had spoken, although he sounded gruff and unlike himself. Everyone turned to him. He'd sat up in the hammock, and he swayed side to side with the motion of the *Annika*.

"We haven't," Baltasar said.

I hoped he was right. In that maelstrom of magic, it was entirely possible that the *Annika* could have been dragged out of the true world and into the Mists. But the ocean sparkling around us didn't seem like the Mists. This cold, sharp air didn't seem like the Mists, either. It felt like home.

"Don't mind him; he's still recovering from the magic-sickness." Asbera bustled over to him and pressed her hand to his forehead. He closed his eyes at her touch and leaned back in the hammock and murmured something I couldn't hear.

"Leave them." Baltasar sidled up beside me. "They've still got the panic from last night. Come, let's see about repairing those old sails. It's something to do while we wait."

I nodded, feeling numb, but I still followed him down below.

The rest of the day was spent largely in silence. Crewmen drifted up from down below in ones or twos, and Baltasar set them to work whenever they appeared on deck. By lunchtime, everyone was awake and accounted for, and to all our great relief, no human had been touched by the magic-sickness.

Together, we repaired and hung the old sails. We cleaned up the wreckage from the storm as best we could—Zakaria was the only one brave enough to touch the shiny mirrored patches on the deck, and although he stayed unharmed, the rest of us left them alone, sweeping and mopping around them instead. Benedict, Finnur, and Asbera counted our food stores and reported back that they had largely survived the storm as well. We had about four days' worth of food and water, more if we rationed.

Baltasar nodded grimly. "Depends on where we are, doesn't it?"

And we all knew that no wages were waiting for us when we returned to Tulja, even if we did get back within a few days' time. Nobody spoke about it much that first day, but it was heavy on my thoughts, and I imagined it was the same for the rest of the crew.

Eventually, the sun sank into the horizon—the west, I hoped. We all gathered on deck to watch the stars come out.

The day had been clear, but as night fell, clouds drifted across the sky, long dark streaks that blotted out the moonlight. I cursed beneath my breath, and for the thousandth time that day, I wondered why this had happened, and why it had happened to us. A denala on the same day that Kolur was to leave for the north?

Fear gnawed at my insides.

"It figures," Finnur said as we crowded around the ship's bow, "we'd get a cloudy night."

"It's not so cloudy," Asbera said, and she was right. Pricks of light appeared against the black sky. I held my breath as I tilted my head back, my body shaking, afraid of what I might see.

Beside me, Asbera let out a long sigh.

The Jolix Lion stretched out in the northeastern corner, languorous and bored as always. Nora's Pot was in its usual place as well, cooking up that healing balm Nora used to save Petra. Although I couldn't see all of the constellations in the patchy sky, I saw enough to know we were in our world.

"We're still here." Asbera drew me up in an embrace. "We haven't crossed over."

Relief rippled across the boat as the crewmen spotted the usual constellations. I dropped my head all the way back until I was able to see the Ice Star, burning bright and brilliant like a flame. It always rested near the top of the sky; I'd heard that if you looked at it from Jandanvar, it would lie directly overhead. It wasn't directly overhead now. Another relief.

Baltasar had already pulled out the sextant and was peering through it at the horizon. "At least two days' north," he barked. The crew muttered to itself. Then, "Reynir! Throw the damn bones."

"You sure?" Reynir asked.

The Ice Star was enough to tell us how far north or south we'd gone, but it wasn't enough to give our exact location. It was risky to throw the bones when the boat had been transformed with the magic-sickness only last night—maybe not dangerous in and of itself, it was such a weak magic, but the reading might not be accurate.

"Yes, I'm sure." Baltasar tossed the sextant aside. "I want to know where the hell we are."

Reynir sighed and shuffled forward, pulling his sack of fish bones from around his neck. He glanced around the deck and then moved over to the stern, away from the silvered patches. Everyone followed him, and we moved into a circle around where he knelt on the deck.

"Give me some room," he said.

We all shuffled back a pace or two. Reynir grunted. He dumped the bones in his palm and shook them like dice.

Everyone held their breath again.

"Stand back," he said again, more harshly this time. We stumbled backward. Asbera clutched at Finnur's hand, their knuckles turning white. I rubbed at my bracelet.

The bones clattered across the deck.

I stared at them, trying to read the symbols—it was nonsense, all nonsense. I didn't recognize any of the configurations. I wanted to weep. But Reynir leaned back on his heels and made a *hmm* sound. The crew stirred, voices rising up out of the darkness.

"It's Anfinn's Rocks!" Zakaria called out. "Look, it's exactly like the map."

"I see it," Reynir snapped, although I suspected he hadn't.

The crew jostled forward. I'd never heard of Anfinn's Rocks, but the arrangement did look something like an archipelago, islands trailing off into the sea.

Baltasar knelt beside the spray of bones. "Someone get me the damn map!" he shouted.

A flurry of activity. The navigation map drifted down from overhead. Baltasar spread it out on the deck.

"Give us some light," Reynir said, and a candle was produced, the wax burned down low. Harald handed it to Baltasar, who set it between the map and the stones. I stood up on my tiptoes, trying to see. So did everyone else.

Baltasar leaned forward. His eyes flicked back and forth between the map and the bones.

"Identical." He glanced at Reynir. "What do you think, fortuneer?"

"It looks the same, but that doesn't mean much."

Baltasar nodded and then clambered to his feet. "You heard him. Light up the ship, men! Look for signs of Anfinn's Rocks. We've got to confirm."

"With what?" someone called out. "Ain't gonna be able to see far enough with candles."

Reynir rubbed his forehead. "Magic-cast lanterns ought to be safe, after this long."

Baltasar looked at me. "What do you say, girl? Think it's safe to cast the lanterns?"

I fumbled for a moment, surprised that Baltasar was asking for my opinion. Reynir seemed surprised too, and a little angry about it. "Yes, it should be safe. As long as we don't light too many."

"You heard 'em. Light the lanterns!"

Lanterns shimmered on across the boat. The sudden surge of magic made me dizzy, and I swooned for a moment. Maybe this had been a mistake.

Finnur caught me. "Did the same thing to me," he said. "It'll pass."

"Do we want to be close to Anfinn's Rocks?" I asked. My head was still fuzzy.

"Oh yes," said Asbera. "It'll only be two days' sail from there to get back to Tulja, and it's an easy voyage."

I nodded. Lanterns swung around us. Zakaria brought one over to Asbera, and she set it onto a nearby hook and slid it over the side of the boat. A circle of light appeared on the water, bobbing with the waves.

Even with the lanterns lit, I couldn't see much beyond the confines of the boat. But then Seimur shouted, "Land in the distance! Port side!"

I turned around. Seimur hung over the railing with the lantern, pointing off in the distance. It took me a moment to see the outline of something jagged and dark against the stars, like a distant mountain.

Baltasar stomped over to Seimur. "Too far away to tell," he grunted. Then he turned around to speak to the crew.

"We'll wait till sunup," he shouted. "We've waited this long; a few more hours won't kill us."

Reynir ran over to him and whispered something in his ear. Baltasar nodded.

"You gotta choose between the lanterns and the heat spheres," he added. "We don't want any surprises. Better to light a fire if you're cold, anyway."

Asbera pulled in her lanterns and muttered the familiar incantation. The lantern's glow faded into darkness. "Don't want to make things worse for you," she said to Finnur.

"So that's it, then?" He sighed. "We've got to hang around for another night?"

"It's not so bad," Asbera said. "We should be home in a couple of days, like Baltasar said."

Finnur shrugged. I didn't blame him for seeming doubtful. He was still weak, deep down inside him, from the Mists attack, and now he was trapped aboard a ship half transformed from the magic-sickness. There was no guarantee we were anywhere close to the Anfinn's Rocks.

Reynir and Zakaria dragged the brazier up on deck and broke up an empty water barrel for the firewood. The brazier was supposed to be for cooking, I was told, but no one ever used it anymore, since the *Annika* didn't take the long voyages she used to. It was nice to have a spot of warmth to gather round, and nicer still to know that warmth wasn't bringing even more magic aboard our boat.

I sat with Asbera and Finnur as the crew took to telling stories, mostly old Tuljan folktales. A few of them I recognized, although they were different from the stories I knew in small ways—here a character was a yak herder, on Kjora he was a blacksmith. But the basic idea was the same. A story of the north. Mama'd told me this once, that all the island stories were the same when you got down to it, that to her Empire ears they were all northern and she couldn't tell them apart. She was teasing, I think, but I thought of her now, hearing those similarities. And my heart about broke.

No one noticed when I slipped away from the fire. I pressed

against the boat's railing and closed my eyes against the wind. We were moored without our sails, and the *Annika* bobbed up and down with the motion of the waves and didn't do much else. I looked down at the dark water, sparkling with the reflection of stars.

Something moved beneath the surface.

I gasped and jerked back, although my first thought was of Isolfr, not the Mists. I'd seen him the same way, hadn't I, all those months ago? A flash of movement beneath the waves.

"Isolfr?" I kept my voice low, surprised by how hopeful I felt. It would have been a relief, in a strange way, to see him now. A bit like how the stars reminded me that we hadn't crossed over.

The shimmer came closer to the surface. "Isolfr," I said, a little louder now. "Is that you?"

But the water went dark.

I sighed and pulled away from the railing.

The next day was cloudy and gray, the sky threatening sea-snow. The crew gathered along the port side of the boat, where we had the clearest view of the land in the distance. It was dark and rocky and not particularly welcoming. But the crew was thrilled to see it.

"That's Anfinn's Rocks for certain," said Harald. "I ain't gonna forget that coastline any time soon."

Baltasar blustered up to us and peered through his view glass. I'd no way of knowing if the land was Anfinn's Rocks or not, and so I watched him and looked for some sign that we'd be on our way home soon. I didn't trust Harald's assessment.

Baltasar slid his view glass shut. "It's the Rocks," he said, with the gravelly authority of a sea captain. "We're on the northern side. Have to sail around, but it won't be too much trouble."

The crew cheered and slapped one another on the backs. Finnur dragged me and Asbera both into a hug.

"Nice to have everything turn out, huh?" he said. "Didn't get blown too far off course, and now we're on our way home."

"Yeah, yeah," said Asbera, laughing. She kissed him.

I smiled, but I wasn't so sure everything had turned out. Why had we sailed into a denala in the first place? Such things only happened when powerful wizards were casting powerful spells. The rest of the crew seemed to agree that it must have been someone on Anfinn's Rocks, especially now that we'd confirmed our location—apparently, Tuljan priests trained there—but I wasn't so certain.

"Hanna, ready the sails," Baltasar shouted. "Asbera, Reynir, and Zakaria, grab the ropes in case there's a problem with the magic. We're heading home."

More cheering, but I couldn't shake the cold, creeping feeling that something was wrong.

I walked among the masts and held out my hands and felt for the magic on the wind. It blew in from the southeast, with a sweetness to it that reminded me of summer sunshine. Perfectly safe.

I repeated that to myself as I shifted the winds in our favor. *Perfectly safe, everything is perfectly safe.*

It was a simple matter to call the necessary winds to drive the *Annika* southward, and I didn't have to expend much energy holding the spell. The denala had made the magic more malleable, like soft clay, and this far from the storm, the threat of magic-sickness was no longer a concern.

For the first time in days, we sailed forward.

The crew's good spirits lingered, even when the clouds thickened and snow fell across the ocean. I spotted Benedict and Harald tipping their heads back and trying to catch flakes on their tongues. Enough of it fell that it started piling up on deck.

"Clear it off," Baltasar shouted from the helm. "Before it freezes."

The crew took care of the snow largely by shaping it into balls and throwing them at each other. Even though I was managing the winds, I joined in, flinging a clump of snow at Finnur's head. He roared with laughter and came chasing after me. I kept expecting Baltasar to shout at us to quit, but he seemed as amused as anyone else. Pretty soon, the *Annika* was the scene of a great snow fight. The winds carried us home, and we just kept flinging snowballs at one another.

And then something changed.

I was back at the stern of the ship, reaching behind some of the crates we stored there to get to a pile of fresh snow, when I felt the wind snap, like it had broken in two. I stood straight up, the snow forgotten. All around me, the crew were shrieking and laughing, but there was a buzzing whine in my head that made it sound like screaming.

I grabbed on to the railing and squeezed my eyes shut, feeling for the wind. But I couldn't grasp it. It squirmed around me, slippery and just out of reach.

"You okay, Empire girl?" It was Harald. I opened my eyes and looked at him, pink-cheeked and grinning. He had hoisted up a snowball and was aiming it at me, but he didn't throw it.

His grin melted away.

"What is it? What's wrong? Should I get Reynir?"

Something moved out of the corner of my eye. I looked out at the water, but all I saw were the coruscating waves.

"Hanna?" Harald stepped closer to me. I was trembling. Something was wrong with the magic. It twisted away from me, vibrating as if it spoke—

Voices—

They communicate on veins of magic.

"Something's wrong," I said.

Harald's eyes widened.

And then something shot out of the ocean and grabbed Harald and pulled him overboard. It happened so quickly that all I saw was shining silvery water and the bright, bright red of blood.

Screaming.

Harald was screaming.

He slammed back up over the railing, his body limp. Blood splattered across my face and it was hot and wet and I screamed and stumbled backward into someone's arms—the thing that had grabbed Harald?

No.

Baltasar.

The ship was silent save for Harald's screaming. His body dripped blood. I realized that Baltasar had one arm around my chest, his hand clutching a knife.

"What the hell is that?" he whispered.

"I can't see," I gasped. And I couldn't—I couldn't see what it was. It looked like the ocean had grown claws.

They can blend in with their surroundings.

Harald dropped out of sight.

There was a splash.

The screaming stopped.

That sudden silence hurt my ears.

"Harald!" Baltasar shouted. He shoved me away. "Get away, girl." Then, louder, "Have you all gone stupid? We need weapons! Get down below and grab the pistols!"

"What happened?" someone shouted. "What happened to Harald?"

I kept stumbling back and back until I was standing among the masts. The sails fluttered and snapped. My face was wet. When I went to dry it off, my fingers came back red.

I choked back vomit.

"He's dead." Baltasar stomped back to the helm. I didn't understand how he could be so calm. "Something dragged him into the water."

All the voices of the crew started up at once.

"What—"

"How could—"

"I didn't even—"

"Get the weapons!" Baltasar jerked the wheel away from Reynir and shoved him in the direction of the lower deck. "Put a fucking protection spell on this boat and get the *damned weapons!*"

"Hanna." Asbera's voice sounded far away, and when she grabbed my hand, it was like she grabbed it through fabric. The magic chattered and vibrated. It was close. *They* were close. *They* had taken Harald, and they were still here. "Hanna, we have to arm ourselves. Come on."

She tried to pull me toward the hatch, but the flood of crewmen heading in that direction made me dizzy. I shook my head. "You go," I said. "I need the air."

She frowned but she did as I said, letting go of my hand and disappearing down below. I leaned against one of the masts and took a deep breath. Harald's blood was sticky on my face. I kept hearing his screams on the air.

I closed my eyes and tried to shut everything out. Voices drifted up from down below as the crew dug out whatever weapons Baltasar kept aboard the boat—it couldn't be many. We weren't a warship, just a fishing vessel. We could hardly defend ourselves against pirates, much less what monsters waited in the depths.

And then the magic shifted again, melting into the air, growing slippery and hard to grasp. And I heard something. Not voices, not screaming. Something else. Like water bubbling in a pot.

I stared into the darkness beyond the boat. At first, I thought I was the only one who heard it, but all around me, the crew stopped in place, looking out toward the water. The sound grew louder. Our fear strung the air out as tight as a wire.

The crew's terrified whispers picked up. I slid forward, moving on a thread of magic, my eyes on the railing. The sound was everywhere.

The ocean had learned how to breathe.

I came to the railing and looked down.

The water churned, wild with froth and still pink with Harald's blood. I shrieked and stumbled backward into Baltasar. He dragged me to the center of the boat.

"Stay away from the edge!" he shouted. "How do you think Harald got killed?"

"I know how Harald got killed!" I screamed, but Baltasar was gone, his feet pounding over to the other side of the boat. The rest of the crew clumped around the masts. I whirled around and found Asbera and Finnur pressed close to each other. Asbera's eyes were wide and determined, and she clutched an old-fashioned rough-hewn sword in one hand. Finnur had a dagger, a small silver blade.

"I got you this," Asbera said, drawing a knife out of her belt.

"I don't know how to use anything." My voice shook. "I'll just use my magic."

Something thumped against the side of the boat.

Finnur dragged me behind him. Asbera shoved the knife at me and lifted her sword over her head in a fighting stance.

Another thump.

"Stay quiet," Baltasar whispered.

Through the haze of my fear, I concentrated on the wind. It was still blowing us south, back toward home. I reached in deep. I didn't have much experience with magical weapons beyond protection spells, and there was already a protection spell on the *Annika*, one more advanced than any I could cast.

I tightened my grip on the knife. It was small and felt unsteady in my hands.

Another thump. Another.

"Ready your weapons," Baltasar whispered.

I wondered how many of the crew actually knew how to fight. I wondered if it even mattered.

The thumping grew louder. More persistent.

It was joined by a scratching like dead leaves against rocks.

The crew pulled closer together.

The wind's magic flowed through me, even though I had no idea what I would do with it.

A face appeared over the railing.

For half a second, I thought it was Isolfr, and I had no idea if I should be terrified or relieved. But then the sails snapped out of the way and the thin afternoon sun shone across the face, and I saw it wasn't Isolfr at all. He had at least tried to look human.

There was nothing human about this face.

It was long and narrow, with a pointed snout and sharp teeth that glowed against the gray light. It scrabbled on deck, flinging off water, its body thin and low to the ground. It moved like a snake, even though it walked on four legs, each of its feet ending in a spray of huge, curved white claws.

It was the color of water, and mist curled around its body, creating a trail that led back to the ocean.

The magic whooshed out of me. I wasn't a witch. I was just a fisherman's apprentice. And I was going to die.

A pistol popped, and the creature slammed up against the side of the railing. Liquid light oozed out across the deck.

"We can kill them," Asbera gasped. She hoisted her sword higher. "We can kill—"

The creature lifted its head and jumped back on its feet. It threw back its head and let out a shrill, rattling cry. I slapped my hands over my ears. My knife clattered to the deck. The crew shrieked and fumbled with their weapons. Pistol shots echoed across the boat, smoke drifting up along the sails.

More creatures appeared over the railing.

The crew dispersed. Most of them scrambled up into the masts. Benedict ran screaming down below. Baltasar shouted for order, but we weren't soldiers, and we weren't going to listen. I would have been running for the masts too, if it hadn't been for Finnur's hand on my arm.

"Stay," he said, his voice hard. "We need your magic."

The creatures spilled over the railing. There were too many to count. They wriggled across the deck, their claws clicking against the wood. One after another after another. Like insects.

Baltasar fired his pistol into the onslaught. White blood splattered the wood. Zakaria and Seimur fired from up in the masts. With each shot, the magic reverberated and I got a taste like rot on my tongue.

The creatures squirmed closer.

Finnur and Asbera and I stumbled back.

"Climb up!" Asbera shouted. She swung her sword and sliced one of the creatures in half, and it rolled away into the shadows. The magic roiled. I knew it was drawing itself back together. "Get to Reynir."

Yes. Reynir. He'd know what magic to use. I crawled up the masts, my body slick with panicky sweat. One of the crew grabbed me and pulled me up to the crosstree before firing back into the churn of creatures. From here, I could see Asbera and Finnur and Baltasar cutting their way through the swarm. Thick gray mist curled over the railings, wrapping around the deck like ghosts. And that blood, that blood like light—it was everywhere.

"Hanna!" Reynir swung down beside me. "Please tell me you can feel it. The magic?"

I nodded and blinked back tears.

"We won't get rid of them, but we should at least be able to protect the boat and send them back to the ocean."

I nodded again.

"If you can't do this, you better tell me."

My heart pounded. I'd beat back the Mists when we were attacked in the village (*with help, you had help*) and the winds were even stronger here, especially so high above the deck.

"I can do it," I said. I almost believed it.

"Take my hand." Reynir grabbed mine. "Pull out the magic. You'll have to cut through the Mists first. You use the wind, right?"

"Yes." I couldn't look away from what was happening on deck. The mist was thicker now, thick enough that Asbera and Finnur were silhouettes in the dim light.

"I use the ocean. That should be enough to expel them. Concentrate!"

I squeezed my eyes shut. It was easier when I couldn't see the monsters snarling and snapping down below, even though I could still hear the pistol shots and the creatures' horrible screeching. The wind roared against my ears. Slowly, it shifted, until it blew in from the south, until it was *my* wind. The boat tilted and turned and I tightened my grip on the masts. It was hard to find clean magic, though, magic that hadn't been corrupted by the Mists, and as I searched, my chest constricted and my throat swelled up.

"Keep—looking—" Reynir sounded strangled. "Just—keep—"

The wind. I shut him out, I shut out the screams down below, and I focused on the wind. It was the wind of my father and mother both: my father's birthright and my mother's ancestors. And for that reason, it was mine. It did not belong to the Mists. Its *magic* didn't belong to the Mists.

And then, there, beneath that cold, thick Mists enchantment, I found it, a glimmer of power, warm like the sun.

"I've got it!" I screamed.

Reynir squeezed my hand more tightly and began to chant in the old language. Through his strange dialect, I recognized the spell. It was a plea for protection.

I joined in, and our words blended together even if we didn't speak them the same. The wind flowed around me and flowed through me, and the magic lit up my blood and became a part of me.

My eyes flew open.

For a moment, I didn't see the world as it was, mist and blood and violence and terror. I saw only the magic. It suffused everything with light: the boat, the creatures, the rest of the crew. And I was aflame.

"—protect us all," Reynir and I shouted at once, our voices ringing out in unison. And there was a sudden, sharp intake, a sudden, sharp stillness—

And then a blast of light.

It knocked me back. Reynir's hand slipped away from mine, and for a moment, I was falling, serenely, through the open air. I stared up at the cloudy sky through the forest of sails. I didn't realize what was happening.

My arm burned.

I'd stopped, midair, and was dangling from the bottom crosstree. Seimur had caught me. His face was strained. I grabbed hold of the sail rope.

"I got it!" I said. "You can let go."

He did, leaning back with a sigh of relief. I swung out on the rope, arcing out over the deck. All the creatures were gone from the *Annika*, but I could see them out in the ocean, frothing up the water. One of them launched itself at the boat, but there was a shudder of magic and it slammed backward.

I swung back to the mast and climbed down. The deck was splattered with light and streaked with smears of red blood. Human blood.

"Asbera!" I shouted. "Finnur!"

"Hanna!" Asbera's voice was a beacon. I stumbled toward it, exhausted from the spell-casting, my thoughts thick and unclear. "Hanna, I need your help!"

Her words were slurred. My feet slipped over the spilled blood. Light flung up and clung to my trouser legs. I ignored it. Asbera was over by the starboard side of the ship, hunched over a dark lump. No, not a dark lump—Finnur. And he wasn't moving.

"What happened?" I shouted. I slid over beside her and fell to my knees. Finnur's eyes were open, his mouth twisted open in an expression of horror and surprise. He was bleeding from his shoulder, blood soaking through his coat.

"He's still alive." Asbera's face shone with tears, and her voice shook. "I can feel his heart beating." She pressed her hand against his chest and closed her eyes. "I can feel it."

I put two fingers on the side of Finnur's neck. His pulse fluttered against them, faint but steady. I lay a finger underneath his nose and felt him breathing.

"If he's still alive," I said, "we can save him." I had no idea if this was true but I had to say something. Asbera looked up at me, her eyes blinking back tears.

"How?" she said.

"We'll come up with something." I pressed my hand against his wound. "We need to stop the blood. Could you get me some water?"

Asbera nodded and bounded away. Finnur had dropped his knife beside him when he fell, and I picked it up and used it to cut away his clothes. By then, Asbera had returned with a bucket of drinking water. Baltasar was with her, carrying an Empire-style sword covered in glowing blood.

"What's wrong with him?" he asked.

"I don't know." I pulled off my scarf and dipped it in the water bucket, then wiped away Finnur's blood. His wound was small, a cluster of sharp punctures arranged in a circle.

"He was bitten," I said.

Asbera knelt beside me. She cupped Finnur's face in one hand.

I looked over at Baltasar, hoping for guidance. But his face was set in stone.

"Can you cure him?" he asked.

I listened to Asbera sniffling beside me.

I shook my head.

"Well, then, we'll have to make good time back to Tulja," he said, and he walked away.

CHAPTER FOURTEEN

We moved Finnur to the captain's quarters, laying him out on a hard, wobbly cot. Reynir dug up some dried herbs that I pressed against Finnur's wound before dressing it with scraps of fabric. "If there's any poison from the magic," Reynir told me, "the herbs should suck it out." But he didn't sound too convinced.

Asbera sat with Finnur through the night, not sleeping. I didn't sleep either, just paced back and forth across the cabin, going through all the spells I knew, trying to find one that could help. The winds aren't much for healing—it's sailors' magic, explorers' magic. Sea-magic could heal, but Reynir told me it was impossible to get to the water with those Mists monsters trailing behind the boat.

"I wish I knew what they were doing here," he told me. We were sitting up on deck, next to the brazier. The rest of the crew was sleeping, and I'd told Asbera that's what I was going to do, too. But I went up on deck instead and found Reynir staring into the flames. I don't know why I sat down beside him. I guess the terror of those monsters was enough for me to set aside our differences.

"The Mists always have some purpose when they come through," he muttered. "They don't do it just for kicks. But what could they possibly want from us?"

I drew my legs in close to my chest. The wood crackled and threw off sparks of yellow light that reflected in the glowing blood-stains that still splashed across the *Annika*.

"I think I know who sent them," I said.

Reynir looked over at me, suspicious. "What?"

I frowned and rubbed my hands together.

"What do you mean, you know who sent them?"

"My old captain." I looked at the flames. "He did something to anger a lord of the Mists. Foxfollow."

"But your captain's not on the boat."

"Does it matter? The Mists already attacked me once. I should have seen it coming." The thought made me queasy with guilt. I stood up. The monsters shrieked out in the water. At least none of them broke through the magic. "Now Finnur is going to die."

"We're sailing as fast as we can." Reynir pointed up at the sails. "You're seeing to that, aren't you? More impressive than I expected."

I looked up. The sails were stiff from the north wind. I wasn't controlling it at all; the direction had shifted not long after the battle with the creatures. But I could see how Reynir might think I had, because it blew so strong and sure and unwavering. I didn't feel like correcting him.

"I just wish there was something more I could do to help."

"If I can't help, you certainly can't," Reynir said. "But the priests can do something. We'll be there soon."

Even his insult sounded empty. I thought of the priests in their stuffy cave. I couldn't imagine them saving Finnur. This was Mists magic, and they couldn't even keep Mists magic out of their own town. Out of their own rituals.

Isolfr, a voice whispered in my head. *Isolfr will be able to save him.*

I scowled. No. Isolfr could barely save himself. And besides, he would be gone by the time we returned, him and Kolur and Frida, all of them.

I had to find a way to save Finnur on my own. He'd gotten me this job aboard the *Annika*; he'd helped me find a place to live. Saving his life was the least I could do.

I walked back to the captain's quarters. Asbera knelt at Finnur's side, clutching his stiff hand in her own. I sat down beside her. Finnur's expression hadn't changed; his eyes were still open, his face still terrified.

"If we weren't at sea," Asbera said softly, "we'd could at least gather the moon moss and prepare the healing draught." She closed her eyes and took a deep breath. "But there's *nothing*—"

I didn't tell her there was something. The sea. We had the sea. But we couldn't get to it, not with those creatures following alongside us as we sailed home—

Home. Sea and sky, we were leading them back to Tulja.

I looked down at Finnur. In truth, he was more important to me than Tulja. Let Baltasar worry about bringing the creatures to dry land. Let the priests use their magic to keep them at bay. I just wanted Finnur to live.

"Are you sure there's no moon moss on board?" I asked.

Asbera sighed, ran one hand through Finnur's hair. "It's not something we typically keep on boats."

I frowned. Then I slid off my bracelet and placed it on Finnur's heart. Asbera looked up at me in surprise.

"I bought it in a magic shop in Skalir," I said. "It's brought me some luck." Not enough, but I didn't think I needed to add that. "It could only help."

She nodded, her face blank. I stood up. "I'm going to see if I can find anything. I don't know much about earth-magic, but if there's anything that I think will be useful, I'll bring it to you."

She nodded again. Then she wiped at her eyes and said, "Thank you."

I made my way to the storage room. I didn't think I would find anything, but I couldn't stand the thought of sitting around, watching Finnur not move. Reynir had gone looking for supplies, but his focus was on ocean-magic. Asbera had been too distraught to look for herself.

One of the few things I did know about earth-magic was that it could be eked out of ordinary materials—cooking spices and flowers from a vegetable garden. Surely we had some of that on board.

The galley was empty, although I could hear the snores of the crewmen through the wall. I didn't find much. Mostly drinking water and crackers and salted fish. I collected one of the empty fish jars, thinking the leftover salt might be useful. A line of small wooden barrels was lashed against the far wall, and I pried open their lids. Most of them were empty, but I did find a few sprigs of dried lavender in one, probably left over from a longer voyage. It crumbled when I touched it, but I was able to sweep the remains into the fish jar.

I didn't know if Asbera would be able to do anything with what I'd found, but it had to be better than nothing.

I took the fish jar back to the captain's quarters. Asbera looked up when I walked in, and I held out the jar like an offering.

"Salt," I said stupidly. "And lavender."

Asbera blinked.

"Plant-magic?" I pulled the jar up close to my chest. I felt like I'd made some terrible mistake. "To help with—"

"Oh." Asbera shook her head. "That's sweet of you, but I can't—there's nothing we can do with salt and lavender."

I looked down at the jar. Worthless. Everything was worthless.

"I do appreciate the thought." She smiled, just a little. "But earth-magic can be so complicated, particularly when you aren't on dry land."

"Oh. Of course. That makes sense."

"I think your bracelet's helping a little, though. Come look."

I set the jar on the floor and went to Asbera's side. The bracelet was glowing. Not enough to cast light, but enough that even someone not touched by magic could see the enchantment in it, fighting with the magic that had poisoned Finnur's blood.

"His heartbeat is stronger." Asbera laid her hand against his neck. "See?"

I felt his pulse. Stronger, yes, but not what I'd call strong.

There wasn't much more to say. I put my hands in my lap. The *Annika* rocked back and forth. Every now and then, I'd hear scratching from the creatures in the water, but our shield held firm, even if nothing else did.

The north wind continued to blow us home, great strong gusts so powerful, they could have been produced with magic. This left me with little to do the next day other than watch over Finnur so Asbera could sleep. She didn't want to—I think she was afraid he would slip away while she was gone. But she curled up in the hammock at my insistence, and a few minutes later, her breathing had grown steady and even.

The bracelet's glow was dimmer than it had been earlier. Asbera probably hadn't noticed; otherwise, I doubt she would have fallen asleep. But I could see it, and feel it too: the bracelet had fulfilled its capacity.

The thought made my chest hurt, but I knew I shouldn't expect so much, not from a cheap trinket from a magic shop.

I knelt down beside Finnur. He skin was waxy and almost translucent, and if I looked hard enough, I saw the glow of magic in his veins. It wasn't the soft glow of the bracelet—this was harsh, violent light. Poison from the Mists.

My heart twisted. I lay my hand against the side of his neck and felt his heartbeat, faint and unsteady. I closed my eyes. Even his skin was cool to the touch, like ocean water. The bracelet had staved off the inevitable, but he was dying.

Something stronger would have to save Finnur.

The boat's rocking lulled me into exhaustion. The creatures scrabbled against the boat's hull. I thought of the warning that Isolfr had given me about Lord Foxfollow: *You need to recognize those creatures that are particular to the Mists.*

Thinking on Isolfr gave me a weird, sharp pain in my chest. I stretched in my chair, trying to shake it off. Part of me still thought he was responsible for all this, that he was the reason the Mists were after Kolur, that he'd *led* us to the Mists—

But that didn't explain Gillean.

I didn't want to think about Gillean, but I did anyway. I couldn't even think about him as he'd been in that space between worlds. Couldn't think about him alive. No, I had to think about him as he'd been in death, his face twisted up in anguish, his body stiff, silver blood everywhere.

Like Finnur, in truth.

Except Finnur wasn't dead. I hadn't been able to save Gillean, but I still had the opportunity to save Finnur. Even if I didn't know how yet.

I played over the future in my mind, unwinding it like Mama's spool: we would arrive back at Tulja, but we wouldn't be able to approach land, not with the creatures tearing up the sea. We'd have to get rid of them first. I didn't care about Tulja, but I did care about Finnur.

And even if we did get rid of the creatures and brought Finnur on land, he'd still be at the mercy of the priests or the healers, and who knew if they had to skill to run up against Mists magic.

Hopelessness threatened to swallow me whole, like the ocean itself. I looked over at Asbera, still sleeping in the hammock. She twitched, groaning a little. Both of them had shown me so much kindness and here I was, doing nothing, *nothing* to help Finnur.

There had to be something.

I thought.

I thought.

I thought of Gillean.

Gillean—face twisted, blood shining. Gillean, standing in a room made of light, terrified.

Gillean.

I sat straight up, my heart racing. Isolfr had called Gillean from the Mists and met him in that in between place. It had been simple magic, too: a song, a gesture. And the north wind.

Wind-magic.

I looked back at Finnur. Blood rushed through my head. I was teetering on the edge of a precipice, trying to find my balance. When I thought about what I wanted to do, dizziness swept through me.

Use Isolfr's spell and call whoever's responsible.

My cheeks burned. *Call whoever's responsible.*

It was stupid. Dangerous. And on some level, I understood that. But I was too exhausted and too overwhelmed to really think on my actions. For the last day, I'd sat by and watched as Finnur slipped away from us, and all I'd done to help was lay my bracelet on his heart.

I left the captain's quarters and went up on deck. Reynir was sitting next to the fire, listening to Seimur play a tune on his flute. They were probably trying to drown out the screeching and splashing of the creatures.

Reynir stood up when he saw me. "Is something wrong?"

I shook my head. "I just need you to go down and watch Finnur for a little while. Asbera's still asleep and I—I need a rest." My voice wavered. Reynir narrowed his eyes, but he didn't comment on it.

"Of course." He nodded once. "You need your rest too."

He walked away. The rest of the nighttime crew had their attention focused on Seimur and his melancholy flute. A sad song at a sad time.

While they were all distracted, I crept over to the stern end of the boat, taking care not to get too close to the edge. The wall of magic that Reynir and I had built was still in place, solid and potent, and I didn't worry too much about being dragged out to sea by one of those creatures. But I was aware of them, aware of their sharp teeth and the poison those teeth carried, and I knew they were aware of me, too.

The wind was cold and icy and rattled through the sails. I knelt down on the cold deck. Closed my eyes. I sang softly, barely above a whisper, afraid one of the crew would hear me and come asking questions.

No one did.

I concentrated hard on the lyrics, the alien consonants of the old language clumsy on my tongue. The magic in the north wind was stronger than I expected, and stranger—more refined than wind-magic should be, like a tamed lion. But I was able to catch it easily enough and intertwine it with the music.

Power shuddered through me, the start of something.

The gestures came to me like second nature: the thumping on the deck was the thumping of my heartbeat, and the arc of my hand was the arc of my breath. The wind grew colder. Dots of snow melted on my face. The screech of the creatures fell away.

I opened my eyes.

The *Annika* was gone.

I stood inside a mirror. The walls and ceiling and floor reflected me back into myself, and so I felt hollow and transparent. I'd done it. I'd come to the world between worlds.

"Whoever's responsible for the attack on Finnur of Tulja," I shouted into the cavernous space, "I call you!"

I was met with silence. I turned in place, and my reflection moved with me. With Isolfr, this place had been golden and full of light, but now I felt like I stood on the surface of the moon. Maybe I'd done something wrong.

Footsteps.

I froze, my heart pounding. I couldn't tell where the footsteps came from, and the sound of them bounced all around the room. For a moment, I was certain an army approached.

And then the footsteps silenced.

"Now, what's this, then?"

The voice was as silvery and liquid as the room itself. It didn't echo, only fell dull and flat like a heavy stone to the soil.

Slowly, I turned. I had no idea what I expected to find: a monster like the creatures surrounding the *Annika*? A beautifully inhuman boy with starlight skin? The Nalendan? But it was a man, just a man, tall and slim and dark-haired. He wore a charcoal-colored jacket cut in a style I'd never seen before. Not Empire and certainly nothing like what the men of the north wore, not even wealthy ones.

His eyes were gray.

I could only stare at him. He strode forward, swinging a wooden cane in time with his steps. Each one fell as flat as the other.

I forced myself to speak. "Are you Lord Foxfollow?"

He stopped again. Tilted his head. "Who are you?" he said.

I knew better than to tell him my real name. "A girl from Kjora."

"I don't know this Kjora." He swung his cane and settled it across the back of his shoulders. "How do you know the name Lord Foxfollow?"

"It was given to me by a friend." I felt like I couldn't catch enough breath, much less speak. My words were miracles. My heartbeat pounded in every part of my body.

"A friend?" The man smiled, slow and easy and unsettling. "Not a friend from your world, I wouldn't think. Was this the same friend who taught you to flatten realities?"

"What?" His question caught me off guard. "Flatten realities?"

"Yes. All of this." He gestured and drew in the room with his arms. "How could a little *human* girl like you call me here?"

I drew myself up, gathering all my courage. "I guess little human girls aren't as weak as you think."

The man laughed. "I suppose not. Tell me, are you the one who beat back my operatives in the human village?"

"Your what?" I frowned. "You mean the costumed men?"

The man waved his hand dismissively. "Yes, yes, they took the form of that silly human magic. Their defeat was no real trouble for me, at any rate. I was merely curious. I sincerely doubt you're the one who *actually* defeated them."

I didn't say anything, remembering the rush of the north wind, my own stilted confusion.

"You must have had help bringing me here, then, as well."

"I didn't." I glared at him, a colossal act of bravery. "I called you on my own. I have questions for you." I took a deep breath. "You never told me if you're Lord Foxfollow or not."

A pause. The silence amplified my fears.

"Of course I'm Lord Foxfollow," he said. "That was who you called." His voice shifted into a woman's voice—my voice. *"Whoever's responsible for the attack on Finnur of Tulja!"* He grinned, rakish. "Or do you not trust your own magic?"

I wanted to falter, but I stood strong. "Why did you send those monsters after us?"

Lord Foxfollow's smile stayed fixed in place. "My deepest

apologies," he said. "I never meant to send my menials after you."

"What?" I said.

Lord Foxfollow waved one hand dismissively. "It's a dull story. Now, why did you call me here?"

I looked up at him, at the lovely carved planes of his face. He smiled at me and his gray eyes glittered. "Come, my dear," he said. "You went to all this trouble to bring me to this space. And you claim you did it all on your own too." He strode over to me and trailed his fingers down the side of my cheek. His touch was cold and damp, like ocean spray or winter humidity. Or mist.

I shivered and pulled away from him.

"My friend." I tried to choose my words carefully. "His name is Finnur Corra. He was bitten by one of your mons— by one of your menials, and he's fallen into a coma. I need you to help me." I lifted my chin defiantly, but I felt like I was caught in a web. A silvery, gossamer, glittering gray spider's web.

There was a long silence.

And then Lord Foxfollow roared with laughter.

"Oh, my dear, my dear, you collapsed realities to try and save your friend? That's sweet, it really is."

"So you'll help him?"

"Look at me," he said.

I did as he asked without thinking. In the shining light of that reflective space, his skin was suffused with a pale, moonlight glow. His eyes roiled like storm clouds. The silvery web tightened, and I looked at his mouth to get away from his eyes.

"I'm afraid I can't do anything to help your friend." I saw his answer more than I heard it, the words rising off his lips. "I could, of course, my powers are . . . quite impressive. But I simply don't feel the need to waste them on a human, particularly when it's a human's fault he's hurt."

"What?" My legs and arms burned, and I realized that tears were dripping down my cheeks. "What are you talking about?"

"My dear, my dear." Lord Foxfollow smiled and wrapped his arm around my shoulder. I wanted to get away, but I couldn't move. He pointed his cane at the mirror across from us. Our reflections were a pair of smeared blurs, distorted by mist. "Why talk when I can show you? I can re-create the past much more easily than you can remember it."

The mirrors melted away and revealed the Rilil docks at night. Stars swirled overhead. The boats were tucked in their usual places. Everything was quiet and empty.

"I'll show you," Lord Foxfollow whispered, his lips pressed close to my ear. I trembled from the pain in my heart. "I'll show you . . . the *Penelope II*."

The scene blurred and the jagged, uneven lines of the *Penelope II* appeared, illuminated by the soft blue light of a magic-cast lantern. Lord Foxfollow squeezed my shoulder more tightly. He smelled like cold, damp steel and men's perfume, and it made me dizzy.

"Watch close," he whispered. Even his breath was cold.

The water around the *Penelope II* began to churn in a way far, far too familiar to me. I shrieked, and Lord Foxfollow clamped one hand over my mouth. "You don't want to miss anything," he said.

The water rose up around the boat, solidifying into the gleaming, cold shapes of the monsters. They crawled aboard, one after another.

I yanked his hand away from my mouth.

"Why are you showing me this?" I sobbed. "What does this have to do with not helping Finnur? Stop. Stop it!"

Lord Foxfollow flicked his cane, and suddenly I could see aboard the ship. Frida and Kolur were crouched beside each other under the masts, firing pistols into the onslaught of monsters. Isolfr was nowhere to be seen. Of course.

"We have to send them away," Kolur shouted. His voice sounded strange, tinny and distorted. "Like we practiced back in Jandanvar."

"Send them where?" Frida shouted back.

"Does it matter?"

Everything in my body went cold.

"Ah." Lord Foxfollow's arm slipped away from me. "She understands."

"This is a trick," I whispered. "This is a lie."

Across the room, Frida climbed up the highest mast and Kolur fought his way to the bow of the boat. The wind buffeted them, knocking the boat around in the bay. Ocean water splashed over the side. I knew they were doing magic, even though I couldn't feel the ripples of it in my own body. I could see it, a swirl of wind and water and starlight.

The monsters disappeared.

Kolur collapsed across the deck.

Lord Foxfollow brandished his cane, and all I could see now was my reflection again. Lord Foxfollow smiled at me in the glass.

"He sent them to you," he said. "He's strong for a human. Much stronger than he looks."

For the first time, I noticed a hardness in Lord Foxfollow's voice, like a vein of ice running through water.

Lord Foxfollow grabbed my chin and jerked my face toward his. My whole body was numb. He tilted my gaze up until I met those flat gray eyes. I was falling into them, tumbling through them, and I knew with a shuddering certainty that Kolur had sent the monsters to me on purpose. It was punishment. Punishment for not helping him.

Lord Foxfollow's fingers dug into my face. His nails were sharp.

The pain bled spots of light into my vision.

"Don't blame me," Lord Foxfollow said. "Blame Kolur Ice-break."

The memory of those images flickered through my thoughts, one after another. The monsters swarming the boat. Isolfr gone. The pop of pistol shots.

Send them where?

Does it matter?

He didn't do it on purpose. My certainty otherwise was a cold mist inside my head, but it didn't come from me. It came from Lord Foxfollow.

"You're a monster!" With a tremendous force of will, I pulled away from Lord Foxfollow. My feet clattered across the mirrored floor. He couldn't hurt me here, he couldn't hurt me here. "Just like your menials. A monster."

Lord Foxfollow tilted his head.

"No," he said. "I'm just different from you."

Rage bubbled up inside me. I thought of Kolur standing at the wheel of the *Penelope*, the wind blowing his hair away from his face. I thought of Asbera weeping over Finnur, and of Finnur himself, frozen and tormented because of one bite to the shoulder.

And although there was no wind in that place, I gathered up what magic rested inside of me, a residue from all the spells I'd cast, all the winds I'd called down. I gathered it up and I wove it into a hard knot of fury and then I cast it at Lord Foxfollow, a cyclone of light.

It struck him in the chest and dissipated. Of course it didn't hurt him. Lord Foxfollow looked at me sadly.

"My dear," he said, "that was highly uncalled-for."

All my anger turned to fear.

"Begone," he said.

The mirrored room disappeared, Lord Foxfollow disappeared, and I drifted, dazed, through a cold and dark space.

He had undone my magic with a single command, and I understood then that he could have done that from the very beginning. That he was only humoring me.

The dark space brightened. Spots of light appeared overhead. I blinked at them. Stars. They were stars. I was lying flat on my back, staring at the stars.

No, not lying.

Floating.

I flailed, my heart racing. I caught a glimpse of what lay below me: dark ocean and the *Annika*, so small it looked like one of Henrik's toys.

"No." I struggled against invisible bindings. "No. Foxfollow!"

My voice carried on the wind. The wind, sweet-smelling and gentle—that wasn't Foxfollow's doing. He would have just dropped me into the maelstrom of monsters down below. No, this was the north wind, buoying me along, keeping me adrift.

I stopped struggling. The wind caressed me. It was cold, yes, but it was a comfort, too.

"Thank you," I whispered, although I wasn't sure who I spoke to.

The wind whistled in response, and then it floated me down slowly, gently, and laid me to rest in the bow of the *Annika*.

CHAPTER FIFTEEN

Lost. Everything was lost.

I sat up. The familiar creaks and moans of the *Annika* were drowned out by the shrieking of the monsters in the water. The boat rocked back and forth as the north wind blew us steadily home.

But we couldn't go home.

"Hanna!" Asbera's voice rang out in the crystal night. She ran over beside me, Reynir at her side. "What happened? Benedict said you disappeared—"

"I was trying to help Finnur," I muttered. "But I can't. I can't."

"Trying to— *How?*" Reynir threw his hands up. "By just *disappearing*? Can you take the rest of us with you? Or take *Finnur* with you, at least?"

"I didn't go somewhere that could help Finnur." I stood up, shaky after flying on the wind. The monsters thrashed against the side of the shield.

"I was worried," Asbera said. "I thought something had happened to you, too."

"Something did. But I'm fine." I stalked away from the railing, back toward the brazier at the boat's center. Baltasar sat beside it, staring into the flames. He glanced up at me when I joined him.

"Worried about you, girl," he said.

He sounded exactly like Kolur. I looked down at him, at the firelight bouncing off his skin, and felt like crying. What if Lord

Foxfollow hadn't been lying? What if Kolur had sent the monsters to me on purpose?

I shook my head. "I just wanted to help. But I didn't find anything." I sat down in front of the brazier and stuck out my hands to warm them.

Reynir and Asbera walked over to the fire, although they hung back, sticking to the shadows.

"Isn't anyone watching Finnur?" I asked.

"Seimur is." Asbera frowned. "I was—we were worried. What were you trying to do?"

I took a deep, shuddery breath. The night howled with sound, clawing and shrieking, and so I focused my attention on the crackle of the wood inside the brazier.

"Find the person who hurt Finnur."

Baltasar gave a bitter laugh. "Did you?"

"He's of no use." I closed my eyes against the tears. "What are you going to do when we get back to Tulja?"

Silence. When I glanced over at Baltasar, he was staring into the flames.

"Well?"

"Been trying not to think about it," he said. "Enough to worry about."

Behind him, Asbera gasped. "No," she said, and stumbled over beside us. She knelt beside Baltasar and grabbed his hand, her eyes big and imploring. "No, you can't—we have to go home. Finnur's dying."

"I know he is." Baltasar wouldn't meet her in the eye. "Told Reynir to come up with something."

Asbera and I both looked over at Reynir at the mention of his name, but he was looking down at the deck.

"I don't have anything yet," he said in a cold voice. "But perhaps

Hanna can find a way, if she can meet with our attacker in some realm in the sky." His eyes glittered in the firelight. "I'd prefer not to see my home destroyed and my family murdered."

"Oh, stop it," Asbera said. "That doesn't help."

"You aren't helping. You're the reason we're going home in the first place. I told Baltasar we should sail in circles until we found a way to get rid of them."

Asbera's eyes flashed with anger.

"Enough!" Baltasar roared.

Magic flooded across the deck of the ship, bright and hot and smelling of the south wind. I jumped and drew into myself, searching for my own magic. Asbera grabbed for my hand. Baltasar hoisted up his pistol.

The enchantment faded away, twinkling on the air. One of the monsters had almost broken through our shield.

"They're getting stronger," Reynir said in a flat voice.

I scanned across the magic, sucking down breath, trying to steady myself. Over on the starboard side, the shield was marred by a thin line of light, illuminated by the stars.

A crack.

"Whatever you did," Reynir said, "it made them worse."

"Maybe you made it worse," Asbera said. "You're the one being cruel."

I slumped back down in front of the brazier. Baltasar didn't say anything, but he didn't put his pistol away, either. One of the monsters let out a long, echoing howl that sank down into the marrow of my bones. I imagined that howl sliding over the empty ocean and disappearing into the cracks between worlds. I imagined Lord Foxfollow whispering spells to his monstrous little pets, giving them the strength to break through our stupid human magic.

"He's right," I said. "It is my fault."

"Hanna——"

Asbera reached out one hand toward me, but I stood up and glided out of her reach. The shields hummed, but the churning on the other side was louder and more urgent.

I'd called Lord Foxfollow to me; I'd shot him with my magic. And all I'd done was give him reason to send his monsters after us in earnest.

Morning dawned, the sun a pale white disc hanging high in the sky. I felt like I'd only just fallen asleep, and I had; the nights were getting shorter. This far north, soon they'd be gone completely.

I had slept down in the crew's quarters, curled up in a hammock so that no one would speak with me. When I woke, I went up to check on Finnur. Asbera was sitting with him, a plate of salted fish in her lap. Untouched.

Finnur was still pale, still cold, still breathing.

"Baltasar says we'll be home by this time tomorrow." Asbera didn't look at me. "But we still don't know what to do about the monsters." Her voice cracked, and she took a deep breath and straightened her spine. "He's right; we can't go back to Tulja, not until they're gone." Her hands trembled as she pushed Finnur's hair aside.

I felt empty. Finnur looked like a corpse, his skin was so pale, so bloodless. Once again, I thought of the vision that Lord Foxfollow had shown me—Kolur and Frida gathering up the strength of their magic and sending the monsters straight to us. I shivered. Why would Kolur do such a thing?

He wouldn't.

The voice whispering to me wasn't my own. It sounded like the wind. I went very still, straining to hear it.

He wouldn't hurt you on purpose.

Asbera kept stroking Finnur's hair. Her cheeks glimmered with tears.

He wouldn't hurt me.

Foxfollow would.

It was an accident. Foxfollow showed me something that had truly happened, but he had been trying to frighten me, to make me feel abandoned. Except the voice on the wind was right—Kolur wouldn't have hurt me on purpose.

He didn't know where he was sending the monsters. But he had sent them away.

And I had seen it.

I bolted out of the cabin, into the bright wash of sunlight. A handful of the crew tended to the sails, and Baltasar stood up at the wheel. The shield shimmered in the sun.

Everything was quiet except for the monsters' screeching.

The sound was horrific, like listening to an animal die, and louder than it had been even last night. I walked over to the masts. Zakaria looked up at me and nodded. He had shoved strips of fabric into his ears. All of the crew had. I didn't want to do the same, though. I thought I should listen. There might be something in the screams that could help.

There was still no need for me to call the winds—that was the only good thing about this trip, that the winds had been on our side all this time. Or maybe it wasn't the winds themselves. Maybe it was that presence in the wind. I couldn't feel it, exactly, but I'd heard its voice down below.

I looked over at the port railing, at the shield. Off in the distance, the ocean was steely and calm. It was only around the boat that the water thrashed.

I walked closer. Slow, careful, cautious steps.

"What are you doing?" Zakaria shouted. I ignored him. "Don't get too close!"

The air was thicker around the railing. The shield sparked out at me, touching the magic in my blood. I took another step closer.

A monster leaped out of the water and slammed into the shield. Magic flared. Ocean water landed at my feet.

The monster slid away.

"Told you not to get too close." Zakaria was at my side now. He pulled the strip of fabric out of his ears. "They've been doing that all day."

"Where's Reynir?"

"Up in the masts, strengthening the shield." Zakaria pointed. "Could probably use your help, you know."

I squinted up into the sunlight. Reynir was a burst of enchantment among the sails, a silhouette wreathed in a halo.

"No," I said. "I need *his* help."

I left Zakaria. Reynir was fully enveloped in his magic, his eyes closed, a stretch of rope knotted around his arm. I waited until he finished, standing there amidst the cries and shrieks of the monsters.

It didn't take long. Eventually, his light faded, and he sagged against the rope, his chest rising and falling. I climbed up the masts.

"Hanna?" he said, squinting at me. "Is that you? The real you? You know how it is with magic—"

"Yeah, it's the real me."

"What are you doing here?" He leaned against the mast and unwound his arm from the rope. "Has something happened with Finnur?"

"No, he's the same." I leaned forward. "Reynir, I need your help. Probably Asbera's, too."

He looked at me with his tired eyes. "For what?"

"To get rid of the monsters."

A pause. The wind whistled around us. It smelled sweet, like honey, nothing like the cold steely scent of the Mists.

"Have you known how to do this the entire time?" His voice was low and accusing.

"No! Well, not exactly. I learned something when I went to the in-between place."

"I knew it."

"I didn't realize I'd learned it until just now. I thought I'd been betrayed, but it was—a trick. Kolur, my old captain, he's the reason they're here in the first place. But not—" I stopped and took a deep breath and told him what Lord Foxfollow had showed me.

"How do you know it's not a trick?" Reynir said.

I glared at him. "I don't, all right? But we have to do something. The monsters are just getting stronger, and if we circle around trying to figure out something else, not only will Finnur die but the rest of us will too, because those monsters are going to break through the shields."

Reynir looked at me. The boat rocked back and forth, and the monsters' screeching bore into my brain.

"Do you know how your captain did it?" Reynir asked. "Sent them away?"

I took a deep breath. "Not exactly—"

Reynir sighed.

"Will you let me finish? No, I don't know how he did it exactly, but I do know it's possible, and I know that Kolur's a seawizard, like you, and Frida, who was with him, she's a windwitch, like me—" I trailed off. *Isolfr.* But he wouldn't have done anything outright, not if he was still refusing to reveal who he was. "And we'll have Asbera, who can work a bit of earth-magic. When you get down to it, magic's just strength of will, right? So together, we ought to be able to throw the monsters someplace else, out at the open sea—"

"So they can attack some other poor ship the way they attacked us?"

"We'll have to throw them farther. The Green Glass Sea, in the south. My mother told me those waters are laced with magic, dangerous magic, and that should be enough to destroy the monsters."

I stopped, breathing hard. Reynir watched me. He looked worn out: dark circles under his eyes, lank hair. But I imagined I looked the same way.

"Have you spoken to Asbera?" he asked.

I shook my head. Reynir sighed. "This isn't going to work."

"We have to at least try."

"We don't even know what to do."

"I saw them do it from a distance. I can figure it out. *Please*, Reynir. Please. Even if you don't care about Finnur, the whole boat's in danger—"

"I care about Finnur," he snapped. "Fine. But I'm not taking the blame when you make things worse."

"Thank you," I said, ignoring his slight. Fighting with him wouldn't do any good right now.

I climbed back down and Reynir slowly followed, wiped out from repairing the shield. We walked into the captain's quarters together.

It was quiet in there, the walls shutting out most of the monsters' wails. Dark, too, since Asbera had drawn the curtains over the windows. Asbera was curled up in the hammock, her eyes closed. I doubted she was sleeping. Not if there was no one else to watch over Finnur.

We crept in. I looked to Finnur, the way I always did. No change. Asbera's plate of fish sat beside his cot, half eaten.

"Hanna." Asbera's voice drifted through the shadows. "You're back."

"I need to talk to you." I knelt down beside her. "Me and Reynir, we may need your help for something—"

She frowned and sat up. She looked even more worn-down than Reynir did. She looked like she'd died and been reanimated.

"What?" she said, voice barely a whisper.

"I think I know how to get rid of the monsters," I said.

"What?"

"I—I saw it. In the in-between place. Kolur did it."

"Your old captain?"

I nodded. "I couldn't see all of what he did, but I saw enough. Enough that I think Reynir and I can do it ourselves. But I want your help, your extra magic, just in case."

Asbera looked over at Finnur. Tears streaked down her cheeks. Finnur didn't move.

"Of course I'll help you," she said. "Why wouldn't I?"

We waited until nightfall. Magic is stronger at night, when the world is wrapped in shadow. Kolur had sent the monsters our way at night as well, and I figured we needed to do it as much like him as possible.

But waiting until night left us little time. The *Annika* would arrive at Tulja soon—already we'd begun to pass the tiny rocky islands that marked the edge of Tuljan waters.

Baltasar cleared the deck for us. All the crew were told to wait down below, and he waited with them, at my request. Without the crew, the deck was even eerier. The shield cast a yellowish glow over everything, and the monsters shrieked and howled like they knew what was coming. Every now and then, one of them flung itself at the shield, and magic would scatter across the deck like flaring embers from a fire.

"Is everyone ready?" I asked. I'd already explained what I'd seen in the in-between place. It wasn't much to go on, but it gave us a sense of where to stand and what to do.

They both nodded. I took a deep breath.

And then we took our positions.

Reynir stood up at the bow of the ship, where the ocean splashed up around him. Asbera was at his side. Her magic wasn't as strong as his, but she could supplement it.

I climbed to the top of the main mast, just as Frida had done, and faced north, into the wind. I didn't call the south winds, not when we were so close to home and with Finnur's life so close to ending—I didn't want the *Annika* to blow off course. The north wind had been sweet to me these last few weeks, and that presence seemed to like me well enough. I should be able to use its strength.

The wind blew hard, rough and cold against my face, and I closed my eyes so it wouldn't draw out tears. Besides, wind-magic works best when you go by feel.

"North wind," I whispered. "I call upon you, cold brother of the south. Drive us forward. Bring the ocean to our feet."

The wind lulled.

My heart lurched inside my chest. "No, no, no," I whispered. "No, please, north wind, I need your—"

And then the wind gusted so strongly that it knocked me backward. I grabbed hold of the rope to keep from falling, and my eyes flew open and I could see the stars, swirling overhead, beautiful.

The north wind had saved my life once again.

"Thank you," I whispered.

The wind flattened out the sails, and the *Annika* plowed forward, dipping into the black, icy ocean. The monsters howled their protest. I held on tighter to the rope and concentrated on pulling the magic from the wind into myself, so I could transform it and unite with Asbera and Reynir.

I didn't dare look at anything but the stars. I didn't dare break my concentration. The wind poured over me and poured through me, and it was transformed into a beam of energy, cold and strong.

"Come on, Reynir," I whispered. "Come on, come on."

The wind blew harder. I tightened my grip on the rope. The magic drained out of me like blood, but I held on, and for a moment I thought I saw Isolfr's face—

A force blasted across the ship and slammed into me. Magic. It was wild and tumultuous like the sea, and it left me damp, my hair curling at the ends. That magic twisted together with my magic, sea and wind. Just like in Kolur's spell.

As our power combined, I saw glimpses of Asbera's face alongside Reynir, and I could feel the two different strains of their strength.

The magic flowed between all three of us, an arc of power. Everything fell away but the rushing of enchantment, which roared like the ocean, like the wind. I couldn't let myself think consciously anymore, and so I let the magic think for me. Think *through* me. Together, we sent it running over the sides of the ship, a waterfall of light that caught the monsters like a spider's web. They howled and thrashed. But they were trapped.

We had to act fast, before the Mists became aware of what we were doing. "To the Green Glass Sea," I whispered, and my voice was Asbera's voice, and Reynir's voice. "To the GreenGlassSea. TotheGreenGlassSea. Tothegreenglasssea. Tothegreenglassseatothe- greenglassseatothe—"

The air cracked with a great thundering tension. Our magic drew tight like a coil.

"Release!" I screamed, and the wind tasted like saltwater.

Distantly, through the rush and roar of enchantment, I heard Reynir's voice shout, "Release," and then Asbera's, layered on top of each other like we were singing a melody.

A pause, long enough that I could feel the texture of the magic all around me, damp and cold and strong and shimmering like starlight.

The monsters let out one last howling screech, all in unison.

And then the magic transformed into an explosion of light brighter than the sun. I screamed and shut my eyes, but the dazzle stayed, burned against my eyelids. In the flash, I saw bright green waters, far away in a warm part of the world, stirred up by a denala. The storm rained monsters into the sea.

And, thank the ancestors, there were no ships on the open ocean to witness it.

Then even that image was swallowed up by the brightness.

The boat rocked. I leaned into the rope and took deep breaths as the magic subsided, pulling back like the tide. The wind died down, and the sea quieted. My eyes fluttered open. There seemed to be more stars than when we began.

I had forgotten what silence sounded like.

"Hanna." The voice drifted in on the wind. It wasn't Asbera's and it wasn't Reynir's. For a moment I thought it was Finnur, but no, the accent was wrong. "Hanna, I'm so glad—"

"We did it!" Asbera's head poked up on the mast. "They're gone. Those awful creatures are gone!" She climbed up on the mast beside me. I straightened up and untangled my arm from the rope. It had seared a red line into my flesh.

"I saw it," I said, feeling dazed. "The Green Glass Sea. Did you—"

"Yes." She pulled me into a hug. "I saw it too. They're gone. *Gone.*" When she pulled away, her eyes shone with tears. "We'll be able to disembark," she whispered. "We'll be able to save him."

I nodded. Everything felt fuzzy. Distorted. Had I really seen Isolfr's face in the swirl of magic? That didn't make sense. Had he been following the *Annika* after all?

But I didn't have time to think on those questions. Asbera pulled me down the mast. After the brightness of the magic-burst, the darkness was too dark, and we both stumbled through the shadows. I banged my knee against the unlit brazier and gave a sharp cry of pain. It echoed in the silence of the open ocean, a comfort.

No more monster cries.

A faint blue light appeared on the deck, bobbing along through the darkness.

I thought of the Mists, disguised as the costumed men.

Then voices rose up, chattering and relieved. The crew. I slumped against Asbera in relief.

"Did you see that?" Reynir bounded up to us, a magic-cast lantern swinging from one hand. "That light? Oh, and the Green Glass Sea—never thought I'd live to see the Green Glass Sea."

Asbera laughed, although it was too strained, too frenetic, to be mirthful. I smiled. Truthfully, I never thought I'd see the Green Glass Sea either.

The crew crowded around us, stomping their feet and cheering. Baltasar slapped Reynir on the back. "You sure they're gone?"

Reynir looked to me. "You can't be sure about anything with magic," I said. "But everything played out the way I saw it."

Baltasar nodded, satisfied. "Well, then. Let's see if we can't make this boat go any faster, eh, boys?"

The crew cheered again, and there was a mad scramble to pick up the ropes and angle the sails to best catch the wind.

Which was still gusting in from the north.

Asbera slipped away from the crowd, moving through the

liquid light of the magic-cast lanterns, toward the captain's quarters. I followed her.

Finnur was still frozen in place. Asbera hung the lantern on the hook above the bed, and as the light slid over him, I almost thought he moved.

"How's he doing?" I asked.

"The same." Asbera lifted up my bracelet and laid her hand on his heart. "Part of me thought—well, I thought that when we cast the spell . . ."

Her voice trailed away. I walked over to her and wrapped my arm around her shoulders. Finnur screamed silently up at the ceiling.

Asbera laid the bracelet back on his chest.

"It's not long now," I told her. "We'll be there by dawn."

"You'll help me, won't you? Take him to the priests?"

"Of course." Even though I didn't know if the priests would be of any help. Kolur knew how to beat back the Mists—but he would have sailed away to the north.

I gave Asbera a hug, squeezing her tight, and listened to the waves crashing up against the sides of the *Annika*. The crew and the winds had us going fast, like we were driving straight into the dawn itself.

Asbera and I stood side by side in our embrace, waiting for the sun.

CHAPTER SIXTEEN

Benedict spotted land just as the sun peeked above the horizon. I was asleep when the call went out, and the clanging of bells wove through my dreams, which were of starlight and the wind. I opened my eyes to find the crew scrambling up on deck.

"Land!" Benedict shouted. "We're home!"

My heart leaped at the word *home*, even though Tulja wasn't home, not really, not for me. But it was home for Finnur. There had to be someone here who could bring him back to life.

I ran up on deck and found the crew preparing to make port, so I grabbed a rope and started tying down the sails. We worked largely in silence, the gray dawn lighting our way. Asbera wasn't on deck, but the captain's quarters glowed with the light from a magic-cast lantern.

"How's Finnur?" I asked Reynir when he joined me at the masts.

"Still alive." Reynir nodded. "I watched over him last night." He hesitated. "Asbera insists there's no change, but I took his pulse and it was weaker than it was yesterday."

I kept winding the rope around my wrist. "At least we're back," I said after a time.

Reynir grunted in response.

The *Annika* sailed through the still, calm waters of the bay, missing one of her crew and nursing another, but not trailing any monsters to land. As the docks appeared in the dim light, I checked over the side of the railing, afraid one of the monsters had found its way back to us. But there were only the dark waters.

"Listen up," Baltasar shouted from the helm as we approached the docks. "Gather round."

We did as he asked. The wind pushed us gently toward the shore.

"I know you're all relieved to be home," Baltasar said, his rough hands gripping the ship's wheel. "But first thing we need to do is to send word to the priests. Finnur's our priority, but you need to tell them about Harald as well. Reynir, I'm putting you in charge of that. Compose the message yourself. Benedict and Seimur, I'm asking you to rent a pair of yaks and take the message in person. You know how the priests can be."

There was a stilted pause at Baltasar's blasphemy. He pulled a couple of stones out of his pocket and tossed them down to Benedict and Seimur. "For the yaks," he said.

They nodded.

"The rest of you can clear the boat. But stay close—head over to the Yak's Horn if you want. Don't know what the priests'll need to get Finnur better. May be sending you out on errands."

The crew muttered their agreement.

The *Annika* slowed as she sailed into the docks proper. I stayed up on deck to help with the wind, standing by the railing so that the crew could scramble up and around the masts. The light peeked over the horizon, illuminating the boats lined up in the bay. There were five of them, more than I expected. Fishing vessels, mostly.

Including one lined with spiky, Jolali-style icons.

I gasped and clutched the railing so that I could lean out over the water. The *Penelope II*. She was still docked at Tulja. They hadn't left after all. Lord Foxfollow's attack must have left them weak.

I whirled around. "Baltasar!" I shouted. "Baltasar, I may be able to help Finnur, faster than the priests."

He had all his concentration focused on bringing us to the docks, like a good captain, and he didn't look at me when he answered. "What are you on about, girl?"

"I know someone who might be able to help. I thought he'd be gone by the time we arrived, but his boat's still here."

"And who's that?" Baltasar adjusted the line of the boat as we moved closer to land. "Your old captain?"

My blood vibrated in my body. Finnur; we'd be able to save Finnur.

"He's a powerful wizard," I said. "It's worth a try, and he can come faster than the priests—"

"Right you are on that. Go fetch him when we get to land. I'm willing to try anything."

I nodded and turned back to the starboard side. The *Penelope II* gleamed in the encroaching dawn as the *Annika* settled into her customary place at the docks.

When the crew were dropping anchor, I raced into the captain's quarters, grinning with the good news about the *Penelope II*.

Asbera sat at Finnur's side, laying damp cloths on his forehead. My grin vanished.

"What's wrong?" I slid into place beside her. Finnur's expression was the same, still that frozen terror, but his skin was pale and tinted blue. Horror crawled over me. "Sea and sky, is he—"

"Not yet." She tucked a cloth around his throat. "His temperature has risen. I'm not a healer, but it feels too hot—"

I immediately laid the back of my hand against his cheek. His skin burned.

"Maybe it's a good thing," I babbled. "Maybe it means he's coming back around."

Asbera shook her head, her hair falling into her eyes. "It took too long," she whispered, and draped another cloth, this time across his chest. "I know you got us here as fast as you could, but the priests will take at least a day——"

"We may not need the priests." I grabbed her hand and squeezed it. She looked over at me, confused. "The *Penelope II* is still here. Kolur might able to help. I know he's familiar with Mists magic."

She didn't say anything, but a light came back into her eyes. A glimmer of hope.

"You should open up the windows," I said. "Maybe the cold air will help bring the fever down. The wind's still blowing out of the north."

She nodded. "Thank you," she whispered.

"I won't be long," I said. "I promise."

I raced along the docks, my hair streaming out behind me. A few fishermen stood scattered around their boats, and old Muni with his fish stand was already set up in the usual place. They all stared at me as I ran past, but I didn't care. I was only focused on getting to the *Penelope II*.

Her masts poked up against the horizon, dark against the pink dawn. Her sails were down. I breathed with relief—she wasn't going anywhere yet. But I didn't slow. My feet pounded against the old saltwater-soaked boards, and I sucked in cold salty air until my lungs burned. When I finally came to the *Penelope II*, I stumbled to a stop and I leaned over, trying to catch my breath. Everything was quiet here except for my panting. Even the ocean seemed to have fallen silent.

The gangplank was down, so I climbed aboard. No one was on deck, but I could smell the residue of magic, like burnt salt. A scrap of woven blue fabric had been nailed to the boards beside the ship's wheel. A Kjoran protection charm—I'd grown so used to the Tuljan ones that the sight of it startled me. I wondered how new it was.

"Hello!" I shouted. "Hello, is anyone here?" I walked across the deck, my voice lifting with the wind. "It's Hanna. Please! I have an emergency!"

No answer. I turned slowly in place. The waves sloshed out in the bay. A cold fear gripped at me. Maybe they weren't here at all. Maybe Lord Foxfollow had killed them, or dragged them away to the Mists. Or done worse, somehow.

"Hello!" I screamed again, panic turning my voice ragged. I ran to the hatch and flung it open. The underbelly of the boat was lit with a faint blue glow. A lantern. I scrambled down, taking deep breaths every time my foot touched the rung of a ladder. "Kolur!" I shouted when I made it down. "Frida! Anyone?"

The *Penelope II* was not laid out like the original *Penelope*, and the corridors twisted off in strange narrow angles. It must have been the Jolali style, but the confusing layout just made me frustrated. I could hear the ocean everywhere, but nothing else, no human voices, nothing. "Kolur!" I screamed. My voice echoed like I stood inside a cavern, not a boat. Another side effect of the magic that had been done here.

"Be quiet."

Frida. I recognized her voice.

I whirled around. I couldn't see anything but blue-lit darkness. "I can't see you," I said, lowering my voice. "I need to speak with Kolur."

"He's resting." Frida ducked through a low-hanging doorway. She was dressed in sleeping clothes. "What are you doing here?" She looked at me. "You shouldn't come with us, if that's what you're thinking. It's too dangerous. Stay here until you can find passage home."

Her voice was sharp-edged and it made me shiver. *Too dangerous.* At least they were being honest now.

"It's not that." I shook my head. "I need Kolur's help. The magic he did a few nights ago, when Lord Foxfollow attacked—it hurt one of my friends."

Frida froze. "How do you know that name?" she hissed. "Lord Foxfollow."

"I know everything that's been happening." I jerked away from her. "Plus, I *talked* to him. He showed me what Kolur did, sending the monsters into the open sea. He sent them straight to the *Annika*."

Frida's hand went to her mouth. "No," she said softly. "No, we didn't mean—"

"I know you didn't." I slumped down. "But one of those monsters bit my friend and put him into a magic-sleep and I have to know if Kolur can help him. Please? They sent for the village priests, but it's almost a day's journey for them to leave their cave and I don't think Finnur—that's my friend—I don't think he has enough time. So will you please let me talk to Kolur?"

The words spilled out in a tumble, and when I finished, I had to steady myself against the wall and catch my breath. Frida looked away from me, her hand still covering her mouth.

"What?" I asked breathlessly. "What's wrong?"

The lanterns threw liquid light across us both. I wanted to scream. Finnur was dying, and Frida wouldn't help me.

"Kolur can't go to your friend," she said softly.

"What? Why not?"

"Magic-sickness." Frida looked back at me. "Parts of him changed—he can't leave the ocean, not for the time being. Pjetur and I wove a spell to reverse the effects, but it will be at least a week's time before he's able to breathe air again."

The world fell away. I heard a rushing in my ears like the air was pouring out of my body. I hadn't seen *that* in the vision Lord Foxfollow gave me. Only the magic.

I pressed up against the wall, my whole body shaking, Sea and sky, we were lucky the magic-sickness hadn't infected us on board the *Annika*.

"I'm so sorry," Frida said. "I am."

"You can heal him," I said. "You're powerful, I've seen it—"

She stared at me sadly. "I've never had the ability to heal," she said. "I wouldn't feel comfortable, not against Mist magic. I'd likely cause more harm than good."

Panic hammered through my thoughts. "What if we put Finnur in the ocean?" My voice echoed around the strange corridors of the *Penelope II*. "We could put him in a rowboat and Kolur could look at him that way—"

Frida shook her head.

"Why not?" My voice trembled. I didn't want to cry in front of her, but I was afraid I was going to anyway. "Please, I swore to his wife—"

"He's too weak to work magic," Frida said. "Yes, he could look at your friend, but he couldn't do anything about it. Not in his current state. It would destroy him, turn him into saltwater."

I couldn't hold back my tears any longer. I stalked away from Frida and ran through the corridors, choking back my sobs even as tears streaked down my face.

"Hanna!" she called out, but I ignored her. I stumbled through the murky shadows until I came to the square of sunlight illuminating the ladder leading back up on deck. Finnur was going to die. Kolur couldn't help him, and the priests would never get there in time.

The burden of my responsibility hung like a weight around my neck.

I climbed back onto the deck of the *Penelope II*. The sun had risen completely, lemony and bright like the summer sun back home. I felt like it was mocking me.

"Hanna, don't go yet."

I stopped. I almost recognized the voice. It was more human than I remembered.

Isolfr dropped down from the masts, landing softly on his feet like a cat. The sunlight refracted through my tears, and in that liquid haze, he shone the way he had when I first saw him.

"I was just leaving," I said, trying to hold my head high. I turned away from him.

"Wait."

There was an urgency in his voice that I didn't expect. I stopped, staring off at the dock in the distance. The wind blew my hair into my eyes. I was blinded.

"My friend's going to die," I said. "I can't stay."

"What?" Isolfr walked over to stand beside me. I thought he was going to put his hand on my shoulder, but he didn't. "Why? What happened?"

"Don't you know?" I snapped. "Don't you know everything?"

Isolfr looked down at his feet. His cheeks reddened. "Not in this body." He lifted his eyes, peering at me through his lashes. "But I heard you yelling, and so I know that it must be serious."

I hesitated. The wind blew harder, gusting in from the west. I thought I smelled summer on it, the fresh scent of berries and wildflowers.

And then I told Isolfr everything. I was desperate.

He stared at me as I spoke, not once looking away. His eyes were the same color as ice. They were the only part of him that didn't seem human.

"I can help," he said. "Take me to him. But we have to move quickly."

I stared at Isolfr, taking in those blandly handsome features, those unsettling eyes. It made sense, in a way. Isolfr was not human, and Finnur had been struck down by inhuman magic.

"You don't trust me," Isolfr said.

"Why should I?" I snapped. "I won't put my friend in any more danger—"

"I want to help him!" Isolfr shouted. "I want to help you."

I'd never heard him raise his voice before, and I took a step back, shocked.

Isolfr seemed to shrink down inside himself, back to the soft Isolfr I knew from our time at sea. "I'm not from the Mists," he said.

"You've certainly told me that enough times," I snapped. "Not that you'll say where you *are* from—"

"I'm from this world," Isolfr said. "From the north."

"Jandanvar?"

He hesitated, and that was how I knew. Somehow, he came from Jandanvar.

"I know what to do to help your friend," he said.

The wind gusted again.

I nodded.

"Show me the way." He ran toward the gangplank. I followed, too scared to let myself get hopeful.

"We kept him on board the *Annika*," I said. "It's moored at the usual place—the seventh dock."

"All right, yes. I know where that is."

We ran. I focused on the line of Isolfr's back ahead of me. Then the *Annika* rose up against the docks. With the masts empty, she looked haunted.

Zakaria and Reynir were standing guard next to the ladder. They looked up at us as Isolfr and I skittered to a stop.

"Who the hell is this?" Reynir asked, jabbing his thumb at Isolfr. "Baltasar said you were going to get your old captain."

"He couldn't come. This is—Pjetur. He can help."

Reynir narrowed his eyes at me.

"We don't have time for this! Move!" I shoved Reynir aside, and he let out a surprised cry of protest that made Zakaria laugh. But neither of them tried to stop me.

I let Isolfr climb up the ladder first. *Please don't betray us,* I thought. *Please please please.*

The deck was empty except for Baltasar. He sat over by the ship's wheel, smoking a pipe and staring off into the distance. He glanced at us when we scrambled on board.

"This is Pjetur," I said before he could ask any questions. "He's not my captain, but I know he can help." *I hope he can help.*

"Where is he?" Isolfr stopped in the center of the boat and sniffed at the air. "He's far gone. I need to see him *now*."

"Captain's quarters." Baltasar blew out a ring of smoke. "Sure hope you can help him, boy."

Isolfr nodded. The way the sun shone on him, he didn't look human at all but like some manifestation of the spirit world, a creature of light and magic.

A creature of wind.

I went very still, thinking of the north wind, the whistling, whispering voice, the way it had cradled me down from the stars—

No. It couldn't be.

Isolfr disappeared into the captain's quarters. Baltasar studied me through the haze of his pipe smoke.

"What is he?" Baltasar asked.

I decided not to lie. "I don't know."

Baltasar turned back to the sea. "You better get in there. He might need your help."

My entire body felt shaky and indistinct, and the world didn't seem real. But I nodded and walked over to the captain's quarters with careful, quick steps. Cold, brittle magic was already seeping out through the walls. It wasn't human magic. But it didn't belong to the Mists, either.

The door swung open when my hand passed by it.

The scene inside the room was a quiet one, not the wild display of enchantment that I'd half expected. Asbera stood pressed up against the far corner, her arms wrapped around her torso. Finnur's shirt was peeled away from his chest, which gleamed pale and weak in the lantern light. I slid over beside Asbera.

"It's that boy," she said, her voice flat. "The one at the mead hall. I don't remember his name."

"He didn't give you a real one." I hesitated. Isolfr was tracing patterns on Finnur's chest with his fingers, runes that I didn't recognize. They glowed in the darkness. "His real name is Isolfr."

"He's not human."

"No, I don't think so."

But Asbera didn't seem to be talking to me, not really. "He's kjirini."

"What?"

Asbera blinked. Isolfr ignored both of us, all his concentration focused on painting those runes on Finnur's body, working with light and magic.

"It's a Jandanvari word." She looked at me. "I don't know how to translate it, not exactly. Sometimes they use it to mean 'wind,' but a particular kind that sweeps in from the north."

I went very still.

"It also means 'magic,'" Asbera said. "But a certain ki—"

And then Isolfr began to sing.

Asbera cried out and grabbed my arm. She never finished what she was going to say.

Isolfr's voice was not a human one, and he did not sing a human song. The notes were low and whistling and mournful, somehow just like the wind, and it filled up the room with a presence strange and eerie and—familiar.

A word that means "wind."

The north wind.

And so, I finally understood completely: Isolfr was the presence in the north wind; the presence in the north wind was Isolfr.

I didn't know how and I didn't know why, but I *knew*.

Magic materialized on the air and dotted across my arm like snow. Asbera moved to my side. I wrapped my arm around her. We pressed close together.

Isolfr's voice grew louder. The music seeped into me and drew out my emotions: loneliness and fear. Homesickness. A yearning for something beyond home, for something larger than just me. Tears streaked down my cheeks. When I looked at Asbera, she was weeping too.

Across the room, Isolfr flickered. In one second he was Pjetur, a dull and handsome human boy, and in another he was Isolfr, shining like the moon, sharp-eyed, elven, too delicate to be real. He shifted back and forth between the two. The song grew louder and louder.

And then Isolfr's hand slid into the skin of Finnur's chest.

Asbera shrieked and moved to lunge forward, but I caught her and held her tight. This was not evil sorcery. I could sense it deep inside me, a hard echo inside my bones. It was the magic of the north wind, the magic that brought me home from the in-between world, the magic that drove the Mists away outside the mead hall. He was helping.

Isolfr's hand disappeared completely.

He shut his eyes and flickered once, and then remained Isolfr, his skin glowing with foreign light. The song shifted, abruptly, into something faster and more howling. It didn't even sound like music anymore, just the shriek of wind in a storm. The enchantment in the room thickened. The walls rippled like sails. I squeezed Asbera tighter.

He was using wind-magic, but not any that I'd ever seen.

And then, with a gasp and a cry, Finnur sat up.

Asbera screamed and tried to lunge forward again, but I stopped her. I didn't want her interfering with Isolfr's spell—his hand was still tucked inside Finnur's chest, and the magic still vibrated around us.

Finnur's twisted expression hadn't changed, and even though he sat up now, he was as still and waxy as before. The light in Isolfr's skin pulsed. His song fell away, and the silence was like the silence in the eye of a hurricane. He stared at Finnur straight on.

Asbera whimpered.

Isolfr took a deep breath. He seemed to suck in all the air in the room. The lanterns flickered. The walls flapped and snapped, no longer wood but fabric. Asbera grabbed my arm so hard that her nails dug into my skin. But I didn't move. I could only watch Isolfr, transfixed by this strange wind-magic.

With his free hand, Isolfr opened Finnur's mouth.

And kissed him.

But it wasn't just a kiss; I could hear the air passing between them, a roaring rush like being caught in a wind tunnel. The air in the room grew thin and weak. It was hard for me to breathe.

Isolfr snapped his head back and yanked his hand, completely unbloodied, out of Finnur's chest.

There was a long, terrible pause. Asbera sobbed.

And then Finnur blinked.

"Finnur!" Asbera ripped away from me. I didn't stop her this time. Finnur looked over at her, dazed. Then he smiled. It was a smile to light up the darkness.

Asbera threw her arms around him. "I thought you were going to die," she said, sobbing into his hair. "I thought I'd lost you forever."

"I thought of you," he whispered. "While I was trapped. Sometimes I saw your face——"

Asbera kissed him.

Isolfr was lying on the floor of the cabin, stretched out, pale. He looked like Pjetur. I knelt beside him. He dropped his head to the side and blinked up at me.

"Is he alive?" he asked.

I nodded. "And awake."

Isolfr smiled and turned his gaze back to the ceiling. "That was more difficult than I expected. The poisons had gone in deep."

I hesitated. Asbera was still weeping behind me, but I could hear the happiness in her tears. I felt that happiness myself. Finnur was alive.

Isolfr had saved him.

"We should give them some time alone," I said.

Isolfr nodded, though he didn't move. I stood up and held out my hand. When he took it, his skin was cold to the touch. I pulled him to his feet. He was lighter than I expected. There was something intangible about him. Like air, magic, wind.

He didn't let go of my hand once he was standing, and he leaned up against me for balance. I could feel him shaking.

Asbera and Finnur ignored us both; they were too wrapped up in each other to care that we were still in the cabin. So I just led Isolfr out onto the deck. The captain's quarters looked the way it always had, out here. Baltasar was gone. I wondered if the spell from the cabin had frightened him.

"Will they be safe?" I asked. "With the magic-sickness?"

Isolfr nodded. He stumbled over to the side of the boat and slumped down, his back pressed up against the railing. He took a deep breath. "It's not true magic-sickness. It'll fade in time."

"Not true magic-sickness?" I frowned. The air was warm and unmoving, like summers in Kjora. I sat down beside Isolfr. "If you don't mind me asking—what kind of magic was that anyway? It felt like it belonged to the wind—"

"It did." Isolfr looked at me, his eyes clear and pale and icy. "But not the sort you can do. The sort I can do."

I stared at him for a long time, trying to work things through in my head.

"Your sort can stop the Mists."

He nodded.

"It comes from the north wind, doesn't it?"

He sat very still. I didn't think he was going to answer. But then he nodded again.

"So it was you," I said. "The night the Mists attacked in the form of the Nalendan. You saved me."

"No." Isolfr gave a weak laugh. "No, I *helped* you. You were holding your own quite well, but human magic—" He shrugged. "You have a talent."

I shrugged, but I looked away from him, my cheeks burning.

"Thank you," I said, speaking to the air. The ocean glittered around us. "Thank you for everything." *Everything* was such a simple, meaningless word, but I didn't know how else to say it.

He seemed to understand.

"It was my pleasure," Isolfr said.

Two days later, we held a funeral for Harald. I thought it would be at sea, because he died in the water, but Tuljans honor their dead with fire and smoke.

There was a procession from the *Annika*, the whole crew draped in garlands made of dried flowers and summer moss. Harald's family was there too. They were yak herders, land people. His younger brother was only ten or so, and he ran to the edge of the docks and stared out over the sparkling water.

"The first time he's ever seen the ocean, probably," Asbera said softly. "It's rare for us to come so close to the edge of the land."

Because Harald's body had been lost to the Mists, his friends carved an effigy of him instead. They scraped his features into a post of soft pine and painted in his skin and eyes and hair. The effigy was laid down on a cloth of woven yak fur and scattered with the same white flowers the Tuljans tossed at the Nalendan. Protection, Asbera explained. To draw his soul out of the underworld of the Mists.

Finnur was quiet in that time before the procession started. He hung back, sipping a cup of mulled wine to stay warm. Asbera and I helped in the preparations, me following Asbera's directions for how to drape the garlands and how to scatter the flowers. But Finnur just watched us.

"He's been like that since he woke up," Asbera said. We were lighting the candles for the procession, one after another, with natural fire and not a bit of enchantment. "He saw things, you know, while he was under." Her voice hitched. "He was in a prison, he said, wrapped up in cold gray mist. He couldn't move, but they showed him things, showed him terrible things happening to me, to our children—we don't even *have* children." Her hands were shaking. Gently, I took the lighting candle away from her.

"He's back now," I said. "I'm sure it'll take some time, but he'll get better."

Asbera looked up at me.

"He's got you," I said. "He'll be fine."

She smiled, wavering and thin. But then she asked, "Why did this happen to us?"

I paused for a moment, thinking. Then I set the candles aside and hugged her. "Bad luck," I whispered. "But Kolur will be gone soon. He'll take the Mists' interest away with him."

Asbera wiped at her eyes. "I hope so."

I hoped so, too. But at the same time, the thought of Kolur leaving almost made me sad.

The procession started. Musicians led the way, playing the clanging, droning song I associated with the costumed men, although no one wore costumes. Harald's effigy followed, carried on its pallet by three of the crewmen and Baltasar. Then his family. Then the rest of us. We carried our candles close to our chests and stayed silent as the music led the way, winding us through the village. People stepped out of their shops and threw white flowers as if we were the Nalendan. They watched us with solemn faces.

Eventually, we came to the open fields. Here, villagers stood outside their tents, all of them holding their own candles. By now, it was almost dusk and the candles glowed like stars in the purple twilight. I had never seen anything like it, all those licks of flame gathering toward us as we moved deeper into the fields.

Our procession grew as we twisted through the tents. The music never stopped, but it still wasn't enough to cover up the occasional bursts of throaty sobs.

We walked, and walked, and walked, until we came to a clearing paved over with smooth flat stones that were blackened and charred.

The music stopped.

For a long time, nothing happened. We stood in a ring around the stones, me and Asbera and Finnur all side by side. The only sounds were the wind through the grass and the muffled hush of weeping.

Then Baltasar and the crewmen set Harald's effigy on the stones. They stepped back, and Harald's mother took their place. Her whole body trembled as she knelt beside the effigy and anointed it with oil. She had covered her face with a scrap of tattered old lace, and in the flickering candlelight, she looked like a ghost.

She was the first to touch her candle to the effigy. The flame caught and trembled, and she blew out her candle and then stumbled back, into her husband's arms. Baltasar went next, and then Harald's father and brother. Then the rest of us. One at a time, villagers touched their candles to the effigy, even as it was already consumed by flames. By the time it was my turn, I could only see the fire. But Asbera whispered in my ear, "Just hold your candle to it," and I did, grazing its tiny flame against the fire's huge one.

I felt something, a tremor of magic inside me. The release of a small part of Harald's soul, from the Mists back to our world.

I stepped back into the cold night air, my face stinging with the fire's heat. I blew out my candle. That was a sort of magic, wasn't it? That transfer of a small light into a large one.

We watched the fire burn. It rose higher against the starry sky, letting off flares of sparks and a great tail of dark smoke that, to my surprise, smelled sweet, like incense. Finnur stared into the fire, the light staining his skin orange. His eyes seemed to glow. Looking at him gave me a hollow feeling, but then he reached over and took Asbera by the hand.

I knew, looking at them, that it was enough.

That night, the *Crocus* was hung with dozens of tiny floating lanterns, the deck covered in dried sea lavender. Seimur played Tuljan songs on a carved guitar while Benedict sang along, both of them perched on the empty helm so their voices carried across the deck. All of the moored boats were lit up that night. A funeral in the evening and a celebration at night. It was the Tuljan way, Asbera told me.

I sat in one of the chairs that we'd dragged up from down below and sipped a glass of honeyed mead, watching as Asbera and

Finnur spun each other around in an elaborate Tuljan dance. All of the *Annika* crew was there, and most of the folk from the docks and the people who lived in their tents out on the tundra. Almost all of them were clapping and stomping time to the music as Asbera and Finnur danced. It was reassuring to watch: Finnur's skin was full of color, and he moved with a liquid grace that didn't suit someone who had, two days ago, been trapped in an eternal sleep.

Finnur tossed Asbera up in the air and caught her at the waist. Everyone erupted into cheers, and Asbera laughed and covered Finnur with kisses. The music jangled on.

Cold whispered against the back of my neck, just for a moment, and then it was gone. I glanced up and saw Frida crawling up the ladder, her hair twisted into a dark, knotted braid.

Isolfr was with her.

No one else had seen them yet. I stood, mead sloshing over the side of my cup. Frida lifted her hand in greeting. Another cheer went up and rippled into the night.

"You still haven't left," I said when Frida and Isolfr walked over to join me.

"No," Frida said. Isolfr didn't look at me, only watched the dancing, the lights shining in his eyes. "Kolur hasn't recovered." She smiled. "He can at least come out of the water for a bit at a time now. So it should be soon."

Isolfr looked over at her when she said *soon*, and then over at me. His expression was grave. "Yes," he said. "Soon."

"Don't look so sad," I told him. "You're at a party."

"I'm not sad." He smiled. "But I don't go to many parties."

Frida shifted her weight. "I'd like something to drink."

"Talk to old Muni there." I pointed up at the bow of the ship, where Muni was perched with a great towering barrel. "He's got the mead."

Frida thanked me and slipped off into the crush of people. Finnur and Asbera were still dancing, both of them spinning wildly in tandem, although now their crowd of onlookers was dancing, too. For a moment, Isolfr and I watched them in silence.

"Finnur and Asbera haven't noticed you're here yet," I said.

"I haven't let them."

I looked over at him. He looked like Pjetur, more or less, but the light of the lanterns seemed to strip his disguise away, revealing the imprint of his real features.

"Why not?" I said.

"I don't want to steal the attention away from them." Isolfr nodded. "It's their party."

I wasn't certain if I believed him, but I decided to accept his answer. After a pause, I walked back over to my chair and sat down. Isolfr followed and crouched down beside me, one hand on the armrest.

"Why aren't you dancing?" he asked.

"I don't know any of these songs." I took a drink of my mead. It had cooled in the chilly night air. "And I don't know any Tuljan dances."

"So if you were on Kjora, you'd be dancing?"

I smiled a little. "I guess."

Isolfr was looking hard at me. He squeezed the armrest. "How much longer until you're able to go home?"

Silence. The music played on, Seimur's singing growing louder and more riotous. In the flash of dancers, I spotted Frida spinning around with Reynir. She held her drink high over her head, and her mouth was open in a continuous laugh.

"What did you tell her and Kolur?" I said. "About being able to heal Finnur?"

He stared off into the darkness beyond the boat.

"Isolfr!"

He sighed. "I made them forget." He looked down at the floor. "I—I actually made all of them forget. Asbera and Finnur and everyone else in the village."

"You what?" I sat up, knocking my drink over. It spilled across the floorboards in a gleaming amber strip. "Why? Why would you do that?"

"It's easier." He kept looking down. "They think the priests healed Finnur. What does it matter?"

"You didn't make me forget."

"No." He looked up and his face was nothing like Pjetur's. I was transfixed by it, caught in a spell. I couldn't look away.

"Stop that," I said.

"Stop what?"

"Holding me in place like that. Whenever I see the real you—"

"I can't help it," he sighed. "I'm sorry. I didn't take your memory away because—because I need you, Hanna."

I closed my eyes. The music flowed around us, and so did some vague, unfamiliar magic. His magic. I wondered if he'd made us invisible to the party. If we were shades now, or spirits. Ghosts.

"Not this again," I said.

He put his hand on my arm, and I was shocked at how cold it was. Like ice water. I looked over at him.

"I'm not here because I want Kolur to win back the Jandanvari queen," Isolfr said. "I'm here because we can't let the Mists through to our world—"

"This isn't your world." I snatched my arm away from him.

"Yes, it is."

The party twinkled on without us.

"You aren't human," I said softly. "That's all I meant—"

"I'm not human, but this is still my world. My home. And

I won't see it destroyed by Lord Foxfollow." Isolfr stared at me. "That's what he wants, you know. The queen of Jandanvar will bring him here, and then he can hurt everyone the way he hurt Finnur."

I trembled, remembering the horrors of the prison where Foxfollow held Finnur. I thought of Asbera weeping at Finnur's side as he screamed in silent anguish.

I thought of that happening to everyone, north and south, east and west.

"You know that I'm right."

"Why me?" I was shaking—I was cold, despite the heat globes drifting around the party. But I knew I wasn't at the party anymore. I wrapped my arms around myself, trying to keep warm. "What do you need me for? I'm no one special—"

"You have ties to the south wind," Isolfr said. "And you have a talent for magic. You're exactly who I need."

"But I'm not even a proper witch. Just a fisherman's apprentice." I glared at him. "And you wanted *Frida* in the first place—"

"And I was too much of a coward to work with her, yes. Is that what you want to hear? That every time I look at her, I remember what she did to my brother?" Isolfr's eyes shimmered, and for a moment, I was afraid he was going to cry. "I am a coward. That's why I need you. Because you're brave."

I stared at him. "I don't think you're a coward," I said.

"He's tried to do it before, you know."

"What?"

"Lord Foxfollow. He's tried to come into our world before. And he was stopped. Twice." Isolfr straightened his shoulders. His Pjetur disguise was melting away. "You're named after one of the people who stopped him."

I realized then that I couldn't hear the music anymore. The party had receded into the darkness. Isolfr and I sat on an island of shadow, and the *Crocus* and all my friends were a dot of light far in the distance. But I didn't care.

"What are you saying?" I said.

"Your mother served aboard the *Nadir*, didn't she? Surely she told you the story about how Ananna stopped the Mists from crossing over into our world."

"Yeah, I've heard the stories." I felt very cold. "Are you saying *that* was Lord Foxfollow? The lord she defeated?"

Isolfr nodded.

"So you want me to help you because Ananna and I have the same *name*?"

Isolfr scowled. "No. I want you to help me because you're talented and brave. I already told you that."

"Fine. But I'm not Ananna. She was a pirate queen when all that happened."

Isolfr leaned close in close. He smelled of honey and ice flowers. "How well do you know the stories?"

"I know them fine."

"Then you should know she wasn't a pirate queen when she defeated Lord Foxfollow. She was your age." Isolfr leaned back.

I stared at him. "What? Are you sure about that?"

"Of course. The problem is that story usually gets entangled with her later adventures. But she was your age when she sent Lord Foxfollow back to the Mists. Now it's your turn to do the same."

I looked away from him. All around was a thick inky blackness, darker than night, and the faint glow of the party.

"All I want," I said, staring at that glow, "is to go home."

Isolfr grabbed my hand. This time, I let him. His sharp inhuman features gleamed like a star.

"I swear to you," he said, in a voice like ice and snowfall, "that I'll see you safely returned to your family. All I ask is that you sail to the north and stop Lord Foxfollow from permanently entering our world."

For a moment, I was struck dumb. Isolfr squeezed my hand tighter.

"Make sail with us," he said, and this time his voice was normal, musical, the voice I knew. "Make sail with us and join your magic with mine. It's the only way."

The only way. I looked at the party again, shrunken and bathed in light. It seemed like a wizard's trick, a toy to enchant children. I thought about the jar of stones sitting aboard the *Cornflower*. Half empty. Nowhere close to enough to buy a ship and a crew.

I thought about the chill of speaking with Lord Foxfollow in the in-between world. I thought of the torment he had visited upon Finnur.

I'd never thought of myself as brave.

I looked at Isolfr. My heartbeat rushed in my ears.

"You can't guarantee my safety," I said. "But I'll go with you anyway."

THE NOBLEMAN'S
REVENGE

CHAPTER ONE

The *Penelope II* sliced through black-green waters, heading north toward Jandanvar. I sat at the bow of the ship, perched on top of a wooden barrel, and stared at the place where the sea met the sky. The air was as cold and bright as diamonds, but I was bundled up tight and Frida had already set several heat-spheres to glowing around the ship.

"Are you waiting for Foxfollow?"

I jumped at the voice. Even after the last few weeks at sea, I still wasn't used to how dull and human it sounded. Isolfr walked up beside me and leaned against the railing, looking awkward in his bland human skin. I still didn't know exactly *what* he was, but I'd seen him as he was supposed to look, shining like silver moonlight.

"No," I said, and I knew I was lying.

"Did you feel something?" Isolfr frowned and leaned close to me. Right now he was disguised as Pjetur, a human boy. Frida and my captain, Kolur, had no idea he was anything *but* Pjetur.

I shook my head. "I just like watching the waters. It's dull out here, without any fishing to do." I drew myself down deeper into my coat. Isolfr turned and looked out at the water.

"This is the longest I've been on a boat," he said. "Fifteen days."

Fifteen days. I'd given up counting off the days a while ago. It just made me anxious, thinking on where we were going. All the way up north to Isolfr's home, Jandanvar, to stop a creature of the Mists from marrying a queen of our world.

"Me too," I said.

He laughed. "But you're a fisherman's apprentice!"

"I mean fifteen days at *once*." I shook my head. "I've certainly been on a boat for more than fifteen days total."

Isolfr and I stood side by side in silence. I was aware of Kolur and Frida tending to the actual sailing behind us—Kolur at the wheel, Frida calling down winds to drive us to the north. It was a Jolali ship anyway, not something I was familiar with, although when you get down to it a ship's just a ship, really.

"If you sense anything," Isolfr said, "you should tell me."

"I know that." I sighed and glanced over at him. "Don't you have some chores to do or something?"

Isolfr shook his head. "Sailing's a fairly ineffective method of travel."

"Compared to what?"

Isolfr's eyes glittered, and for a second I saw a flash of him as he truly was, beautiful and ethereal and far from human. But then he went back to being boring old Pjetur and didn't answer me.

"Flying?" I said.

"Don't say that too loud," he hissed.

I laughed. "They're not paying any attention. You know that better than anyone."

Isolfr glared at me. I just laughed again.

"Oh, come off it," I said. "I know that spell's still working."

"I don't like risking it."

"Hey!" I shouted, my voice fluttering out on the wind. "Pjetur's really some magical wind creature and he—"

Isolfr launched at me and put his hand over my mouth and we tumbled over the barrel, landing in a tangle on the deck.

"What the hell are you two doing?" Kolur shouted. "Is there a problem?"

"No problem!" I called out, laughing. Isolfr perched on the balls of his feet. He wasn't glaring anymore, and in fact I could see he was trying not to smile. Kolur hadn't heard a word I'd said. Neither had Frida. Isolfr had made sure of that, through a spell so subtle I couldn't even feel it. He didn't want them knowing who he was. Not for any dishonest reason; mostly, it was because he was scared of them.

"See?" I said. "Didn't hear me."

"Maybe you two could find something more worthwhile to do with your time," Kolur said.

"There's nothing!" I counted off on my fingers the meager chores Isolfr and I shared. "We've got fish to last the next few days, and we've cleaned the decks and down below, and the sails are all in good repair. What more do you want?"

"It's not dinner time, either," Isolfr said, "or else we could start cooking."

"The storeroom could use some cleaning," Frida said. "I've noticed some water on the floors down there. Don't want anything to mildew."

I sighed in frustration. Cleaning out the storeroom. Wonderful. Back on board the *Penelope* I'd never had to do anything so unpleasant. Of course, we'd never been out at sea for longer than a couple of days, either. But that's because the *Penelope* had been for fishing and nothing else.

"I think that's a fine idea," Kolur said. "Both of you. Get down there."

Isolfr said, "Aye, captain," and hopped up straight and proper. I rolled my eyes.

"You could learn something from him," Kolur said.

"Not as much as I should," I muttered. Kolur didn't hear me, although Isolfr shot me an irritated look. Which was fair——he'd gotten a lot better about keeping me informed since we'd left Tulja.

Isolfr and I climbed down below. The corridors twisted around onto themselves, turning into weird labyrinthine knots that I found unnerving. It was the Jolali way, but I was a Kjoran girl and we didn't go in for that sort of trickery in our boats. Supposedly, it was meant to befuddle pirates.

I followed Isolfr though the dank, narrow corridors. Our footsteps echoed and rebounded off the walls.

"So," Isolfr called out, "do you remember what to watch for?"

"I wasn't looking for him. I told you, I was just looking at the water."

"I know. I'm asking just to be sure."

The corridor ended abruptly. The doorway leading into the storeroom was small, and you had to crouch down and crawl through to get inside. But at least the storeroom was spacious compared to the corridors. I crawled in after Isolfr and leaned up against the wall. Barrels half-full of drinking water and hard biscuits were lashed to the floor so they wouldn't slide around, and a cask of salt dangled from the ceiling, swinging in time with the boat. A single magic-cast lantern shone a dull green light over everything.

"It doesn't seem that damp down here," I said.

"They were trying to get rid of us." Isolfr hopped up on one of the barrels and swung his feet, heels knocking against the barrel's side. The boat lifted up a little, wood creaking, and seawater sloshed out of the corner, slapping at my boots.

"Oh," Isolfr said. "I see what Frida means."

"It's not that much." The boat righted itself and the water slid back to its hiding place in the corner. I climbed onto my own barrel and watched the salt cask swinging back and forth. "A wind spell ought to clean it up."

"You can do the honors," Isolfr said.

I looked over at him. In magic-cast light he always looked more like himself. The light filled his skin with a faint luminescence that you don't see in humans.

"You sure you don't want to?"

He didn't answer. I knew he wouldn't. I'd never actually *seen* him do magic, although I'd felt it—or rather, felt him, when he was riding around on the north wind. But that was only ever in dire emergencies. Which the threat of mildew was not.

"I'll get magic out of you yet," I said.

He glanced at me and smiled a little. I called down the wind.

It was tricky to do, being down below like that, but Isolfr being there made it easier. It was as if the wind wanted to be close to him. A southern breeze came whistling down through the ceiling in a faint, humid trickle—southern because I have an affinity with the south wind. It was just enough for me to draw the magic out of it. That magic was warm, balmy, the way magic from the southern winds always is. I drew it up into a knot and then spread it out over the storeroom. The air sparkled. The water sloshing in the corners turned to steam that drifted up among those sparkles and disappeared.

"Nice job," Isolfr said when everything finished.

"No thanks to you," I said, although his compliment did make my cheeks warm.

Now that the storeroom was dry, I used the last bit of magic to cast an anti-dampness spell, a simple one that would wear off after a few days. Once all that was done, I hopped back on my barrel and crossed my legs. The boat rocked and creaked.

"And we're back to where we started," I said. "I hope we get to Jandanvar soon." I didn't mean that. Lord Foxfollow waited for us in Jandanvar. He was the creature of the Mists Isolfr had been tasked to stop from entering permanently into our world. As one of the spirits of the winds, it was his role to protect this world from dangers; a sacred oath taken by all the spirits in his family. And because Foxfollow threatened the north, Isolfr had been chosen. He was the north wind. He was the north's totem.

I had agreed to help not two weeks ago, leaving behind the home I'd created for myself in Tulja, and the friends I'd made there, Finnur and Asbera. Sometimes I regretted it. But mostly I knew it was something I needed to do. I had to be like my namesake, like Ananna of the *Tanarau*.

Isolfr looked down at his hands. "You never answered my question," he said.

"What? What question?" I laughed, a nervous titter. "And it's not like you ever answer my questions, so I figure that makes us about even."

Isolfr shook his head. "About what to look out for. You remember, don't you?"

I sighed. "You're worse than Kolur, I swear." He'd been nagging me about the warning signs too, ever since we made sail. "Mist on the water," I said. "Monsters like the ones we sent away—"

Isolfr opened his mouth to speak but I held up one hand. "And I know they won't necessarily look like *those* monsters! Sea and sky. But I know how the magic changes when they're close by and that's all that matters."

Isolfr snapped his mouth shut and kept watching me.

"People with gray eyes," I said. "Warships like the one—"

"Not just warships," he said. "It could be any kind of ship. But you won't see the crew up in the sails."

"Right, I know." I slumped back against the wall and wrapped my arms around myself. "Really, that's the worst thing about not having anything to do. The fact that I have to sit around thinking all the time."

I could feel Isolfr staring at me because it made my skin prickle all over. That was another way I knew he wasn't human. Because even his gaze felt like magic.

"I know what you mean," he said.

It was reassuring, hearing him say that.

"What do you think we're going to find there?" I asked. "When we get to Jandanvar?"

He didn't answer right away, and it didn't matter because we'd had this conversation before. We both knew we were going to find Lord Foxfollow. He was a murderer and a tyrant, and if he married the Queen of Jandanvar, then he would have a foothold of power in our world. And that was no good; Ananna and her lover, Naji, had already sent him back to the Mists twice before. Now it was my turn to face him, to live up to her name. Which meant fighting. It meant being brave when I didn't remotely feel it.

That was what we were going to find in Jandanvar.

Isolfr looked over at me, his eyes the blue of glaciers.

"I don't know," he said.

He was lying. But it was an easier answer, and I didn't mind.

Two nights later, I woke to the sound of whispering.

I sat straight up, throwing my gaze around the darkness, seeing nothing but shadows. "Light!" I cried, and the magic-cast lantern flickered on. My cabin was empty, although the light slid across the walls, rippling over the Jolali carvings of unfamiliar gods and making them seem alive.

The whispering started again, as soft as the sea. It seemed to be saying my name, *Hanna Hanna Hanna*, over and over.

"Isolfr?" I said, tossing the blankets and furs aside. I crawled off my cot. "Sea and sky, why didn't you just come down?"

The whispering swelled—gusted really, just like the wind. "Isolfr!" I said again. Louder.

DANGER, the voice said.

I went cold all over. Silence came back into the cabin. The shadows kept moving over the walls. Something was wrong. Isolfr never came to me on the wind anymore.

I pulled on my coat and boots and then, after a second's thought, grabbed the narrow knife I used for cleaning fish. It still glittered with scales but it was better than facing the Mists empty-handed.

I edged my cabin door opened and stepped out into the corridor. The boat was silent save for the usual creaks and moans of life on the sea. I didn't hear any disturbance up on deck—no screams or footfalls. My heart pounded and I wanted to slink back into my cabin and bar the door and cower in the corner.

But that wasn't an option anymore.

I crept through the corridor, one hand on the wall to steady myself, calling for light as I moved past the lanterns. Up ahead, a square of moonlight illuminated the stairs leading up to the hatchway. It was open.

We never left it open.

I closed my eyes, took a deep breath, whispered to myself that I had to be brave if I wanted to get home. Then I lunged forward and clambered up the ladder, my knife clutched tight in one hand, my palm slippery with sweat.

Cold wind blasted me as soon I stuck my head through the hatch. Northern wind. My chest tightened. The deck looked empty, although I could feel Frida's magic winding its way through the sails. I recognized the texture of her sailing charm—and her protection charm.

I heaved myself up. The wind sang its low, mournful song, and for a moment I thought I heard Isolfr's voice, rising and falling like a melody. Then I realized I *did* hear his voice, only not in the wind, but on it—his voice came drifting in from the bow of the ship. He was talking with Kolur.

I tightened my grip on my knife and moved forward. I spotted them on the other side of the masts, huddling close together with Frida. All three stared at some dim moonlit spot on the horizon.

"What's going on?" I said.

They turned toward me as one. Their faces were pale and frightened, but that might have just been the eerie nighttime darkness.

"What are you doing up here?" Kolur asked.

I glanced at Isolfr. He looked the most frightened of all of them.

"I heard something," I said. "Voices. I thought—I thought the worst."

Kolur sighed. "And you came up here? There's a thin line between bravery and stupidity, girl."

I glared at him. "You don't seem to be in any trouble."

"I saw something," Frida said. Her voice cut like the wind. "Or I thought I did."

I shivered and looked out at the black water. Waves crested in our wake, their white caps the same color as the moon. I remembered Lord Foxfollow's monsters, how they shimmered on the air, blending in with their surroundings. But I didn't see anything.

"We're going to have to strengthen our protection charms," Kolur said. "I'm not taking any chances."

The rest of us stayed quiet, a silent acceptance of what he'd said. I nodded and pulled my coat tighter.

Then Frida spoke.

"You know I've exhausted most of my power," she said in a low voice. Isolfr and I both looked at her. She tilted her head toward Kolur, and she didn't look back at us. "You know we'll need something stronger—"

"The Svastin," Kolur said abruptly.

Frida stared at him, unspeaking. I'd never heard of the Svastin. It was Jandanvari magic, most like, something they had learned in their time there studying at the Undim Citadels.

But then I noticed Isolfr. He had gone pale, almost white, and his eyes were wide and fearful. He gaped in horror at Kolur, although Kolur didn't notice.

"What?" I asked Isolfr in a low voice. "What is it?"

He shook his head. "This is bad."

Frida and Kolur paid no mind to our conversation. Probably because of Isolfr's spell. I didn't know what that implied about this new protection spell, this Svastin.

I shivered. Up here on deck my little cleaning knife seemed small and ineffectual in the face of that vast dark ocean, and I felt stupid for even bringing it with me. If there had been Mists monsters, my knife wouldn't have stopped them. I knew that. I'd seen what the monsters could do.

"Go back to sleep," Kolur told me. "The both of you." He jerked his head at Isolfr. "Frida and I'll keep watch."

"Are you going to cast the Svastin?" I asked. "What is it, exactly?"

Kolur's face darkened. "We're using it for protection. But no, we won't be casting it tonight. We'll need a day to prepare." A pause. "It's not the sort of thing you should watch anyway."

"What? Why not?" I glanced at Isolfr. He still looked pale and frightened. "I thought I was supposed to be practicing my magic."

"Go to bed, girl!"

I glared at him. So here we were. Back to keeping secrets, just as he'd done when we sailed north from Skalir instead of south back home to Kjora, the way he'd pretended.

I stalked back over to the hatch. Isolfr tagged along beside me. Once we'd climbed down the ladder and were safely out of earshot—not that it mattered—I asked, "So I take it you're not a fan of the Svastin."

He stopped walking. The boat rocked around us. "No," he said, his voice rough and serious. "And you shouldn't be either. It's dangerous magic."

"You think everything's dangerous," I said, even though he was serious enough that his concern frightened me. "At least it'll protect us from the Mists."

"At the very least," he muttered, before continuing on his way down the corridor, leaving me alone in the dark. With questions.

The next morning, Kolur set me and Isolfr up on deck. Isolfr got the wheel and I was in charge of controlling the winds.

"You're going to sail us," he said, "while Frida and I get the preparations done."

Something about the way he said "preparations" made my heart skip a beat. And Isolfr looked as if he might throw up.

"If you don't mind me saying, sir—" he started, but Kolur interrupted.

"I do," he said. "I'm aware of the dangers, but we don't got much of a choice."

Isolfr looked down at the wheel, his pale hair falling across his face. As scared of Kolur as he was, it must have been a big step to say even that much.

"Keep us going due north," Kolur shouted over to me. "I threw the bones and they promised easy weather."

And with that, he slipped down the hatch and disappeared.

I took a deep breath, closed my eyes, and felt around on the wind for Frida's magic. It was easy work—all I had to do was take over control of the south wind from her. The transfer went quickly. There was a sudden rush of magic through my veins, and then I felt the south wind, strong and laced with the memories of my ances-tors. The sails bulged, and the *Penelope II* shot forward through the waves, heading north toward Jandanvar.

It took some effort to maintain the wind—the natural wind was actually blowing in from the northeast, blustery and laced through with frozen daggers—but I was grateful for the work. I leaned up against the railing and concentrated on the warm spice scent of the south wind, trying not to think about what Kolur and Frida might be doing belowdecks.

Things went that way for most of the morning. Eventually I grew tired of holding the wind so close to me, so I muttered an incantation Frida had taught me to control the wind in my stead. Then I walked over to Isolfr. He stood stiffly at the wheel, his eyes straight ahead on the horizon.

"Having fun?" I teased.

He glanced at me, shook his head. "This is serious," he said in a low voice. "I can feel them down below, calling on darkness."

The way he said that stopped me cold. I'd been so wrapped up in the winds that I hadn't noticed any dark magic bubbling up belowdecks. I stood still, concentrating, but all I noticed was the magic veining through on the wind.

"I don't feel anything," I said. "Maybe it's just your imagination."

Isolfr glared at me. "It's Jandanvari magic," he said. "And it's *dark*. You haven't been trained to feel it."

I slumped against a nearby mast. We bounced along, water spraying up over the sides of the boat. Not exactly the clear weather that Kolur had promised, not with that northeasterly fighting against the navigation wind.

The rest of the day carried on. After a time, it became as dull as our empty days previously; lunch was a relief, just to have a break in the monotony of controlling the winds. I expected Frida and Kolur to join us, but they didn't, and when I moved to fetch them Isolfr grabbed my arm and shook his head, his face grim.

"You shouldn't," he said.

I stared at him for a moment, my heart pounding. The *Penelope II* rocked against the waves, and the movement made me dizzy.

"Fine," I said after a moment, and I walked away from the hatch, back over to the food and water that Isolfr had brought up that morning. We ate in silence, sitting beside the ship's wheel, our magic roiling around the ship and guiding her north. Isolfr just picked at his food.

"What exactly are they doing?" I finally said after I finished my serving of salted fish. "What's got you so spooked?"

Isolfr lifted his face to me. "I don't like talking about it."

I would have been annoyed—more damn secrets—but something in his expression sent chills shuddering through my body. I didn't press him.

That afternoon, I took to singing songs from my childhood, the Kjoran hymns I learned from Papa and the pirate shanties I learned from Mama. Isolfr didn't join in, but every now and then I'd turn around, catch his eye, and grin, trying to lift his spirits. It didn't work. He kept frowning and fretting, his hands gripping the wheel so tightly his knuckles turned white. His fear had me nervous, even though I knew it was probably just him. He didn't trust Kolur and Frida. That was the whole reason he'd latched on to me in the first place.

But still. I couldn't help but wonder if Kolur and Frida really were doing dark magic down below.

I stopped my Kjoran ballad mid-song and shifted over to one of the pirate songs, a song calling for safety on the seas. It was a mournful tune, and the south wind caught my voice and distorted it so the melody was even more haunting. I stared out at the horizon as I sang. The sun sparkled against the water, but the moon had come out, a pale disc hanging in the corner of the sky.

When I finished, my voice echoed for a few seconds more, hollow like the wind.

"You have a lovely singing voice."

I shrieked and whirled around, almost dropping my hold on the magic. It was Frida. She was pale, with circles under her eyes so dark she looked as if she'd been in a fight. Her appearance gave me a chill, and I thought about Isolfr grabbing my arm and telling me not to go down below.

"Um, thanks," I said. Kolur was on deck too, rearranging barrels at the stern of the ship. Isolfr frowned over at the wheel, like he was trying not to look at either of them.

"We need you to go down below," Frida said.

"For the spell?" I wrapped my arms around my chest. "Are you sure you don't need my help?"

Something like panic crossed Frida's features, and she shook her head. "No. You aren't familiar with this kind of magic."

She said this as if it were a kind of magic I should never be familiar with. Kolur was talking to Isolfr now, probably telling him the same thing. Go down below.

"Go on then," she said, jerking her head toward the hatch. "It's our responsibility to keep you safe."

That was the first time I'd heard anything of the sort—neither of them had exactly done a bang-up job of keeping me out of harm's way. But I did as Frida asked. Isolfr was already climbing down the ladder. Nobody ever had to tell him twice when it came to hiding.

Kolur stood beside the hatch, watching us file down below. "What are you going to do?" I asked him.

"Protect the ship," he said in a grave voice. "Now, don't come up until we tell you it's safe."

I watched him for a moment longer, but he didn't say anything more. So I started down the ladder. Kolur slammed the hatch shut once my head was clear. Squares of sunlight lit my way down. The lanterns in the corridor were still burning, a low bluish-green. It wasn't their typical color. An unfamiliar scent wafted on the air as well. I couldn't quite place it—there was a hint of wood smoke, and burnt flowers, and something vaguely sinister.

Isolfr materialized out of the shadows.

"Sea and sky!" I cried. "Don't scare me like that."

"Sorry." He looked paler than usual. "I wanted to make sure you'd come down."

"Didn't have much choice, did I?" I slumped against the wall and felt the rocking of the ship in my spine. "What is that smell?"

"Ghosthair," Isolfr said.

"Never heard of it."

Isolfr shifted uncomfortably. "It's a Jandanvari herb. I don't really like talking about it."

"About an herb." I sighed. "Why would they even have something like that on board?"

"I don't know." He wore a vague, distracted expression. "We should go to the brig. That's the farthest away from the deck you can get."

"The brig." I stared at him. "You want me to go down to the brig." I'd forgotten that the *Penelope II* even had a brig—the first *Penelope* didn't, it being a fishing ship and nothing more. But Kolur had bought the *Penelope II* from a group of Jolali men and I had never been clear what it was used for prior to that. Something that involved taking prisoners. I didn't care for the brig. I'd only gone down there once, and found it damp and mildewed and reeking of misery.

Isolfr nodded.

"Nope." I shook my head. "I'll stay in my cabin, thank you very much."

"I really don't think that's safe—"

A wave of magic crashed over the boat. It was like a lightning storm, sudden and bright and terrifying, and the strength of it sent me wheeling across the corridor. The lanterns flickered and deepened their color to a rich, unearthly emerald.

"They're starting," Isolfr said. "We have to go now."

"Starting?" I looked over my shoulder, toward the hatch. A breeze seeped through the grating, blowing in from the west. Frida's affinity. The wind was laced with a magic I'd never felt before, something wild and vast like the winter ocean. I could sense the danger on it, but I was overcome by curiosity as well. It had to be dark magic. Frida had taught me some Jandanvari magic, but I'd never felt anything like this before.

I moved toward the hatch.

"What are you doing?" Isolfr darted in front of me. "You can't go up there! It's dangerous!"

"I just want to *see*. I'm not going to actually go above deck." I pushed past him and scurried over to the ladder. An eerie greenish light filtered through the grating, mingling with the white-gold summer sunlight that we'd been sailing through since we left Tulja. The magic prickled against my skin. I lifted the grating a few finger widths and peered through.

"No!" Isolfr grabbed my arm and tried to pull me away from the ladder.

"Shush!" I whispered, glaring at him. "Let me watch."

"It's *dangerous*." He paced back and forth, wringing his hands. "It's—cruel."

"If you're so scared, go hide. I'm staying here." I turned back. Through my vantage point at the hatch, I had a fairly good view of the ship's deck, where Frida and Kolur had set up. A heat-sphere burned between them. That was where the green light came from. I'd never seen a heat-sphere that color before.

"Hanna!" Isolfr hissed below me.

I ignored him. Learning the few spells I had from Frida as we traveled north was the closest I'd ever come to going to the Undim Citadels. I wanted to know more. I wanted to know what sort of darkness might defeat Lord Foxfollow. I wanted to know how to protect my family, if it ever came to that.

Both Frida and Kolur stared into the light of the sphere. Their eyes glowed green, and I couldn't tell if it was because they were reflecting the light or because of the magic boiling inside of them. The sphere sent flares of light into the air, and with each flare I felt the magic surge, and I smelled it too, a strange and unpleasant scent, overly sweet like rotting flowers.

Then Frida began to chant in a low, humming voice. She hardly sounded like herself. I didn't recognize the language, but it made the space between my eyes crackle.

"Hanna, we have to get to the brig now," Isolfr said.

I twisted around to look at him. "You go," I said. "I'm going to watch this."

He looked at me with worry, but I could tell that he didn't want to be there. I didn't exactly blame him. But my curiosity was making me brave.

"I'm sorry for what you're about to see," he said, and then he turned and raced down the hallway.

His words left me anxious, but I didn't follow him. When I looked back out the hatch, Kolur had stood up, and the green sphere had swollen. I thought I saw something moving inside of it, dark shadows against the light.

Frida's chanting grew louder and louder. It sounded like an

insect's incessant whine, like nothing human. I hunched forward. My calves were cramping from perching on the ladder, but I didn't care. I wanted to *see*.

The sphere cracked.

My heart jumped. Kolur froze, his eyes on the sphere. He was behind it now, and all I could see was his face, unfamiliar in that harsh green light.

Frida's chanting began to sound like shrieking. Her whole body trembled. Hair clung to the sides of her face.

Another crack. Another. The lines were fine, like the cracks in an egg as it begins to hatch.

Another crack appeared, this one larger than the others. And then a piece of the sphere fell away, and I realized an egg was exactly what this was.

I let out a gasp and immediately jerked away from the hatch, afraid that Frida and Kolur had heard. Isolfr was gone, vanished into the bowels of the ship. But my fearful curiosity got the better of me, and I peered through the grating again. Frida had her head thrown back, her body racked with spasms. Pieces of the sphere lay scattered across the deck of the ship, and a face poked through the shell. I wouldn't call it human exactly, but it had the features of a human, only more refined, more beautiful, even beneath the thick greenish slime coating its body.

I thought of Isolfr as I'd seen him the first time, wet with seawater and beautiful in the moonlight, and a tremor of unease shuddered through me.

A large piece of sphere fell away, shattering when it hit the deck. An arm shot out. The side of a bare torso. A single, tiny foot.

The sphere-creature jerked its head around the ship, eyes wide and blinking. It looked over at the hatch. Looked right at me.

I pulled away and slid three rungs down the ladder. I clung

to it, breathing heavily, listening to Frida's horrible chanting.

Something screamed.

I gripped the ladder more tightly, my heart pounding. It screamed again, this time long and drawn out, full of panic. I scrambled up the ladder and looked through the grate, and then I almost screamed myself.

Kolur was dragging the sphere-creature across the deck by one arm. It kicked and fought back, but I could see a shimmer of magic hovering over it, weakening it and holding it in place. Horror snaked through me, a low and insidious fear—*Kolur is doing this; that person looks like Isolfr.*

Kolur stopped. I hunched down lower, too afraid to look away. Frida's chanting filled the air like a snowstorm.

The sphere-creature kicked and twisted and tried to free itself from the spell.

Kolur lifted a knife and it glinted in the sunlight, long and mean. I'd never seen the knife before. It wasn't one we used to clean fish. A stupid thought in that moment, but it was the only thing that broke through the wall of terror: I'd never used that knife to clean fish.

In one clean motion Kolur drew the knife across the sphere-creature's throat. In that same instant, Frida fell silent.

I was paralyzed. I wanted to run to the bottom of the ship with Isolfr and beg for his protection, but I couldn't move. The creature's blood seeped out of its wound. It wasn't red, but a pale pearly green, faintly luminescent. Not light, not like the blood of the people of the Mists, but closer to that than to human blood.

Kolur set the body down and dipped his hand in the widening pool of blood. He walked over to Frida and knelt beside her and touched his hand to her forehead. There was a surge of unfamiliar magic, strong enough that I slipped down the ladder again, catching myself before I fell completely. Nausea washed over me. I couldn't tell if it was because of the magic or because of what I'd seen or because of both.

Another surge of magic, one that radiated across the entirety of the *Penelope II*. I could feel it working its way through the wood in the ladder, a tingle against my hands. I yelped and let go and this time I landed with a thud on the floor. Magic vibrated everywhere. I hated it. I didn't see how a protection spell could emerge out of an act of violence.

I struggled to my feet. My nausea had worsened and my stomach roiled like the sea. I stumbled down the corridors, heading toward the brig. The deeper into the boat I went, the more my nerves settled, even though I could still feel that crackle of magic in the walls.

When I burst into the brig, Isolfr sat curled up on the floor of one of the cells. He'd even closed the door, although it wasn't locked. I pushed it open. He lifted his head when the hinges creaked. His cheeks were wet, and something twisted up in my chest, a pang of empathy.

"Is it over?" he asked. "Did you see?"

I leaned up against the bars. "Yes."

We fell into silence. The magic wasn't as strong down here— he'd been right. I could still sense it up above us, though. Lurking.

"What was that?" I whispered, after a time.

"Jandanvari magic," he said. "A particularly cruel kind."

I let go of the bars and walked across the cell and sat down beside him. I wanted to be as close to another person as possible after what I'd seen.

"Kolur killed someone," I said, and it was the first time the thought really solidified in my head, and it was terrible.

Isolfr looked over at me. His Pjetur mask was slipping, and the real Isolfr kept flickering through, incandescent beauty shimmering beneath the surface. "Not killed exactly," he said, setting one hand on my shoulder. "The spell works with the spi—with the spirits of the elements." His voice wobbled and he dropped his hand and looked down at his feet. "You can't kill an element, but you can remove its human form and send it back into the air." He closed his eyes. "That's what they did. Converted the spirit to magic, then used that magic to protect us. A transformation more than a death. But it's—it's a kind of slavery. The spirit can never go free of its own accord now."

I felt sick again. The boat rocked against the waves and the lanterns swung back and forth. Isolfr stared down at his feet, his hair hanging in his eyes.

"Is this why you're scared of Frida and Kolur?" I finally asked, after a long time had passed.

Isolfr never answered.

CHAPTER TWO

It was hard to get back into our earlier routine after what had happened. I couldn't look at Frida and Kolur in the same way, and every time I went up on deck, I'd find reasons not to stand too close to them. They made it easier, too. Frida never spoke to me, never even met my eye, and Kolur would only bark out orders for me and Isolfr to complete whenever he could think of something. We always did as he said. There was nothing else to do.

One night, I dreamed the ocean was full of pearly green blood. The *Penelope II* sat in the middle of it, caught in a still spot, and Kolur had a long thin knife, and he stabbed Isolfr through the heart, and Isolfr dispersed on the air and turned into sea mist.

I woke up with a shout and drew my legs in close to my chest. My blankets were piled up on the floor and I chattered from the cold. I reached down and grabbed one and pulled it around my shoulders, although it didn't do much to keep me warm. The ship was moving, rocking with the motion of the waves, but I knew I wasn't going to fall back asleep. Not until I made sure that Isolfr was okay.

I pulled on my boots but kept the blanket wrapped around my body. It was too cold to get dressed properly. Then I called up the light in my lantern and carried it out into the corridor. The boat seemed empty, abandoned. Flashes of my dream came back to me: the green sea, Isolfr's face, his expression frozen in fear.

The door to the crew quarters was shut. I knocked once, but

my heart was beating too fast and I had to know if he was still alive, so I opened the door without waiting for any answer. Even awake I couldn't escape the sick fear of the dream.

But when the door swung open, I found Isolfr sitting on top of his cot, mending his coat.

He looked up at me, startled. In the light of the magic-cast lanterns he looked more like Isolfr than Pjetur.

"You're okay," I said, and then immediately felt stupid.

"Why wouldn't I be?" He frowned, and then his eyes widened. "Did something happen? Are we under attack?"

"No." I slipped into his room, closed the door, and hung my lantern on the hook in the wall. "I had a dream."

Isolfr picked up his mending again, although he was still looking at me.

"That's all?" he said.

I hesitated. Now that I knew he was fine, my earlier fear seemed absurd. "I dreamed that Kolur killed you. Like he did the water spirit. And I just wanted to make sure——"

Isolfr stopped mid-stitch. "Oh," he said, and then pulled the thread the rest of the way through. He set the coat aside.

"Yeah, it was stupid." I hugged myself tighter, still not completely warm. "But I knew I wasn't going to be able to sleep——" I slumped against the wall, suddenly exhausted by the weight of my emotions. I hadn't talked to anyone about what I'd seen up on deck. Isolfr dodged the subject, and I certainly couldn't bring it up with Kolur or Frida. I was back to where I'd been before Tulja, when I didn't know who to trust.

"I just didn't think he was capable of doing something like that," I whispered.

Isolfr went back to his mending, the needle drawing in and out of the coat with measured, even movements.

"You did, though," I said, peeling away from the wall. I perched beside him on the cot. He continued mending and didn't look at me. "This is what you were talking about, wasn't it? When you said that Frida was dangerous—"

Isolfr paused, the thread stretched taut. "Yes," he said. "She tried to cast the same spell with my brother."

My chest felt hollow.

"Tried?" I said.

"She didn't succeed. I stopped her." He was still sewing, the needle moving faster and faster. "That's why I hide myself from them."

I gaped at him. "I'm so sorry. I didn't realize." I couldn't imagine how he could be on the same boat with Frida all this time. How he could *work* with her. I could barely stand to look Kolur in the eye because of what he'd done. I looked down at my hands, shameful heat rising in my cheeks.

Isolfr set his mending aside. "Do you at least understand now?" he said. "If they knew what I am, they might try to use me for my magic as well."

I looked at Isolfr then, in his Pjetur disguise, and tried to find the glimmers of the Isolfr I had first seen floating in the sea. He had swum up to the *Penelope* knowing the danger.

"It's all right," Isolfr said. "I took my precautions." He gestured at his disguise. I thought about all the times I'd tried to tell Kolur about Isolfr and felt sick to my stomach. It was a good thing that Isolfr had cast that charm after all, the one to keep Kolur from hearing me whenever I tried to betray him.

"I don't understand how you can work with them. How you can help them," I said. "If I had known—" I shuddered, remembering the spill of green blood. I swore to myself I would never be that kind of witch. "If I had known, I wouldn't have teased you so much."

"I'm not helping them." Isolfr looked up at me. His blue eyes sparkled and for a moment they were his, the eyes of a spirit and not those of a human boy. "They're helping me."

I didn't say anything.

"Kolur can get me to the queen," Isolfr went on. "I could never do it on my own." He hesitated. "I need them."

We lapsed into silence. Isolfr didn't pick up his mending again, and so we sat side by side on the cot, the green light of the lanterns washing over us. I felt safe next to him. Safer than I would have if I was alone.

Out in the water, something thumped against the side of the ship.

"What was that?" I tensed, all my nerves on edge.

"A wave?" Isolfr's voice squeaked.

"That's not what a wave sounds like." I looked over at him. "You've been on the boat long enough, you should know—"

Another thump.

Isolfr jumped and grabbed at my arm. My heart pounded.

"You're right," he said in a low voice. "It's not a wave."

Another thump, and this time it was accompanied by the scrabble of claws against wood. I jumped to my feet, my muscles tight. The blanket I'd wrapped around my shoulders pooled on the floor. I wasn't cold anymore.

"We need to go up on deck," I said. "To make sure—to cast another protection spell if this one doesn't hold—"

Isolfr looked over at me with big pale eyes. "Go up on deck?" he whispered, and I wasn't sure if he was more afraid of the threat of the monster, or of Frida and Kolur.

"What else are we going to do?" I said. "Cower down below?"

I ran out of his cabin, hoping he would follow me. I didn't want to go up there alone. For a moment I was afraid he had stayed behind, that I would have to decide whether I should drag him out to help me or not. But then I heard footsteps. Isolfr jogged up beside me.

"It'll be fine," I told him.

He didn't answer.

We made our way through the crooked corridors and up the ladder, through the hatchway. I could hardly breathe. The deck was awash with thin silver moonlight. We didn't have much in the way of nighttime this far north, and I'd almost forgotten what it looked like. Frida and Kolur were both still asleep. Waves slapped against the side of the boat. I didn't hear any thumping.

"They slept through that?" I muttered. "Figures."

"It's the spell Frida cast," Isolfr said. "It's probably muffling the noise up here. We only heard it because we were down below."

I nodded, although I was unconvinced. I moved to wake Kolur, but Isolfr had gone over to the railing. He stood a few paces away, staring at the water.

"Isolfr!" I hissed. I couldn't imagine him going to the railing on his own accord, not with the threat of monsters, but when I ran over to him he didn't seem enchanted by the Mists.

"What are you doing?" I said.

"I'm looking for signs." He stood up on the tips of toes, peering out over the black water. There was nothing to see but a faint churning of waves.

"Maybe it was just our imagination," I whispered.

Isolfr looked over at me and I knew he didn't agree.

"I'm going to wake Kolur," I said. "He needs to know."

Isolfr didn't answer. I looked back at the water one last time— and saw a splash, a flash of silver.

"Isolfr," I whispered, grabbing his arm.

"I know, I saw it."

Both of us kept our eyes trained on the water. Another splash. Maybe it was just a fish.

I knew it wasn't a fish.

Isolfr trembled beneath my grip. "Come on," I said. "Let's get Kolur."

I dropped my hand, but he grabbed it in his and squeezed. "Let's hope Kolur can do something," he said in a dark voice. He let go of my hand. I moved over toward Kolur, but Isolfr remained staring down at the water.

"I'll be right back," I said, and I turned and ran to where Kolur was still sleeping beside the ship's wheel.

"Kolur!" I shouted. "Sea and sky, why haven't you woken up yet?"

He let out a little snort. I shoved at his shoulder, shaking him hard. Eventually his eyes fluttered and then opened.

"What do you want, girl?" He tilted his head up toward the sky. "Still dark."

His eyes closed and his head sank back down.

I whirled around, hopeless. Frida was still asleep as well. Isolfr hadn't moved from his spot by the railing.

"Isolfr!" I shouted. "They won't wake up." I jogged over to him. "You didn't do this, did you? It's not part of your blocking spell?"

"No." Isolfr's gaze remained fixed on the water. "It's him."

The way he said "him" sent cold shivers racing up and down my spine.

Another splash out in the water.

"The protection spell," I whispered, frantic. "It's keeping us safe, right? It's still working——" I thought of the spirit's blood splashed across the deck. The idea of the spell's failure made me sick to my stomach.

So did that splashing out in the water.

"It's still up," Isolfr whispered. "But he——he's doing something,

something to the magic in the water." He turned to me. "You can feel it, can't you?"

I stared at him, fear quaking through my body. Then I shook my head.

"You don't?" Isolfr turned back to the water. He was trembling again. There was another splash, and this time I caught a glimpse of something pale and sharp. I stumbled backward and reached out to the wind, testing its magic. *That* I could feel, but there was nothing poisonous about it, like what I'd sensed when Lord Foxfollow attacked before. A surge of panic washed over me.

"What's happening?" I said. "What do we do?"

"They never should have used that spell," Isolfr spat. "It's too dark. Lord Foxfollow is finding a way to manipulate it."

My stomach flopped over. The spirit's murder had been in vain. Kolur was a killer and there was no reason for him to be.

"Can we keep him at bay?" I said. "We'll need to wake Kolur and Frida; maybe they can reverse the spell."

Isolfr nodded. His eyes were wide with fright but I could tell he was trying to be brave. "The protection spell is making them sleepy," he said. "If Lord Foxfollow can change it that much, he'll probably be able to come through——"

"We can't think about that right now," I said. "What can we do to wake up Frida and Kolur?"

Isolfr shook his head. Of course he wouldn't know. I sighed and turned over to where Kolur was slumped in his hammock. That was clever of Lord Foxfollow, to make the spell work against the only people who could reverse it.

But I was a witch, even if I hadn't trained in the Undim Citadels or the Koljan capital. And I knew that all magic, whether Jandanvari or northern, whether dark or not, worked the same way. It was all about transformation.

I knew I couldn't reverse Kolur and Frida's spell completely, but maybe I could change it just enough to wake them up.

I ran up the stern of the ship, where the southerly winds were pushing us north. I breathed them in and felt for the magic twisting through them. Found it: a vein of warmth on the chill of the air, a hot sun in an eternal summer. I braced my feet hard against the deck and concentrated on isolating the magic. After a moment, the wind shimmered in the moonlight, and the magic started to glow, faint and golden. My heart pumped and my blood burned. The magic flowed through me, and I was changing it, willing it to wake Frida and Kolur.

The wind gusted, swelling the sails, and the *Penelope II* lurched forward over the choppy water. Wind buffeted the deck. I whirled around. Isolfr was still staring out at the water, his arms wrapped around his chest. The magic avoided him, gathering instead in golden clouds over Kolur and Frida. It wrapped around them, cocooning them, and I braced myself against the railing and thought, *Wake, wake, wake*, over and over.

Through the glow of magic, Kolur's eyes opened.

"What the hell is going on?" he shouted.

Frida stirred over on her cot, pushing up on one elbow. She looked around the ship, blinking, the magic still winding around her. I trembled against the railing. The magic sluiced out of me, taking my energy with it. But I wanted to make sure they were awake. I didn't want them to fall back asleep the minute the magic ended.

"Hanna!" Kolur turned to me. "Hanna, are you doing this?"

"You—sleeping—" My voice croaked.

"We're up now!"

With a sigh, I dropped my hold on the magic. The wind gusted again and blew the golden light away, and I dropped down on the deck, exhausted. Feet clattered against the boards. They sounded distant and far away.

"Hanna?" It was Kolur. He knelt beside me. "Hanna, look at me."

I lifted my head. My vision blurred. There were two Kolurs, two Fridas.

"She's spent herself," Frida said. "But she should be fine. Just needs to rest up." She looked at me, her brow knitted. "I don't understand why you couldn't just wake us—"

"Your spell!" I shouted. I didn't like how close they were to me; I kept remembering the spill of green blood. "Your horrible, murderous spell! Lord Foxfollow used it against you!"

Both their faces turned cold and stony.

"You weren't supposed to see that," Kolur said in a low voice. "I told you to go down below."

"Well, I did see it. And it doesn't matter now. Because Lord Foxfollow used the magic to make you fall asleep."

"How could you possibly know that?" Frida said.

"Isolfr felt it—" But I stopped myself. They wouldn't hear his name.

"It doesn't matter," Kolur said. "She's a smart girl, she figured it out. We need to get you down below, Hanna. It's not safe up here, not if Lord Foxfollow's about."

"Is it safe down below?" I snapped. "Is it safe anywhere on this boat. With *you*?"

Kolur gave me a sharp look at that, but he didn't say anything.

"He's right," Frida said. "We need to get you and Pjetur both—"

A sphere of magic flared up around the ship.

I screamed, the force of the magic knocking me down. I landed hard on the deck. A pale green aura surrounded the boat, shifting and sliding like Jandanvar's lights. Pale green. The color of the spirit's blood.

"We have to get you down now!" Kolur shouted. "Pjetur, get over here!"

Isolfr was still by the railing. He turned around, his face ashen with fear.

Something flew out of the water behind him and slammed up against the aura.

Kolur shouted and dragged me toward the hatchway. I struggled against him, trying to throw him off. Frida was shouting in the distance, shouting *Pjetur* over and over, and cursing at him, telling him to get away from the railing.

Another flare of magic, stronger than before. It seemed to shatter the air into pieces. Kolur was flung away from me, and I slammed up against the deck. Pain shot through my left ankle. I rolled over onto my back. The sphere of magic was cracking open, like an egg. Dark shadows wriggled across its surface, growing large and small, oozing like liquid. I stared at them in horror. One of them passed over a fissure in the magic, and it narrowed itself to a tiny drop and squeezed through our shield.

For a moment it hung in the air, dropping longer and longer. Then it broke free. I watched it fall, my chest so tight I could hardly breathe.

It landed, splashing up like black water.

Distantly, I heard screaming.

The black water gathered up on itself, growing tall, squirming and undulating. I fought back against the urge to vomit. It was forming into a shape. A long thin snout, a narrow body. Four sets of sharp claws.

"Hanna!"

Isolfr grabbed me and dragged me over the deck, his panicked breath cool against my neck. I didn't take my eyes off the monster. It didn't look like the monsters that had attacked the *Annika*.

"What is it?" I whispered, fear strangling my voice. "Where's Kolur and Frida? What about the magic they did? I don't understand—"

"It found a way through." Isolfr sounded as scared as I felt. "They're trying to patch the magic. You need to help them."

My stomach roiled. The monster was stalking toward us with slow, even steps, its mouth stretching open to reveal all its teeth. Its claws gleamed.

"I'll take care of this," Isolfr said. "Go!"

He dragged me to my feet and shoved me in the direction of Kolur and Frida, who stood at the bow of the ship, their veins glowing through their skin. I turned back to Isolfr. His Pjetur mask had fallen away completely, and the north wind was swirling around him like a cyclone as he stared down the monster.

"Go!" he shouted, not looking at me. When he lifted his hands, I could see them trembling.

I ran over to Frida and Kolur. The glow in their veins had reached their eyes, and they didn't see me. I doubted they saw anything in our world.

Isolfr had told me to help them, but I had no idea what to do. This wasn't wind magic, it was something stranger and darker and I had no idea how my spell would interact with theirs.

I whirled around, back to Isolfr, where the wind, sparkling with magic, struck out at the monster. It snapped back, howled, and then lunged forward, knocking Isolfr to the deck.

"Isolfr!" I ran a few paces toward him, not thinking, but then the monster roared, a loud, trumpeting sound that rattled the boards of the ship. I lurched to a stop and skittered backward. The monster fixed its steely eyes on me. They were flat and silver, like plate armor.

It roared again. The *Penelope II* rattled and shook.

"Hanna, get away!" Isolfr shouted. He crawled over the deck. "I can take care of this——"

He didn't sound so sure of himself.

"I can help you," I said, although when I glanced back up at the monster, I didn't know if that was true.

Still, I took a deep breath. I gathered up my courage and the strength of the south wind. The wind was faint, a thin current of warmer air, but I grabbed hold of it and leached the magic out. The monster charged toward me, and with each step the air sparked and vibrated.

"No!" I shouted, drawing the wind up around me like a shield. The monster slammed up against it and roared. Its dagger teeth were only a few hand widths away from my face.

I gathered up the wind and flung it at the monster. It shattered across its snout. The monster hardly seemed fazed.

"Hanna!" Isolfr was at my side, glowing with starlight. "Combine our winds. It might be enough——"

The monster roared again, cutting him off. But I didn't think. I just called down the south wind, let it swirl and weave around me. Isolfr did the same with the north wind. Then he reached over and grabbed my hand. The moment our palms touched, our magic combined, infused with the power of opposites. It erupted into a riotous spray of light, magic showering all around us like rain.

The monster flew backward.

At the same time, there came another wash of magic, pale pearly green and charged with a sense of malice and wrongdoing. It was like needles on my skin, and it dragged me forward across the boat, following the trajectory of the monster. Isolfr didn't let go of my hand. I screamed, feeling that terrible magic soak into my body, mingling with my own magic, creating something new, something terrible.

Isolfr and I slammed up against the railing. We tipped over the side. Isolfr was screaming. The water below was pale green and calm, which I didn't expect.

We tipped farther. I knew we were going to fall. I didn't know how to stop it.

"Frida!" Isolfr shouted. "Stop the spell!"

That was the last thing I heard before Isolfr and I, still holding hands, fell overboard and splashed in that eerie emerald water.

Everything went green.

And then everything went dark.

CHAPTER THREE

My head ached with a sharp pain that came rippling through the darkness. I groaned and rolled over onto my side. A pale light seeped in at the edges of my vision, growing wider and vaster until I realized it was just sunlight bouncing off the ocean.

I rolled over again and hit up against something hard and flat—a wall. No, not a wall. The side of a boat. I blinked, trying to force things into focus. It didn't look like the side of the *Penelope II*. It was too short, for one, and for another it was covered in slick red paint.

Fear jolted through me. I sat straight up. The haze of waking up was gone, and every one of my actions was propelled by fear.

I was in a boat. A small, narrow one, big enough for only two or three people. Isolfr was with me, thank the ancestors, sprawled out on his stomach. The bow and stern curled up into fancy, decorative spirals, and we didn't have sails or oars or any way to direct the boat away from this one spot, which was in the middle of the ocean.

Sea and sky. For the first time I really became aware of the enormity of the water. It was a dark glassy green and so calm it was like sitting on the surface of a mirror.

Another jolt of fear, this one sharper and more pure than the last.

"Isolfr!" I scrambled over to him. The boat tilted back and forth. "Wake up! Isolfr!"

I shook him by the shoulder, praying to every god I knew that he wasn't dead. He didn't move. I shook him harder, then rolled him onto his back. This elicited a groan of protest from him, and I slumped back, relieved that he was at least alive.

His eyes fluttered open, but then he squinted against the brightness and flopped back over onto his stomach. He moaned into the painted wood of the boat.

"You've got to get up," I said to him. "Something's happened."

He lifted his head and blinked at me. For a moment Pjetur flickered through his features before disappearing permanently. He was only Isolfr now.

"What happened?" he said.

"I was hoping you would know!" I felt a pang of dread. Maybe it was expecting too much from him, but Isolfr had always seemed to know more than he let on. Surely he could tell me where we were.

Isolfr gripped the side of the boat and heaved himself up to sitting. The boat rocked. Isolfr cried out, then tightened his grip on the boat, his knuckles whitening.

"Yeah, it's not the *Penelope II*," I said.

"I see that." Isolfr looked around, his eyes wide. He tilted his head back at the sky and gave a little yelp.

"What? What is it?"

He pointed up at the sky, and I followed the path of his finger. Nothing but pure, empty blue.

"I don't see anything."

"Exactly."

I glared at him. "Stop talking in riddles! What the hell's going on?"

"There's nothing there! No sun."

Fear shot through me. Immediately I craned my head back. He was right. The sky was empty and full of light but there was no sun, no burning disc of fire.

"I don't understand." I stared at him. "What does that mean?" A horrible thought struck me. "Sea and sky, are we dead? Is this the ocean of ghosts?"

Isolfr stared at me. "I can't die," he said. "Not the way you can."

I looked over the edge of the boat, down at the glassy, unnatural water. Of course. He was a spirit of the north wind. He couldn't come to the ocean of ghosts.

"Then where are we?" I looked over at him again. "You know, don't you? Just say it." I had my own suspicions, but I wanted desperately to be proven wrong. "Please. Isolfr. Where are we?"

Isolfr's eyes clouded. He looked away.

"Tell me!"

"The Mists," he whispered.

I couldn't breathe. The air seemed tainted, thick, poisonous— of course it did, it was Mists air, laced with unnatural magic.

"How?" I finally said.

Isolfr shook his head. "I don't know. If Lord Foxfollow meant to do it on purpose, we wouldn't be here." He swept his arm across the vista of the sea. "We'd be imprisoned. Or—or dead."

I looked out at the expanse of ocean. We were alone, a tiny boat floating amid saltwater, no provisions, no protection from the cold.

"We're basically imprisoned right now," I said. "And we'll be dead soon enough."

Isolfr shook his head. "This isn't Lord Foxfollow's doing. It's not his style."

I crossed my arms over my chest. "You know so much about his style?"

"I do, actually." Isolfr hesitated. "This—this was probably the spell that Frida and Kolur cast." He shivered at the word "spell." "It must have combined with Lord Foxfollow's magic somehow." Isolfr turned his attention toward the horizon. It was a dark line in the distance, a seam between the green ocean and the pale sky.

"That's it?" I said. "It combined with Foxfollow's magic *some-how?*" Anger rose up inside me, trying to smother my fear. It wasn't working. "This isn't the time to start keeping secrets again," I said.

"I'm not keeping secrets." Isolfr turned toward me. He looked paler than usual in the odd, fractured light, and even more impossibly beautiful. That made me angry too. This was not the time for Isolfr to be beautiful. "I told you everything that I know." He paused. "That I think I know. I'm only guessing about the magic mixing. But it seems the most likely answer."

I slumped down against the side of the boat. We rocked gently over the water. "We're trapped here." I looked up at him. "And we're going to die. Just admit it."

"No." Isolfr shook his head. "Frida and Kolur's spell"—another shiver—"for all its darkness, it was a protection spell. It's likely still protecting us."

"It put us in a pleasure boat."

"A gondola," Isolfr said. "A favorite of the Mists nobility. I'm sure there's a reason for it."

I rubbed my head. "Well, what are we supposed to do while we wait for the magic to start *helping* us?" I glowered. "So what do you think we'll die of first? Thirst? Or the cold?"

Isolfr looked over at me, his eyes glittering, silver and pale blue. "I don't need to worry about either of those things."

"Congratulations. *I* do." I sighed and ran my hands over my hair. "I'm not just going to sit here and hope the protection spell protects us. Can we try calling the winds?"

Isolfr hesitated. "I don't know if it will work."

"Well, can we at least try?"

Another pause. I could tell from his expression that he thought this was a stupid idea, and I knew, when he nodded, that he was just humoring me. But I didn't care. I wanted to prove him wrong.

I steadied myself and lifted my hands. The air was so still that even that small movement seemed a massive disruption. I'd never felt this kind of stillness before.

"Together," Isolfr said. "One, two, three——"

I reached deep into myself, deep into the memories of my father's ancestors, and then my mother's too, because I always thought my magic worked the best when I pulled from both sides of my family. The air stayed still. I tried to feel for the magic, for the whisper of spice and warmth, for *anything*, but there was only that stone-dead stillness.

I looked at Isolfr. His eyes were closed and his face was scrunched up in concentration. But I didn't even feel the brush of a north breeze.

This was not good. He was a spirit of the north wind, and he shouldn't have to concentrate the way I did.

"Fine. You're right. It's not working."

Isolfr's eyes flew open. "I'm sorry, Hanna," he said, and he seemed genuine.

"I'm going to freeze to death," I said. "And I can't even call the winds, which, you know, is the *one* thing I can do to protect myself——"

"It's a different world," Isolfr said quietly, "with different winds."

"Wonderful."

"Jandanvari magic will likely work here," he said.

"I don't know a single useful Jandanvari spell." I drew my coat tight across my chest. The Jandanvari magic Frida had taught me was fisherman's magic, simple stuff to let you know where to cast a net or how to hold a spell. Nothing that would help us. I shivered. The still air felt like shards of broken glass. Soon, the cold would be too much.

But then Isolfr knelt down on the bottom of the boat with his palms up and his eyes closed. He began to hum, a low, throaty melody that rose and fell like the wind. As he hummed, a glow brightened inside of him, and he was illuminated like a magic-cast lantern, pale blue light competing with the Mists brightness. I couldn't take my eyes off him. He was beautiful, casting that eerie blue light, but I was also afraid. The magic crackling across my skin was unfamiliar. Not at all like the spells Frida had taught me.

I expected the winds to blow in from the north, for the gondola to rise up on the waves and rush toward shore. Instead, a heat-sphere materialized in the middle of the boat.

"All that for a heat-sphere?" I muttered.

Isolfr opened one eye. It was nothing but light. "Test the ocean water," he said, his voice echoing and thrumming. "It should be fresh."

I hesitated for a moment, thinking of the cold.

"Please," Isolfr said. "I'm trying to keep you alive." He shut his eye, a light going out.

My cheeks warmed, and I felt the way I did whenever Mama chastised me for dawdling on my way home and making her worry. He was right. This magic, he didn't have to do it.

I pulled off my gloves and leaned over the side of the boat and dipped my hands into the water. I cried out at the shock of the cold, but I managed to scoop up a handful of water and splash it on my tongue.

Fresh.

"It worked!" I cried, and I held my stinging hands up to the heat-sphere. The warmth spread over them like a blanket.

Isolfr let out a sigh that sounded like a gust of wind. The light faded out of him and he dropped forward, his face pressed down into the boat's bottom.

"Isolfr!" I pushed over beside him, still keeping my hands held up to the heat-sphere. "Are you all right?"

He groaned in response, and I felt a rush of relief.

"You better not have hurt yourself," I told him.

"I'm fine." He lifted his face and blinked at me. His eyes seemed too big, wide and guileless. "That should hold you over until the protection spell directs us to help."

"We still don't know for sure that it will." I dropped my gaze down to my hands, still warming by the heat-sphere. "I mean, thank you. For the fresh water."

In response, Isolfr sat up and leaned against the gondola's edge. The light bounced off the water, sending sparkles into the air. There was no warmth anywhere except for Isolfr's heat-sphere and in the panicked drumming of my heart.

I'm not sure how much time passed. The boat floated in the glassy sea, not moving forward, only side to side, rocking us like a cradle. I sat close to the heat-sphere, my knees drawn up to my chest. When I felt thirsty, I'd scoop up water from the side of the boat. I'll give Isolfr credit: it was as sweet and sparkling as water from a spring, even if it did my freeze my hands to drink it.

We didn't talk much. There just wasn't anything to say. Casting the spells to get me warmth and fresh water seemed to have exhausted Isolfr anyway, and he curled up at the bow of the gondola, his head resting on the railing, his eyes closed. I did ask him if he was all right, early on; he fluttered his eyes and said, "I'm fine," and that was that.

We sat.

We waited.

My stomach grumbled. I sighed and dropped my head back to look at the broad expanse of blue sky. My stomach grumbled again.

"I don't suppose there are fish in these waters." I looked over at Isolfr. He stirred, opened his eyes. His expression was sleepy.

"Probably not," he said.

I sighed. "What sort of ocean doesn't have fish?"

"An ocean in the Mists."

Those words chilled me more than the frigid air. For the first time, I was struck by exactly how dire our situation was. Because it wasn't just a matter of being stranded on the open sea—that would be bad enough, as it's nearly impossible for a man to come back from the emptiness of the ocean—but being stranded in the Mists. The *Mists*. The land that I'd been taught my whole life to fear. Ever since I was a little girl, my parents had whispered to me the signs of the Mists, in case its people ever came trailing through our village. Mist on the water, unnatural gray eyes. And here I was. Trapped.

Not that anything in this place looked like what I'd been taught to fear. The sky was bright, the water sparkling. I tilted my head back again. Not a single cloud drifted overhead. I wondered why they called it the Mists when there wasn't a wisp of mist in sight.

My stomach grumbled more loudly, and this time the grumble was accompanied by a sharp pang of hunger. Isolfr was staring down at his feet, not looking at me. Lucky him, not having to eat.

I leaned over the side of the boat and brought water up to my lips to drink. It was so cold that it set my whole body to chattering, but I thought that if my stomach was full of water, maybe I wouldn't feel the hunger as much. And part of me hoped I'd see a fish flickering through the water.

I didn't.

I kept drinking, even as my fingers turned blue. My hunger hadn't subsided. I wasn't sure it was going to, but drinking water gave me something to do. I tried not to think about what would happen when I needed to relieve myself. There wasn't exactly much privacy on the gondola.

I scooped my hands in the water one more time, my arms raised with goose bumps and my body shivering with the cold. When I lifted my hands up, the surface of the water rippled and an image formed. It looked like a reflection.

The water drained through my fingers. The reflection was of a boat, a sailing ship.

"Isolfr," I said.

"Yes?"

"Isolfr, get over here." I didn't tear my eyes away from the image of the ship in the water, not even to look up to see where the reflection came from. It was a grand-looking ship, with wide golden sails and a carving of a woman at the prow, her hair falling all the way down the length of her body in curls and waves.

"What is it?" His voice was right next to my ear. I pointed at the water.

"There! Look! Please tell me you see it!"

There was a pause, and for a moment I was afraid I was going mad. But then Isolfr shouted, "We're saved!"

I looked over at him. He was leaning over the side, a huge smile plastered on his face. He reached down and touched the reflection, and it shimmered over the water.

"It's real," he said, looking over at me. "It's real!"

"What is? The reflection?" I looked from him to the boat in the water. The horizon was still empty. "I don't see an actual boat anywhere."

"Because it's underwater." Isolfr hopped to his feet and then dove over the side of the gondola. He hardly made a splash.

"What in the name of the ancestors are you doing?"

"Moving us. That ship'll be surfacing soon, and we don't want to be in its way."

"Surfacing?" I looked over the railing again. The reflection was still there. Isolfr positioned himself beside me and began pushing the gondola through the water. It clearly wasn't easy for him. He pressed his shoulder against the boat and heaved, his legs kicking up a froth under the water. The boat inched forward.

"Is there anything I can do to help?"

Isolfr grunted and shook his head. "The water's too cold for you."

We lurched forward. I reached down and paddled with one hand, trying my best to ignore the numbness working through my fingers. The gondola broke the stillness of the water with a faint ripple, and the water licked against the side of the boat, keeping time to Isolfr's occasional grunts of exertion.

The reflection of the sailing ship still floated in the water.

"How do you know it's going to help us?" I said. I drew my hands up and knotted them in my coat; the water had gone too cold for me to stand. "The ship?"

Isolfr gave one last push and the gondola launched forward on his momentum and then stopped dead in the water.

"Well?" He climbed over the side of the boat, and the water evaporated off him immediately. To my eyes, he was completely dry.

"It's a fishing boat," he said. "There's no guarantee that they'll help us—"

"But you said!"

Isolfr shook his head. "I know what I said! I was thrilled that it wasn't a warship, that it's not something of Lord Foxfollow's—"

The name sounded different in this place. It seemed to echo in upon itself.

"We'll have to talk our way aboard," Isolfr said. "But we have a chance." He slumped down against the boat's side and wrapped his arms around his chest. He'd said it was impossible for him to feel the cold, but looking at him drawn together like that, I wasn't sure I believed him.

"Would you like my coat?" I said.

He looked over at me and frowned. "You know I don't need—"

And then the ocean ripped in two. An enormous, glassy wave crested and lifted up the gondola. I tumbled forward, slamming against Isolfr, who shrieked in surprise. I flipped around, flailing about to grab onto the railing, certain that we were going to capsize.

Isolfr went paler than usual. "Let me speak," he said.

"To who!" I shouted, my voice nearly drowned out by the rush of water showering around us.

The top of a mast appeared against the sky, drawing up and up and up. Next were pale gold sails, masses and masses of them like clouds, and then the woman at the prow, her hair shimmering.

The sailing ship of the reflection emerged out of the ocean, water streaming down its sides. The gondola was knocked back on the ship's wake, and I held tight to the railing as we plummeted backward. Water splashed over the side, soaking through my coat and my boots and extinguishing the heat-sphere.

Sea and sky, I hoped Isolfr would be able to get us aboard. No heat-sphere would be able to dry this out.

The ship rose majestically, glittering in the sunless light of the sky. It was so bright that it hurt my eyes, and I had to turn my head away, blinking against the dots of light. Beside me, Isolfr stood up, despite the unsteady rocking of the gondola.

"Fishermen of the undersea!" he shouted. "May I speak to your captain?"

There was no answer but silence. I wondered how Isolfr knew

to address the ship. He was a spirit, yes, but I knew he was of my world and not the Mists.

Isolfr took a hesitant step forward. The gondola rocked. "Fishermen of the undersea!" he shouted again.

This time a voice drifted down from the ship's deck.

"Who's out there? Identify yourself!"

Isolfr glanced over at me. He looked scared, which was no surprise, although I couldn't do much but chatter at him, I was so cold. If he thought I could give him answers, he ought to know better.

Isolfr turned back to the boat. "We're from the Sun Realms," he called back.

The Sun Realms. He must mean our world. I'd never thought it had its own name.

"The Sun Realms?" A face appeared over the ship's railing, small and pale and fringed with a shaggy mane of thick dark hair. "You here to steal from us?"

"Of course not!" Isolfr shouted. "We just want passage back to dry land."

The fisherman scowled down at us for a moment longer, then disappeared. I slumped back.

"Where'd he go?" Isolfr asked.

"Leaving us here to die," I muttered.

But then another man appeared at the railing. He had the look of someone important—golden skin, long black hair pulled into a ponytail, a rather ostentatious blue hat. He leaned over the railing like he was examining us. Neither Isolfr nor I moved.

"How did a pair of sunners wind up with such a fine gondola?" he finally called out.

Isolfr and I glanced at each other. He took a deep breath—trying to rally his courage, no doubt. He squinted up at the man in the blue hat.

"Magic gone wrong," he called back.

The man snorted. "I doubt that. You aren't really sunners, are you? No need to be lying, mind. That's a Boluda-style gondola there, and the *Shira* is friends of the Boluda family. You're welcome aboard, no questions asked." He gave a shallow bow. "Wait a moment and I'll send some of my men to fetch you."

And with that, he vanished from the railing, leaving Isolfr and me alone again.

"I told you the protection spell was still working," Isolfr said.

"Coincidence," I told him, although I didn't believe that myself.

We waited for a few moments, and I heard a splash in the water. A rowboat, as golden as the ship's sails. Two men rowed over to us.

"Now keep in mind it's the gondola that's getting you on board." The man speaking was a different one from the man in the blue hat, although he wore a uniform of the same color, tassels hanging from his shoulders. "The captain doesn't want to risk angering the Boluda family. But any sign of trouble, we're tossing you overboard."

"That sounds fair," Isolfr said.

I wasn't so sure about that—after all, they might start the trouble and lay the blame at our feet—but I was so cold by that point I didn't see much reward in trying to speak.

The rowboat made its way toward us, the oars rising and falling like the beat of a drum. The man in the blue coat stood with a booted foot propped up on the boat's edge, his big arms crossed over his chest. He was dry. The ship had just burst out of the ocean, and he was dry.

"You stay where you are," he barked as the boat approached. "I need to check you out, make sure you're decent."

I held up both of my hands. "We're decent," I said, teeth chattering.

The man glanced at me and laughed. "You look like you're no

danger, then. Not safe, getting your clothes wet in these waters."

The two rowers drew in their oars and the man sprang off his boat and landed in ours, a leap too wide for a human to make. The gondola barely dipped into the water. "I'll need to check you for weapons," the man said. "Hold up your arms."

Isolfr did. The man patted Isolfr through his clothes. When he didn't find anything, he made a disappointed grunt and turned to me. I unwrapped my arms from around my chest and held them up, shivering in the cold air. The man must have taken pity on me, because he didn't search me as thoroughly as he had Isolfr.

"All right then," he said. "Into the boat with you."

The rowboat was still too far away for me to climb into it. I looked at the water and my stomach quaked at the thought of jumping into that icy bath. It would probably kill me.

But then the man looped one arm around my waist and one around Isolfr's and jumped, bouncing into a high arc through the air, taking us with him. The air froze against my face. I cried out, startled, and then he landed us in the rowboat with all the agility of a cat.

"Onward!" he barked, and the two oarsmen dropped their oars into the water and turned us around.

I sat backward in the rowboat, my shivering more violent. The gondola was grander than I'd realized when we'd been inside it. The hull was painted with images of faces with large green eyes and long billowing hair. It took me a moment to recognize that all the faces were the same, that they belonged to the spirit Kolur and Frida had killed back onboard the *Penelope II*.

I turned away.

"Where you from?" the man asked Isolfr. "You didn't get water-logged like that one." He jutted his thumb out at me.

Isolfr's eyes went wide, and his mouth opened and closed.

Despite the cold frosting over my thoughts, I spat out, "He's a great wizard from Tulja, of the Sun Realms. All Tuljans know how to protect themselves from the freezing ocean."

The fisherman looked at me, his eyes drawn tight and beady. "I'm with the captain," he said. "I don't think you're from the Sun Realms. But hey, Boluda business is Boluda business, as long as it doesn't mess with our ship." He held up to hands. "Which reminds me. Keep any spells to yourself onboard the *Shira*. Doesn't matter what kind. We've got magic enough in the storage holds." He turned away from us, toward the oarsmen. "Faster!" he barked. "We want to make it back to Llambric by tomorrow, don't we?"

"Excuse me," Isolfr said. "Did you say you're going to Llambric?"

"We are indeed. That gonna be a problem?"

"No." Isolfr shook his head and sat down beside me. He radiated a faint chill that just made me shiver harder. "No problem at all."

The boatman turned away from us, and Isolfr leaned over and whispered in my ear. "The protection spell is still working. Of all the places in the Mists, Llambric is where we'd most want to be."

The name meant nothing to me. I was more interested in what the man had said.

"Why can't we use magic onboard?" I asked Isolfr.

"They're magic-miners," he said, as if that explained everything.

"Then why are they on a *ship*?"

"Ladder coming!" shouted a man from the *Shira*. "Clear the water!"

"Clear!" the fisherman shouted back. Well, not a fisherman. A miner.

I still didn't understand what he was doing on a boat.

A rope ladder splashed into the water beside us, flinging more damp across my lap. I wasn't sure I'd ever get warm.

"Hope you can climb," the fisherman said. "Otherwise, we're leaving you here."

"I can climb." I stood up, grabbed hold of the rope. It was sturdy and strong, and when I pushed myself up onto it, it stayed in place. I heaved myself up, rung by rung. The exercise didn't do much to warm me up.

At the top, a stout, muscular man was waiting for me, bearded like the others. He took me by one hand and dragged me over the railing.

"Oh, girl, you've caught the dampness." He clapped twice. "Change of clothes for the lady! Bring her heat!"

I muttered a thank-you and stumbled away from him. The ship's deck gleamed. It looked more like a ballroom than a sailing ship. The sails threw off rays of light, and the ship itself shimmered gold, the way the figurehead had. Men scurried up the masts and around the deck, chanting together in a language I didn't understand, their boots and palms clapping out a rhythm.

"This way, girl." Another man came up beside me. He didn't have a beard, but he did have long matted hair, and rough sailor's skin, and gray eyes.

Gray eyes.

He blinked at me, those gray eyes looming. "Come along," he said. "We'll get you dry. That dampness, it can kill you."

I felt dizzy. The brightness of the ship was too much. Isolfr hadn't climbed over the railing yet. My heart started to race.

"No time to dawdle," the man said, and then he took my hand, gently, and led me toward the upper cabins. I was too dazed, too cold, too exhausted, to try and resist, but I did look over my shoulder at the place where the ladder attached to the ship's side. It was empty. Empty—

Isolfr's head appeared over the edge. His pale golden hair seemed like an extension of the ship itself.

"Isolfr!" I cried.

The man glanced over to where I was looking. "Don't worry, lass, we'll bring him to you soon enough. But that cold—" He shook his head, made a clucking sound. "Not good, not good for you at all."

I watched him, cautious. In all the right ways he looked like a human. He looked more like a human than Isolfr did. And yet I couldn't think of him as human at all.

He led me into one of the upper cabins. It shone just like the deck, and the furniture looked as if it were all carved out of stone.

"I want to see Isolfr," I said, looking over to the door. The man had left it hanging open, and I could see out to the deck and the sailors bustling around. Their chanting drifted into the cabin.

"He'll be here in just a minute." The man opened a drawer underneath the bed and pulled out a pile of folded clothes and set them on the bed. "Why don't you change up, and I'll bring you something warm to drink." He gave me a pleasant smile and nodded down at the clothes. "Go on, don't want you to die out here! It'll taint the magic."

I felt dizzy. *Taint the magic.* The man turned and left the cabin, shutting the door behind him. There was the sound of a key turning in a lock. I ran up to the door, tried to push it open. It didn't move.

I cursed and choked back a flood of tears. I might have been in the most beautiful ship cabin I'd ever seen, but I was trapped here. Imprisoned.

And shivering violently.

Moving by rote, I stripped off my wet clothes and stepped into the dry ones the sailor had left behind. They were cut for a man, and so a little too big, but the fabric was thick and warm and soft. I sat down on the bed, sinking low into the mattress. Where was Isolfr?

A few moment later, someone knocked on the door.

I looked over at it, my heart pounding.

"Are you decent?"

"Yes." I dug my fingers into the mattress. I had no weapon, nothing to defend myself.

The lock turned, the door swung open. The man in the blue coat stood in the doorway, Isolfr at his side. He carried a steaming mug in one hand.

"Just as I promised, I brought you a warm drink." He stepped into the room, and Isolfr followed. For once he didn't seem that frightened. The man handed me the drink, then turned over to an alcove set into the wall. "You didn't light the fire?"

"I didn't—didn't know how. You said not to do magic." I glanced over at Isolfr, the steam from the drink billowing around my face. It smelled of honey and spice, and I wondered if the stories were true, the ones that said eating and drinking in the Mists would trap you there. Nothing else about this place had been what I expected. Not so far, anyway.

"Not big magic. You can light a fire."

Isolfr knelt beside the fireplace. "I can take care of it," he said. "I'm familiar with this sort of magic."

"Ah, good, good. Keep her warm." The man straightened up, smoothed down his clothes. He nodded at me. "If you spoil our haul for today, there'll be a worse fate in store for you than freezing."

And with that, he stepped out of the room, locking us in once again.

"What's he talking about?" I demanded. "Spoil the haul? Magic? How can you gather up magic?"

"We're in the Mists. Things work differently here." Isolfr looked over his shoulder at me. "You should drink that."

"Is it safe?"

Isolfr turned back to the alcove. There was a pause and a tremor on the air, and then flames erupted inside the wall. They were the same golden color as the rest of the ship, and not like any fire I'd ever seen. But they gave off warmth, just as you would expect.

"It won't trap you here, if that's what you're thinking. That's a story." Isolfr stepped away from the fire. "Here, sit close."

I slid off the bed and pooled down beside the flames. Their heat was a relief, even if nothing else on this ship was. "How do you know it's just a story? Everything else has been true, about looking for mists and gray eyes—"

"Those are warnings. Things you see in your world. The idea that if you eat in the Mists, you'll be trapped—that's just a myth." He sat down beside me and offered the mug. The scent of spices floated up around me. "I swear to you."

I looked up him. He'd never given me a reason not to trust him. That much, at least, was true.

I took the mug and stared down at the surface. The drink was dark and creamy, not like any drink I'd ever seen before. I breathed in the spices one more time, and then I took a sip.

Warmth flooded through me.

CHAPTER FOUR

All night, we weren't allowed to leave the room. One of the fishermen came by to see that I had warmed up—he felt my pulse and leaned his ear against my chest to listen to my heartbeat, nodding like he was satisfied. I sat very still and watched Isolfr.

"Glad to see you've recovered," the fisherman said. He straightened up, smoothed down his beard. "Looks like you won't be tainting the magic after all. Cassius will bring you food shortly. We all eat dinner at the same time aboard the *Shira*."

He left, locking the door behind him.

"I don't understand," I said, staring at the strange licking flames of the fire; they had a tendency to hypnotize. "Why are they so kind to us if they're keeping us prisoner?"

"They're fishers of magic." Isolfr paced across the room, his arms crossed over his chest. "The dive under the surface and collect the magic from the sea, and then sell it in port." He stopped and looked over at me. "Just like you do with actual fish."

I didn't say anything. I remembered fishing aboard the *Annika*, swapping conversation with Finnur and Asbera.

"I've spoken with fishers of magic before," Isolfr went on. "It's a tricky business. They saved us because of some obligation to the Boluda family, but now that we're on board, they have to keep us content. Our unhappiness would taint the magic. But there's still that risk we're here to rob them, so—" He jerked his head toward the lock on the door and resumed his pacing.

I watched the flames. His explanation made an odd sort of sense. I wondered if that was how everything would be here in the Mists. I wondered if the rest of my life would be making this odd sort of sense.

As the fisherman had promised, someone brought food to our room later, although I didn't know how much later—it was hard to sense time passing. When the door swung open the deck was bright, but the sky seemed darker. I only saw it all for a flash though.

Our meal was a stew that reminded me a little of lisila, a dish Asbera had prepared for me back in Tulja. It shimmered blue-gold in the firelight, and I stirred it, still not sure if wanted to eat, even though my mouth watered and my stomach grumbled. But then Isolfr sat beside me and lifted his spoon to his mouth.

"Both of us," he said. "I may not need to worry, but I don't want you to worry."

And then he took a bite and stared at the fire. The flames cast golden light over his pale skin.

I looked down at the stew.

"It's pretty good," he said.

That was enough for me. I took one tentative bite and then another and another, slurping down the stew in gulps. I hardly tasted it, but I was so hungry I had to stop myself from slurping it straight from the bowl.

Isolfr laughed at me.

"Shut up," I said. "You have no idea what's it like."

He went quiet. "That's true," he said.

We watched the flames together, our empty bowls sitting at our feet. I could hardly feel the *Shira* moving over the water, and part of me wondered if we were moving at all, or if we were just trapped out at sea in a larger ship than the gondola. But the rest of me didn't care. The rest of me only wanted to watch the flames licking at the alcove, golden and enticing.

A face appeared in them.

I recoiled. "Sea and sky, did you see that?"

Isolfr didn't answer, just kept staring at the fire.

"Isolfr!" I grabbed his shoulder to shake him, but he brushed my hand away.

"Shhhh," he whispered. "It looks like someone has cast the Flames of Natuze."

"What?" I'd never heard that name before. "Do you mean I really did see a—"

The face appeared again, materializing out of the lines of fire, the flames twisting together to make cheekbones and eye sockets and a strong, pointed noise. It sort of looked like Kolur.

The eyes opened. Sparks flew out of the alcove and scattered across the floor. I yelped and jumped backward, but Isolfr held his place. And then I became aware of magic shimmering in the room, a blanket of enchantment falling over us both.

"—Tur?" the face in the flames said. "Is that you?" The voice faded out, faded back in. "—She make it through? Han—"

"Yes," Isolfr said. "It's me. Pjetur."

"You look different." The face pushed out from the flames, and it was Kolur, his features carved out of gold. I stared at him, not knowing what to think.

"The Flames of Natuze can distort perception," Isolfr said quickly.

I shot a glance over at him. He looked different because he looked like Isolfr, not Pjetur. But Kolur seemed to accept this explanation without question.

"Where's Hanna?" he said.

I slid into view of the alcove. "I'm here."

"Oh, thank the ancestors." The flame-Kolur closed his eyes. "Are you both safe?"

"For now," Isolfr said.

The flame-Kolur shimmered. "I can't hold this for long," he said. "Frida and I are trying to find a way to get you home. We're going to Jandanvar at full speed—we think it will be easier there. There's a group of rebels—outlaws, really—that we're going to meet with. We think—"

His voice was fading again, his words turning into the crackle of the flames.

"—Find you," he said. "Do not try anything—pid."

"What do you want us to do until you can bring us through?" I said, hearing the panic coming through in my voice. "How are we supposed to avoid Lord Foxfollow?"

Isolfr put his hand on my arm. "Kolur's gone. That sort of spell between the worlds can never last long."

I pulled away from him. He was right. The flames were just flames again.

"What are we supposed to do?" I asked.

Isolfr pushed himself back until he was sitting beside me. He didn't answer for a long time.

Then he said, "The *Shira*'s taking us to Llambric. We can find help there."

I didn't like that answer.

A day later, we made landfall.

The crew let us out of the room shortly before we pulled into port. It was a relief to breathe in the fresh, brisk air, to smell something other than the stale mustiness of being trapped in such a small space. A burly man stayed close to us, though, and he wielded a huge, gleaming ax that he swore he had no intention of using. "Assuming, of course," he said, "you don't change my mind."

"Oh, we won't," Isolfr said.

The three of us walked to the bow of the ship, where we would be mostly out of the way in the bustle of pulling into port. I wrapped my arms around my chest and watched the land appear on the horizon. Not just land—a city, glimmering in the light.

"Where are we?" I said, turning to our guard.

He grunted. "That's Amkal City. Finest magic port in all of Llambric." He nodded once, short and definitive.

Isolfr looked over us, the wind blowing his hair across his face. It kept glinting like flecks of cold. "I'm sorry, did you say Amkal City?"

"I most certainly did." Our guard pointed with his ax at the docks spreading themselves across the sea. "I was born and raised right there, on a boat aligned to one of Lord Llambric's own fishing ships. Fine childhood, it was."

Isolfr smiled. "Amkal City. That awful spell was good for something."

"Does that name mean something to you?" I said.

"Perhaps."

I sighed, trying to stifle my frustration. I'd have laid into him for keeping secrets, but I didn't want our guard to hear. And maybe that was why he was keeping secrets in the first place.

The *Shira* glided into port. Up close, Amkal City was like no city I had ever seen. The buildings rose tall and spiraling. They were built of stone and glass, and despite the cold air, flowering trees cast drops of color all over the city streets. I could feel the magic wafting off the place, a strange and unfamiliar magic. One that was clearly not human.

Someone called out to our guard, and he turned, shouted back in a language I didn't understand.

"What's this about Amkal City?" I whispered to Isolfr. "How do you know this place?"

Before Isolfr could answer, our guard clamped a heavy hand on my shoulder. "Captain wants you off first," he said. "So there's no chance of you making off with our catch. You understand."

"Of course," Isolfr said primly. I nodded in agreement. Like I even wanted to steal magic from the Mists.

Another fisherman, different from our guard—younger and skittish and always casting frightened glances at me out of the corner of his eye—led us down the gangplank. The docks were bustling with people. Merchants selling food and women pushing trinkets and jewelry on passersby. We passed a ship unloading barrels glowing with a pale green light that made all the hairs on my arm stand on end.

"Is that what the *Shira* was transporting?" I asked Isolfr, pointing.

"No ma'am," said the fisherman. "That's magic from the Isles of Yalisu. Much more dangerous than ocean magic. Unstable."

I nodded, grateful when we were clear of the ship.

The fisherman led us to the end of the dock and gave a quick two-fingered wave. "This is where I leave you," he said. "No need for kindness now that we've made land." But he hesitated, and his gray eyes flashed. I shivered in spite of myself.

"Good luck," he said, and trundled off.

Isolfr and I stood in the middle of the tumult of the docks.

"Now what do we do?" I asked him. "Are you going to explain this Amkal City thing to me? And what's Llambric anyway? Why are you so excited to be here?"

He didn't answer, just craned his neck to look down the direction of the main street. I rolled my eyes and turned away from him. The city rushed around us. It wasn't like any city I'd ever seen, that was true, but at the same time I didn't feel like I was in another world. The people looked mostly the same, except for their gray eyes, and when they spoke I could understand them. The woman a few feet away was selling fish pies, and she shouted, "Fish pies, fish pies!" like the rhythm of a melody.

"I know someone who might be able to help us," he said.

I turned back to him. He blinked at me, his eyes bright and guileless.

"What! Who?"

He hesitated.

"No secrets, Isolfr. We're trapped here. And you promised."

He sighed. "I didn't want to get your hopes up. If anything has happened to him since we spoke last—"

"Tell me now."

He paused. The city glimmered and threw off its strange strains of magic.

"Lands in the Mists are tied to the nobility," he finally said, speaking in a low voice. "We're in the lands of Llambric now. I know that name. A boy, Trystan Llambric—he's a friend of mine. Or was."

I stared at him. "You had a friend from the Mists?"

Isolfr nodded. "Our families knew each other. He liked to call through the veils between worlds. It was a game. I think he'll be able to help us. But I know he lives in the countryside, not in a city, so we'll need to find out how to get to his house."

I rubbed at my arms, not out of cold—the fishermen's lent clothes were quite warm—but out of fear. I didn't want to place our fates in the hands of someone from the Mists.

"Can't we just stay here?" I said.

Isolfr's expression darkened. "No. The lands are tied to the various nobility, but Foxfollow has taken them over. For the most part. Trystan would be able to protect us, but even Llambric . . ." His voice faded away. "We need to be careful."

Suddenly, the city seemed sinister, and I crowded in close to Isolfr, certain that every face that passed us belonged to some Foxfollow spy.

"Should we be out on the street then?" I finally said.

"We don't have much choice, do we?" Isolfr sighed. "But we do need to find our way to Trystan as soon as possible. He can help us pass through into our world."

"What, we can't just wait for Kolur under this Trystan's protection?"

Isolfr scowled. "I'm not waiting for Kolur."

"Why the hell not?"

"What sort of magic do you think Kolur's going to use to pull us through? Do you have any idea how hard it is to move between worlds—especially to move someone else—"

"You do it!" I snapped. "You took to me to the world between worlds."

"Exactly," Isolfr said. "A liminal space. This is different. This is harder."

We glared at each other. The woman sang out *fish pies, fish pies* and the sound of her voice made my head hurt. We were in a city of people from the Mists. It might remind me of my world, but that was only the surface. Deep down, it was different. It was dangerous.

But at the same time, I knew Isolfr was right about the sort of magic Kolur might use. And the thought that a spirit might lose its existence, might suffer in pain, just to save me—I wasn't sure how I felt about that. I tried not to think about the gondola, the happy accidents of the *Shira* finding us floating in the water and bringing us here, to lands owned by someone Isolfr used to know.

"I'm not going to leave you here," Isolfr said. "But please don't be stupid."

"How am I being stupid?" I said. "You're the one wanting to go after some Mists lord who used to contact you as a *child*." I stepped away from him and knocked into a woman dressed in elaborate finery, pale gold silk dripping with jewels. She whipped around and pulled her lips back and hissed at me. Her gray eyes bore into mine, looming larger and larger.

Isolfr stepped between us.

"Pardon her, madam," he said with a bow. "She's a bit simple-minded."

The woman hissed again. But then she lifted her skirts and billowed away, giving me one last lingering glare over her shoulder.

I sucked in a deep breath and covered my face with my hands. My body trembled. A presence moved close to me, and when I dropped my hands, I saw that it was Isolfr, frowning down at me in concern.

"I trust Trystan," Isolfr said.

"Why?" I was still shaking from my encounter with the jewel-dripped, hissing woman.

Isolfr sighed. He glanced around, his gaze jumpy and nervous. "Let's get away from the crowd," he said. "I'll tell you when we aren't in such a busy place."

I nodded. He made a good point, even if it pained me to admit it. The docks were crowded, swarming with Mists folk. It wasn't a good place to talk.

"So where are we going?" I said.

"Trystan's lawyer." Isolfr took a deep breath and straightened his shoulders. "He handles Trystan's business in the city. We'll just have to find him." He hesitated, then glanced over at me. "Let me do that, though. You give yourself away too easily."

"I give myself away because of my dark eyes." I glared at him. "And your eyes are blue. They know what we are."

Isolfr had nothing to say to that, of course. Still, I followed him when he took off down the bustling street. Together, we wove through vendor stalls and clumps of gray-eyed people who sometimes spoke a strange, hissing language that made my blood curdle. To my eye, all these people seemed the same, regardless of the state of their clothing or the way they carried themselves. They were all from the land beyond lands, and I knew that if I cut them, all would bleed light instead of blood.

But to Isolfr, there was some distinction, because he peered up at folks as we passed them, frowning, like he was trying to make a decision.

"Just ask someone," I hissed, poking him in the back. He glared at me. We'd left the docks at that point, and the glass buildings towered around us, throwing off fragments of light.

Isolfr glared at me. "I'm trying to find the right sort!" he said in a low voice. "You don't want Foxfollow to know we're here, do you?"

We moved on. I wasn't used to cities, much less Mists cities, and the chatter of voices and clatter of shoes against the cobblestones made my head spin. Every now and then a cart would clank down the street, its driver hollering to clear the way. The crowd would surge to the side, and the cart would rattle past. The carts were never drawn by horses or oxen, but by sleek, moonlight-colored creatures that flickered against the waterfall of light from the buildings. They reminded me of Lord Foxfollow's monsters, and every time I saw one I'd press close to Isolfr without thinking.

When I thought I wouldn't be able to stand it much longer, Isolfr pulled me into a narrow side street tucked between two short stone buildings.

"There's no one here!" I cried. "Why didn't you ask one of those thousands of people out there?"

"Because I don't trust them," Isolfr said.

"Yes, but we're not getting anywhere."

"That's what you think." Isolfr grinned at me. "But I think the protection spell is still working. Look."

I peered down the street. A sign jutted out into the alley, swinging on its hinges. MASTER JULIO FORMENTI, LAWYER-IN-SERVICE.

"It doesn't say *Trystan* anywhere on it." I frowned and looked over at Isolfr. "How do you know this is the right person?"

"Trystan's my friend. We were close. I've heard him talk about his lawyer before."

"How could you be close to someone from the *Mists*?"

Isolfr sighed, darted his gaze around. Then he lowered his voice and leaned in close to me. "His family has been engaged in a feud with the House of Foxfollow since before Trystan was born. When he was a boy, his family called on the magic of my family to help them in fighting off Lord Foxfollow. They're the only noble family who ever openly defied him—all because of some feud that they couldn't even remember the source of." He shrugged. "But I know Trystan would never betray us. Family loyalties run deep here. That's assuming we can find him."

Another enemy of Lord Foxfollow's. I thought of Gillean, how frightened and kind he'd been to me. He was from the Mists, and I'd trusted him. I'd trusted him, and he'd never betrayed me, but he still dragged Foxfollow to the *Penelope*. Just because he didn't mean to didn't change what had happened.

Of course, Foxfollow only found the *Penelope* because of my kind-heartedness, because I hadn't wanted to see Gillean turned into a ghost.

"Come on," Isolfr said. "We shouldn't linger."

We went through the door below the sign, stepping into a room that smelled faintly of roses. A gray-haired man sat writing at a wooden desk, and he lifted his face to us as we came in. The air was very still. My heart beat too fast.

At least the man's gray eyes didn't loom large, the way Lord Foxfollow's had.

"Yes?" he said, setting down his quill.

"We're friends of Lord Llambric's," said Isolfr.

The man didn't move. "You aren't of this world."

Isolfr didn't say anything, just kind of shrank into himself, as if he didn't know how to respond. I watched him for a moment, my heart racing, waiting for him to say something.

The man did the same thing.

Finally, I took a deep breath and stepped forward, knowing I would have to be the brave one. The man flicked his eyes over to me, which startled me. Still, I was able to find my voice.

"We aren't from this world," I said. "But my friend here, he's spoken to Lord Llambric." I gestured with one hand and added, "He's a wizard."

The man frowned.

That was enough to jar Isolfr into action. "Yes, I'm a wizard," he said. "Lord Llambric and I had correspondence some years ago—" He straightened his spine and stuck out his chin. "We were great friends. He answered my questions about the ways of the Mists."

"Yes, I'm sure you were curious about that," Mr. Formenti muttered. He picked up his quill and peered at us over the bridge of his nose, not looking remotely approving. "What is it you want, exactly? Understand that I will have to communicate with Lord Llambric before we go any further."

"Directions to Llambric Manor," Isolfr said promptly.

Mr. Formenti stared at us. I wanted to cringe away from him.

"Very well," he said with a sigh, and then he reached into a desk drawer and pulled out a fresh sheet of parchment. It didn't look like any parchment I'd ever seen before, though; the surface shimmered and reflected light like a mirror.

Mr. Formenti dipped his quill into the well sitting in the desk's corner and began to write.

I glanced over at Isolfr, wanting to ask what Mr. Formenti was doing, knowing that I shouldn't. Surely in the Mists they had the capacity to send messages quickly; after all, a wizard could do the same back in Kjora.

I fidgeted, shifting my weight from foot to foot. Mr. Formenti stopped writing, his quill poised over his paper, his eyes scanning what he had written. Then he looked up at us.

This time, his eyes loomed huge and gray. My head swam, and the room spun around in circles. I reached out and grabbed ahold of Isolfr, afraid I'd fall. And even Isolfr looked pale, his skin tinted greenish instead of silver.

We shouldn't have come here. We shouldn't have spoken to this man, this Mr. Formenti. He was a spy for Lord Foxfollow. He was killing us—

And then, abruptly, that swirling, sick sensation vanished. Mr. Formenti looked back down at the paper, blinked twice, and then looked back up at us.

"It will be a moment," he said. "Lord Llambric may not see the message right away." He gestured to a pair of round-backed chairs upholstered in dark velvet. "Please, have a seat." He said this with a slight sneer, as if he didn't like treating us as guests.

I didn't move, not trusting anything Mr. Formenti did. Isolfr, however, stumbled over to the chair and collapsed. The green tint had disappeared from his skin, but he looked exhausted. Worried, too.

Maybe I wasn't alone in my anxiety after all.

I joined him, trying to sit in the proper lady's fashion, as I'd seen Bryn do a hundred times. *Bryn*. Sea and sky, I wondered if I'd ever see her again. She'd live out her whole life, marrying some wealthy suitor, raising children in a garden house in the capital, going to dances on pleasure boats during the summer's long daylight. And the whole time I'd be wasting away in the Mists, turned to steam or light or the very essence of magic. Gone.

Mr. Formenti glanced at his sheet of parchment.

"Well," he said, "it seems Lord Llambric does remember the gentleman. Isolfr Witherjoy, welcome to the Llambric Lands of the Mists. The lady, however—"

My fear returned with a sharp stab, and I knew I was going to die.

"The lady is named Hanna," Isolfr said, "and she's accompanying me. I'm sure Lord Llambric understands."

Mr. Formenti sighed. "You're quite right in that respect, Mr. Witherjoy. His exact words were," he peered down at his parchment again, frowning, "'any friend of Isolfr's is welcome at Llambric Manor.' Very well." Mr. Formenti folded his hands over his parchment, and for the first time, flushed with relief, I wondered how the magic worked that he was able to communicate with Lord Llambric through the paper. When he looked at us and the room spun—had he been capturing our image, sending it across the air of the Mists to Llambric Manor?

I shivered at the thought.

"I will arrange for transportation to take you to the manor," Mr. Formenti continued. "Nothing elaborate, of course, not for—" He stopped himself. "It will be comfortable, however. You'll leave tomorrow morning."

My head buzzed. I really didn't want to stay in this city any longer than I had to. Not that traveling across the countryside in some sort of Mists mode of transportation was much better.

"And what about tonight?" Isolfr said. He gestured at me. "She needs a place to eat and sleep."

I glared at him. He couldn't pretend that he needed to eat and sleep too?

Mr. Formenti wrinkled his nose. "Of course, yes. There's an inn two streets over. They accept magic as currency." He waved one hand at us. "I can sense the magic wafting off both of you, even if it isn't Mists magic. It'll be enough."

I didn't like the sound of this. I didn't like the idea of the Mists extracting my magic out of me, or of using it for some ill will. But Isolfr seemed to accept this answer, because he said, "Very well," and stood up as if the transaction was finished.

"It's called the Three Anchors," Mr. Formenti said. "I'll send the cart there tomorrow morning."

"Thank you," Isolfr said. "And thank Lord Llambric as well." He nudged me with his foot.

I sighed and stood up. "Yes," I muttered, "give my thanks to Lord Llambric."

Mr. Formenti just snorted in disapproval. Isolfr and I glanced at each other. He seemed pleased with himself.

"After you, Mr. Witherjoy," I said.

Isolfr's eyes sparkled like he wanted to laugh, an urge I didn't remotely understand. I couldn't imagine being delighted in this place.

He walked out of Mr. Formenti's office, and I followed. Being outside in the cold, sea-soaked air was actually a relief; I hadn't realized how stuffy the office had been, how it seemed to squeeze in on me and choke out my breath, until I was outside.

"Is this going to get us killed?" I asked Isolfr.

He looked at me. His eyes weren't sparkling anymore.

"I don't think so," he said.

It wasn't the most reassuring of comments. Still, I didn't have much choice, and together we walked down the narrow street to find the Three Anchors.

CHAPTER FIVE

I didn't sleep well that night. The Three Anchors was nice enough—clean and warm against the cold, blustery winds outside—but all night I lay awake listening to the unfamiliar noises creeping through the walls. Sometimes they sounded like voices, sometimes they sounded like claws scrabbling against the wood. I tried to feel for magic, but whenever I did my head would buzz and my skin would prickle, and it frightened me enough that I decided I would rather not know. So I pulled the thick blankets tight around me and didn't move; just stared straight up at the ceiling, which was fragmented by an odd, greenish light spilling in through the window.

Isolfr stretched out on a mat on the floor and closed his eyes and didn't move once all night. I wasn't sure if he was sleeping, the way I needed to sleep, or if it was some spirit-trance. He'd done the same thing occasionally when we were onboard the *Shira*.

Eventually, the greenish light faded and was replaced by the pale gray-white light of daytime. The sounds in the walls were replaced by more familiar noises—laughter, humming, the clatter of breakfast dishes. I sat up, throwing my blanket off to the side. When I put my feet on the floorboards, Isolfr sat straight up.

"Is it morning?" he asked.

"Apparently." I nodded toward the window. Everything had a hazy quality to it, like my mind was trying to dream during the day since it couldn't dream at night. I sighed.

"The carriage should be waiting for us downstairs," Isolfr said.

I nodded and my stomach grumbled. "I hope breakfast is, too."

Isolfr smiled. "I'm sure Lord Llambric will have seen to all our supplies. He's a good man."

"He's not a man," I murmured, "he's from the Mists." But even as I spoke, I knew I didn't completely believe that. Gillean, he had been a good man. And Isolfr's friend besides.

"The Mists are dangerous," Isolfr said, "which is why we need someone from the Mists to help us."

I didn't say anything, just pulled on my stockings and boots. I took one last look around the room, at its sparse, clean furnishings, its curtains hanging over the window. They were woven out of green fabric, I realized. Maybe that accounted for the odd light last night.

No, I didn't think it did.

We went downstairs. The dining room was crowded with Mists folk, their voices carrying over the clamor of dishes. I peered at their breakfasts as Isolfr and I walked past. Strips of fish, a sturdy, dark brown bread. Just like on the *Shira*, the food could have come from home.

Isolfr went up to the innkeep. I lagged behind, my arms wrapped around my chest. If we didn't have food in the carriage, as Isolfr had promised, I'd have to buy something here, trading my magic for a meal. I didn't really want to do that. Last night Isolfr had paid for our room, and I had hung back and watched as the innkeep—the same one he was speaking to this morning—had laid his hand on Isolfr's head and drawn up a thin, shimmering line of ice-colored light. The room had gone freezing for a few seconds. My breath turned to steam. And then the light had drawn up in the innkeep's hand, and he had nodded and said, "Room fourteen."

"A traveling carriage is waiting for us," he said, "courtesy of Julio Formenti."

The innkeep grunted. "It's out there." He jerked his head toward the door. "Only one drawn by irri. Can't miss it."

Isolfr nodded, but my chest clenched up. Irri?

We threaded through the dining room together. The smell of breakfast made my mouth water, but I tried to push it aside. "What's an irri?" I asked Isolfr in a low voice.

"It's not a thing. It's a type of magic."

"Is it dangerous?"

"Trystan is skilled in its practice."

"You don't sound so sure."

He glanced over at me, and he didn't look so sure either.

"It'll be fine," he said.

We pushed open the inn doors and stepped out onto the busy, bustling street. That sunless white light poured over us, and I squinted against it, my eyes hurting. I was too exhausted to be out in such brightness. Still, I was able to see well enough to notice that there wasn't a carriage waiting in front of the inn.

"It's not here," I said.

"Of course it is." Isolfr frowned. "It's just not *here*. They must have taken it behind the inn, over to the stables."

"Why didn't the innkeep say that?"

But Isolfr just veered off down the sidewalk, following the path around the side of the inn. The path was narrow and darkened by the surrounding buildings, and I was grateful for the rest it gave my eyes.

"How could the carriage even get back here?" I said. "There's not another path, is there?"

Isolfr glanced over his shoulder at me. "We're in the Mists," he said.

His answer made me shiver. I thought about the long beam of light that the innkeep had extracted from his forehead.

The path ended abruptly, bumping up against a big stone-and-wood building that smelled of animals and dried grass. Isolfr pulled open the side door and stepped in. I followed him even though I didn't want to. My heart was racing, and I was hungry and tired and I didn't know what animals we would find waiting for us, but I doubted they would be any I was familiar with.

The inside of the stable was dark and hazy. A few beams of sunlight, bright against the dark, pushed their way through the cracks in the walls, illuminating the stable in dappled patches. I saw a round, orange eye, a swish of a tail, the complicated straps and buckles of a carriage harness. I stayed close to the wall, twisting my coat up in one hand, trying to calm my anxiety. Isolfr strode across the scattered dirt and grass of the stable floor. At one point, he stepped too close to one of the creatures in the pens and it reared back, a flash of silver in the shadows, and let out a loud shrieking-snort that didn't sound like any animal I'd ever heard. I slammed against the wall and Isolfr crouched down, one hand up like a shield. But nothing happened. He looked over at me sheepishly.

"It's fine," he said. "Come on, I see our carriage." He gestured to a dark corner of the stable.

"I don't see anything," I hissed back, trying to whisper. "Isn't there a lantern in here? Can't you cast a light spell?"

Isolfr sighed. "Not with the moon horses stabled here." He nodded at the silvery flash that had reared up when he came too close. "But you can see better when you're closer, I promise. Besides, we don't want to stay any longer in the city than we have to."

He spoke that last part lightly, but a cold chill rippled down my spine. He was right. There was too much of a chance that Lord Foxfollow's spies would see us. Maybe they already had.

I took a deep breath and moved forward, trying to keep myself as contained as possible. It worked, because when I passed the moon horse's pen, it only exhaled a puff of air, nothing more. Isolfr smiled at me in the darkness, and then together we picked our way through the straw to the carriage waiting in the corner. All I could see of it was a misshapen dark lump.

"How does the irri work?" I moved closer to the carriage. It wasn't very big.

"It's part of the design," Isolfr said. "Built into the walls. You'll see."

I looked at Isolfr and then I looked at the carriage, doubtful.

"We can't walk," Isolfr said. "The carriage will give us protection against—you know."

I shivered, although I knew he was right. "Fine," I said. "But you can get in first."

"Very well." Isolfr walked up to the carriage and pulled open the door. A creamy light issued from inside, casting Isolfr's face in long, eerie shadows. He looked back over at me, grinning. "Oh, you're going to like this."

"Don't make fun of me."

"I'm not." He climbed in, then stuck his head out and gestured for me to join him. "Come on! I promise you, we'll be safer in here than we've been since we arrived."

I took a deep breath. Isolfr smiled at me from the carriage door, his skin bathed in that strange light. I trusted him. I also knew this was the only way I was going to get back home.

I crawled through the carriage's open door—

And into an opulent, spacious lounging room, much, much bigger than the carriage was.

"Sea and sky," I whispered.

"Trystan's quite handy with Mists magic," Isolfr said, pulling the door shut. It made a loud clicking noise as it latched. I jumped. Because I *could* jump—the interior of the carriage was big enough for me to stand. I could have reached up on my tiptoes and not even been able to touch the ceiling. The floor was layered with thick tap-estried rugs and large silk pillows. One wall—because this carriage had *walls*—was lined with shelves full of jars and stacks of fabric.

"Are those new clothes?" I walked over to the shelf and pulled off one of the pieces of fabric. It unfurled into a suit jacket of the sort that Mr. Formenti had been wearing. I turned around to face Isolfr. "Is this all for us?"

"I imagine it is." Isolfr was smiling, his whole face lit up in a way it hadn't been since we arrived.

I turned back to the shelves, marveling at them in wonder. I selected another piece of fabric, this one a rich, mossy green. It unfolded into a thick brocaded gown, the fabric luxuriant against my bare skin.

"I can't believe this," I said. "I can't—" I turned around to face Isolfr. "Are you sure this isn't a trick?"

"I'm sure." Isolfr laughed. "I'd think it was a trick if the carriage wasn't like this." He clapped his hands together. "Of course, now we need to get her moving."

"How do we do that?" I set the dress down carefully on a stack of pillows.

"It's easy. You just have to feed the irri."

"How do you know all this?" I watched as Isolfr walked over to the shelves and pulled down a tall, narrow jar. It glowed when he touched it, a pulsing that reminded me of a heartbeat.

"I told you, Trystan and I were friends. And this design is his own, so he explained how it works." Isolfr made his way through the pillows to a lever on the far wall. He pulled it down, and a win-dow opened, revealing a gaping, empty darkness. Fear crawled up my skin. It was like looking into the end of the world.

Isolfr tilted the jar against his palm. A few gray flakes fluttered out, and he tossed them into the window. Then he pulled the lever to close it again, and the wall smoothed over.

"That's it?" I said.

Isolfr nodded. "The irri knows where to go."

"And we can trust it?"

"Yes," Isolfr said, his voice firm. "It's one of the only things we can trust in this world. One of the only things that hasn't been tainted by Lord Foxfollow."

A shuddering, creaking groan rippled through the room. Everything brightened, bathing us in a warm, lemony light that reminded me of the sun. The carriage lurched. I lost my balance and tumbled headfirst into the pillows.

"It must take a little getting used to," Isolfr said. He sounded unsure of himself.

The carriage lurched again, and I realized we were moving. All the jars on the shelves rattled and shook, although none of them seemed in danger of falling.

"How do we know where we are?" I said, looking around from my place on the pillows. With the lights up the room was even more extravagant. Everything sparkled like moonlight on the sea. Isolfr looked as he had the first time I ever saw him, drifting in the water like a ghost. Too beautiful to be human.

"Hmm," he said, putting his hands on his hips. "There should be a hatch somewhere for lookout purposes." He gazed around the room, squinting up at the ceiling. "Ah, there it is!"

I looked to where he pointed. A small, round doorway was set in the middle of the ceiling.

"How exactly are we supposed to get up there?"

"Tell the carriage what you'd like."

I looked at him. We trundled along. Through the walls of the room, I could hear the chatter of the city, voices shouting and laughing. I'd wanted to be a witch all my life, and I was familiar with magic. But I'd never seen magic like this. Not in our world.

"*Now* you're making fun of me," I said.

"No! Here, I'll show you." He held out his hands awkwardly and said, "Carriage! We'd like to look outside."

Nothing happened.

But then I noticed a lightness in my body, as if I were underwater. The lights in the room dimmed. My feet lifted up off the floor.

"Sea and sky!" I shouted. "What's happening?"

Isolfr laughed. He floated a few finger widths above the floor too, but it didn't seem to concern him at all. He pushed his arms out as if swimming and propelled himself upward, toward the round door in the ceiling. I did the same, tentative, afraid that the magic would fail and I would drop to the ground. I doubted those pillows would do much to break my fall.

"What's doing this?" I called out to Isolfr.

"The irri," he said. "It controls everything. It had to take a little energy from the lights to lift us up, but that's okay. Everything's perfectly in balance. Trystan saw to it."

He was too enamored with Trystan. I just hoped Trystan would actually be able to help us.

Isolfr undid the latch and pushed the door open. A patch of pale blue sky appeared, and he pushed himself up and out of the carriage, then leaned back down, holding out one hand. "Here, let me help you."

I took his hand, shivering at the coldness of his touch. Connecting with him made me feel tethered, although it also made me more aware that my feet were dangling above the floor, that I was embroiled in magic I doubted I'd ever understand. But at the same time, the breeze blowing in through the hatchway was crisp and clean-smelling.

I kicked my legs hard and pushed myself up, and Isolfr pulled me out the rest of the way. There was a platform at the top of the carriage where we both could sit, although we had to press close together so we'd fit. Narrow pipes jutted out from the front of the carriage, belching gray mist. The cold dampness of it settled on my skin, making my hair curl, but I turned myself away from it, looking out at the road as we receded.

The view was spectacular.

We were up on a hill in what must have been the outskirts of the city. The buildings and people were sparser here, and I could see those huge glass structures rising up in the distance. Already trees were starting to sprout off the ground, strange ones with long, twisting white leaves that trailed over the pale, golden grass. We passed a little stone building that might have been a house—it was strange to think of the people of the Mists living in houses like anyone else, but there was a clothesline stretched between two trees, the line flapping with gray fabric. A little boy peeked out from behind a piece of the fabric, his eyes big and curious. He reminded me of Henrik, even if he was a child of the Mists. I waved at him, and he yelped and dove back behind the laundry.

"Don't do that." Isolfr looked over at me. The wind tossed his hair into his face, and I was caught again by the nature of his strange, inhuman beauty. "He could have been a spy."

"A little boy?"

"Maybe."

I shivered, drawing my knees up to my chest. The house drew farther and farther away in the distance. The city sparkled.

"Maybe we shouldn't be up here then," I said.

"Maybe not." But Isolfr didn't make any move to go back inside, only turned his gaze toward the city, falling away into the horizon.

The carriage huffed and steamed and rolled us over the stone pathway. The countryside stretched out around us. For all my fear of Lord Foxfollow, I didn't want to go back inside either.

Traveling in the carriage was much easier than traveling on the *Penelope*. In either of her incarnations.

The food, although it was preserved in jars and there was no way to heat it up properly, was still delicious. We ate salted lemons and strips of some sweet-tasting fish that reminded me of the lisila that I'd had back in Tulja. There were fruit preserves to spread on butter-bread and packages of sharp yellow cheese and vegetables soaked in brine. We also had clean clothes, enough that we could change every day of the trip, and as it turned out, there was a small room set off from the main one with a ceramic tub that refilled itself with fresh warm water whenever we needed it. That first day, I soaked in the water until it turned cold, and when I stepped out, my skin smelled sweet, like flowers I couldn't identify.

The one drawback, of course, was that there was nothing to do. I liked the varied food and the nice clothes, but even on the *Penelope II* Frida and Kolur would find chores for us from time to time. I thought things were dull enough then, but they were even more dull in the carriage.

"How are we supposed to bide our time?" I asked Isolfr one afternoon. I knew it was afternoon because we had taken to leaving the ceiling hatch open so we could watch the sky change its light.

"There are books to read," Isolfr said, which was what he was doing, stretched out on the pillows.

"Dull ones," I said. "About the great House of Llambric in its glory days." I'd tried reading one of those books when I first grew bored, but the book actually bored me even more. "You'd think the history of noble houses in the Mists would be more interesting than that."

"The really interesting part of their history can't be recorded," Isolfr said. "Lord Foxfollow saw to that. Anything written about his takeover has to be presented in a positive light, or else the writer will be killed." He settled into a melancholy silence. I didn't blame him; I didn't much want to think about Lord Foxfollow either.

Isolfr turned back to his book. He stared down at the pages, his brow furrowed.

Then he tossed it off into the pillows.

"Why don't we stop for a rest?" he said.

"Are you sure that's a good idea?"

He hesitated. I could see him thinking it over in those lovely blue eyes of his. "It's not the best," he said. "But I do think it will be good for us to stretch and walk around a bit. We're in the country-side, so we don't have to worry about spies." He stood up and straightened his coat. "And if we go up and it looks like there are any houses or other travelers, we can wait until it's clear."

I considered this. I wasn't used to spending all my time indoors, and it would be nice to breathe fresh air—even if it was fresh air that belonged to the Mists.

"Yes," I said. "I'd like that."

Isolfr grinned, although I could see the flash of anxiety in his eyes. I realized with a jolt that he probably didn't really think this was a good idea.

"If it's not safe," I said, "we don't have to go out."

Isolfr shrugged. "I don't like seeing you bored."

My cheeks warmed. Isolfr looked away. "Carriage! We'd like to look outside," he said, and then he drifted up in the air. I did the same. I still wasn't used to it, that weird feeling of weightlessness. Just like I wasn't used to Isolfr saying he cared about my happiness. More or less.

He climbed out to the viewing platform first, then ducked

back inside. "It's clear," he said. "Carriage! Could you stop for a moment?"

A loud wheezing bellowed from the walls, and then the familiar, droning rattle ended. The light dimmed down to silver.

We had stopped.

"Come on," Isolfr said. "It's a nice day."

I lifted myself through the hatchway. The carriage sat in the middle of an endless, sweeping grassland growing wild with lavender flowers. The sunless sky was pale blue overhead, glowing its infused light. The flowers rippled like the sea.

"We're not even on a road," I said, feeling breathless. The cold air burned in my lungs, but it did so with a sharp pleasantness, something I realized I'd missed since being trapped inside the carriage. I looked over at Isolfr. "How do you know we're even going to Llambric Manor?"

"We are." He smiled at me. "We're just not taking the roads. It's safer that way. Which means it will be safer for us to stop for a bit." Then he looked back out at the landscape. "Those are eye-of-amories," he said. "The roots are good to eat."

"How do you know that?"

"I've heard Trystan talk about them."

"Trystan, Trystan, Trystan." I rolled my eyes. "I hope this Trystan actually exists, you know."

Isolfr gave me an irritated look, but in the bright air I couldn't be bothered by it. I knew it was dangerous being out here, even if we were off the roads and the grassland was empty. But it was just so lovely. It reminded me of the spring that I'd missed back in Kjora when Kolur whisked me away to the north.

"Let's pick some of these eye-of-amories," I said, standing up on the platform. I tottered in place, looking down at the swirling, silky grass. "And hope your Trystan has good taste in food."

Isolfr laughed. I took a deep breath and jumped off the carriage. My dress fluttered around me and the wind blew across my face and for a moment I felt as if I was flying.

I landed on all fours. The grass waved in the breeze, tickling at my nose. I straightened up and when I looked over to my side, Isolfr was already standing there, his hands shoved in his pockets.

"I didn't hear you jump," I said.

"Because I didn't." He gave me one of those crooked, nervous smiles.

"Show-off."

He laughed, ducking his head, and for some reason that made my stomach feel like it was full of butterflies. It wasn't an unpleasant feeling.

"So the eye-of-amories are the purple ones, right?" I said, trying to make things go back to normal. I had no business turning into a swoony court girl over a spirit of the north wind.

Isolfr nodded. "Just make sure you pull them up by the roots. And keep the flowers, too. Trystan says you can suck the nectar out of them."

"Right." I lifted up my skirts and plunged into the grass. It came up nearly to my waist, but walking wasn't as difficult as I'd imagined. The grass glided aside for me, clearing a way through the landscape. Isolfr rustled behind me, and I turned around, looking at him over my shoulder.

"You're not going to turn into the wind out here?" I teased, "and blow through the field?"

"You're about to step on some flowers."

"Stop avoiding my questions." I stopped and looked forward again. Purple blossoms swelled out in front of me, so thick that it was as if the grass had changed color.

"Pull them up by the roots?" I said.

Isolfr stepped up beside me and nodded. "And pull hard. They can be tough to get up."

I knelt down. The grass rose up around me, a soft whispering cage. The stalks of the eye-of-amories were actually quite a bit thicker than the grass, and the flowers themselves hung off several silvery strands at the stalk's top, fanning out like a tree. I grabbed the stem, braced myself against the ground, and pulled.

The eye-of-amorie came out easily. I wasn't expecting that and so I sprawled backward and landed on my back, clumps of damp dirt scattering across the bodice of my dress.

"Ancestors damn you!" I said to Isolfr. "You knew that was going to happen."

"Knew what?" He laughed. "I didn't think you would fall over." He leaned over and ripped out a flower of his own, then another. Our thievery didn't even register in the vast pool of lavender.

"Is all of the Mists this beautiful?" I said.

Isolfr yanked out another flower. "I've not seen very much of it. But from what I can tell, much of it is rather striking."

I draped my arms over my knees and gazed up at the empty sky. "It's just not what I pictured. I thought it would be dark and wrapped in mist." I shrugged.

"I always thought that too." He smiled down at me, his arms full of flowers.

Behind him, I saw a smudge of darkness against the sky.

"What's that?" My heart started pounding, and I stood up, careful to keep my eyes on the dark smudge.

"What is it?" Isolfr's face lost all of its incandescent brightness. He whirled around. "What do you see?"

The dark spot grew bigger.

"It's him," I said, the fear growing slow and thick in my chest. I couldn't breathe.

"We need to get back to the carriage. Now."

I didn't want to turn my back on the dark spot, but Isolfr took me by the hand and pulled me toward the carriage. I looked behind me the entire time, not taking my eyes off the dark spot in the sky. My feet tangled up in my skirts as I ran. Grass slapped against my waist. The carriage was perched up on a hill, surrounded by acres and acres of rippling grass. It seemed like part of another world.

The dark spot was beginning to take shape. It had wings like a bird, but I could tell it was much bigger than any bird I had ever seen, and it threw off glints of light that fell into my eyes and blinded me.

"Hurry!" Isolfr shouted.

My foot caught on a loose patch of soil and I tumbled forward, landing in the prison of grass. I kicked, trying to right myself, but my skirts wrapped around my legs and I could see the dark creature barreling toward us, light flashing all over the landscape. Its wings were the only way in which it really resembled a bird. In all other respects it was like some kind of lizard, its scales charred black except for a handful that shone like diamonds.

The creature opened its mouth, revealing a lolling red tongue, rows of sharp teeth.

"Hanna! Move!"

Isolfr's voice jarred me out of my paralysis. I scrambled to my feet, the dress ripping as I stood up. Isolfr took my hand and pulled me through the grass.

The creature was silent save for the constant beating of its wings. They created a breeze that lifted the ends of my hair and chilled the back of my neck. I stifled a scream.

Lights danced across the grass.

A shadow fell across the two of us, me and Isolfr.

The carriage waited on the hill.

The creature swooped down, one huge wing knocking me to my back. For a moment there was only a tangle of wing and fabric and grass, and then I heard Isolfr scream.

Isolfr floated in midair, one dark claw wrapped around his waist.

"Hanna!" he shouted.

For a moment I could only stare at him, stricken. He was my one connection to the Mists, the one who knew who to speak to, who to trust. If he died, I would be alone. I'd never survive.

And so without thinking I felt for magic. Any magic, not just wind. And I found it, a sudden slamming burst of it, cold and wet like mist. I breathed it in and let it burn in my lungs. It intertwined with the magic inside of me, twisting and changing and melding into something new.

The creature flapped higher. Isolfr wasn't moving. I hoped he wasn't dead.

But I knew I couldn't think about that now. I could only think about the magic, churning inside of me, igniting my veins with enchantment. The power rose up heavy and strong and I lifted my hands and flung the magic, my magic, my transformed magic, out into the world.

There was one moment's calm peace. The grass fluttered, tracing the path of the magic as it arced overhead.

And then my spell slammed into the creature with a flare of gray mist and white liquid light. The creature spiraled out of its trajectory, wings flapping wildly and then not flapping at all. It slammed into the ground with such a heaviness that I felt the earth shake beneath my feet. For a moment nothing seemed tangible. Everything seemed like mist.

And then the sensation passed. The creature lay in an unmoving lump among the grass.

"Isolfr!" I screamed, and I bounded forward, swiping at grass and flowers to get them out of my way. I slowed several paces from the creature, not wanting to get too close. It still hadn't moved, but I didn't think I would be able to blast magic at it again—certainly not with the strength I had just done.

"Isolfr?" My voice cracked. "Please tell me you're all right."

There was no answer. I crept around the creature, looking for some sign of Isolfr. The brilliant diamond scales flashed and shimmered. The rest of the creature was blackened, charred, like burned coal.

And then I saw a strip of blue fabric, a sharp contrast against the creature's scales.

"Isolfr!" I dropped to my hands and knees, crawling forward. The fabric stuck out from underneath one of the massive black wings. I reached out, hand trembling, and brushed my fingers against the wing's membrane. I snatched my hand back in preparation—but nothing happened. The creature didn't move.

I reached out again, lifting the wing up, my breath coming hot and fast. I peered underneath it. Isolfr was there, curled up like a snail, his hand thrown over his head.

"Isolfr?" I whispered. "Can you hear me? Please?"

I stared at him, my heart pounding, waiting. He didn't move.

He didn't move.

He didn't move.

And then he did.

It was a small movement, just a twitch of his fingers, but it was enough for me to know he was still alive. I ducked under the wing. The air there was dank and dim and smelled like a dampened fire, like wet smoke. I wrapped my arms around Isolfr's chest and dragged him out into the light. His head lolled against my arm, and I could see his eyes moving behind his lids, a rapid back and forth like he was dreaming. He was heavier than I expected, and as soon as he was clear from the creature I had to drop him into the grass to catch my breath. The creature didn't move, just rose up out of the earth like a boulder. I glanced over my shoulder at the carriage, my breath coming short and fast. The carriage hadn't moved either.

I turned back to Isolfr and knelt down beside him. His eyes moved back and forth. I pushed on his shoulder. "Isolfr," I whispered. "Isolfr, wake up."

He didn't.

I looked over at the creature. I wasn't certain if it was dead, or if others would arrive soon, blackening the sky and throwing off points of diamond light. So I took a deep breath, picked Isolfr up under his arms, and slowly dragged him back to the carriage.

It took a long time.

At least the creature never stirred, and the sky remained empty. But I had to stop every few paces to readjust my grip or steady my breath, and by the time we'd made it back to the carriage my skin was slick with sweat. I laid Isolfr down in the dirt and pulled on the handle of the carriage door. For a moment I was afraid it wouldn't swing open, that it had been locked from the inside—but then the latch turned and the door swung out, revealing the soft light of the interior.

I frowned, hands on my hips, uncertain how I was going to get Isolfr inside. I didn't want to risk using magic the way I had against the creature—I wasn't sure *where* that magic had come from, and I didn't want to use too much and fling him up against the wall. Eventually, I climbed inside, then reached down and heaved. Something wrenched in my back, sending up a sudden ripple of pain, but I gave one last violent pull and Isolfr tumbled in.

I slumped back among the pillows, staring up at the circle of blue sky cut out from the ceiling. Sweat dripped into my brows and I didn't bother to wipe it away. I was exhausted, not just from dragging Isolfr to the carriage but from drawing in that strange magic out of the air. It had wrung the vitality out of me, like water wrung from a rag. I prayed to the ancestors, unsure if they could even hear me in these strange lands, that I hadn't destroyed myself in the process.

"Carriage," I said, my voice weak, "we would like to continue our travels."

The lights in the room brightened, the side door slammed shut and locked into place. Isolfr gave a little moan. I dropped my head over toward him, too tired to drag myself out of the pillows but sick with the fear that I had hurt him irrevocably.

He stirred, curling up into a ball, and then fell still.

The walls wheezed and hissed. The sky began to glide past the opening in the ceiling.

We were on our way to Lord Llambric once again.

Except I didn't know what else we'd find on the journey there.

CHAPTER SIX

I fell asleep in the pillows and didn't dream. When I woke, the sky had darkened into that eerie gray-green color, the shade of nighttime here. I couldn't see any stars. You never could. I thought of Papa teaching Henrik and me the constellations after dinner. He'd sketch them out on the floor with a stick he'd blackened in the fireplace, the shapes of our collective ancestors: Hilga and Kjartan and Valdi and Asta.

"If you look up in the sky," he'd say, looking straight at Henrik and me, his voice grave, "and you don't see these constellations, you've sailed into the Mists."

Funny how those stories were so much more true than I'd ever expected. It wasn't just the constellations that were missing. It was everything that made up the sky: the sun and moon and stars and clouds. All of it, gone.

I closed my eyes to stop the tears. It didn't work.

And then I heard a shuffling in the corner. Isolfr.

"Are you okay?" I wiped at my eyes, hoping he wouldn't know I'd been crying, and slowly eased myself to my feet. My entire body ached, my joints creaking like old cabinets, my muscles burning with the intensity of standing. The pain in my back twinged.

Isolfr stood over at the counter near the shelves that we used to prepare our food. He lifted his head, the movement too slow.

"The magic," he croaked.

"The magic? What magic?" I stumbled forward, kicking pillows out of my way. Isolfr lifted a tiny red vial and tapped its contents into a stone bowl. Everything seemed to be happening underwater. "What are you doing?"

"Magic," he said again in that harsh, raspy voice. He tried to set the bottle down on the counter and ended up knocking it on its side; pink powder fanned out across the surface. Isolfr looked down at it in dismay.

"You need to be resting," I said, and I stumbled over to him and wrapped one arm around his shoulders. He immediately leaned his weight into me, his eyes closing and his whole body sighing with relief.

"I need—I won't recover from this. I'll turn into the Mists."

His voice was right in my ear, soft, not panicked or urgent at all. It took me a moment to register what he was saying. *I'll turn into the Mists.* To the place itself? A shudder of revulsion rippled through me.

"I'll fix it," I said. "You can lie down and tell me what to do."

He mumbled something unintelligible against my ear. His breath was as cold as the north wind, and there was a dampness to his skin I'd never noticed before. *The Mists.*

"Did I do this to you?" I asked quietly, leading him toward the closest pile of pillows.

He didn't answer. I suddenly felt very hollow.

"I'm sorry," I whispered, easing him down.

"You saved me from the dragon," he said. "You saved—I just need your help again."

"All right," I said, kneeling to help him lie down on the pillows. He stretched out and his head dropped back. His eyes closed. He didn't move.

"Isolfr?" My breath grew sharp with panic; Isolfr didn't need to sleep and I didn't know what it meant if he fell asleep now, after

I blasted him with foreign magic and knocked him out of the sky. "Are you okay?" I shook his shoulder. "You can't slip off like this. I need you to tell me what to do!"

His eyes fluttered. He gazed up at me through half-closed lids.

"Add sysab and coral powder to the bowl," he said, speaking slowly, with long gaps between his words. "Mix them. Then—"

"You rest," I said, afraid he was going to fall asleep, or die, or drift off permanently into the ether. "But stay awake. Tell me what to do as I'm doing it."

He nodded. It was a small movement and looked painful. I rose to my feet, shaking, not wanting to turn away from him. He was pale, but not in the moonlight way I'd gotten accustomed to. Instead, he looked sickly, especially in the eerie magic light of the carriage. His eyes were glassy and overly bright, his lips cracked and flaking.

"Hurry," he whispered.

I stumbled over to the shelf and scanned up and down, looking for the spell ingredients. Every now and then I would glance over my shoulder at him, to make sure he hadn't closed his eyes, hadn't drifted away. He watched me, slumped there among the pillows, hardly moving.

Eventually, I found both vials on the bottom shelf, labeled neatly in an elegant, aristocratic hand. I scooped them off the shelf and bounded over to the counter.

"How much of each?" I said.

Isolfr stirred. "Equal parts to the kuzar. It's already in there. I didn't measure—"

"I've got it." I frowned down at the bowl. This was basically earth magic, all this mixing and stirring, and I hadn't practiced it much except for when I helped Mama cook dinner. But I knew messing up a potion like this was much worse than messing up a meal.

Still, I measured out the sysab in my palm, holding it up against the kuzar in the bowl. When it looked equal, I added it in, then did the same with the coral powder. I used a long metal spoon sitting beside the bowl to mix them together.

"Now what?" I said, looking over at Isolfr. My chest was tight and I was anxious that he'd fallen asleep, but he lifted his head and blinked at me.

"Add the milk of maelys," he said. "It's on the shelf there." He pointed vaguely with one hand before his arm dropped against the pillows like a weight. He leaned back and took a deep breath. I heard the wheeze in his lungs and knew I had to hurry.

"How much?" I said.

"If it's an apothecary's bottle, the whole thing—"

"An apothecary's bottle?" I was in over my head. I could control the wind if I was in my world, but I couldn't control the strange magic of the air here, and I should not be mixing up potions like an earthwitch. I was just going to make Isolfr worse.

"The same size as the dry ingredient vials," he said. "If it's larger, it'll be twice the size, so half of it."

I fumbled around on the shelf, the roughness of his voice scraping against my thoughts. My heart beat too fast and made my hands shake. Fortunately, it didn't take me long to find the milk of maelys—it was sitting on the same shelf where the dry ingredients had been. It was the same size bottle, too. I dumped it in.

"Next?" I called out, urgency turning my voice to a whine.

"Mix together."

I did, whisking the liquid into the powder. It turned frothy like beer.

"Keep mixing," Isolfr said, "until it changes color."

My chest constricted. "What color? It's dark red now."

"Yes, good." Isolfr sucked in a long breath of air. I clutched the spoon more tightly and stirred more quickly. "It will change to pale green. Keep——" His voice faded away. I looked up over the bowl and saw that his head had sagged down into the pillows.

"Isolfr!"

I was about to drop the spoon and run over to him when he jerked his head up and said, "Don't stop!"

"What?"

"The spell! Don't stop stirring."

I whipped the liquid into a frenzy. "I won't."

"Good." He slumped back. His wheezing was louder, a sound emanating from deep inside his chest. I kept stirring the potion, one hand pressed against the counter to brace myself. I stared down at the frothy liquid and willed it turn to green. It wasn't red anymore, at least, but a murky brown color. I stirred harder.

"Isolfr," I said, because I wanted him to keep talking to me, wanted to know for sure he was still alive. "What were those things?"

"The dragons?"

"Is that what they're called?"

He made a soft grunt of affirmation. "They were created by wizards of the Mists a long time ago." He took deep a breath. "Mists magic, mostly, with some magic from our world—the essence of fire."

I frowned down at the potion. It was still brown, but the brown was starting to lighten, to turn the color of maple bark.

"Were they sent by Lord Foxfollow?"

Isolfr didn't answer.

I looked over at him, still stirring. "Isolfr?"

"I don't know." His voice was quiet, distant. "Perhaps. Or maybe they just live in these skies."

"Would Trystan send us this way, if there were dragons?" The word was vaguely familiar—someone in the village had told me stories of dragons when I was a little girl. Not Mama or Papa, but one of the elders. They were not a creature of our world, she'd said, but of the Other. A creature of heat and mist.

"No." Isolfr wheezed. "Not if he knew."

Then he wheezed again, a long whistling sound, louder and more painful than the others. I stirred faster. My arm was growing tired but I didn't slow down. The brown was turning yellow-gold, like autumn grass.

"It's yellow," I said. "Is that close—"

"Keep stirring." Isolfr took deep gasping breaths. "You're close. Concentrate. Concentrate."

I stared down at the potion, hypnotized by the constant circular path of the spoon. The yellow lightened. I thought of all the green I'd seen in my world. Spring leaves and the stems of flowers. The dress I wore to the midsummer celebrations last year. Grass stains on the hem of my skirts. The leeks Mama chopped and simmered for dinner. The sea in sunlight.

Slowly, the potion began to streak with that same pale green I was imagining.

"It's changing!" I cried, breathless. "What do I do next?"

"Feed to me," he croaked. "When it's green, it's ready."

I kept stirring, whisking out the last of the yellow. Then I tapped the spoon against the side of the bowl the way I'd seen Mama do and laid it down on the table. The potion gleamed in the light, letting off a scent like crushed flowers, sweet and earthy. I picked the bowl up and carried it over to Isolfr.

He'd gotten worse in the time it took me to stir up the potion. The waxiness had left his skin and been replaced by an eerie translucence, and his eyes were filled with a dull light. I gasped and fell to my knees beside him. He turned his head toward me, hair falling across his forehead. His mouth moved, tracing the shape of my name, but I couldn't hear his voice.

"It's ready." I shoved the bowl at him. "Is it all right? Is that the right color?"

Isolfr's gaze drifted down to the bowl. He nodded. I tilted the bowl up to his lips and let him drink. He gulped at the potion, his eyes closed, the line of his neck moving up and down. Some of it dribbled down the side of his face, staining the pillows. When he finished he slumped back and let out a long breath.

"Thank you," he said. Already his voice was stronger, clearer.

"What was that?" I stood up, weak with relief. I set the bowl on the counter and grabbed a washrag and sat down beside him. "What sort of spell?"

Isolfr didn't answer right away. I dabbed at the green lines tracing out of the corners of his mouth, and his head tilted toward me, eyes searching. I pulled the rag away.

"What happened to you?" I whispered.

He stared at me. I felt a hollowness deep inside my stomach.

"I fell out of the sky," he said. "Thanks to you. You saved me."

I shook my head, wrung the rag around in my hands. "I blasted you with magic. I'm sorry, I was just—"

"You were trying to get me away from the dragon." Isolfr shifted among his pillows and rested his hands on his stomach. "I know that. It was Mists magic, though." I heard the hitch in his voice, the hesitation. "How did you—"

"I don't know. I was trying to find the magic on the wind and that was what I got." I tossed the rag up on the counter. The carriage rumbled along, the dark patch of starless dark green sky staring down at us. "I wasn't thinking. I'm sorry I hurt you."

"I'll be fine." Isolfr propped himself up on his elbows, moving as he if wanted to sit up. But the exertion must have been too much for him, because he collapsed down again, taking in deep breaths of air.

"You have to rest," I said, as if I knew.

Isolfr nodded. "I know. I just wanted to show you that you don't need to worry." He smiled up at the ceiling, although it was a bitter, frightened smile. "If the dragon had carried me off, that would have been much worse. It would have sucked the essence out of me to fan the fire burning in its belly." He sighed and dropped his head down again. "They'd do the same to you, windwitch. Although it seems you've got a bit of earthwitch in you too."

I blushed at that and shook my head. "It was just adrenaline. I couldn't have you dying. This Lord Trystan's never going to listen to me on my own."

Isolfr chuckled. "Well, you're a pretty girl, and he likes pretty people."

My blush deepened, heat rushing up through my face. I looked down at my hands, heart hammering in my chest. I couldn't imagine that a creature like Isolfr, with all his otherworldly beauty, could possibly find me pretty.

I snuck a glance at him, fumbling around in my head for the right words. He was staring up at the hatch in the ceiling and looked lost in his own thoughts. Maybe he hadn't even realized what he said.

Still, I cleared away the stained pillows and stretched out beside him, watching the night go by.

I stayed up with Isolfr during the night, although after drinking the potion he didn't seem to need my help. Mostly I brought him water to help his dry throat and sat with him as I nibbled at my meal. I didn't have much of an appetite after everything that had happened, but I knew I needed to keep up my strength.

We kept the hatch open, and every now and then I glanced up at it, afraid I'd seen a shadow pass overhead. But the sky, as far as I could tell, remained clear.

"What exactly did that potion do?" I asked Isolfr at one point, after we'd finished sharing a cup of sweet berry-flavored water. "You never explained it to me."

Isolfr looked over at me. He was still too weak to move around, but at least his skin was no longer transparent, and his eyes had gone back to normal—as normal as someone like Isolfr could look, anyway.

"Counteracted the magic of the Mists," he said. "You channeled Mists magic as if we were back home, but the Mists *are* magic, so doing that just intensified the effect." He paused, hesitating. "You sent the magic right into me. Made it a part of me."

I stared at him, a cold horror rising in the back of my throat. "I'm so, so sorry," I said.

Isolfr shook his head. "You don't have to apologize! Your intentions were for the dragon, so he received the full brunt of it."

I slumped down against the pillows. "I should have known better," I said.

"No one told you." Isolfr shook his head. "If anything, it's *my* fault; I should have warned you."

I smiled at him. "Yeah," I said. "Let's make it your fault."

He laughed.

Isolfr rested most of that first day after the attack. He stretched out on the pillows, staring blankly up at the ceiling or the wall, his eyes gleaming like twin moons. He didn't move, didn't snore, didn't mumble to himself the way humans do in their sleep. He only stared into infinity with his silver eyes.

I wandered around the carriage, trying to decipher its secrets. Mixing up the potion for Isolfr had made me more confident in my magic, but after what had happened with the dragon, I wasn't going to risk testing anything in the carriage. I had no idea what made it run or how it had been built, and my curiosity, combined with my boredom, threatened to drive me crazy. So I did things like pressing my ear against the wall to listen to the wheezing and huffing inside it, a strange mechanical noise that almost reminded me of the creaking onboard a sailing ship. I took everything off one of the shelves and felt around for a latch or a hidden cubby, and I searched for runes along the floors and walls, something to explain how the carriage was larger on the inside. I never found anything. The carriage hid its secrets well.

I slept during the afternoon, waking up again in the middle of the night. Isolfr was no longer stretched out on the pillows. I sat up and twisted around, trying to spot him.

The carriage was empty.

My heartbeat quickened. The ceiling hatch was closed, and the carriage was still rumbling us toward its destination, but Isolfr was *gone*—

I heard the gentle splash of water inside the bathing room.

I stood up and stumbled over to the bathing room door and knocked once. "Isolfr?" I called out. "Are you okay?"

Another splash. "Yes, thank you for asking! The potion worked so quickly—you've got a touch."

Butterflies fluttered around inside my stomach. I thought of Isolfr saying I was a pretty girl and they flapped their wings even harder.

"Well, I'm glad you're up," I said. "I was getting bored without you. It was like being back on the *Penelope*."

Isolfr laughed, and I left him to his bath. Talking to him through the door made me think of him bathing, sitting naked in the water. And thinking about Isolfr naked was a strange thought indeed. Not bad, exactly. Just—strange.

I fixed myself a plate of dried sausages and hard cheese and fruit preserved in a sweet honeyed syrup, and sat down against the wall to eat. I was sick of cold food. The hot meals aboard the *Shira* had me spoiled, and at least on board the *Penelope II* we had fresh fish to supplement the powdery, stone-hard biscuits.

Isolfr emerged from the bathing room, the woodsy scent of oakmoss trailing behind him. He was dressed in a dark tunic, his hair turned burnished gold from the water. He didn't move with his usual unsettling grace, but the wobble in his step just made him seem more human.

"Thank you again," he said. "For the potion. I'm not sure—" He waved one hand around vaguely.

"Not sure you'd have been able to mix the sysab and the coral powder together?" I grinned at him. "Yeah, my arm was pretty tired."

Isolfr laughed, then sat down beside me. He didn't say anything as I ate, and he didn't eat anything himself. No need to keep up pretenses with me.

"How much longer till we arrive?" I said.

"A few more days, I think."

I sighed and pressed my head against the wall. "You'd think Lord Trystan could have left us a can and some dice. *Something* to pass the time."

Isolfr smiled a little. "It wasn't Lord Trystan who set up the carriage," he said. "It was Mr. Formenti. I suspect he was unhappy about having to tend to us, so he left out the entertainment."

I rolled my eyes and popped another piece of sausage in my mouth.

The carriage jostled.

I froze, my heart pounding in my ears. *It's just a rut in the road*, I told myself. *We just ran over—*

It jostled again, more violently this time. The walls let out a long, clanging wheeze as the carriage tilted over to one side, then slammed back upright. My meal flew off my plate and scattered among the pillows.

"What's happening?" I said in a panicked rush. "What's—"

The carriage tilted again, dropping down into a sharp angle. The pillows went sliding across the floor. Jars and bottles fell off the shelves. I braced myself against the wall, the plate sliding off my lap and cracking into two pieces.

"Isolfr!" I shouted. "What the hell is happening?"

We tilted farther. I slid against the floor, and I knew that soon the floor was going to be the wall, and the wall was going to be the floor.

"I don't know," Isolfr said. He pressed himself against the floor too, his hands splayed out, the knuckles turning white.

"It's Lord Foxfollow," I said, just as the carriage finally tipped. For a moment I felt as if I was flying. There was a half second of peace.

Then I slammed against the far wall—the floor now. Pain shuddered up through my spine. Isolfr landed beside me, light on his feet like a cat, and crouched down, his eyes wide.

"He shouldn't have found us," he said.

"Well, he did!"

The carriage tilted again, rolling back the other way. The light flickered and went out. This time I tucked my head into my arms and screamed as I tumbled over the pillows and the food jars—strangely unbroken—landing with another sharp shudder of pain on the other side. Isolfr shouted, his words blurring together. My ears rang.

"—Right yourself—"

I blinked, not understanding. Right myself? I sat up hesitantly. The carriage was still again. Isolfr floated in the middle of the room, his hands clenched into fists. He shouted up at the ceiling.

"Right yourself, carriage!" he shouted. "Activate your protection spells!"

I waited to feel something, some trickle of magic, but it never came. Isolfr looked over at me, his face drained of color and full of fear.

"Are you hurt?" he said.

I shook my head even though I wasn't sure if that was true. My body ached all over. When I looked down at my arms, bruises were blossoming under my skin.

"Right yourself!" Isolfr shouted again. Nothing happened. I hunched in the dark, my muscles tensed. The air felt thick and stale.

"Carriage!" Isolfr shouted.

"It's pointless," I said. "The magic's gone."

Isolfr shook his head. "No. No, it can't. We'll never make our way across the empty—"

And then, outside the carriage, there came a whomping roar like the sound of a fire igniting. Isolfr paled and dropped out of his place in the air. When he hit the ground he vanished.

"Isolfr!" I screamed, trying to scramble up to standing, feeling my way along the wall. The air stirred, a cold, sweet-smelling breeze. The north wind. The north wind of my home. Isolfr.

He coalesced a few paces away from me, transparent and fuzzy at the edges and looking absolutely terrified.

"We have to get out of here," he said in a voice like the moan of the wind. "We have to get away."

"What is it?" I was shaking, my heart thundering inside my chest. "Is it him? It's him! Are we going to die?" I paused, horror squeezing the breath out of my lungs. "Am I going to die? How could you turn to wind like that when I don't have that option and *he's* out there and—"

A sweltering wave of heat washed over the carriage, heat like nothing I'd ever felt before. It sucked the air right out of me and left me gasping and sweating and leaning up against the wall.

Isolfr vanished again.

"Damn you!" I shouted into the empty carriage. "Gods and ancestors both! Don't you dare leave me—"

I felt a cool trickle of air against the side of my cheek. It felt like a kiss of respite against the smoldering heat.

"Isolfr," I gasped. "Please—"

Another blast of heat, like the Empire sun itself was enveloping the carriage in its embrace. I screamed. The cold air wrapped around me, cooling the heat in my skin. Smoke crawled along the walls. A fire flickered in one of the corners.

The wind—Isolfr—lifted me up, cradling me, gentle against my bruises, cold enough that I felt relief from the heat wavering in the corner of my vision. We flew over to the side door—it was on the ceiling now. I reached out and flung it open. Light and heat poured in, bright and spangling. It hurt my eyes. Isolfr grew colder, cold enough that my teeth chattered, but I didn't care.

"Wh—what are we going to see—" I began, but he didn't answer, not even in the wind's howling whisper.

Another roar, closer this time.

Isolfr shot straight up into the air, barreling us both toward the pale sky. Wind buffeted against my face, tugging on my skin. I clenched my teeth to choke back my fear. I didn't know it was possible to move so fast.

And then we stopped, suspended in the middle of the air.

"Isolfr?" I whispered.

His voice fluttered in my thoughts. *We must—*

I heard the flapping of wings. Spots of diamond-bright light fell across my eyes.

A dragon.

I craned my head around and saw it, the dark shadow winging toward us. Its blackened scales glowed like embers.

"Isolfr!" I screamed.

He dropped down, taking me with him. For a moment I was sure we were falling, the swell of grass rising up to meet us. Then he lifted me up before we hit, skimming just above the surface. The dragon let out its thunderous, horrifying roar and released a shimmering wave of heat that made Isolfr's cold wind steam. We swooped around in a billowing arc, over the carriage burning to ash beneath us. More dragons crawled among the flames, their diamond scales glittering.

Hanna, Isolfr whispered around me, his voice billowy and soft like the steam. *Hanna, I can't——this heat is too much.*

"Isolfr!" I shouted. We were dropping toward the earth, toward the violet flowers that only a few days ago I had found so beautiful, the dragon flapping behind us, belching heat. I closed my eyes and concentrated on the cool velvety sensation of Isolfr wrapped around me, the assurance of the wind, the reminder of Kjora. My home. My parents and brother. My friends. Everyone I'd ever known, ever loved.

I would never see them again. Isolfr had tried but it wasn't enough against the heat of the dragons. I was going to burn here in the Mists.

I tumbled into the grass. For a moment it was all I could see. Isolfr's cool touch disappeared. I rolled my aching body onto my back and stared up at the pale sky and waited for the dragon to consume me.

It appeared overhead, the long reptile snout with teeth glowing red.

I lay shaking in the grass, too terrified even to scream.

The dragon opened its mouth, and I could see the heat rising up in its throat.

I closed my eyes and said a prayer to the ancestors, begging them to welcome me among their ranks.

But then there was a horrible, piercing cry, a sound like glass shattering. My eyes flew open just in time to see the dragon slamming sideways away from me. The scent of strange, steely magic drifted on the air.

I lay still, too dazed too move. A soft thumping echoed in the distance, hooves against the ground, but I couldn't see anything through the wall of grass.

A shadow passed over me, not a dragon but a creature like a reindeer, long-limbed and sprouting antlers. It leaped over me and went racing in the direction of the dragon. I forced myself to sit up, all my muscles screaming. A man sat on top of the creature, cradling a narrow staff in his arms, the top end streaming ribbons of pale mist. I stared as the man galloped toward the dragon. The dragon crawled to its feet and spread out its wings, blocking the light from the sky. Its throat glowed orange-gold.

The man thrust his staff toward the dragon, and the mist slammed up against the wave of heat. Mist billowed out over the grass. The man held his staff tight, his body leaned forward, one hand tangled in his mount's thick, shaggy mane. The mist grew thicker and crept through the grass. I crawled backward, trying to get away from it. I could smell the magic, that scent like cold metal, but more than that I could *feel* it, interacting with the magic inside of me. It was too close to the magic I had accessed when I had saved Isolfr, and I was afraid of creating another blast that I couldn't control.

Up ahead, the dragon reared up on its hind legs and let out one of those frightening, *whomping* roars we'd heard before the carriage was attacked. I clamped my hands over my ears and curled up in the grass, my head ringing. The man lifted his staff and more mist belched out, gray and shimmery and thick. It wrapped around the dragon, concealing it. The dragon roared again. The man shouted something I couldn't understand. The staff was shaking, rattling back and forth with the force of its magic.

Another shout, and then the mist converged into a towering silvery column. The magic inside of me rioted. I felt like my insides had turned to insects, buzzing and chattering.

Everything went as still as death.

And then the column of mist flattened out, swooping over the ground with such speed that I'd hardly realized what had happened until the cold, damp mass was on me. I screamed and when I did I breathed, sucking the mist into my lungs. It burned the inside of my nose and the back of my throat. I scrambled to my feet, whirling around, dizzy with magic. The landscape had turned gray and hazy with the fog, and the light from the sky was diffuse and pale. I couldn't see much more than shapes in the grass—the shapes of mounted men, of our broken carriage. No dragons.

I lurched forward with my head down, trying not to breath in the mist. Distantly, I heard heroic cheers, and then a strange, unearthly chant in men's voices—it reminded me of the victory chants boys at home would shout together. I stumbled through the grass, trying to get away from the sound of the chanting.

"Isolfr!" I shouted, and my voice bounced around oddly, echoing and distorting. "Isolfr, where are you?"

I was answered with the sound of his name bouncing back to me through the mist. I choked back a sob of fear. He had to be here. Even if he was in the form of wind, so he couldn't be hurt by the dragons, he wouldn't leave me—

I tripped over a patch of loose grass, stumbled, caught myself. The mist swirled around me. For a moment it thinned, revealing a dark, unmoving shape up ahead. Too small to be a dragon.

"Isolfr!" I conjured up my strength and raced forward. It was Isolfr. He lay stretched out in the grass, unmoving, his arms twisted at strange angles.

Not again, I thought. *Not when the carriage has been destroyed—*

And then something gripped me from behind, jerking me back by my arm.

"Oh, no you don't. The lord's gonna wanna talk to you."

The voice was harsh and rough at the edges and male. I screamed and thrashed against his grip, but he only hauled me up closer to him, at which point he wrapped his arm around my waist and pinned me in place. I twisted around to look at him. He was tall and broad-shouldered, with long black hair and looming gray eyes. A scar, pale against his dark skin, ran in a jagged line over one eye.

"No use fighting," he said. "Flynn's got the mist working on you. You'll be calm as a kitten in a few breaths' time."

"No!" I kicked against him, trying to aim my blows between his legs. He laughed and jostled me so that my legs flew out into the empty air.

"Flynn!" he bellowed over his shoulder. "You got that spell changed? This one's gonna be a heap of trouble, I can already tell."

A voice called out through the fog: "Takes time, Quinton."

Quinton grunted. "Wizards," he muttered. "They're always taking their time."

I kept kicking and struggling against him, even though my thoughts were growing hazy. I knew it was from magic: It was *my* magic that was doing it, in fact, bewitching me without my permission. The mist. I'd felt the interaction.

I kicked one last time with all my might, trying to swing my way out of Quinton's grip. He squeezed me tighter. Through the fog, a dark mountain of a man approached Isolfr. He stopped and looked down.

"Got another one!" he shouted, and Quinton laughed, and the voices poured into my head as the magic finally worked its way through my system, dragging me down, down into darkness.

Lord Foxfollow, I thought, *he's found us.*

And then the world vanished into mist.

CHAPTER SEVEN

I woke up in the back of a cart, my wrists bound behind my back. My head throbbed and every time I breathed I felt something move inside my lungs, as if I was struck down with winter sickness. It was nighttime, the sky murky green and starless overhead, the air freezing against my bare face.

Isolfr lay beside me, eyes closed, hands bound.

The cart rattled and jostled. The wheels clacked as if they were striking against stone, not grass and dirt, and so I pushed myself up, trying to see over the side of the cart. But I couldn't see anything in the dim shadows.

I collapsed back down, taking a deep breath. Men's voices drifted up from the front of the cart. I couldn't make out what they were saying, but every now and then they'd erupt into gales of raucous laughter. They sounded like they'd be more at home in a mead hall, slamming their cups together and flirting with the serving girls.

After a few moments passed, I tried to sit up again. My body screamed in protest, but I managed to lurch myself up so that my shoulders were leaning against the side of the cart. I wriggled my hands, trying to get comfortable. The ropes binding me weren't so tight as to be painful, but they weren't loose enough that I'd be able to pull my hands free, either.

I stretched one foot across the cart and nudged Isolfr in the side. I didn't like it when his eyes were closed like that, knowing he didn't have to sleep.

"Isolfr," I hissed, trying to keep my voice low. "Isolfr, are you all right?"

I nudged him again. Up in the front of the cart, one of the men shouted, "And it turned out it was the merchant's daughter!" and they all roared with laughter. I flopped back. Despite the freezing air, my hands were sweaty and hot from being tucked behind my back. I thought maybe if they were slick enough I'd be able to pull free—

No. The rope scraped against my skin, burning it. I gave up and nudged Isolfr again.

This time, his eyes fluttered open.

"You're alive!" I said, more loudly than I intended. Isolfr frowned, then twisted his head up to the sky.

"Where are we?" he said in a low voice.

"I don't know."

Something long and thin slammed down into the cart with a thud—the handle of an axe. "Quiet back there!" roared one of the voices, and I glanced up at its owner, a hard-looking man with thick brown hair. He scowled at me.

"We just want to know where you're taking us," I said, drawing my chest up. Isolfr cowered in his place in the corner.

"Where the hell do you think we're taking you to? The lord's manor." The man jutted his thumb over his shoulder. "You were trespassing on his lands. The two of you are worth a sweeter price than those dragon carcasses."

With that, he disappeared from my view. I couldn't move. *Worth a sweet price. The lord's manor.* I looked over at Isolfr, who was still staring at me with that fearful expression of his.

"He's found us," I said. "Lord Fox—"

"I told you two to be quiet!" The same voice from the front. Isolfr recoiled and then fixed his gaze back on me.

"We don't know for certain," he said.

I kicked out at Isolfr in frustration, although I had no intention of actually hitting him. "Your friend sold us out!"

"Never." Isolfr shook his head. "He hates Lord Foxfollow more than I do. More than anyone in our world, I'd wager, and he would never have sent our carriage through his lands."

"So where are we going?" I hunched forward, hoping the constant rattle of the cart would mask our discussion. The men up front hadn't seemed to notice again. "Would your Lord Trystan truss us up like this?"

Isolfr glared at me. "If he took us on an out-of-the-way route, we might have passed through another lord's lands before we could arrive at Trystan's. That's likely where they're taking us. Calixto, I think, is the lord's name."

"Is that going to be a problem?" My heart fluttered hard against the inside of my chest, and my breakfast from earlier roiled in my stomach.

Isolfr looked away from me. "I don't know."

I sighed and leaned back, dropping my head against the side of the cart. I hated that starless sky. It was like looking straight into infinity.

"Are you hurt?" I was changing the subject because if we were riding to our deaths, I'd rather not think about it.

Isolfr shrugged. "I guess that's one way of putting it." He shifted against his ropes. "The magic they used to immobilize the dragons—it had the same effect as when you—" His voice trailed away, and I looked down at the floor of the cart, at the scatter of dried grass and dirt, and felt sick. We didn't have the carriage and its shelves of ingredients to patch him up this time.

"They didn't strike me directly," Isolfr went on. "So I could recover on my own in time—"

"But you won't be able to make a daring rescue," I said. "I get it." I gave him a half grin. "Guess it'll be up to me, then."

Isolfr didn't return my smile.

"Do you want me to help you sit up?" I asked.

"No," he said. "I don't have the strength. Lying here—is better."

I didn't have anything to say to that. The cart rattled along, our captors' voices rising and falling. Isolfr and I didn't speak much, although I watched him, ready to nudge him again if his eyes closed.

They didn't.

And together we rode in that cart toward an unknown fate.

We rode for a long time. We stopped twice, and both times the burly brown-haired man from earlier led Isolfr and me out to the fields to relieve ourselves. "Don't want you soiling our cart," he said. They never gave us any food or water, though, and as soon as I had finished—since Isolfr apparently had no need for that sort of thing, a fact he disguised as best he could from our captor—the man would drag us back up to the cart and we'd be on our way.

I watched the sky change, something I'd never seen in its entirety in my time in the Mists. It wasn't like watching a sunrise— there was no ball of light creeping up over the horizon. Rather, it was as if the color simply drained out of the sky. The dark green went away and was replaced by the paler shade of daytime.

My stomach was empty, my throat dry and scratchy. In the daylight it was easier to the see the stretches of grasslands surrounding us. The landscape never changed.

And then, without warning, the cart rattled to a stop.

I assumed the brown-haired man was going to take us out to the fields again, even though I didn't need to do anything. Instead, I heard the sound of hooves clopping against stone. Isolfr stirred, lifting his head. His skin was growing paler, coming close to translucent. He slumped back down and let out a sigh.

"How much longer can you make it?" I whispered to him. "I thought you just needed to rest—"

"So did I," he slurred.

I sat up as best I could with my hands tied behind my back. My limbs were stiff and sore, and it was hard to even get up on my knees—but I managed. I peered over the top of the cart. Our captors had climbed down and were waiting on the road for a rider ambling toward us on a shaggy, thick-furred horse. He wore a long cape of luxurious blood-colored fabric that fluttered and snapped out behind him.

"Name your business," the rider shouted in a rich, sonorous voice.

"Dragon hunters, sir." It was the black-haired man who spoke, the one who had dragged me across the field. Quinton. "Killed three adults. Come for our reward."

"Evidence?" The rider drew closer and pulled his horse to a halt a few paces away from the men. He peered down at them, his face fixed into a disapproving frown.

"Three diamond scales. Turned the rest back into mist." Quinton reached into his coat and pulled out a packet of burlap, which he unfolded there on the road. The diamond scales burned like fire in his hand.

"Very well. We'll see about your reward." The rider sniffed. Then he jerked his head up, and his eyes latched onto the cart.

They latched onto me.

I dove back down and tried to make myself as small as possible. Isolfr frowned at me, and he looked like he wanted to say something. But before he could speak, the rider's voice drifted over on the wind.

"And what else do you have with you today?"

A pause. I sat very still, holding my breath so I didn't miss any of Quinton's answer.

"That's between us and the lord," he answered.

"I'm afraid it's between you and me right now," the rider said. "Who do you have in your cart?"

Footsteps clattered against the road. I trembled in the cart, trying for the first time since daybreak to work my binds free. Isolfr lifted his head, his face twisted up in exertion.

"Don't do it," I hissed at him. "If you destroy yourself, then you can't help me anymore."

"I'm trying to help you no—"

"And what do we have here?"

The rider's voice was right behind my head. I froze.

"Well?" More hoofsteps. "Explain yourself, Quinton."

The rider stopped at the back of the cart. He peered in and looked from me to Isolfr and back again. I thought of Lord Fox-follow, how he'd looked when I met him in the in-between world. Handsome and slippery like you'd never be able to put a finger on him. This rider reminded me of him, with his sharp gray eyes and his slicked-back hair.

The rider's brow furrowed. "Well?" he barked.

"Found 'em with the dragons, sir." Quinton's voice boomed out into the still air. "Thought they might be spies."

"Spies?" The rider looked down at Quinton, then gestured back at the cart. "You think they're spies? They're from the Sun Realm! Did you not notice their eyes?"

"Exactly," the black-haired man said. "We thought the lord would be interested—"

"I dare say he'd be interested." The rider drew up his shoulders and lifted his chin. "Tell me, what was their mode of transportation?"

Isolfr perked up at that, and he managed to swing himself up to sitting. I still didn't dare move.

"Was it a carriage, perhaps? Enchanted? Of his lordship's design?"

Isolfr broke into a big grin.

"Well, it's hard to say, sir, it'd been destroyed by the dragons—it was burning when we got there—"

"Oh, bollocks," the rider said. "You've kidnapped his lordship's guests! Bring them out of the cart and untie them immediately."

For a moment I didn't understand what the rider had said. I was so petrified that I could only expect the worst. But Isolfr leaned forward and shouted, "Are you an aide of Lord Trystan, sir?"

The rider glanced over at him. "I am indeed. And you are in his hallowed lands as we speak." The rider turned back to the dragon hunters. "Why haven't you untied them yet?"

The back of the cart slammed open. The browned-haired man stood on the other side, his arms crossed over his chest. Behind him Quinton was glaring at the rider, who didn't seem to notice. Or care.

"Well, come down with you then," the brown-haired man said. "You heard his honor. We're to cut you free."

Finally, belatedly, the relief rushed through me. I let out a long breath as Isolfr scooted forward over the straw.

"Stop dawdling!" the rider shouted. "Get in there and free them."

The brown-haired man glowered, but he jumped up into the back of the cart in one easy motion—surprising, given his bulk. He pulled out a knife and brought it down behind Isolfr's back. The ropes fell to the cart, and Isolfr swung his arms forward and wriggled his fingers.

"Thank you," Isolfr said.

The brown-haired man ignored him. He turned to me and said, "Come along then, you heard his honor."

My relief made it hard to move. I was trying not to laugh and trying not to cry at the same time. I turned around as best I could, and the brown-haired man must have grown impatient because he hauled me up to my feet and sliced through my ropes. Immediately I shook my arms out, relishing the stinging tingle as feeling rushed back into them. Shakily, I made it to my feet. Isolfr was already on the ground, hunched over a little, standing beside the rider's horse. The rider watched me with his glittering gray eyes.

"I'll take you up to the manor," he said in that aristocrat's voice. "Separate from these overzealous fools. I *am* sorry to see that you were so badly mistreated, and I'm sure Lord Trystan will be sorry as well."

I crawled out of the back of the cart. The road was made of dark polished glass. It felt strange beneath my feet, slippery like ice.

"Take your dragon scales to the usual place," the rider said to the dragon hunters. Then, to Isolfr and me, "Come along."

His horse trotted off. I glanced over at Isolfr, feeling dazed and uncertain. "Are you sure this is a good idea?" I whispered to him.

He smiled at me, despite his pale skin and shaky countenance. "Yes," he said, "I think it is."

I took a deep breath. The rider glanced over his shoulder at us. "Don't delay!" he said. "Lord Trystan is waiting for you."

Isolfr made his way down the road. I took a deep breath and followed him, keeping my head down as I walked past the dragon hunters. They didn't say anything to me.

I looked back up as soon as I was clear of the cart—and gasped. A manor rose out of the sweeping grass, its windows glittering in the sun. I'd never seen anything like it in my entire life, not even in the capital, where the wealthy of Kjora made their homes. Even when I'd attended a dance with Bryn, it had not been held in a place like this, with turrets and towers.

I stopped in the middle of the road and gaped for a moment. Isolfr and the rider continued on their way, and I stumbled after them to catch up.

"That's where Trystan lives?" I murmured to Isolfr. I didn't like the idea of the rider listening in on our conversation.

"Yes," Isolfr said. "It's a nice home, don't you think?"

"Nice?" I squeaked. "It's a palace!"

Isolfr laughed. "That's not a palace. It's not grand enough."

I smacked him on the arm. "I've never seen anything grander. This looks like the palace at Jokja, the one Mama told me about in her stories."

Isolfr grinned. "Well, we better make sure we never take you to Jandanvari Palace, then," he said. "Because you might completely pass out in wonder."

"Stop making fun of me." I scowled at him. He made a face back at me, then laughed. He was still as weak as before, but our approach to the palace—I was going to keep thinking of it as a palace, no matter what Isolfr said—seemed to have brightened his mood.

We didn't have to walk long before we reached the outer gate. It was carved out of black stone, statues of dragons perched on the top, their tails and wings swirling around in strange, elaborate designs. The palace rose up behind the gate, throwing off light like the dragon's diamond scales.

I shivered. I didn't like that this Lord Trystan seemed so fond of the creatures that had nearly eaten us.

The rider trotted his horse right up to the gate and whispered words in a language I didn't understand. They swirled around me like mist and fog, sparking with the magic inside of my system.

The doors slid open.

"In you go," the rider said. He turned his horse around so that he faced away from the palace.

"You aren't coming with us?" I asked, peering up at him. "How will we know where to go?"

The rider flattened out the line of his mouth. "I'm not allowed past the gates," he said. "Go to the front door, ring the bell, and tell Master Illsey that you're here to see Lord Trystan. He'll recognize your faces."

Before I could ask any more questions, the rider clopped away, back down the shining black road.

"Why can't he go past the gates?" I asked Isolfr. "What's going to happen to us in there?" I peered inside, but inside didn't look much different from outside. Just the road, more grass. And the manor, looming overhead.

"It must be a Mists tradition," he said.

I glared at him. "We don't know that. It could be dangerous—" I pressed close to him and lowered my voice. "We still don't know if we're even *in* Lord Trystan's lands, you know. The rider could have been lying."

Isolfr looked over at me. He looked even more drained than he had been earlier. His eyes were like two dull stones, and I could already start see the path of veins beneath his skin.

"I need aid," he said. "We have to take this risk."

"You never want to take risks!"

"But we don't have a choice." Isolfr's voice wavered. "With Frida and Kolur—we had a choice. Now—" He turned toward the gate. "Besides, I don't think this is how Foxfollow would trick us. He wouldn't trick us at all." A pause. "He'd just attack."

And then Isolfr stepped through the gate, crossing over to the other side.

Nothing happened to him. He turned around and blinked at

me. The air stirred, a wind that didn't prickle the magic inside of me like any wind I felt at home.

"It's fine," he said.

I gathered up my strength. Then I walked forward, closing my eyes as I passed under the gate. I stopped. Opened them. I was inside.

At first, nothing happened.

Then there was a screeching clang and a wheezing like the sound I heard inside the walls of our carriage, and the gate slammed shut behind us.

I jumped. Inside the enclosure, everything was quiet. There was no chatter of voices, no laughter or singing or shouting. Nothing.

The place seemed abandoned.

"Let's go," Isolfr said. "I'm not sure I can stand much longer."

That was enough to drive me forward. I didn't want to see him collapse in the grass, knowing I didn't have the ingredients to save him.

We walked down the road, our shoes clicking against the smoky glass. Slowly, the grass gave way to a garden overgrown with strange glowing flowers that let out little puffs of white mist. They turned on their stalks to follow us as we walked past. I wrapped my arms around my chest and concentrated on my magic, on keeping it safe from those sinister flowers.

Eventually, the road ended at a set of stairs leading up to a pair of elaborately carved black stone doors. A frayed silk rope hung down beside the door, puddling on the stairs. Isolfr climbed up the stairs and gave it a hard tug.

Deep inside the manor, bells rang.

"Get up here!" he called out to me. I hesitated, frowning at the stone doors. Isolfr beckoned me. "You need to be up here—" But he was interrupted by a loud scraping creak. He whirled around to face the door, drawing himself up straight. I swallowed my fear and bounded up the steps, arriving at the top just as a thin little man appeared in the doorway. Master Illsey, I assumed.

"May I help you?" he asked.

"My name is Isolfr Witherjoy," Isolfr said, bowing at the waist. "This is my traveling companion, Hanna Euli."

I fumbled with my skirts and sank into a wobbling curtsy.

"We're here to meet with Lord Trystan."

Master Illsey sniffed like he didn't approve, but he said, "Ah yes. He said you would be arriving soon. Come in, please."

He stepped out of the doorway. Isolfr and I exchanged glances. I still couldn't shake the feeling that we were walking not into Trystan's manor, but into a trap set by Lord Foxfollow.

Isolfr slid into the gloomy darkness. Master Illsey stared at me from the doorway, his gray eyes thick and heavy.

I took a deep breath, and I crept inside behind Isolfr.

It took a moment for my eyes to adjust to the dim light of the foyer. A chandelier hung from the ceiling, although it wasn't lit, and a statue of a dragon lurked up against the wall. I noticed that it was coated in a layer of dust.

"This way," Master Illsey said, breezing past me. He smelled of cold winter air, of mist. I shivered. At least the house itself didn't smell of mists, but of cloves and oranges, a bright spicy scent that tickled at my nose.

Master Illsey's footsteps echoed in the cavernous hallways. Isolfr and I followed without speaking. We threaded deep into the house, turning left and right and left again until I was certain that I'd never find my way out on my own. Everything was covered in dust, as if this Lord Trystan couldn't be bothered with housekeeping.

Isolfr shuffled beside me. The burst of energy when he greeted

Master Illsey seemed to have drained the rest out of him; I was afraid he would pass out before we made it to Trystan.

And I prayed to the ancestors that we really were going to see Trystan.

Eventually, Master Illsey stopped in front of a shut door. He turned around to us and his eyes gleamed silver, like twin moons at night. I jumped, unsure what light they were reflecting—there wasn't any in this hallway.

"You may wait in here," he said. "Lord Trystan will see you shortly. Feel free to tell the housekeeper if there's anything she can fetch for you."

He shoved the door open. Light poured out into the hallway, and I threw up my arm without thinking. My eyes stung.

"In you go," Master Illsey said, sounding annoyed.

I stumbled into the room. It was larger than my entire house back home, and windows stretched all the way across one side, amplifying the daytime light from outside. A trio of chairs was set up in the center of the room, angled around a small round table. Everything was elegant but, at the same time, shabby, as if it were also very old.

Isolfr immediately shuffled up to one of the chairs and sank down in it, head lolling back. I slid into the seat beside him.

"Are you all right?" I whispered.

"I'm fine," he said, even as he shook his head. "I just—I need some more of the spell we cast earlier, the potion. I'm sure Trystan will have so—"

The doors clanged open, and I jumped, my heart pounding. A woman bustled in. She wore flowing violet robes and she carried a silver tray containing a long, thin bottle and a pair of glasses.

"Would you care for a glass of brandydown wine?" she asked in a smooth, liquidy voice.

I stared at her, blinking. I'd never heard of brandydown wine—the fishermen aboard the *Shira* hadn't served it to us. But the woman didn't wait for an answer. With one free hand she poured our drinks. The wine was pale and silvery, little bubbles crawling up the sides of the glass. She handed one to me and one to Isolfr and then she swept out of the room.

"What is it?" I asked, staring down into my drink. It fizzed and popped.

"I'm not sure," Isolfr said. He set his glass on the table. "I shouldn't drink it, not in my condition. I don't know what effect it'll have."

"Well then, I'm not drinking it either." I slid the drink away from and crossed my arms over my chest. "We still don't even know for certain if we're in Lord Trystan's manor."

Isolfr pitched forward in his chair. I dove forward and caught him before he could fall to the floor. He leaned up against me and took a deep breath. His skin was freezing, so cold it almost hurt for me to touch him.

"I'm all right," he said, straightening up. "It was just a—point of weakness."

I didn't like this. We needed to find him a cure soon.

The doors opened again, revealing a man.

It was not Lord Foxfollow, and relief slammed into me like an ocean wave. This man was much younger, with pale brown hair that curled around his ears. He wore a dark blue suit cut long and lean through the legs, with a jacket that nipped in at the waist.

"Isolfr!" he cried, throwing up his hands. "It is you!"

Isolfr peered at him, trembling in his seat. "Trystan," he whispered.

Trystan frowned. "What's wrong?" he asked, and then he darted over to Isolfr's side, kneeling beside his chair. "What's happened to you? I heard that you were mistreated by the dragon slayers—"

Isolfr shook his head. "I've exhausted my magic," he said, his voice scratchy, "from trying to flee the dragons."

"I mixed a potion for him the last time this happened," I said. "I don't know what it's called, but he needs it."

Both Isolfr and Trystan looked over at me. I was struck by the concern on Trystan's handsome face, the depth of worry in his looming gray mist-man's eyes. Then he broke into a charming smile.

"And who's this?" he asked. "Your companion?"

"Hanna Euli," Isolfr coughed out.

"Ahh, the lovely Hanna." Trystan leaped to his feet and bowed deeply. He lifted my hand from my lap and said, "It's a pleasure to meet you," and then brushed his lips against my knuckles. I gaped at him.

"I don't mean to be rude," I said hesitantly. "And it's lovely to meet you, but Isolfr needs—"

"Yes, yes, I know." Trystan beamed at me with one of his bright smiles. "The house knew what Isolfr needed the minute he passed through the door. The potion should be here shortly." He patted Isolfr on the shoulder and then sat down in the third chair, drawing one leg over his knee. He leaned back, and his movements were easy, practiced. They reminded me of the way wealthy sons danced at cotillions in the capital. As if they've spent their entire life learning how to move.

"So how did you enjoy your trip?" Trystan said. "Before the dragon slayers interfered. I *am* dreadfully sorry about that, of course, but we were trying to keep your identities secret and the carriage was enchanted so that anyone who stumbled across you would think you mere farmers. Unfortunately," here Trystan heaved a weary sigh, "the dragons burned the spell, and so the slayers saw

you as a bandits and thieves instead. A threat to the lands of Llambric, you see. My subjects are very loyal, even if we are all, technically, in Foxfollow's service."

Trystan's eyes glittered. For a moment the breezy nobleman
had vanished, replaced by something darker and angrier.

Beside me, Isolfr chuckled—a hollow, rattling sound. "You
could have at least warned us."

"I didn't think it necessary." Trystan threw his hands in the air.
"Oh, you are looking poorly, Isolfr. That potion should be here any
mom—"

A chime sounded deep in the walls of the house. Trystan leaped
to his feet, tugged down his coat, and bounded over to a painting of
a rather dour-looking man with thick gray eyes. I hardly had time
to question what the hell he thought he was doing when he plunged
one hand into the painting. His arm disappeared up to his shoulder.
He rolled his eyes up, concentrating, and then pulled out a little
round apothecary's bottle.

"Here you are!" he said. "Freshly prepared by my own personal
spell master."

He handed the bottle to Isolfr, who pried out the stopper and
gulped down the contents. He drained the bottle completely, and
when he finished, he looked up, saw us staring at him, and shrank
back a little.

"Thank you," he said softly. Then, straightening his spine, "Oh.
Thank you a great deal. I can already feel my magic reforming."

"My spell master is the best in the Mists." Trystan settled back
in his chair. "And I'd hate to have my dear friend from the Sun
Realms die in my gathering room! That would be awkward."

Isolfr smiled. "Yes. Very much so."

"I see you haven't tried your brandydown wine," Trystan said,
gesturing down at the glasses. "There's nothing to worry about it,

you know. You're perfectly safe from the machinations of Foxfollow as long as you're in this house."

I picked up my glass of brandydown wine and looked down at its contents, still bubbling and fizzing.

"I guarantee," said Trystan, his eyes gleaming, "that a daughter of the Sun Realms has never tasted anything like it."

Isolfr reached over and picked up his own glass of brandydown wine and took a small sip. His eyes immediately lit up. "Oh," he said. "It's delicious."

"See?" Trystan grinned. "And it has healing properties as well. That's why I wanted you to try it. I'm sure you've had a terrible time in that cart with those dragon slayers." He shook his head, curly hair falling into his eyes. "Brutes! I *am* so sorry about all that."

Isolfr was still sipping from his drink and nothing had happened to him—but then, he was a spirit, so it would be harder to harm him. On the other hand, he was weak from overtaxing his magic, and I could feel the dull sting in my wrists from where the rope had bound me, and my muscles ached and twinged whenever I moved. I could certainly go for wine with healing properties right now.

I picked up my glass and drank.

Isolfr was right; it *was* delicious, fresh and bright like the citrus fruit I'd once eaten in the capital. It was as sweet as honey and tickled my nose when I swallowed. Immediately, the ache lessened in my muscles.

"Thank you," I said to Trystan. "It's very good."

"I told you." He smiled. "We aren't all monsters here, you know."

My cheeks burned.

"It's just that the monsters are the only ones who go through the boundaries." He scowled. "And I assure you, those monsters are as much monsters here as they are in the Sun Realms."

"Actually," Isolfr said, setting his empty glass on the table, "one of those monsters is why we're here—"

Trystan jerked up his head. "What?" he said. "No." His expression darkened and his eyes loomed, making me dizzy. "No, he *wouldn't*. Not again. Not after what happened the last time—"

"Yes," Isolfr said quietly. "He found another way through. A—permanent way, although it hasn't become permanent yet. I've been tasked to stop him, but—" He looked down at his hands folded in his lap.

"He brought you here." Trystan gaped at Isolfr. "And you *survived?*"

I hated how they were talking over me—it reminded me of Kolur and Frida when we'd first left Skalir all those weeks ago. "I don't think he realized that he'd done it," I said. "It was a protection spell that counteracted with his magic, and that's what dragged us through."

Trystan finally looked over at me, his gaze piercing. I didn't turn away.

"A protection spell," he muttered. "That would explain why he hasn't found you yet. He may not even know you're here." He grinned at that. "Oh, that is a delight, the idea that two children of the Sun Realms could come through and he doesn't even *know*." Trystan clapped his hands together. "Well, you're under my protection now. You're welcome to live here at the manor. We don't have much, at least not as much as we used to—and you can thank Foxfollow for that, just as you can thank him for all the ills in both our worlds—but I swear you will be safe and well cared for. The dragons don't cross the boundaries."

A weight slammed into the pit of my stomach. Live at his manor? Didn't he understand? Wasn't he supposed to help us home? I looked over at Isolfr for help, but he looked as stricken as I felt.

"Does that not suit you?" Trystan asked, frowning. "I do apologize that I can't offer the luxuries the Llambric household once—"

"It's not that." Isolfr fumbled around with his drink, stuttering a little. "I mean, I've been *tasked* to stop him from coming through to our world. Hanna's helping me. And we can't let that happen."

Trystan stared at Isolfr with a bland expression. It was like he was trying to stop himself from showing his true feelings.

"That's an awfully difficult task," Trystan said.

"I know," Isolfr said. "But it's not impossible. It's been done before."

Ananna. He was talking about Ananna of the *Nadir*, and her lover, Naji. They had stopped the Mists. They had stopped Foxfollow himself, if Isolfr was to believed. She was the entire reason I had agreed to sail north in the first place.

And now this Mists lord was telling me I couldn't.

"He's right," I said. "It has been done before. But we have to be in our world to do it." I had no idea if this was true. "Lord Foxfollow is set to marry the Queen of Jandanvar, which will get him a foothold in our world. That's what we're trying to stop. We can't do it if we're in the Mists."

Trystan settled back into his chair and tapped his fingers on the armrest in a quick, staccato rhythm. Silence fell over the room, apart from his tapping. He looked back and forth between us, considering.

"You don't understand," he finally said. "I'm not keeping you here out of cruelty. I don't want to see you hurt. Either of you." He turned to me and gave a bow. "Even though we've just met, my dear, I couldn't live with myself if I handed you over to Lord Foxfollow."

"But you aren't," I said. Isolfr was shrinking back in his chair, looking defeated. I knew he was worthless right now. "We just ask that you find a way to help us get back to our world." I took a deep breath. Trystan kept staring at me with his gray Mists eyes. "Jandanvar holds the weakest boundaries between the two worlds. What we call Jandanvar, I mean," I added. "I'm not sure what you call—"

"The City Across the Way," Trystan said. "Yes, Jandanvar, I know it."

"That's all we're asking," I said. "To take us there."

Trystan fell silent again. He stopped tapping his fingers. Light poured in through the windows, casting everything in a hazy golden glow. The brandydown wine had worked its way through my system and I felt vivified, as if I could march on Lord Foxfollow's forces myself, with nothing but my magic roiling inside of me.

"Please," Isolfr said, breaking the silence. He pushed forward on his chair, his hands clasped together. "She's right. We just need passage to Jandanvar. We can pass through there. I'm not asking you to march on Lord Foxfollow again—"

Again. I looked over at Trystan, frowning. His face gave nothing away, but he fidgeted with the button of his coat, twisting it around his finger. When he saw me looking, he snatched his hand away.

"I don't like thinking about that," he said, "and you know it."

"Yes," Isolfr bowed his head in apology. "I'm sorry, I shouldn't have brought it up. I was only emphasizing that Lord Foxfollow wouldn't have to know of your involvement."

Trystan stood up and smoothed down his lapels. Isolfr peered up at him. He looked too hopeful; he had none of Trystan's regal countenance, none of his ability to hide his emotions.

"A trip to Jandanvar," Trystan said slowly. "That would be expensive. I'd need the finest carriages, of course, the finest protection spells. A squadron of traveling guards. Not easy to pay for in these times, but I could manage." He walked over to the windows and stared out through the glare of light. I sat still, my heart pounding.

"We have magic," I said. "We can pay with—"

"Oh no, I don't want your magic." Trystan looked over his shoulder at me. "You'll need all of it, my dear, if you hope to defeat Lord Foxfollow." He turned around and stood with his hands on his hips, haloed by the light. "I can afford it. He took my ancestral lands, but he wasn't able to steal away *all* of my wealth." Trystan smiled without humor. He looked back at us.

I held my breath.

"If you do this," Trystan said, "all I ask for in payment is that you defeat Lord Foxfollow. That you kill him."

Isolfr nodded slowly. I could see him trembling against the seat.

"Take my revenge for me," said Trystan. "I can't do it on my own without risking censure from the capital. But if you do it— that will be payment enough."

CHAPTER EIGHT

Isolfr and I stayed the night in Trystan's manor. He gave me a huge room on the third story that looked out over the sweeping fields of purple flowers. The furniture was carved out of the walls and floors and garnished with fluffy pillows and throws of threadbare silk. A set of clean sleeping-clothes lay draped on the bed. And, just like in the carriage, a little room waited for me off to the corner, containing a tub filled with steaming, rose-scented water.

I was too tired, sore, and exhausted to worry about my paranoia anymore. I stripped out of my filthy clothes, crawled into the tub, and sank low beneath the water. The warmth was a welcome balm against the chill in the air and the ache in my muscles. I think I would have fallen asleep right there in the tub if the water hadn't grown cold and prickled my skin with goose bumps.

So I heaved myself out and dressed in the clean clothes and draped myself across the bed. It was like curling up on a cloud. It was like balancing in midair. It reminded me of the way I'd felt when Isolfr-as-the-north-wind buoyed me above the ground. I closed my eyes, remembering. Now that I wasn't in danger from dragons or other Mists monsters, I could focus on just the pleasant part of the memory, the way I'd felt so safe and secure despite the threat of death. I imagined the two of us at a dance in the capital, Isolfr and me spinning together in one of the big ballrooms, our feet barely touching the ground.

I drifted off to sleep with that image in my thoughts, and

although I didn't remember my dreams the next morning, I woke feeling bright and happy and safe.

The walls of my bedroom were lined with windows, and the light of the sky pouring in like water woke me up. I felt refreshed for the first time since I had left home with Kolur, and I rolled over onto my back, stretched, and gazed up at the ceiling, where I found paintings of small gray figures battling swirling, monstrous dragons, lines of red heat radiating out of the dragons' mouths.

I didn't want to get out of bed. I was safe here, and warm, and knew I wouldn't be when we began our journey to the Mists side of Jandanvar. Getting out of bed meant facing the future—meant facing Lord Foxfollow.

But of course I had to face him. I'd promised Isolfr. And I needed to protect my family from the horrors of his monsters.

Still, I let myself lounge in those silk sheets for a few moments longer. When I finally did crawl out of bed, I found a fresh change of clothes draped over the nearby chair. I stopped and stared at it with discomfort. Had someone come in while I was sleeping and laid out those clothes? Had someone watched me? Some person of the Mists?

But in the golden light I couldn't stay nervous for long.

My new day's outfit was a dress, cut simply and dyed a dull shade of brownish-blue, with a second layer of thick cream-colored fabric that was as warm as wool but not nearly as itchy. I pulled on the dress and did up the buttons running along the side. It wasn't much to look at it, but it was comfortable. And warm.

A pair of boots and stockings sat beside the chair, and I pulled those on too, and ran my fingers through my hair a few times to get out the tangles.

I supposed I had nowhere to go but downstairs.

The hallway was empty but bright, light streaming in through windows set into the ceiling. I followed the path from last night: down the hallway and then down two flights of immense stone stairs that ended in an enormous circular room filled with statues. At that point my memory failed me. There were six doors set into the walls, and I couldn't remember which one we'd come through.

I stood awkwardly in the center of the room, tugging on my dress. It was too heavy for this big room, which was warmed by some mysterious magic I couldn't see or sense. There certainly wasn't a fire burning anywhere close by. I peered up at the paintings, which were all portraits of men and women with dour expressions and gray eyes. I assumed they were the previous lords and ladies of Llambric, and I thought I saw strains of resemblance between them and Trystan.

One of the doors on the far side of the room clanked open. A man appeared—a guard, his staff burning pale blue.

"Miss Hanna," he said, "I see you're lost. Please, come with me."

He glowered at me from across the room. I wiped my palms against my dress, hesitating. The guard thumped the floor with his staff.

"Lord Trystan and Master Witherjoy are waiting for you," he said.

I let out a breath of relief. "Thank you," I said.

The guard didn't respond.

I threaded my way through the statues, all those big silver generals and lords and screeching dragons. The guard watched me as I approached. When I was at his side, he turned sharply on his heel and led me through the door.

It wasn't the same way we'd come last night. The hallway was narrower and darker, without any of the tapestries we'd passed before. But it felt quicker, and soon the guard was ushering me into the same room where Isolfr and I had met Lord Trystan for the first time.

"Hanna!" Isolfr called out. "Finally! I thought you were going to sleep all morning."

I would never have guessed that only yesterday afternoon Isolfr had looked in danger of dissipating into the Mists. In the light of the room, he seemed to glow, and his incandescent beauty was so dazzling it almost hurt to look at him. I was reminded, suddenly and sharply, that he wasn't human—that no one was human in this manor except for me.

My chest tightened.

Trystan stood up and bowed. "My lady," he said, whipping his hand around in a flourish. "Even in those dull servant's clothes you look lovely. Forgive me for not laying out the finest ballgowns in Llambric, but I thought it would be more prudent for you and Isolfr to dress as my servants."

I blinked at him. For the first time I noticed what Isolfr was wearing—he was so beautiful in the Mists light that he outshone his coat and trousers. But they were the same dull blue-brown color as my dress, the cut simple and plain.

"Are you hungry, Miss Hanna?" Trystan asked. "Breakfast is laid out in the second dining room. Isolfr and I were just discussing the plans for our trip, but we'll be happy to accompany you." He smiled, as handsome as a hero in a song.

"I can wait until you're done," I said, feeling dazed.

Trystan nodded and turned back to Isolfr. "Shall you fill her in or should I?" he asked.

I frowned at that. Of course they were old friends, and Trystan knew this world in a way I didn't. But the two of them making plans without me reminded me of being onboard the *Penelope*.

But then Isolfr said, "I wasn't trying to keep things from you. I promise. We just planned while you were sleeping, and we thought it should be done as soon as possible—"

"It's fine," I said, more curtly than I intended. Isolfr glanced down at his lap, and I softened my voice and said, "I understand. We need to hurry."

"Yes," said Trystan. "Exactly. We want to travel under cover of disguise—you and Isolfr will be my servants as I take a caravan to some of the great houses of the Mists. It's been some time since I've gone visiting, so no one will question it."

"The great houses?" I frowned. "But we need to get to Jandanvar! And you said we needed to hurry."

"We do," Isolfr said.

"And we will," Trystan said.

"But if Trystan simply takes a carriage into Jandanvar, it will look suspicious." Isolfr leaned forward in his seat and looked at me. "He has no reason to go across the border. We've been lucky so far that Lord Foxfollow hasn't found us. But we can't trust that luck to hold for much longer."

"Yes," Trystan said, "that's exactly it. Rest assured that the minute he gets word of two children of the Sun Realms visiting our lands, he'll have his little beasties flying through the mist to find you. But if those beasties only see Lord Trystan visiting the houses of Tattersall and Penverne and Dumvir, he'll think nothing of it, and he certainly won't care that Lord Trystan is winding a trail up to Jandanvar. Because Lord Trystan simply *has* to visit Lady Garrowglass, whom he hasn't seen in *years*. And there will be no question as to why Lord Trystan saw fit to schedule in a side visit to the City Across the Way. It's a tradition, to go over the boundary into the Sun Realms. That I promise you." Trystan bowed his head, his eyes closed and his expression solemn. "You will have to travel as servants, of course, in order to go unnoticed. But you'll be traveling as my personal valets, trainees of Master Sedrick, my current valet. You will not be expected to do anything *too* unsavory, that I promise." Another solemn bow.

Silence fell over the room. I considered the plan. It did make sense in its convoluted way. It was certainly a better course of action than Isolfr's original plan back in our world, which involved swimming alongside the *Penelope* and nagging me into talking to him.

"We'll be taking my best carriage," Trystan continued. "Enchanted with the finest protection spells. It is—if you'll forgive me for being so dramatic—the only way."

I glanced over Isolfr, looking resplendent despite his plain servant's clothes. He smiled bravely at me.

"Won't the noble families ask why you have servants from the, ah, the Sun Realms?" I asked, turned back to Trystan.

"Oh, no need to worry," Trystan said, waving his hand around in the air. "It's a bit of a fad to bring in children of the Sun Realms to serve in the great houses. That's the real genius of this scheme. I assure you that they'll find you a novelty and nothing more."

I was discomfited by that admission, and by how breezily Trystan divulged it. *Bring in children of the Sun Realms.* He meant kidnap, surely.

I thought back on the servants I had seen in his house, scurrying through the hallways on quiet feet. Had they possessed colored eyes, brown and blue and hazel? Or had they all been that oppressive gray?

I couldn't remember.

"Please, Hanna," Isolfr said, leaning over the space between our chairs. "Trystan's right, this is the best plan we have—"

"It's going to delay us getting to Jandanvar," I said. I didn't say, *It's going to delay us getting home.*

"Better delayed than—than stopped completely."

We looked at each other. The light was almost warm on my shoulders, a lemony brightness that seemed at odds with all that I'd learned about the Mists in my childhood—with all the dangers of the Mists we were about to face.

"Well, I think that settles it," said Trystan, clapping his hands together. "A spot of breakfast before we leave, then?"

I wasn't hungry, but I nodded anyway.

The carriage we were to travel to Jandanvar in was, on the outside, the same size and design as the one Isolfr and I had ridden to Trystan's manor. On the inside, however, it was larger than my cottage back home in Kjora, with a labyrinthine hallway and individual rooms, like cabins on a ship. There was a large sitting room, furnished not with pillows but with lush, high-backed chairs, and a small kitchen staffed by a surly looking woman who scowled at us whenever we passed by.

"That's Miss Cordelia," Trystan explained. "One of the greatest cooks in the Mists, but she does have a nasty temper, so stay on her good side. Sedrick can tell you more."

The mysterious Sedrick had not boarded the carriage yet, although I had seen him from afar, helping to order the entourage of servants' carriages that would travel behind us. He was a tall, broad man, with long dark hair pulled back into a neat ponytail at the nape of his neck.

"The extra carriages make the trip more authentic," Trystan explained to me. We were up on the roof of the main carriage, sitting in the riders' seats and watching the proceedings below. "It's customary to bring as many servants as one can afford when one goes visiting." Trystan brushed one hand through his hair. His expression hardened. "That's a large part of the reason I haven't gone traveling in recent years. I didn't want the other great houses to know how close to ruin my family was." His eyes glinted like flints of steely rock. "I'll be glad to see Lord Foxfollow gone.

From this world, from your world. From all worlds."

I didn't know what to say. Isolfr was down below—he claimed the odd light of the Mists did not agree with him—and suddenly I wished I wasn't alone with Trystan. He was depending on me to avenge his family, his *lineage*, and I was a fisherman's apprentice and a fisherman's daughter. For the first time, I wondered, really wondered, how I'd come to be here.

An elegant voice called Trystan's name from down below. Trystan leaned over the hatch. "Yes, Sedrick?" he called out.

"It's time, my lord. The servants' carriages are ready, and if we delay much longer then we won't be out of the dragon lands by nightfall."

"Very well, very well." Trystan glanced over at me. "I suppose it's time."

"The dragon lands?" I said. "But won't they attack during the day? That's when we were attacked—"

"That wasn't the dragon lands," Trystan said. "They travel, the same as we do, and you were attacked by travelers on *my* lands, hence my right to kill them. But if we travel through the little sliver of dragon lands at night, well—" He looked out at the horizon. "It violates certain ancient treaties. Nothing you need to worry about." He gave me a handsome smile and then jumped down the hatch, drifting on the magic already activated inside the carriage. I followed, floating down like a falling leaf. I still wasn't used to it, that drifting, tumbling sensation.

Master Sedrick waited for us in the common room. Isolfr was there too, standing at attention. He'd disguised himself to look more human, just in case, and I found myself missing the real Isolfr. His new face—his Pjetur face—made me feel alone.

Then Isolfr smiled at me, and for a moment I saw a flash of the real him glimmering beneath the surface.

"Very well," Trystan said. "What do you need me to do?"

Master Sedrick flicked his fingers in a gesture too quick and complicated for me to follow. The hatch slid shut overhead, and the walls began to hum.

"Everyone's waiting for your command," he said.

Trystan sighed like a little boy asked to do chores. "Carriage of Llambric," he said in a bored tone, "let us begin our journey."

Master Sedrick gave a satisfied nod, and the humming in the walls turned to steamy wheezing. We rumbled forward.

"No turning back," Trystan murmured. Isolfr looked over at him as if he wanted to say something, to offer some words of condolence, but Master Sedrick made a disapproving cough in the back of his throat.

"You're not to address Lord Trystan when you're acting as his servant," Master Sedrick said. "Wait until he addresses you."

"Oh, leave him be." Trystan scowled. "We're alone in the carriage save for Miss Cordelia, and you know she can keep a secret better than anyone in the manor."

Master Sedrick demurred, tilting his head toward the floor. "That's very much true, my lord. But it's better to develop the habit now, when a mistake won't be an issue. It would be devastating when we are among the great houses."

I gazed at Master Sedrick with a vague sense of surprise. Of course he knew about our little ruse, but I hadn't expected him to be so conniving.

"I suppose you're right," Trystan said. He slapped one hand on Isolfr's back. "This is it, then, my old friend. We'll have to reconnect in Jandanvar."

"It's for the best," Isolfr said.

Trystan nodded. He had a distant air about him, as if our conversation up on the carriage top had taken him someplace else.

"The protection spells are making me feel a bit woozy. Travel always gets to me anyway."

"Why don't you lie down," Master Sedrick said. "I can see to Isolfr and Hanna."

I wondered what that meant, *see to us*. We were supposed to learn how to be servants on the trip, but I wasn't sure I wanted to start my lessons yet. What I really wanted was time to think about what we were going to do once we made it to Jandanvar. I'd been reminded that this entire trip, the carriages and the aid of Master Sedrick, came with a price.

And I didn't know if I was capable of paying it.

"Yes, lying down, that would be lovely." Trystan gave a short nod to me, then to Isolfr. "I suppose I need to get used to treating you as my servants, as well. My endless apologies, both of you."

"It's what we have to do," Isolfr said.

Trystan nodded and then drifted out of the room, carrying his aura of nobility with him.

Master Sedrick cleared his throat.

Isolfr and I both turned toward him and were met with a thin, forced smile. He didn't seem practiced in smiling.

"I have duties to attend to," he said. "Certain documents to arrange in order to pass through the dragon lands. But tomorrow, we will begin discussing your behavior as servants. We'll arrive at the first great house in two days' time. Tattersall Manor, the ancestral home of Lord and Lady Alfara." He looked us up and down, his nose wrinkled. I felt myself diminishing into my clothes. "We'll have to find a way to keep you out of sight until you're ready."

Before either of us could answer, Master Sedrick stalked out of the room.

"Well," I said, after a moment's silence, "that was reassuring."

"He's looking out for us," Isolfr said. "Master Sedrick, he's helping us not get caught."

I sighed and slumped down in one of the nearby chairs. My weight sank into its cushions and I realized I didn't ever want to climb back out again. "Did you ever think that we're in over our heads?" I asked. "That this plan might be too complicated? Why couldn't we just travel in secret, alone?"

"It's too far." Isolfr slid into the chair beside me. He leaned in close enough that I could smell something sweet about him, like flowers coated in ice. "We need to be cautious."

"You always say that, and you're always too cautious." I glared at him. "You refused to tell Frida and Kolur about what you were doing, and dragged everything out instead of just *explaining*—"

"I'm not wrong about this," Isolfr said. "Lord Foxfollow is looking for us. He has to know by now that we're here—that protection spell wouldn't have lasted that long. We'd never be able to travel the distance to Jandanvar without Trystan's aid. And all this," he waved his hand around the cavernous sitting room, "is what Trystan has to do in order to travel without arousing Lord Foxfollow's suspicion."

I slumped down in my chair. I hated everything about this plan, but I knew there was no way to protest it. I wasn't about to travel through the Mists alone.

"We'll be there soon," Isolfr said. "Sooner than we'd like, I imagine."

I looked over at him. His bland human face made it even easier to read his expression. He was afraid.

I was afraid too.

I nodded in agreement.

CHAPTER NINE

We arrived at our first great house two days later.

The journey itself was dull, with only the occasional lessons from Master Sedrick to break up the monotony. Even those were few and far between. He'd sweep in while Isolfr and I were lounging in our quarters, dispense a bit of nonsensical advice—*Always keep your gaze downturned, never look anyone in the eye, never speak unless spoken to, try and stay out of eyesight unless called upon*—on and on. I'd never known anyone who had proper servants, and I couldn't imagine a world where you ignored most of the people living in your house.

Despite our lack of preparation, it was almost a relief to arrive at the first house, since it meant a break in the routine. It was also a reminder that we were closer to Jandanvar than we'd been two days ago, which was not so much a relief as a sharp twist of anxiety in my chest.

"Do you want to see it?" Trystan swept into my quarters, fluttering around like a butterfly in his long flapping coat. It was a nicer coat than the one he'd been wearing, with sparkling gold buttons at the cuffs. That was how I knew we'd arrived.

"We're here? At Tattersall Manor?"

"That we are. It's quite a grand sight, if you've never seen it before." He gestured for me to join him. "It was always my favorite part of visiting," he added, "seeing the houses for the first time."

I slid out of my bed and followed him out into the hallway. Isolfr was waiting for us, his arms crossed over his chest.

"Come, come," Trystan said, "or we'll miss it and then what'll be the point? I'll have to dine with Lady Alfara and listen to her inane stories for nothing."

I stifled a laugh at that, but Isolfr looked too nervous to be amused.

We all piled into the common room together. Trystan instructed the carriage to float us up to the hatch in his booming spellcaster's voice, and the air swooshed out of me and I drifted upward. Trystan pushed the hatch open and sweet-scented wind billowed inside. I took a deep breath; I hadn't been out in the open since we left, and Master Sedrick had forbidden us from leaving the hatch open as the carriage traveled. Trystan must have dispatched him somehow, so that we could climb onto the roof in peace.

I hung back so Trystan could clamber up first—I was trying to remember my place as his servant. Isolfr glanced over at me.

"I hope this works," he said.

I knew he wasn't talking about going up on the roof. "It was your idea," I said.

"I can't have second doubts?"

"You never have anything but second doubts." I pushed up through the hatch, trying to shove my worry away. The last two days had been nothing but a constant, low-grade anxiety; I wanted for one moment to feel free.

The first thing I noticed when I stuck my head through the hatch was the rush of magic, from the carriage's protection spells and the surrounding air both. The veins of magic were stronger here than they were back in Llambric, strong enough that I could feel the magic vibrating through my bloodstream, that my head spun with the strength of it. And then I was aware of the icy edge on the wind, and a sweet scent like honey and flowers, and the ceaseless brightness of the illuminated sky.

I reeled from the strength of so much stimulation after the dull, dim carriage.

"Look,"Trystan shouted over the wind. "Isn't that something?"

I couldn't see anything, just the glare from the sky, an endless starburst of sourceless white light.

"Amazing," Isolfr breathed, his mouth close to my ear.

I squinted and brought my hand up to shield my eyes. Slowly shapes filtered through the brightness: the curving lines of short, strange trees blossoming with flowers, the pebbly road, and a mountain growing up out of the horizon, asymmetrical and beautiful and ancient and strange.

No, not a mountain. A great house. Tattersall Manor.

"That's where we're going?" I said stupidly.

Trystan glanced over at me and laughed. "Yes. It's something, isn't it?" He leaned back against the carriage's roof and sighed. "The Alfara family grew it, you know. Out of magic and stone." He nodded at the trees lining the road. "Same with those things. They don't grow anywhere else. If you listen closely you can hear them singing."

I stared at the manor and tried to imagine the strength of magic required to grow a house. No wonder I'd been inundated by it when I climbed up here.

"Is it—safe?" Isolfr asked.

Trystan laughed and gently slapped Isolfr on the back. "Of course it's safe, Isolfr. I'm not dragging you into danger. That's the whole reason we're traveling like this, remember?"

Isolfr didn't say anything, just drew into himself, scowling. His cowardice had annoyed me plenty when I was onboard the *Penelope*, but now it seemed practical. I didn't point out that Trystan was dragging us to danger, eventually—he was taking us to Jandanvar.

The three of us rode in silence for a few moments longer, the wind rippling the flowers in the trees, the manor throwing off glints of light up ahead. It glowed like a beacon.

"We should probably go back down and prepare,"Trystan said, sighing. "Well, I'll have to prepare more than you, certainly. Lady Alfara's going to want *all* of the Amkal City gossip and I just am not in a mood to give it to her."

He slipped down through the hatch. I stayed put though, relishing the velvety feel of the magic over my skin. Isolfr stayed at my side.

"Two days closer," I said without thinking.

"Yes," Isolfr said. "That's why I'm afraid."

The inside of the manor was soaked in even more magic than the surrounding estate. It wasn't an unpleasant experience, exactly, and although I was aware of the magic, its sweet heaviness like honey, I never felt in danger. Magic-sickness didn't seem to exist here in the Mists. Either that, or the whole land was born of magic-sickness. I wasn't sure which.

Master Sedrick led Isolfr and me through a series of narrow, dark tunnels—he called them *servants' corridors*—until we came to our room. The tunnels were inclined upward and wound round and round like a mountain path. Every now and then we'd pass an opening in the tunnel that branched off into proper hallways, where the floors shone with dark wood and the walls were draped with living vines, their flowers glowing in the darkness. I could feel that magic crackling over my skin and I was momentarily overtaken by the strange beauty of those hallways and by the power of the magic that had created it.

"Don't dawdle," Master Sedrick said sharply. "Remember, you are not to be seen or heard unless the lords and ladies require it. Come!"

I tore my gaze away from the hallway and glanced over at Isolfr. He was pale in the darkness, his expression fearful. I was touched by a swift wave of pity. Maybe it was the magic of that place, toying with the edges of my mind, but I reached over and grabbed his hand and squeezed. He jumped, looked down at our hands, looked up at me. And then he smiled, but only a little.

I felt warm despite the chill in the tunnels.

"Here we are." Master Sedrick stopped at one of the tunnel openings and turned toward Isolfr and me. I instinctively dropped Isolfr's hand. Master Sedrick sniffed.

"You were given separate quarters," he said icily. "I see that was probably a wise decision on Lord Trystan's part."

My embarrassment hit me like a fever. Isolfr turned bright red.

"Very well." Master Sedrick marched us through the opening. It didn't lead into another tunnel, as I expected, but rather a large, open room, with windows on the ceiling that let in streams of pale sunlight. The room was empty save for a single enormous flower, the blossom shaped like a trumpet, and the walls were lined with doorways.

"Room number six and room number seven," Master Sedrick said. "You may choose which one you'd like. They're identical, but I'm afraid there's only enough space for one person to sleep."

My face burned. I didn't even dare look at Isolfr this time. All I'd done was take his hand to give him some comfort.

"If Lord Trystan needs you for anything, he will have the family contact you through this," here Master Sedrick gestured at the flower, "and you will hear your name called. Come out and speak as if the person were in the room with you. I don't foresee that happening, however, as Lord Trystan is endeavoring to keep you two out of the way."

I studied the flower, fear and curiosity mingling. I'd never seen enchantment like this. I thought about what Trystan had said—that the entire house had been grown out of magic and earth. Was it a sort of earth-magic? Or something entirely new?

"A bell will chime when it's time for your evening meal," he continued. "I will meet you here to show you the location of the servants' kitchens. Until then, please, stay out of the way."

He whirled around and marched back out the way we'd come. Isolfr and I stood alone in that empty room. The hugeness of the space threatened to swallow me whole, and I was still tinged with embarrassment from Master Sedrick's comments. I glanced at Isolfr out of the corner of my eye. He was staring down at his feet.

"I guess we should go to our rooms," I finally said.

He looked over at me. "Yes. Like Master Sedrick said—"

"We just need to stay out of the way."

"Don't want any of the house servants seeing us and talking to us."

"Exactly."

Neither of us moved. I kept thinking about what Master Sedrick had implied, and I wondered what it would be like to share a bed with Isolfr. I'd never done anything like that before; just kissed a boy at one of Bryn's dances, and it was such a quick, fleeting thing it was like a butterfly landing on my shoulder. Charming, but when all was said and done I hardly noticed it.

"I can take room six," Isolfr said.

"All right." I tried to force my thoughts into something more appropriate. It might not even be possible with Isolfr. After all, he was a spirit.

But Isolfr didn't leave. I realized then that I didn't want to be alone, and probably he didn't either.

"You want to come into my room?" I said, and then regretted it, because of the way it sounded in light of those strange, intrusive—but yes, *lovely*—thoughts. "I mean, not like what Master Sedrick—"

"I know," Isolfr said quickly. Too quickly?

"He was just teasing, I think." My words blurred together.

"Yes, I agree." For a moment Isolfr looked like he wanted to say something, and there was a glint of silver in his eyes, his real form peeking through. But then it was gone, and the room was silent, and I said, "Well, let's go on then."

"Yes."

We walked together to room number seven. The door was unlocked, and it swung open into a narrow room, smaller than the sleeping quarters aboard the *Penelope*. There was just enough space for a little bed and a trunk and a place for someone to dress. At least there was a window in the ceiling to let in light.

I pulled the door shut.

"Now what?" I said, and I thought of Isolfr and me lying side by side in the bed, kissing.

For the love of the ancestors, I told myself, *knock it off.*

"I suppose we should just—oh," he said.

"Oh?"

Isolfr pointed at the shelf above the bed. A single candle burned there, but its flame had widened and flattened into a round shining disk.

"What the hell is that?"

"You can't tell?" He smiled at me. "It's the Flames of Natuze. Frida and Kolur are contacting us again."

"Are you sure?" I frowned at the disk of candle flame. A silhouette moved across it, something sharp and spiky—

The outline of the *Penelope II.*

"You're right." I crawled onto the bed. The silhouette faded away and was replaced by patterns of smudges and shadows that slowly coalesced into Frida's features.

"Thank the ancestors!" she said. "We've been trying to contact you, but every time we thought we'd found you, you'd slide right out of view. We were terrified something had happened."

"We were riding in one of Lord Trystan's carriages," I said. "It had about five layers of protection spells on it."

"Lord Trystan?" She frowned, the lines in her face deepening in the flat disk of light, and I realized I'd misspoken, that I'd forgotten Isolfr was supposed to be Pjetur, an ordinary fishboy who wouldn't have any connection to a nobleman in the Mists. "Who's that?"

"A friend," Isolfr said quickly. He squeezed himself beside me on the bed, close enough that our legs brushed together. The solid-ness of his body gave me a shiver. "He's taking us to Jandanvar, but we're traveling under cover of disguise."

"We're servants," I said.

"You have a friend in the Mists?"

"We made one," I said. "After we were picked up by the fisher-men. The ones who were taking care of us when we talked before."

Frida studied us. I made sure not to look at Isolfr.

"Be careful," she said.

"We couldn't very well travel on our own," I said. "Lord Fox-follow's spies are everywhere, and we have no way of hiding from them."

Frida fixed a disapproving gaze on us through the light. Or maybe she was just worried.

"We're safe," Isolfr said. "I assure you. And if anything happens, Hanna has her magic."

I looked over at him, touched by the sincerity in his voice.

"Yes, well, it works differently there—"

"Already seen that," I said.

Frida's image flickered in the disc of light. "We'll be arriving at the shores of Jandanvar in about a day's time. Our contact has promised us the outlaws have a place we can hide ourselves while we decide what to do next. Kolur wants to run rampaging into the palace, but I've told him not to be stupid. Still, perhaps by the time you've arrived, this will all be over."

She didn't sound convinced.

"So far we haven't run into any trouble," she said, "but we've been casting so many protection spells I can't tell if it's because he hasn't found us, or if we just can't see him." She leaned close, her face looming in the circle of light. Her eyes gleamed with a reddish darkness like coal. It was strange seeing her like this, her features carved out of magic. And yet it suited her at the same time.

"I'm not going to be able to hold the spell much longer," she said. "Where are you staying, exactly?" Her image blurred and flickered again. "No, we don't have time for you to explain. But please, take care. We'll be waiting for you in Jandanvar."

She flickered once and then faded away, leaving only the light. And then, after a few heartbeats, that was gone too.

Isolfr and I sat in silence. The room seemed to hum, although I couldn't tell if that was an aftereffect of the magic Frida contacted us with, or if it was just the blood pumping through my ears.

"I'm sorry I told her about Trystan," I said. "I didn't think."

Isolfr looked down at his hands, dirty-blonde hair falling across his eyes. I missed the brilliant luminescent starlight color of his real hair. "It's fine," he said. "You needed to explain where we were." He shrugged, then looked up at me. "It won't matter anyway, once we pass Jandanvar's boundaries. Everything gets mixed together up there. Our world, the Mists. She'll see me for what I am."

I stared at him in shock. "What! Then why keep it a secret?" I studied him, confused. "If they're going to see you eventually?"

"I was delaying the inevitable. Putting it off. I really am rather cowardly, you know. You were right."

"No—" I flushed with embarrassment. In truth, his confession made me find him braver. He had gone to save the Jandanvar queen knowing he would have to reveal himself to Frida and Kolur, the two people who had tried to harm his brother with dark magic. But I didn't know how to tell him, in this moment, that he seemed as far from a coward as I'd ever known him.

"I accept it," he said, and then he slid off the bed. "It's this form. When I'm on the air, I feel braver. But as a corporeal being, I'm so vulnerable."

I was suddenly aware of the limits of my own body: the outline of my skin, the shape of my fingers. I was aware of my body as something constricting, a shell that crowded all the things that made me into an unchanging shape. It was the reality of being human and I'd never thought about it before.

I looked up at Isolfr. He was gazing down at me, but I couldn't read his expression.

"You're not a coward," I finally said. I wasn't sure if he believed me.

We left Tattersall Manor the next day after lunch. The servants' meal consisted of reassembled scraps from the family's formal dinner last night, but even so, the food was more lavish than any I'd had back home: rice with golden fruit and strips of honey-roasted meat, a salad tossed with edible flowers, a fruit pie. Quite a step up from the bland stew we'd had for dinner.

Isolfr and I didn't speak much as we helped Master Sedrick bring Lord Trystan's belongings down from his room. The Lady Alfara had gifted him a large, cumbersome vase, painted with tiny flowers that illuminated themselves like fireflies. Isolfr and I took turns staggering down the servants' tunnels with it, but that was as much excitement as we shared. I was still feeling shy after our conversation last night.

Outside in the courtyard, I was struck again by the

overwhelming rush of magic. Fortunately, Isolfr was carrying the vase, because I stumbled backward when the magic flooded over me, losing, just for a moment, the sense of myself. I'd gotten used to the magic inside the manor, but the outside magic was different—stronger, more wild.

"Are you all right?" Isolfr peered around the side of the vase, his eyes wide.

I leaned up against the stone garden wall. "It's just the magic. I wasn't expecting it to be so strong."

Isolfr looked at me with concern. "Is there something different about it?" He glanced up, as if the blank sky might give him some kind of answer.

"No. Just a bit overwhelming. I'm fine." I pushed away from the wall to prove this was true, which it wasn't. My thoughts were spiraling, taking paths I couldn't follow, and the magic pounding through my veins left me weak and listless.

"Are you sure?" Isolfr asked, just as Master Sedrick's sharp voice cut across the courtyard.

"John and Mary!" he shouted, the bland servants' names we'd decided to use as we traveled north. "Stop dawdling!"

I resisted the urge to glare at him because I could see the Alfara family drifting across the garden. Lady Alfara walked arm in arm with Trystan, her long silken gown flowing like water over the grass, and she leaned in close to his ear and said something to make him laugh.

Isolfr gave me one last worried look and then tottered away, the vase threatening to crush him.

"It won't do for the Alfaras to see Lord Trystan's personal attendants lazing about in the garden," Master Sedrick hissed at me as he passed. "You must make yourself look busy."

"I know." I took a few hesitant steps away from the wall. I was still dizzy, but at least my body was growing accustomed to the magic. I followed Isolfr in case he needed help with the vase. Voices drifted over the garden, the twinkling sound of women's laughter. I glanced over my shoulder even though I knew I shouldn't. Lady Alfara kissed Trystan on the cheek, and he bowed deeply, smiled, murmured something.

I turned back to Isolfr and the vase, and as I did, a shadow passed over the sky.

I stopped, my heart pounding. A dragon? Lady Alfara was still laughing behind me, and the other servants continued to prepare the carriages as if they hadn't seen anything unusual.

I tilted my head back and squinted up into the sky. There was only that unceasing brightness—

And then the shadow flickered past. Not a dragon—too small, and it didn't throw off any diamond glints of light. This looked more like a bird, a falcon or an eagle or some other bird of prey. It swooped once in a low circle and then disappeared into the blaze of the sky.

I stood for another few seconds, watching, until Master Sedrick shouted my servant name from across the grounds. I startled and jogged to catch up with Isolfr, who was struggling to shove the vase into the carriage.

"Did you see that?" I asked, sliding my hands under the vase to help.

"See what?"

We pushed and the vase lurched a few finger widths forward into the carriage.

"A bird. It was swooping around in the sky." As I spoke, I realized how silly I sounded, worrying about a bird as if I'd never seen one before.

But Isolfr frowned and glanced over at me. We shoved the vase again and it slid completely into the carriage.

"A bird?" he said.

"I thought it might be watching us," I said stupidly. "And I don't know for sure that it was a bird. It was flying, and it wasn't a dragon."

"There wouldn't be any dragons here." Isolfr clambered into the carriage and took hold of the vase's rim and dragged it backward. "I have no idea where Master Sedrick expects us to put this."

I gave the vase a shove to help him. "Just get it inside, let him deal with it." I sighed. "It just struck me as strange. The bird, I mean. I haven't really seen any."

"That's because there are no birds here. But there are other flying creatures."

I shivered. "It just felt—wrong." I thought about the blast of magic. Maybe it had helped me see what I wouldn't have otherwise. "We should watch out for it," I said. "Just in case."

"Yes." His eyes glittered in a way that suggested fear, and I thought he might be trying to pretend at bravery somehow, to make up for what he'd said last night. Or to prove what I'd said.

Together, we gave the vase one last heave before settling it up against the wall.

"He ought to have a carriage just for his gifts," Isolfr said, "if this sort of thing is going to keep happening."

I smiled, trying to mask the quaking in my chest. "And I'm sure it will. Did you see Lady Alfara flirting with him?"

Isolfr rolled his eyes. Outside the carriage, Master Sedrick was ordering the other servants to hurry up, that we didn't want to be delayed. But as much as I tried, I couldn't stop thinking about the dark shadow swirling overhead.

CHAPTER TEN

We had four more stops on our way to Jandanvar—the absolute fewest Trystan said he could get away with it. They proceeded much as that first one had, although none of the other houses had the strength of magic of Tattersall Manor. I didn't hear from Frida or Kolur again, although at the third house I stole a candle from the kitchens, tucking it up inside my sleeve, in hopes that I might be able to conjure up the Flames of Natuze myself. Unfortunately, I couldn't get the candle to light—I had no access to fire and I was terrified of my magic spilling out of me without my permission. The last thing I wanted was to burn one of the Mists' great manor houses to the ground. So the candle remained unlit. I returned it to the kitchens the next morning.

For Isolfr and me, each stop was largely the same: we would help unpack, and then Master Sedrick would stow us away in the servants' quarters, and we'd take meals when called. Of course, each house itself was different. One was made of sprawling white stone that gleamed against the bright green grass. Another was built into the trunk and branches of the biggest tree I'd ever seen; the servants' quarters were underground there, with a roof made of tree roots and a floor made of dirt, and we had to crawl up ladders fashioned out of thick, ropy vines to get to the main part of the house. After that, the next house we visited seemed ordinary by comparison, even though it was enormous, its rooms and hallways and gardens bigger than any in Kjora.

It was almost enough to make me forget that we were traveling to Jandanvar to stop Lord Foxfollow. Almost.

I never saw a shadow in the sky again, although this didn't give me any comfort, because I also hadn't been as inundated with magic as I had back at Tattersall Manor. Our journey took us closer and closer to Jandanvar. The landscape was changing like the houses, turning rocky and flat, grasslands giving way to a hard, frozen ground covered in tiny blue flowers. We'd be there soon. I teased myself with fantasies about Frida and Kolur defeating Lord Foxfollow before we arrived, but I knew that wouldn't happen. Isolfr had sought us out because Kolur could help, not because Kolur could defeat Foxfollow on his own. No single human wizard was strong enough. Not against Mists magic.

I distracted myself by talking to Isolfr. I still couldn't get him to tell me any details about his life beyond those I already knew, but he would listen when I talked about my own life in Kjora. I told him about Mama and her adventures as a pirate aboard the *Nadir*. I told him about all the best places to hide from chores in the forest near the village. He listened with a bright intensity, his eyes never leaving me as I spoke. I wondered how he could find my life so interesting, but at the same time, I was grateful for it, even though talking about my family, about Kjora, about the world beyond the Mists—it made me sad. And in a way, sadness was a relief from the fear of fighting Lord Foxfollow.

And then we arrived at Garrowglass Manor.

We arrived in late afternoon. By that point, Isolfr and I knew what was expected of us. The carriage wheezed to a stop and we made our way into the common room to stand at attention along the back wall with Miss Cordelia. Trystan was already there, dressed in a resplendent dark red coat I'd never seen him wear. He gave Isolfr a weary smile. I didn't know what to make of it.

Once we were all assembled, Master Sedrick opened the carriage door. A heavy gray light spilled in, along with the scent of snow. I frowned. As far as I could tell, it was summer here in the Mists.

"Jandanvar," Isolfr whispered beside me.

A rope constricted around my heart. "What?" I said. "Why didn't you tell me earlier?"

"We aren't there yet," he said. "We're on the boundary. I can feel it close by, though." He closed his eyes and took a deep breath. "I can smell home." But when he opened his eyes they sparkled with fear.

I felt sick to my stomach. The gray light seemed to wash out the color of the carriage, and I felt as if we were trapped in a world without life.

"So we've arrived," Trystan said in a grim, hard-edged voice. I risked a glance over at him. He stood with his hands clasped behind his back. His hair was slicked back in a neat little ponytail. He looked as he had at every great house, save for his expression, which cut a line of fear straight through my heart. He was scared too.

"That we have, my lord." Master Sedrick bowed. "I've sent a messenger to alert Lord and Lady Garrowglass that you will be joining them shortly, so they can prepare for the formal entrance."

"Very good." Trystan shook out the lace in his sleeves. We all stood in silence.

And then Trystan broke the careful protocol we'd been following the past several days. He looked straight at Isolfr. "I know you know where we are. Promise me you'll wait before you go barreling across the border. It's almost certain that Lord Foxfollow has guards stationed. We've been hidden by my protection spells for the journey, but I can't make guarantees as to your safety once we're through the boundaries. We'll have to be very careful about taking you across."

I'd known this already—suspected it, at least, but hearing him lay it out in such detail just amplified my fear. Off to my left, Miss Cordelia stared into space with her usual glowering stare, taking everything in and storing it away until she died. Master Sedrick stood by the door. He didn't act any different, but I realized with a jolt he was guarding it.

"What exactly is the plan?" I said. "To get us across. You know that Kolur and Frida are waiting for us."

"I want you across as quickly as possible, too." Trystan's eyes glittered. "I want to see that creature destroyed. I'm just saying we need to be smart." He looked from me to Isolfr. "I'll tell Lady Garrowglass that I wish to take an afternoon stroll through Jandanvar. It's not an uncommon thing, and the Garrowglasses have always loved that they live at the edge of the world. They think it gives them a certain quality that the other great houses lack. I'll insist on bringing my two devoted servants along—that's the two of you—and we'll get across under Garrowglass protection. It will be stronger and safer than any magic I could conjure—I'm not used to dealing with the magic of your world."

I glanced over at Isolfr. He looked pale, but brave at the same time. Determined.

"We'll get you back to the Sun Realms soon enough," Trystan said.

The Sun Realms, I thought. *Home.*

It did not feel like going home.

Garrowglass Manor was ordinary compared to the other houses. I didn't reel back from its magic, and I didn't have to crawl through the branches of a tree to get into my bedroom. It was simply a sprawling stone house surrounded by gray trees. Snow was falling by the time we disembarked from the carriage, a faint dusting that clung to Isolfr's eyelashes. Trystan rode ahead in a horse and carriage provided by the Garrowglass family. The rest of us had to walk through the snow, our breath forming in white puffs on the air.

In many ways, Garrowglass Manor felt more like home than the rest of the Mists. The gardens were filled with scraggly plants that looked as if they could belong to a house in the capital, and when we went inside, the air was damp and cold and lit not by glowing flowers or streaks of magic, but by torches, burning small and steady in intervals along the soot-blackened walls. Maybe the Mists became more like my world when they met at the boundaries, just as my world became more like the Mists.

Isolfr and I were deposited in our quarters—a single room this time, located on the very top floor. It was small and cramped, the two narrow beds crammed up against each other, but there was a window that looked down over the estate. It was covered with a thick pane of glass, and when I crawled onto the bed to look through it, the magic in my veins buzzed: it wasn't ordinary glass. It rattled around inside me, and I thought it might be something that had been transformed through magic-sickness. Sand, perhaps, blasted by wave after wave of enchantment. I hoped it hadn't been something more sinister than that.

"I wish we weren't here," Isolfr said.

I pulled away from the window, my skin tingling. "Don't go close to that window," I said. Then I sat down beside him on the bed. "And where do you wish we were?"

"Anywhere," Isolfr said. "Back onboard the *Shira*. In Tulja." He closed his eyes. "I'm not ready for this yet. Trystan thought we'd go running across the boundary but I'm not sure I even want to cross at all."

He drew his knees up to his chest as if he were trying to make himself as small as possible. His Pjetur disguise flickered, and for a moment I saw the true Isolfr. My heart clenched. I hadn't seen him like that for a long time.

"I don't want to go either," I said. "But we have to do it. You convinced me to come with you, remember? You said we were going to save the world." He'd gone back to his disguise, bland features and dull hair. "I'm not doing this without you. You want to give up, I'm giving up too."

"I don't want to give up." Isolfr sighed. "I just wish it didn't have to be *me*. My siblings—they're all so much braver than I am. But they'd been weakened, their magic broken." He didn't finish the rest of it, and I knew he was probably talking about what Frida and Kolur had done. I felt a surge of warmth for him. He really was brave. He just didn't show it the usual way.

"At least we don't have to cross the border right away," I said. "We can—prepare. Decide what we're going to do."

Isolfr laughed. "We should have been doing that all along, shouldn't we? But I couldn't stand to think about it."

"I couldn't either."

He looked at me, his eyes bright. "Really?"

"Of course. I'm terrified."

He watched me for a few seconds, neither of us speaking. His gaze made my skin burn, but I didn't turn away. I couldn't. It was like an embrace.

"You seem so brave to me," he finally said, and he leaned forward a little, and I didn't pull away.

Something like magic flowed between us. His lips were very close to mine. My head spun, and I thought, *Can spirits even kiss?*

And then we did.

Isolfr jerked his head back. I was so stunned I couldn't move, although I felt the blood rushing inside of me like the ocean.

"I'm sorry," Isolfr said, and he looked down, his hair falling across his eyes. "I'm sorry, but I'm afraid—there's a chance we might die, and—well, I guess I just wanted you to know."

And you say you're not brave.

"It's all right." It took me a moment to find my words. "I rather—I rather liked it."

Isolfr lifted his face and his eyes met mine. That magic arced between us, sparking and bright. It reminded me of the magic of the west wind, in a way, it was so huge and encompassing and bigger than myself. But I knew it wasn't magic I'd ever known before. It was something special.

"I did too," Isolfr said shyly. He smiled. It was not a Pjetur smile, but an Isolfr smile, a spirit's smile, and for a moment the room spun and I tried to grasp onto the idea that this beautiful creature had kissed me, that he had *liked* it.

And then a loud, insistent banging erupted through the room.

Isolfr and I jumped apart.

"Open up!" shouted a harsh, unfamiliar voice.

We both scrambled backward over the bed. More banging. The door wasn't even locked—I could see the latch hanging open.

"What's happening?" I whispered. Isolfr just shook his head in silence.

The door swung open. Two guards charged in with swords drawn. They stopped when they saw us.

"The hell?" one of the guards said. "They're just a couple of kids."

The other one grunted. "He said not to let that fool you."

He said.

I looked over at Isolfr in horror. He was pale and shaking, staring up at the guards. *He said.*

"Who said?" I demanded. "What's going on? We're just servants of Lord Trystan—"

"Lord Trystan has been taken under arrest by order of Lord Garrowglass. As are you. Please come with me."

"Under arrest!" I said. My whole body trembled, but I was not going to let the guards know. I lifted my chin, forced myself to speak. "On what charges?"

"Conspiracy."

Dizziness swept over me. Conspiracy?

"I have permission to use force if you don't comply. Please come along." The guard nodded at Isolfr. "Both of you."

This time, when I looked over at Isolfr, he looked back at me. His eyes shimmered with tears. I knew we shared the same thought.

Lord Foxfollow.

He had found us.

"Don't drag it out," the guard said, sighing. He pointed his sword at me. "Move along."

I didn't know what to do, so I did as he said. I shoved myself forward on the bed until my feet touched the floor. Hesitated. Stood up. The room tilted. The guard grabbed me by my upper arm and dragged me forward.

"You too," said the other one, jabbing his finger in Isolfr's direction. "Orders are for both of you."

Isolfr didn't move. There had to be some kind of magic I could do—I felt for it on the air, for something, anything, that I could convert into power. Energy surged up inside of me.

And then there was a sharp pain in my side. "We were warned about that too," the guard said in a low, scratchy voice. "You try magic, and I'll cut you and feed your blood to the house."

I choked back a scream. Isolfr stared at me with wide, mournful eyes. I looked down at the root of the pain. The guard held a slim, gleaming knife at my waist.

"You wouldn't want that," the guard whispered.

I whimpered, my terror turning to sound. Isolfr stood up. I was trying not to cry but when I looked at him I couldn't help it. We were right on the border of Jandanvar. We had come so close.

I thought of the shadow I'd seen in the sky at Tattersall Manor. And then I thought of home, of my parents, of Henrik, and I knew I would never see them again.

The other guard grabbed Isolfr and jerked him forward. Isolfr's limbs went limp, like an animal playing dead in the presence of a hunter. His head rolled back on his neck.

"This way," my guard said, and he pulled me out into the hallway. The knife was still stuck at my side, a burning pinprick sting. I stumbled over my own feet as the guard led me through the hallways, his boots clomping on the heavy stone floor. I could hear Isolfr and his guard behind us, footsteps and the occasional gasp of fear, but I was too afraid to look back, too afraid that doing so would make the guard spill my blood.

The guards didn't take us through the servants' corridors, but into the main hallways. The ceiling soared above us. There were faces carved into the stone. In the oozing torchlight they roiled around, glaring at me, mocking me. The hallway was empty save for us, and our footsteps bounced against the walls and sounded like the footsteps of an army.

The guards took us to a set of stairs leading down into the earth. "Move," my guard said, shoving me in the back. "Don't try anything."

I couldn't speak. I could barely see through my tears. I didn't understand why the guard thought I would try anything—I had done as he asked, hadn't I? I walked; I didn't turn around to see Isolfr.

The bottom of the stairs was so shrouded in darkness that it was like descending into the deep of the sea. A cold wind blew up, ruffling through my hair and sending ripples over my skin. The guard shoved at me again, and I stumbled down the stairs, aware of the knife in my side. The cold wind blew harder, whistling a low, tuneless sound. I didn't dare reach out for the magic in it; I didn't know what would happen if I did, and besides, I didn't want the guard's knife to dig deeper into my side.

The guard muttered beneath his breath, a stream of syllables that could only be a language. Immediately, fires erupted at the base of the stairs. Torches. They flickered and sent up spirals of black smoke that crept into my lungs and made me cough. The guard pressed the knife harder against my skin.

"Don't try anything," he said.

I coughed again, shaking my head. My footsteps slammed heavy against stone. We were at the bottom of the stairs, in a dungeon, row after row of empty cells.

"Which one?" asked Isolfr's guard.

"Don't matter, as long as they're locked up." My guard heaved a cell open and shoved me inside. I felt at the place where he'd been holding the knife. A few drops of blood smeared over the tips of my fingers.

The door slammed shut. Metal clanged and reverberated around the dungeon. The guard turned a key in the lock, then tossed the keys over to the other guard, who was dragging Isolfr through the murk. He opened a cell across from mine and shoved in Isolfr.

"What's going on?" I said, feeling braver now that the knife was gone from my side. "You can't do this to us—Lord Trystan is *important*—"

The guards turned and marched up the stairs, leaving us in the sooty glow of the torches.

I shrieked in frustration and grabbed my bars and shook them.

They didn't move, although the lock jangled up against them with a hollow, ringing sound. I screeched and pushed away, my heart pounding. Isolfr leaned up against the far wall of his own cell, head turned down, eyes closed like he was lost in thought.

"Do something!" I shouted at him.

He lifted his face. "I can't," he said.

"You're not even human. You can do *something*."

"Not here," he said. "Not in this house. Not in the Mists."

"Fine." I stalked back and forth through my cell, treading over damp green moss and bits of charred wood. "I'll do something."

"Hanna, no—"

I ran back up to the bars and tried to shake them again. "No!" I said. "No! How can you say that? At least let me *try*."

"No!" Isolfr darted forward until his hands were wrapped around the bars too. "There are protection spells woven in here— Mists ones. You might not have sensed them. They'll only make your spell backfire. Please, Hanna, it's not worth it."

Protection spells? I tightened my grip on the bars and closed my eyes and concentrated, feeling for waves of magic. At first I felt nothing, only the cold unfamiliar wind, the underground dampness. And then, something whispered at the edge of my perception. A strain of magic. I'd felt it before. When Lord Foxfollow sent his monsters after the *Annika*.

I gasped and dropped my hold on the bars. Isolfr looked at me mournfully. I knew then he'd seen the horror on my face. The recognition.

"I know," he said. "Everything's lost."

CHAPTER ELEVEN

Time passed. I didn't know how much. There was no sense of time in the dungeon, only the slow, wet drip of stone. Time spread out over thousands of years. It was no good to me.

Only Isolfr and I were locked up. There was no sign of Trystan, even though the guard had said he'd been arrested too. But the guard could have been lying.

Trystan could have been lying.

Isolfr and I did not speak. There was nothing to say. He curled up in the corner of his cell, head tucked over his knees, and I paced, trying to decide what to do next. Every now and then I would feel for the magic, to see if the trace of Lord Foxfollow and his vicious magic had vanished. It hadn't. He had finally found us.

Eventually, other guards appeared. They brought water and food with them, bowls of beef broth and stale bread, which they slid through the bars in the cell door. They didn't say anything to us. They wore the same Garrowglass colors as the guards who'd brought us down here and who had watched us walk past on our way to the manor grounds on the day of our arrival. Which had been today? This morning? It seemed a thousand years ago.

One of the guards sat down in a stone chair in the corner and the other one clanged his way back up the stairs. Isolfr was curled up in a ball in the corner of his cell, tucked into himself like a cat. I imagined he wanted to appear as if he were sleeping. The guard didn't seem to notice, however, or care. I dragged my broth and bread and water jar close to where I sat on the floor. Sniffed it. I didn't smell anything.

"Excuse me," I called out. "Excuse me, Master—"

"Ain't no master," the guard said, running a cloth over the blade of a narrow knife like the one that had been held to my side. "And my name's of no interest to you anyway."

He sounded bored. I took that as a sign, along with the colors he wore, that he worked for the Garrowglass family directly, and not for Lord Foxfollow. He was not a monster. At least not literally.

"Is this food poisoned?" I said.

The guard stopped polishing his knife and looked up at me. For a moment we just stared at each other.

Then he roared with laughter and picked up his rag and took to polishing his knife again.

"And if it was," he said, "would I tell you?"

My cheeks burned. I looked down at the soup. My stomach felt tight and empty, and my throat was dry. I wanted to eat it. I didn't know what it would do to me.

Footsteps echoed down the stairwell. I jerked my head up. The guard didn't look up from his knife polishing. Shadows flowed over the walls.

Trystan.

His hands were bound behind his back, and his hair hung loose from its ponytail. He peered over at Isolfr, still sleeping in his cell, and then over at me. His expression was worn out, exhausted, frightened.

"I'm so sorry," he whispered, his eyes burning through mine.

"Shut up!" the guard shoved him with the butt of his sword. "Don't talk to the other prisoners." Trystan and the guard shuffled out of sight. A few seconds later, the clang of a cell door opening and closing and locking ricocheted around the room. Isolfr jerked up at the sound, wide-eyed. The first place he looked was me. My skin sparked. I pointed off to the side, to where they had taken Trystan.

"Trystan!" Isolfr shouted. The knife-polishing guard looked up from his work and kicked the cell door.

"Keep your mouth shut, boy."

The other guard marched into view. He nodded once at the knife-polishing guard, then disappeared into the stairwell. I slumped down, my hands still on the cell bars. The guard was staying. There was no way to speak with Trystan now.

I settled on the cold floor. The scent of broth was nearby, wrapping around my senses. Isolfr hadn't touched his food; but then, he didn't need to.

I reached over and grabbed the jar of water. Gave it a good sniff. It smelled metallic, like stone and dirt, but not poisonous. I took a hesitant sip.

It was as sweet as fruit nectar.

That was enough for me to forget my fears about poison. I slurped the water down. Then I turned to my food. It sat there, plain and unappetizing. I broke off a hunk of bread and dropped it in the broth.

I needed to eat. I couldn't wallow in the darkness of the dungeon. Trystan was here. He had not betrayed us.

I had to decide what to do.

I woke up with a jolt. At first I had no idea where I was. My body ached all over, and I was still clinging to the fragments of dreams about life on the sea, leaning over the side of a ship as Isolfr bobbed in the water beside me.

But I wasn't onboard the *Penelope*. I wasn't even in the proper world. I was in the Mists, in a dungeon, and I had slept on the cold stone floor.

I rolled up to sitting. The guard's chair was empty, and all but a handful of the torches had burned out. One of the still-burning torches was close to my cell, and so I was bathed in reddish light while Isolfr lurked in shadows, his pale face floating against the darkness.

"Isolfr," I whispered, "can you hear me?"

He answered almost before I had finished my question. "Yes."

"How long have the guards been gone?"

"I can't say. They left a while ago. No one has replaced them."

"And Trystan?"

"He's in his cell. Sleeping."

We stared at each other through our bars. Water dripped. I could hear myself breathing.

"We have to do something," I said.

Isolfr rubbed his forehead, a shadow passing over his face. "We can't use magic to escape. You heard the guard——"

"Maybe it was a bluff." I pressed myself against the bars, as if I could squeeze myself out and undo all our locks. "We can't just *sit* here, though. We have magic! Both of us! There's got to be something we can do."

"I wouldn't risk trying to escape." Isolfr wrapped his arms around his chest. "You don't know what sort of enchantment they have woven through the bars."

"I can feel it," I shot back.

"It's Mists magic. You can't read it."

I knew he was right. The magic had a cold, metallic hum to it, and a haziness that made it hard to grasp on to. Yes, I knew it was there, I could feel it interacting with the magic in my veins, I even knew it had at its source Lord Foxfollow, but I didn't know how to control it. And that's what skill with magic is. Control.

"So we won't try to escape." I drummed my fingers against the bars, listening to the hollow, empty sound they made, and thought. "But we can do something else. Something smaller." I felt for the magic again, wishing I could find the south wind's familiar gusts, but there was only that strange, horrible Mists magic. "Something the prison wouldn't recognize."

An idea struck me then, hard and sharp as an arrow. I jerked my head up and found Isolfr again. He had slunk away from the bars and was leaning up against the wall of his cell, staring down at his feet.

"The Flames of Natuze," I said.

Isolfr tilted his head toward me.

"It's magic from our world, so the prison won't likely recognize it. But it's not an escape spell, either. It's just *talking*, really."

Isolfr glanced over at me. His eyes flashed silver in the torchlight.

"We can tell Kolur and Frida what happened, if nothing else," I said. "And maybe they can even send help. It's worth *trying*, Isolfr. We don't know what's going to happen in the morning." *Foxfollow.* His name was a threat, a weapon poised in the darkness.

Isolfr shuffled back over to the bars. "The Flames of Natuze," he said slowly. "Do you know how to cast the spell?"

I immediately deflated.

"No," I said. "But you do."

Isolfr fidgeted with the hem of his shirt. "We don't have fire, anyway," he said. "We have to have a flame to cast the—"

"But we do have fire!" I pointed at the torch. "I can grab it—get it over to you—" My words faltered. I could probably grab the torch and snake it into my cell, but the gap of space between me and Isolfr was too vast. The fire would go out before it reached him.

"I'll have to cast it," I said.

Isolfr stopped his fidgeting and looked up at me with huge shining eyes.

"You don't know how," he said.

"I realize that! But you can tell me what to do."

Isolfr moved closer to the bars. The thin strips of torch flame fluttered across his features.

"I don't want you to get hurt," he said.

His words struck me the way his kiss had. I blinked, and my cheeks warmed, and for a moment I wasn't stuck in some filthy dungeon, wearing servant's clothes and waiting to die.

But only for a moment.

"I won't," I said. "I promise."

He hesitated. "If you can get the fire, then I'll tell you how to do it." He spoke softly, as soft as a heartbeat. "Take care not to burn yourself."

"I *won't*." He reminded me of Kolur then, always giving me advice I didn't need. I felt a moment of levity at the thought.

I took a deep breath. The torch flickered off on my left, its flame licking against the stone walls. I squeezed myself up against the side of my cell and slipped my arm through the bars. My forearm fit easily, but my upper arm could barely squeeze through. I closed my eyes and concentrated, willing my arm to shrink. My arms aren't especially slim, but they are certainly narrower than a man's. No wonder the Garrowglass dungeon left a torch so close to the cell.

I jammed my shoulder up against the bars. My arm waved free. I twisted it around at the shoulder, trying to grasp onto the torch. My fingers grazed over the handle. The bars pinched at my skin. I pushed myself a little farther out of the bars, trying to jam my shoulder through the gap. Pain radiated around my collarbone. I ignored it. The torch's light turned my hand orange. I reached—

I reached—

My fingers hooked around the torch's handle—

And then I had it. I tightened my grip and jerked the torch up. It slid out of its holder easily, and for a moment, a second between breaths, I was afraid I had dropped it. But I could still feel the heat of the fire on my fist, and I disentangled myself from the bars and pulled the torch through. The flames swirled and snapped around the bars, leaving streaks of black in their wake.

"I got it," I said to Isolfr.

"I see that." He looked paler than usual. "Now prop it somewhere where you can see the flames burning."

I turned around in place. The walls were starting to crumble, and cracks appeared in the stones of my cell. I ran my fingers over the walls, holding the torch aloft so I had the light to see by, until I found a fairly sizable one. I dusted it out and nestled the torch inside.

It held.

I whirled around, back to Isolfr.

"Find the magic on the air," he said. "It won't matter what sort—just anything to forge the connection. You must be careful, though. Remember what happened with the dragon. This is a small spell, but the danger is still possible."

"I haven't forgotten." I didn't tell him that the memory made me nervous. "What'll I do with the magic once I've got it?"

"Focus it on the fire," Isolfr said, "and concentrate on the person you wish to speak to. Think of their face, their voice. Assuming it works the same with Mists magic, the fire will find them. If it doesn't—" Isolfr's voice trailed away. "I might be able to pull your mind out from here."

"You won't have to." I faked confidence I didn't feel. That was always a risk with magic, wasn't it? That the transformation could overtake you completely, that your mind would be subsumed. But that was magic in our world. Mists magic was stronger, more unreliable—

No. I couldn't think like that.

Isolfr smiled at me, a smile like a gift of courage. I turned back to the torch. The fire was ordinary. I could smell the burning wood and the heated metal flame guard and the smoke. I took a deep breath.

And then I closed my eyes.

I had to find the magic first, but I had to be careful, so that the dungeon wouldn't be able to tell what I was doing. Hesitantly, I reached out, feeling on the air around me. The magic of the prison pulsed. It was old magic, hazy magic. I sifted through it, trying to find something that would interact the right way with the magic inside of me. But everything was slipping away from my grasp. The magic here was as cold and intangible as water. It was magic intended to keep me locked away, not magic put in place to help me.

So I reached farther, through the walls of the dungeon, into the kitchens, the basements where they stored wine and dried meats— anything.

And that's when I felt it. A spark inside my bloodstream.

"I've got something," I gasped, and my eyes flew open. The torch flame loomed in front of me. I focused on the white of its center. The hottest part of a fire was its strongest part. It was the most basic knowledge of any sort of flame-magic.

The spark grew inside of me, wavering out through my bloodstream. Whatever sort of magic it was, it wasn't terribly strong, but it had a touch of the wind about it. A touch of home. I let it shimmer and grow as I stared at the white of the torch flame and thought about Kolur. He was easier to draw up than Frida, for I'd known him longer, even though I hadn't known the true him. I thought of him standing at the ship's wheel, shouting instructions to me as the *Penelope* rocked over the water. I thought of him speaking to Mama outside his little shack on the beach, his hair rustling in the south wind I'd pulled up to torment them both. I thought of our adventures on the open sea, and in Tulja, and Skalir. Kolur. I thought of Kolur.

The firelight broadened, stretching out across the wall of my cell. The flames disappeared. Magic radiated off the light, burning my face the way the heat once had. But it was a different kind of burning, a cold sort, like the burning of ice. The magic beckoned me forward. My heart pumped. Fear crawled up my spine. If I did this wrong, Isolfr would have to save me from his cell. His magic would certainly call the attention of the guards—

The light wavered.

No. I had to keep thinking of Kolur. I stepped forward. Magic rippled over me. I reached out one hand, trembling, and grazed my fingers across the wall of light. I expected it to burn me but it felt only warm, pleasant, like summer sun. I pulled my fingers away. The tips were stained with light.

This had to mean it was working.

I took another step forward. Another. I pressed both hands to the light and pushed. They slid in easily, the light swallowing me up to my wrists. To my elbows. But I couldn't speak to Kolur with my hands.

I leaned forward, and pressed my face into the light.

For a moment, I saw nothing but whiteness, the blinding, brilliant whiteness of the flame's hot center. And then a shape appeared in the distance. A silhouette of a man, tall and lean.

"Kolur!" I shouted. My voice was distorted by the magic of the Flames of Natuze. The silhouette turned toward me.

"Kolur! We were betrayed by Lord Garrowglass. We've been thrown in the dungeon and we've no way of escape. You'll have to come through at Jandanvar—"

The silhouette approached. Shadows rippled and swirled around its feet in a way that did not suggest, remotely, the clothes that Kolur wore. A creeping sick sense of fear rose up in my stomach. Who was I talking to?

"I'm afraid I'm not Kolur." The voice was distorted. It faded in and out, manipulated by magic. It didn't sound like Lord Foxfollow. It was accented in a way that reminded me of Mama.

"Who are you?" I demanded. "Where's Kolur?"

"I don't know." The man glided close enough to me that his features materialized out of the brightness of the Flames of Natuze. He was handsome, but a scar ran down the side of his face, twisting his expression into a sneer of anger. I jerked back. The Flames rippled around me.

"I don't know who Kolur is," he said.

I should have pulled away, gone back into the cell. Except the spell had *worked*. I was enveloped in the Flames of Natuze, and I was speaking to someone through the veils of magic. I just didn't know who it was.

"Who are you?" the man asked, but I didn't answer him, only spun back through the litany of memories I'd revisited while I was casting the spell. My mind had wandered away from Kolur. To home. To Mama.

"Do you know Maia Euli?" I thought about his accent. "Or Maia of the *Na*—"

Even in the blazing light of the flames, I saw the recognition flicker through his eyes.

"You know her!" I cried. "Maia Euli!"

"Why? Who's asking?" His expression grew guarded, careful. He studied me. "What do you want with her?"

"She's my mother," I said.

The man stared at me. "No," he said. "I can't believe it."

"What's to believe?" I snapped. "How do you know her?"

"Maia the pirate?"

"Yes!" And suddenly, I knew who he was.

The scar.

The southerly accent.

"Are you Naji?" I said.

The man's eyes widened. He grabbed the edge of his cloak and twisted it around himself and disappeared in a twist of magic.

"Wait!" I shouted, that sudden flood of hope stopped short by desperation. "Come back! I need your help! Please!"

The Flames of Natuze burned around me. I didn't know if it was possible for me to cry in this in-between place. I didn't know if my body was really here or not, if my tears could even manifest. But I could feel those tears like hanging weights behind my eyes. I'd come so close to finding help—Naji, *the* Naji of all Mama's stories. He had defeated the Mists. He had defeated *Lord Foxfollow*. And now he had just abandoned me.

A shadow shimmered into existence. It was far away, indistinguishable.

"Naji!" I screamed. "Please! I'm not here to hurt you. I wasn't even trying to find you, I was trying to find Kolur, but I thought of Mama instead—"

The shadow moved closer. No, not a shadow—shadows. Two of them. I fell silent. Blood, swollen with magic, thumped in my ears. I wondered what was happening in the cell. I prayed to the ancestors that Isolfr wouldn't pull me back.

Distinctions emerged out of the shadows. One was Naji, his dark cloak swirling. The other was a woman, broad-shouldered and voluptuous, her hair a messy tangle piled on top of her head.

Ananna. I recognized her immediately.

"So," she said as she came into focus, "this is Maia's daughter."

446

I tried to bow, but the flames held me in place. "Captain Nadir?" I whispered.

"That's what they call me," she said. "But your mama, she called me Ananna, and so can you. I can see her in you, you know." She turned to Naji. "Can't you see it? The eyes? The cheekbones, too."

Naji made a grunt of affirmation.

"He fetched me as soon as he figured out who it was." Ananna smiled. She was radiant in the white light, and I saw in her the whole history of my mother and the whole possibility of my name.

"Mama named me after you," I said.

"She'd damn well better have," Ananna said. "Only way I was letting her go."

I smiled.

"Now." Ananna leaned forward. "I figure you didn't show up in my ship's cookstove to chat about your mama." She frowned. "Did you?"

I shook my head. My panic came back to me in a sudden onslaught. "I was trying to find Kolur. He's—my apprentice master. We're trying to fight Lord Foxfollow."

"Who?" Ananna frowned. "Should I know who that is?"

I felt like I'd been punched in the stomach. Isolfr had told me that Ananna had defeated Foxfollow, and that was why I had agreed to help—

But Naji's face had darkened, and he turned to Ananna and murmured something in her ear.

"Kaol and Emki both," she said. "How in hell did Maia's daughter get embroiled in all *that*?"

"It's a long story. Mama doesn't even know. She still thinks Kolur's a fisherman."

"A fisher—" Ananna threw up her hands. "You're in it worse than I was. And I had this one tagging along with me." She jerked her thumb over at Naji, who rolled his eyes. But then she looked at me again, and I could feel the magic of the Flames of Natuze tugging back and forth between us. "Do you need help? 'Cuz I can get Naji to help you, and I'll send my fleet your way, if you need it."

"I'm in the Mists," I said.

"You're what?"

Naji frowned at me. "How did you accomplish that?"

"I don't have time to tell the whole story. We were on our way to Jandanvar—that's how we were going to get back to our world; it's a city that exists in both our world and the Mists—and we were caught by a nobleman who's loyal to Lord Foxfollow, and we've been thrown in prison—"

"Stop." Ananna held up one hand. "Who's *we*?"

"Me and Isolfr—he's a, ah, spirit—and a Mists nobleman named Trystan. We've all been thrown in prison, and Kolur and Frida, she's a witch, they're in Jandanvar and they're waiting for us, and I just don't know what to do. I don't know if I'll be able to cast the Flames of Natuze again. It was hard enough the first time because I couldn't keep my attention on Kolur." Heat streaked down my cheeks and I realize it was tears, even though it didn't feel exactly right. "So I don't know what to do."

"Stop right there," Ananna said. "I get the picture. You're in it for sure. But why'd you need to contact this Kolur?"

"So he could come—get us, or something."

"Mmmm. That ain't a guarantee though. It'd be just as easy to break out of the jail yourself, don't you think? I've done it plenty of times. Your mama too. It's one of those things you pick up when you're a pirate."

Naji made a coughing sound.

"I can't break out of jail," I said. "I can't use my magic. It'll interact badly with the entrapment spells."

Ananna gave me a wink. "You don't need magic to break out of jail."

"It certainly helps," said Naji.

"You would say that, wouldn't you?" Ananna reached over and swiped a hand through his dark hair and Naji looked at her and his eyes glittered like he was smiling. "But this is why I say you learn to do everything without magic. That way—you've got your options."

"You don't understand," I said. "I'm not a pirate. Mama didn't teach me anything like that! I know how to sail a boat and catch fish and draw on the wind and that's it."

Ananna laughed. "This isn't something you learn. It's something you do. Just gotta think about it." She tapped the side of her head. "Trust me. You'll find your way out. There guards down there with you?"

I nodded. I was starting to feel tired, like my body was pulling apart. I couldn't hold this magic much longer.

"Good. Guards are just people. That means you can fool 'em easily enough."

"We're in the *Mists*," I said. "So they aren't just people."

"They're people built of magic," Naji said. His low, rumbling voice rolled around inside my head. It hadn't done that before. "If you know magic, you'll know them."

"You're starting to fade out," Ananna said. "Everything okay?"

"I can't talk any longer," I said. My throat was dry and raspy. "I'm sorry. But thank you—thank you for your help—"

"Give Maia my regards," Ananna said, just as the white Flames of Natuze swam across my vision and enveloped me whole.

CHAPTER TWELVE

I sucked in a long draft of cold, damp air. Someone was shouting my name.

"Ananna?" I muttered. "Captain Nadir?"

"Hanna! Look at me!"

The world was dark. After the brightness of the Flames of Natuze, I couldn't make out anything but heavy, blurred shadows. I was still reeling from my conversation with Ananna. I had spoken to her. And she hadn't looked down on me or told me I wasn't worthy of her name. In fact, she gave me *advice*.

"Hanna!"

With a jolt, I recognized Isolfr's voice, and I turned my head toward him. He was kneeling beside his cell door, reaching through the bars.

"I'm okay," I whispered, but he was too far away to hear.

"Hanna?" He pressed his face against the bars and squinted at me. "Oh, thank the ancestors, her eyes are open!"

"Good," came a voice a few cells away. Trystan.

I pushed myself up onto my arm. The dungeon spun around. The magic I'd used to activate the Flames of Natuze was still lingering inside my veins, churning with power.

"Did you speak with them?" Isolfr asked. "What did they say?"

It took me a moment to remember that Isolfr was not asking about Ananna and Naji, but about Frida and Kolur. I sat up and rubbed my hands over my face. I felt as if I'd been asleep for a long time. Days, weeks, years. But the guard's chair was still empty, and the extinguished torches hadn't been relit. The light in my cell was dim and hazy—the torch I'd used to cast the spell had burned and solidified into black stone.

"No," I said.

"No?" Isolfr frowned. "But you were in the flames for so long! The spell worked. I saw it."

"It didn't take me to Kolur and Frida." I looked at him through the bars. His eyes were on me, heavy with concern. His expression made my bloodstream spark in a way that had nothing to do with magic. "I spoke with Ananna though. Ananna of the *Nadir*."

"Who?" said Trystan, voice rebounding off the dripping stone walls.

"Will she help us?" Isolfr asked.

I shook my head. Isolfr slumped back, looking defeated, but I didn't share his pessimism. She'd told me that I just needed to be like her. I just needed to live up to my name.

Easier said than done.

"We can get ourselves out," I said. "And then run across the border into Jandanvar. Once we're there, Kolur and Frida can collect us, right?" I tilted my head to the left, where I assumed Trystan was imprisoned. "Do you know how far it is?"

"A day's walk," Trystan said.

"We'll never make it," Isolfr said.

"Through the woods," Trystan added. "We'd have cover of foliage, if the two of you know how to handle such things."

"We don't have that much time, either," I said. "Isolfr, you could fly us."

"No," said Trystan sharply. "Lord Foxfollow would expect that. He'll have spells cast to feel if Isolfr transforms into the north wind—that effect would ripple all over the Garrowglass estate. No. Absolutely not."

I pressed my face against the cell bars. They were cold and damp, like everything else in this place. For the first time I felt as if these lands deserved the name the Mists.

A hopeless silence settled around the dungeon.

"Or . . . ," Trystan said. "Or—I might know a way. To get us there quickly."

Isolfr shifted in the shadows. "What is it?" He hadn't protested Trystan's warnings about the threat of him turning into the north wind, and I didn't blame him. Not when we were in the world where Foxfollow gained his strength.

"Lord Gallowglass keeps moon horses. I've got a touch with the creatures, and they don't harbor loyalties to their owner. I might be able to convince one to fly us into Jandanvar."

"A moon horse?" The name sounded familiar, and at first I couldn't place it—but then I remembered a flash of silver in the stable back at the inn in Amkal City.

"The winged horses of Argent Island. Lord Gallowglass collects them, the poor things. They're always happy to rebel when they can."

"You're both ignoring the obvious," Isolfr said. "Even with the moon horses, we still have to get ourselves out of the dungeon. Without magic. You're skipping over the hardest part."

"Ananna said we should trick the guards," I told him. "She said that if guards are people, then they can be tricked." I paused, remembering her smile as she'd spoken to me, indulgent like Mama's when I was first learning how to tie ropes on board Papa's boat. "And that the guards here are people made of magic, so we can know them well."

Trystan snorted in his cage. "Not the highest kind of magic," he said. "Not if they're just guards."

"It doesn't matter!" Isolfr said. "It doesn't matter what sort of magic they are. We won't be able to trick them—"

A door clanged open at the top of the stairs.

Isolfr went pale and silent and dropped away from his bars. I could just see him in the shadows, two eyes sometimes glinting with white light.

I stayed where I was, despite the pounding in my heart. I needed to watch the guards. I needed to study them, figure out their weaknesses. I needed to be like Ananna.

Footsteps, the jangle of keys. It was frightening how easily those sounds became routine. The guards' distorted silhouettes danced across the walls, announcing their entrance; a few seconds later, the guards themselves appeared. They were different from the men the other day. Two of them again, one balancing three trays of food on his arms.

"Morning, morning!" the free-handed guard shouted. "Wake up. Another day in the dungeon. Lord Foxfollow will be arriving later this afternoon, and Lord Gallowglass wants you *well-rested*."

A tray of gray porridge slid through my cell door. It was lumpy and unappealing, but I lost my appetite, small as it was, at the mention of Lord Foxfollow's name.

He would be here today.

I did not have time to formulate a clever plan, like one Ananna would have invented.

I pulled my tray over and stared down at the congealing, unappetizing porridge, fighting back tears. The guard finished distributing breakfast and sat down in the guard's chair. The other one leaned up against the wall, fingering the hilt of his sword. They looked bored.

I took a raggedy breath. All wasn't lost yet—Foxfollow would be here this afternoon, and the guards had made it clear it was morning. I still had time. And so I studied them, looking for clues, for weak points, for *anything*.

I noticed that they both had keys glinting at their sides, but I didn't know what to do with that observation. I knew I couldn't use magic to draw the keys to myself; the dungeon would stop me before I retrieved them. Same with casting a spell on the guards, something to make them pliable and weak.

Ananna was right. I couldn't use magic. I'd have to use my wits.

I stirred my porridge around, trying to decide what to do. If I had something I could use as a weapon, I could lure the guards into my cell, then grab the keys, free the others, and run. But I needed a weapon.

Nothing on the tray would work. Not that I would have expected it to. The guards weren't that stupid.

I pretended to eat, spooning the porridge up to my mouth, one eye on the guards. They were too wrapped up in their conversation, their voices a dull murmur, to pay me any mind. One of them chuckled.

I set my spoon down, glanced around my cell.

And then I saw it.

The torch.

The torch, transformed by the Flames of Natuze into shiny black stone. I had a weapon in my cell.

I scuttled backward a few finger widths at a time, dragging the tray with me. One of the guards glanced over at my cell but didn't say anything, and a heartbeat later he turned back to the other guard. They both laughed.

My spine hit up against the wall. I was wrapped in the dungeon's dark shadows, and the light of those few torches burned a world away. I ate another bite of porridge, just in case. The guards didn't look at me. I crawled over to the torch.

It lay on the floor, blending into the dungeon's dark stone. I turned my back to the guards so I could pick it up, shielding my actions with my body. The transformed torch was heavier than the original had been. The stone was smooth and cool, as if it had been polished like a gem. I tried to imagine using it, slamming the torch down on the back of the guard's head, but I couldn't. My mind went blank at the thought.

But I knew I had to try.

Trembling, I folded the torch up in the skirts of my dress. Then I crawled back over to my bowl of porridge and ate another couple of bites. I might as well have been eating sand. The porridge felt like sand in my stomach, too, heavy and sludgy and weighing me down.

The guards weren't look at me.

I was dizzy with fear.

I hurled my spoon against the floor so it made a great clatter, and then I screamed.

I screamed, and I grabbed at my side and slumped over, howling and shrieking. I didn't dare look at the guards directly, but I heard the jangle of their keys.

"What the hell's wrong with you, girl?" one of them asked.

"I don't know!" I wailed. "It just started hurting!" I squeezed my eyes shut.

Footsteps on the stone. I rolled over the floor, digging my hands into my side. "For the love of the ancestors, help me!" I lifted my head, hair already stringy with sweat—it came from fear, not pain, but the guards wouldn't know that.

They stood in front of my cell door gaping at me. A smear of silver flashed behind them. Isolfr.

"Was it poisoned?" I shrieked.

"Was what poisoned?" asked one of the guards.

"The porridge!" I rolled over onto my back. "You tricked me! What about the others!"

"The others are fine," the guard said. "Stop screaming."

"She looks pretty bad," the other said. "You know it wouldn't do to have her die before his lordship arrives."

I screamed again, louder this time.

The first guard didn't answer.

"I'm going in," the second said. "What's she going to do? She can't use magic down here."

"She can't use *some* magic," the first said. "Lord Gallowglass has never been exactly thorough—"

"You're being a coward. It's just a girl."

I moaned and shrieked and clutched at my side. The keys jangled in the lock and my heart raced and sweat prickled through my clothes. I twisted around on the floor so I could draw my other hand across my body and easily grab hold of the torch.

"Now, tell me what's the matter." The guard's footsteps stopped. I rolled over, gazed up at him. My vision was hazy. He crouched down, put a hand on my forehead. "Elex, she's soaked in sweat. Go fetch the physician to tend to her. You *know* we can't bring them dead."

I screamed again, rolled over onto my side. The first guard hung back in the doorway, frowning. If he would leave, I'd only have to attack one—

The kind one. The one who'd come in to check on me. I reminded myself he only did it because he couldn't bring me dead to Lord Foxfollow.

"Fine," the first said.

"You don't want Foxfollow angry with you," the second said.

"I said I would go." He whirled around and stomped out of the dungeon.

"We'll see what's wrong," the guard said in a low, comforting voice. "Don't you worry."

His kindness was clanging and harsh. I hated myself, and I hated the reason behind that kindness. I knew, too, that I couldn't waste any more time. The echoes of the first guard's footsteps had faded. I didn't know how long he'd be gone.

I tightened my fingers around the torch.

I took one last look at the guard, measuring how far I needed to swing to hit the back of his head.

And then I attacked.

It happened so fast that it felt like a dream. I swung the torch out and for a moment it was whistling through the air and then it stopped, and a sickening jolt ran up my arms. There was a crack like ice breaking. The guard didn't even cry out, just slumped over on top of me.

Revulsion racked through my body. I threw the torch away in disgust, and it rolled out of my open cell and over to Isolfr, who was staring at me through the bars.

"What are you *doing?*" he hissed.

I wriggled out from under the guard's weight. Blood trickled down his neck but I couldn't think about that. Instead, I unhooked the keys from his belt and ran out of my cell and over to Isolfr's. My hands were shaking. I listened for footsteps on the stairs and kept thinking that I heard them. But no one appeared.

I jammed the key into the lock and turned. The door popped open. Isolfr looked stunned. His Pjetur mask had dropped away completely, and he glowed in the darkness like the moon.

"Don't forget me!" Trystan called out.

"Shhh!" I jogged over to his cell. It was at the far end of the dungeon and larger than mine, with stone seats and a straw-covered cot. I unlocked the door and yanked it open, then whirled around, trying to decide how to get out of the dungeon. Isolfr had stepped out of his cell. He looked around, dazed, as if he couldn't believe he'd found his freedom.

His toe knocked against the torch. It clattered across the stone. I dove forward and grabbed it before it could roll into my cell. The guard stirred, groaning, and fear spiked through my heart. I turned to Trystan.

"How do we get out of here?" I said. "Up the stairs?" I imagined us meeting a troop of armed guards and that being the end of our escape.

"No!" Trystan gestured for Isolfr and me to join him by his cell. "Most of the ancient lords installed underground entrances to the dungeons—" He felt along the wall, his fingers skimming over the stone. Isolfr drifted over beside me. Flashes of Pjetur flickered across his features.

"Thank you," he whispered.

I smiled.

"Found it!" Trystan said in a loud whisper. He banged a fist against one of the stones. Nothing happened. Isolfr and I exchanged glances.

The guard groaned again. I whirled around and slammed the cell door shut and turned the key in the lock.

A rough, raspy scraping filled the dungeon. I turned back to Trystan. Cracks had appeared in the stone, threading like bright veins. Trystan cursed and banged his fist against the wall.

The wall crumbled.

"There we are," he said. "Just like at Llambric Manor. Come along then. This should take us up to the gardens. Once we're outside, I can get us to the moon horse stable. Hurry!"

I glanced at Isolfr to make sure he was still all right. He looked small and pale and frightened. Not cowardly, though. Fear was necessary here. It was what would keep us alive.

I understood that now.

I grabbed his hand and squeezed. He lifted his face to me. For a half second I thought of our kiss, the dry cool roughness of his lips against mine.

This was not a time to think about kissing.

Trystan disappeared through the hidden door. I tugged on Isolfr's hand and pulled him forward, and we followed Trystan into the dark tunnel. There was enough light from the flames of the dungeon to illuminate Trystan's form as he glided along the path—and then that light was gone. Winked out.

The darkness flooded over me. I felt as if I was drowning. The only thing anchoring me to the world was the solidity of Isolfr's hand in mine.

"Keep moving!" Trystan said. "There's light up ahead. You only have one path. But I had to tell the wall to rearrange the door—otherwise, this would be the first place they'd look." His voice faded in and out. I squeezed Isolfr's hand tighter.

"I'm not going to leave you," Isolfr said softly.

"I know," I said.

We moved forward. The tunnel was narrow and restricting, as if the house itself was on Lord Foxfollow's side and wanted to squeeze the life out of my lungs. I took deep, shuddery breaths. It was disorienting in the darkness, and I stuck out my free hand—I didn't dare let go of Isolfr—to touch the wall and help steady myself. It was cold and covered in a fuzzy growth like moss that undulated beneath my fingers. I yelped and snatched my hand away.

"Are you all right back there?" Trystan said.

"I think so. I just touched something—"

"The magic makes things grow down here." Trystan sounded far away, and then he sounded right behind me. "Keep walking. We'll be there soon."

After a while, the path tilted upward enough that my breath

quickened. Isolfr and I were still holding hands. I wasn't sure, after this, if I could ever let him go.

Something brushed across my shoulder. I jumped, but Isolfr said, "Shh, it's just me."

I sighed with relief.

"I just wanted to tell you," he said, "that I can hear you breathing."

"Oh. I'm sorry."

"No, no! It's good. It makes me feel—safe."

I glanced toward the sound of his voice. The darkness was so thick I couldn't see anything but two twin flashes, quick as lightning. His eyes.

"I'm glad," I said.

In the silence that followed, I imagined him smiling.

I'm not sure how long we walked. It was a long time, certainly, but it was uninterrupted by guards or danger. Of course, that didn't mean I wasn't terrified. In that darkness we were vulnerable. In that house, that dungeon, we were vulnerable. I wasn't sure if I'd ever be safe again.

And then light appeared.

It was thin and weak, like moonlight back home. It glazed the floor and the walls and Isolfr, draining them of all color. I laughed at the sight of it, laughed at the idea of light. Trystan, only a few paces ahead of us, turned to me and said, "Quiet! We're approaching the exit soon. They may be waiting for us."

My laughter vanished. I'd picked up the torch and tucked it into my belt, but I wasn't sure I could use it again.

The light brightened enough to form long, eerie shadows. Trystan stopped, both hands stretched horizontally across the tunnel to stop us. For the first time, I let go of Isolfr's hand. In case I needed to fight.

I didn't want to think about fighting.

"I don't hear anyone," Trystan whispered.

Up ahead, the path dead-ended into a tangle of briar branches, brown and thorny. Trystan crept forward, ear tilted toward the branches. I clutched the torch and trembled.

Trystan pushed the branches aside. Pale light poured in. He peered outside. My throat seized up.

"It's clear," he said. "We're in the woods. Hurry through." He pulled at the branches, clearing a hole, and crawled through. Isolfr glanced over at me.

"I'll go first," he whispered.

I nodded. I could see in his expression that he was scared. But he still waded into the branches without hesitation. I pushed in after him. The branches slashed at my face, leaving sharp stinging marks on my skin. For a moment I was completely entangled in them, and I was afraid that I was stuck, that we'd all gotten stuck.

But then a hand, slim and pale, reached down through the branches and found mine.

"I've got you," Isolfr said, and with a burst of strength, he pulled me through, out into the damp Mists night.

We stood in the middle of a dense, thickly layered wood. The brambles crawled around the trees and the leaves rustled overhead. It was brighter than I expected, as if we were standing in an open field under full moonlight—in truth, it was brighter even than that. And then I realized the light came from the trees. It shone just underneath their surfaces, crawling up their trunks and branches in swirls and eddies.

"Where are we?" I asked Trystan.

"Asha Forest," he said. "Still on Garrowglass property. The moon horses' stable is not far from here. Climb up into one of the trees to hide. I'll find you."

"What!" said Isolfr. "No. We can't split up—"

"It's the easiest way," Trystan shot back. "I can speak with one of the moon horses more easily if I'm alone, and I can move faster. Hide in the trees. I'll fly overhead to pick you up."

I wanted to protest too. It was a terrible idea for him to run off like that, to leave us in an unfamiliar and magic-enchanted wood in the Mists. But I didn't have a chance to say anything. Trystan had already vanished into the darkness.

"I can't believe he did that," Isolfr said.

"He's a nobleman," I said, knowing even as I spoke I was being unfair. "He's used to getting his own way."

Isolfr stared after the place where Trystan had disappeared. I tucked the torch into my belt again and picked my way through the brambles to the nearest tree. The trunk was thick, much bigger around than I was, but its branches grew low and sprawling.

"We can climb this one," I said.

Isolfr glanced over his shoulder at me. "You don't think he betrayed us?"

Of course I'd thought that. "He's your friend," I said. "You told me you trusted him. That's all I need to know."

Isolfr hesitated. "I do trust him," he said.

"He didn't betray us then." I beckoned for him to join me. "Come on, let's get up here before Garrowglass's men come along."

"His men haven't been in these woods for a long time." Isolfr moved through the brambles with grace, hardly making sound. I grabbed hold of the tree's lowest branch and heaved myself up.

"You sure about that?"

"Quite. The people of the Mists always leave traces behind. And the traces here are all ancient."

"I haven't noticed that. The traces, I mean." I crawled up to the next branch, which was wide enough for me to turn around and peer over the side at him. He had one hand on the tree trunk and was squinting up at me. In the tree's light his skin was transparent and gauzy. He didn't look human at all.

"I've trained in it. Is this hard to do? I've never climbed a tree before."

I couldn't help myself; I laughed. "No, it's not that hard. This is a good climbing tree."

Isolfr frowned and tilted his head, studying the low-hanging branch. "I've never had to climb something before. Not even on the *Penelope II*—Kolur never asked me to."

"You usually just fly?"

"Not fly. Change form. Become the wind." He sighed. "But Trystan was right; I can't risk doing that here. Not just because of Foxfollow. In these woods, with this old magic—" He shook his head. "I'm not sure what would happen."

"Well, it's not so bad, climbing." I braced myself against the tree's trunk. "Just pull yourself up one branch at a time. Make sure you have your balance before you go any higher."

Isolfr screwed up his face in concentration. I watched him with a warm flush of affection, charmed by the idea that he'd never had to properly climb something before.

He pulled himself up to the first branch after a couple of hesitations and false starts, then turned to me, skin blazing in the light.

"Not so bad, huh?" I said.

"I wouldn't exactly say that."

I smothered a laugh. "Well, we need to get higher. Into the leaves at least." I grabbed the next branch and shimmied my way up. I'd had practice climbing trees and mastheads both, and I could have gotten to the top of that tree in no time at all. But I didn't. I waited for Isolfr, never letting him drop more than one branch behind. When we finally made it to the tree's canopy, I grabbed Isolfr's hand the way he had grabbed mine in the briar tangle and pulled him up beside me.

The highest branches were sturdier than I expected, hanging with wide, flat leaves. We carved out a place where we could sit, leaves falling around us like curtains, keeping us hidden. A small patch of sky shone through so I could keep watch.

"Which way are the stables?" I asked.

"Everything is that way." Isolfr pointed over my shoulder. "We're on the edge of the Garrowglass estate. That direction," and he jabbed his thumb over his shoulder, "is the way to Jandanvar."

I shivered. Lord Foxfollow must have been there when he received word that we'd been captured. It was obvious now that Frida and Kolur hadn't managed to defeat him in the time that we'd been in the Mists. I prayed to the ancestors that it was because they hadn't tried yet, and not because they had, and failed.

"Watch for Trystan," I said, drawing my knees up to my chest. "We don't want him to fly overhead and miss us."

Isolfr pushed himself closer to me on the branch. After sleeping in the dungeon and casting the Flames of Natuze and trekking through those dark, inclined tunnels, my entire body ached with tension and exhaustion. But Isolfr's proximity, the soft paleness of skin, and the shivering north-wind breeze of touch, relaxed me. After a moment's pause, I turned myself around so I could lay my head on his shoulder. He didn't move, didn't push me away—in fact, a few heartbeats later, he lay his hand over mine, his fingers curling around my fingers. I lifted my gaze up to the gap in the leaves, watching for Trystan. The sky was the color of old stone.

"I'm glad you were on Kolur's ship," Isolfr said suddenly. "I'm glad I was able to meet you."

The leaves rustled, leaving streaks of pale light in their wake.

"I'm glad I was able to meet you too." I felt breathless. There was a tickle at my ear—Isolfr, readjusting himself, pulling me closer. His body was a comfortable solidity beneath me. Cold, but not in an unpleasant way. Not at all.

A shadow appeared in the sky.

Any sense of calm vanished. I tensed. Isolfr tightened his grip on my hand.

There was a sound, a soft *whomp whomp whomp*, like the beating of wings.

"Is that him?" I whispered. "Trystan?"

"I'm not sure."

Whoever it was hadn't passed by the gap in the leaves. I pulled myself away from Isolfr even though it was the last thing I wanted to do. I peeked my head out into the open. A silhouette dove across the sky. A horse, a pair of wings, a man.

The horse swooped toward me. Its hair shimmered like starlight and its mane streaked out behind it like the tail of a comet. In the light of the trees I could see that the rider was Trystan.

I sighed with relief.

"It's him," I said, bending down to Isolfr.

The beating wings grew louder. I held out my hand to help Isolfr stand up without losing his balance. He smiled at me. The trees formed a veil around us, and without thinking I leaned forward and brushed my lips against his. Immediately, my cheeks flushed hot the way they had the first time.

"Sorry," I muttered.

"You never need to apologize for that," Isolfr whispered.

Now it was my turn to smile.

The leaves rippled. A cold wind stirred up around us. I stuck my head back out into the open, and Isolfr did the same, peering out cautiously. The moon horse hovered a few paces away, wings pumping. The wings were a dark inky black, and I could see them in silhouette against the sky, as wide as the sails on the ships that went north.

"The guards are assembling," Trystan said. "We need to go now."

I nodded. Trystan held out one hand and I took it and he pulled me onto the back of the moon horse, who gave a whinny of irritation but otherwise did not protest. Then Trystan did the same with Isolfr.

"Hold on," Trystan said, and I immediately gripped the sides of his coat. Isolfr wrapped his arms around my waist, squeezing tight. His breath was a cold tickle on my shoulder.

The moon horse swooped up, its wings creating a blasting wind that cooled my hot skin, a wind that was infused with strange and beautiful magic.

We flew up into the sky, as high as the clouds, and fled the lands of Lord Garrowglass.

CHAPTER THIRTEEN

I'm not sure how long we flew. Time seemed to change in the far reaches of the sky. Slow down, speed up—I wasn't sure. But there was a beautiful freedom to soaring through the air. The magic was stronger up here, crackling around us like lightning. I could feel it mingling with the magic inside me; I could feel it dancing on my skin. It wasn't like the magic back home, and it wasn't like the magic closer to the surface of the Mists, either. It was magic like starlight, like rainstorms, like wind.

None of us spoke. We couldn't have heard each other even if we had, with the wind howling past our ears. Isolfr snuggled close to me, his chin on my shoulder, and I leaned into him and felt safe with his arms wrapped around my waist.

No one followed us.

Eventually, the night gave way to morning, the sky lightening and lightening until it was no longer dark green-gray but pale ivory. For the first time since I'd come to the Mists, a cloud moved into view, a thin wisp of a thing, almost invisible against the pale sky. My breath caught in my throat.

"We're here," Isolfr said, his mouth close to my ear. His voice blended with the wind's. "We've passed the border. We're in Jandanvar."

My chest tightened. Jandanvar. The place where my world and the Mists bled together. We had gotten free of the Garrowglass dungeon but I knew we weren't safe. Not yet. The moon horse was flying us into a danger so great I couldn't imagine it.

I closed my eyes against the brightening sky and saw, just for a second, my little cottage in Kjora, Mama and Papa waving at me from the garden.

In my little straw bed in that house I'd dreamed of adventures. Those dreams hadn't matched with reality. In my mind, adventures were like being on the back of the moon horse, a boy like Isolfr holding me close—but without all the other terrible things, the terror of being caught and tortured and killed by Lord Foxfollow, the night spent in the dungeon, the confusion as we sailed toward unknown lands. And even this moment, the wind and the magic swirling around me, was tainted by the cold stab of fear at what I would have to face when we landed.

The moon horse descended. We spun lazily toward the ground, drifting like an autumn leaf. The frozen grassland had given way to a rocky, dark beach, waves crashing along the shore. I looked for the *Penelope II*, but the beach was empty.

"Where are we going?" I shouted at Trystan.

"The shore," he shouted back. "To wait. Senra doesn't want to fly over the sea with us on her back."

As if she understood us, the moon horse threw back her head and whinnied.

"See?" Trystan said.

I didn't, but I wasn't in a mind to argue with him. Down and down we spiraled. The shore loomed ahead. The water was dark like octopus ink, and when the waves slammed into the rocks I could already feel the soft sting of the cold ocean spray.

The moon horse flapped her wings once and then glided the rest of the way to landing. Isolfr squeezed my sides, and I let go of Trystan long enough to pat his hand.

We landed softly, and the moon horse transitioned from flying to galloping with hardly a jolt. She folded her wings up along the sides of her body, covering both of my feet, and then slowed to a stop at the water's edge. Even with the sea breeze blowing in off the ocean, the air felt as still as summer compared to the howling rush of wind during our flight.

"Everybody off," Trystan announced, jumping to the ground.

"What?" Isolfr said. "Here? We're out in the open."

"And it's going to be difficult for Frida and Kolur to fetch us," I said, gesturing at the rocks and the crashing waves. "A rowboat's not going to get through that." I frowned. "How are they even supposed to know we're here?"

The moon horse whinnied and shook her head, silvery mane rippling over my lap like river water. Trystan leaned close to her. I glanced over my shoulder at Isolfr. He looked like himself, just as he'd told me he would. Radiant, unearthly Isolfr. Pjetur had vanished completely from his features.

"Senra's got that all sorted," Trystan said. "But you'll need to kindly get off her back."

"Sorted?" I glared at him. "Sorted how? Don't you dare keep sec—"

"She's going to toss you off if you don't get down," Trystan said.

I sighed. The moon horse tossed her head from side to side and pumped her wings once.

"Fine." I swung my leg over her back—somewhat awkwardly; I wasn't used to riding on the backs of beasts—and slid to the ground. Isolfr followed after me, although he moved with significantly more grace.

The moment we were off her back, the moon horse leaped into the air, soaring out over the ocean.

"Sea and sky!" I shouted. I turned to Trystan. "Is this some kind of trick?"

"Keep your voice down," Trystan hissed. "She's off to find Frida and Kolur. She'll let them know where we are. Which," he paused, craning his head down the beach, "will be down there. She said the water's calmer and there's a natural pier."

"A horse told you all this," I said. I didn't say what I was thinking: namely, my fear that Senra wouldn't be able to find Frida and Kolur, that they were already dead.

"No." He scowled. "A moon horse. Will you please explain the difference to her, Isolfr?"

Isolfr didn't answer. I looked over at him, expectant, with my arms crossed over my chest. I'd come all this way and I wasn't letting anyone keep secrets from me.

"They're creatures of magic," Isolfr finally said, casting his eyes down. "And that means they can communicate in different ways— through thought, mostly. She'll be able to show Frida and Kolur where we are."

"And that's how I spoke to her," Trystan added. He tapped his temple. "Through my mind."

I rolled my eyes. Trystan turned and marched across the beach. He kept his chin high despite his dungeon-filthy clothes and matted hair. With the wind blustering around him, he looked like a nobleman from one of the romantic stories Bryn always loved.

"We ought to go with him," Isolfr said. "We don't want to be out in the open any longer than we have to."

"Do you think Foxfollow knows that we're here?"

It was the question we'd both been thinking, I knew that. But I wanted it out in the open. I wanted it acknowledged.

Our feet crunched over the stones.

"I don't know," Isolfr finally said. "If he doesn't now, he will eventually."

Tall, pale seagrass poked out of the rocks. It rippled in the wind. I drew my hand over it as I passed, and I felt a jolt of magic—not

Mists magic, but the earthy richness of dirt-magic. I pulled my hand away.

Isolfr looked over at me and smiled. "You're close to home," he said.

"And you are home." I smiled back. He shimmered, rippling with the wind. "Are you nervous that you can't disguise yourself?"

Isolfr looked away. "A little. It would be nice to be Pjetur when I see them for the first time, just so they—they can see me change. But the only human form I can take is my own."

I reached over and grabbed his hand. "It's my favorite of your human forms, you know."

Isolfr ducked his head, spots of color appearing on his cheek.

I spotted Trystan a few paces ahead. The water was calmer here, the ocean gently lapping across the sandy soil, not crashing and rioting like it had been farther down. Trystan sat in a patch of seagrass, his arms draped over his knees. He stared out at the horizon. I could just make out the sun behind the clouds. It was a beautiful thing to see.

"I can't go back," Trystan said suddenly.

I didn't know who he was speaking to. From the expression on Isolfr's face, he didn't either.

"Um—I'm sorry?"

Trystan pulled out a clump of seagrass and hurled it into the ocean, where it disappeared beneath the lapping waves. "It's not your fault," he said. "It's that monster Lord Foxfollow's. I can't believe he ordered Gallowglass to make me suffer the indignities of the dungeon."

Lord Foxfollow had very nearly killed one of the only friends I had in Tulja. He had tried to kill me and Isolfr and Kolur and Frida on more than one occasion. He'd killed poor Gillean just for help-ing us. The dungeon had been the least of his crimes.

"You think I'm being absurd," Trystan said without looking at us.

"No," Isolfr said.

"I wouldn't expect you to understand." He ripped another clump of seagrass out of the earth, only this time he let it slip through his fingers so that it showered across his lap. "It's a matter of propriety. Of—*reputation*. I've been branded a criminal and a traitor." He glared out at the horizon. "I can't let him win again."

"He won't," Isolfr said. The certainty of his voice surprised me; it had a strength to it out here, as if it were suffused with magic. I hadn't noticed before. "We're going to stop him." He looked over at me. "Hanna's here."

"Right. Hanna. A little Sun Daughter." Trystan snorted. "At least she's back in her element."

I wanted to conjure up the south wind and slam its power into him, just to show him that I could. But then Isolfr spoke.

"Don't dismiss her," he said. "You don't want to remember this conversation when she's about to save your life."

The wind gusted, cold and chill. It was blowing in from the north.

I looked over at Isolfr and that was when I realized that the strength in Isolfr's voice had the wind in it. The north wind. We had that strength, Isolfr's strength. Trystan was right about me, even if I didn't want to hear it—but he couldn't fathom Isolfr.

We waited for the return of the moon horse in strained silence. Isolfr and I sat away from Trystan, on the edge of the dark soil. He seemed to want to be left alone and I didn't much want to talk to him, although as I thought about it, I realized I didn't blame him for his anger. Lord Foxfollow had ruined his life once before, and now ruined it again—with no guarantee of vengeance.

Isolfr and I didn't talk much either. I was dull with fright, worried that the moon horse was taking so long because Frida and

Kolur were dead. That Trystan and Isolfr and I would have to fight Lord Foxfollow on our own.

Isolfr kept fading in and out with the wind. Sometimes I would look over and see him like always, solid and sure. Other times he would be transparent, or only parts of him would be visible—a spray of blonde hair, a pair of eyes. It would have startled me, but I had more pressing concerns, and anyway, I always felt him. Felt the presence of him, burning on the wind. And that was all I needed.

Sails appeared on the horizon.

Isolfr solidified back into human form and stood up. The boat was only a dark speck next to those expansive sails. The *Penelope II* had sails like that, but my heart beat furiously, and I was afraid this was some kind of Foxfollow trick. Even when a shadow appeared in the sky, swooping like a bird but shaped like a horse, I still wasn't convinced.

"It's them," Isolfr said.

I stood up beside him and watched the boat draw closer. The wind blew my hair away from my face; sea mist brushed over my skin. Strange, jagged figures stuck out of the side of the ship, Jolali-style. It had to be the *Penelope II*. But I didn't allow myself to feel relief yet.

The moon horse made land first, galloping along the shore toward Trystan. He stood up to greet her, and when she stopped beside him, he placed one hand on her forehead and stood still, his head leaning into her forehead. She flapped her wings. Trystan nodded.

The moon horse flew away.

"She's not staying?" Isolfr asked.

"She can't take the risk," Trystan said. "I don't blame her. She wants to free her children from Lord Gallowglass's stable."

I didn't blame her either. If I could fly away, I would. But this was my world, and it was Isolfr's world, and I knew we needed to protect it.

The *Penelope II* sailed up alongside the rocks jutting haphazardly into the water and laid anchor. My fingers were tense with anxiety. It looked like the *Penelope II* but we couldn't be sure, not yet—

Kolur's face appeared over the side of the railing.

"Thank the ancestors," I breathed. "It's him."

Isolfr didn't say anything. He slid behind me.

"You made it through!" Kolur shouted. He was far enough away that I couldn't read his expression—if he was happy, relieved, terrified of Isolfr's true form. He waved at us, then gripped the railing and leaned forward. My heart jumped.

"Who the hell is that?" he asked, gesturing at Trystan.

Trystan gave a deep nobleman's bow, sweeping one arm gracefully through the air. "I am Lord Trystan of Llambric," he shouted over the wind. "Pleased to make your acquaintance."

"Who the hell is that?" Kolur shouted again, this time directing the question at me. Isolfr was still hanging back, behind me.

"A friend," I said. "He helped us arrive at Jandanvar, and he wants to see Lord Foxfollow dead."

"Don't we all," Kolur said in a grim, flat voice. He disappeared from the railing. I reached back and grabbed Isolfr's hand.

A few moments later, the gangway dropped.

"Can that captain of yours be trusted?" Trystan said.

"He can be trusted more than Lord Gallowglass."

Trystan looked over at me and his eyes glittered with a dark ferocity. I hadn't seen it in him before, and it made me want to shrink back, to hide like Isolfr. "I'm not giving up until he's been killed. He'll bleed light in this world, yes? Make him bleed light."

I felt a dull thud in the bottom of my stomach. Of course we'd talked of killing Lord Foxfollow—of destroying him. But now that we were here in Jandanvar, I didn't know if I could do it.

"Your legs broken?" hollered Kolur over the side of the boat. "Get the hell on board. We can't linger here! Ain't safe!"

I glanced over at Isolfr. He gazed back at me, his eyes lambent and sad.

"We can't put it off any longer," he said in a whisper.

"Now that's the most sense I've heard in a while," Trystan said, and he marched toward the gangplank with his back straight and his chin lifted.

I reached over and took Isolfr's hand. He gave me a grateful expression. He didn't need to say anything more.

Together, we walked on board.

Frida was in her usual place by the navigation table. She was hunched over a paper map held down by rocks, tracing across it with a divider. Kolur was tugging up the anchor, a charm to lighten the load twinkling on the air around him. Neither of them looked up from their work.

Trystan gazed up at the masts. At least his presence hadn't activated the protection charms.

Kolur glanced over at us. "Oh, thank the ancestors, you're on—" The anchor rope slipped out of his hands. Even with the charm, the anchor slammed back into the sea, generating a wall of water that splashed against the side of the boat. Kolur cursed and jumped sideways, shaking his coat dry. Then he looked up again. Not at Trystan. He'd known Trystan was of the Mists. No, he was looking at Isolfr.

For a moment, he didn't move, just stared at Isolfr with his mouth hanging open.

Then he reached into his coat and yanked out a knife.

"What the hell is this?" he hissed. "Frida!" he shouted. "Your spell is a travesty to the ancestors! It *let something through*!"

"It did not." I stepped in front of Isolfr, my whole body shaking.

Kolur brandished his knife at me. Behind him, Frida had lifted her gaze away from the map. She let out a shout and covered her mouth with one hand, then fumbled at her belt for a weapon.

"This is Lord Foxfollow's doing," Kolur said. "How the hell did you get on my boat?"

"We're not from Lord Foxfollow." Tears brimmed over the edge of my voice, but I didn't let myself back down. "It's *Pjetur*," I said. "This is Pjetur's real form. Do you even recognize him? You should." I turned my glare at Frida. "You tried to cast dark magic using his brother. The only reason you didn't kill him like you did that water spirit is because *Pjetur* stopped you."

Frida went pale. The knife she'd pulled from her belt dropped to the deck with a clatter.

"You're a trick too." Kolur lunged at me, but Frida lifted both hands and a gust of wind, sweet-smelling and westerly, blasted across the boat. Kolur fell on his side. His own knife went flying across the deck, and the wind lifted it up and sent it sailing back to Frida. She plucked it out of the air and tucked it into her belt.

"What the hell, Frida!" Kolur shouted.

"You know who it is," she said in a low voice. "You remember. Stop play-acting."

My hands were balled into fists, and I couldn't catch my breath. I was aware of Isolfr's closeness to me. I risked a quick glance back at him, and he was shaking, his arms wrapped around himself.

"You don't know what you're talking about," Kolur grunted.

"Don't be a fool, Kolur. We don't need this now." Frida strode over to him and helped him to his feet. The wind had resettled, a soft breeze that rippled the sails. Kolur wouldn't look at me.

"He was scared of you," I said, my voice ringing out clear and true. "All this time. He hid himself. He came to me and asked for *my* help because he didn't trust you."

Frida lifted her head, peering at me through the wisps of her hair that had fallen out of her braid.

"I know what you did," I said.

She looked away.

For a moment, there was only silence, and the wind. I turned back to Isolfr. He was still curling into himself. The wind ruffled his hair. It was a south wind, I realized—I could almost taste the magic of it on the back of my throat. Isolfr looked up at me. His eyes gleamed.

"She thinks you're very brave," he said in a low voice.

I blinked, shook my head: *I don't understand.*

"My sister." His hair danced across his forehead. "The south wind. She likes you."

I'd never thought of the south wind that way. I'd never considered her spirit, only her magic. And I smiled at the thought of it.

"So have we got this sorted?"

I jumped at Trystan's voice. He was still lounging over by the railing, his coat flapping around his thighs. Kolur and Frida both turned toward him. Kolur looked pale. Shaken.

"Are you going to let my friend on board the ship?" Trystan gestured at Isolfr. "Or aren't you? I need to know, because we need him. He's got the magic to weaken Lord Foxfollow." A pause. There was an eerie flatness in his expression. "So I can kill him."

"No," Kolur said. "This is not settled."

Trystan sighed. "We don't have time for this. Once he marries her, he'll be bound to your world. You do realize that, right?"

"I know that." Kolur looked straight at Isolfr and me. I dropped back, grabbed Isolfr's hand, squeezed it tight. "I know that better than anyone. In fact, if it were up to me, I would have killed the bastard already."

Trystan snorted. Frida sighed, rubbed her forehead.

"I'm sorry, Pjetur," Kolur said. Then he closed his eyes. "I mean, spirit of the wind. Which wind are you?" His eyes opened again.

Isolfr squeezed his hand against mine, and I tried to will him all of my strength.

"The north," Isolfr said. "My family calls me Isolfr."

His family. I felt a cold stun in the center of my heart. Surely it wasn't his true name, his spirit name, the name by which he could be controlled, but it was the name his family called him. All this time, even after the kiss, the worry in the dungeon and the tunnels—I'd thought Isolfr was a false name, a name spirits tell to humans.

"Very well, Isolfr." Kolur bowed. "I don't ask your forgiveness for what we did. But we need your help."

"I know," Isolfr said. "That's why I found you."

We sailed for a long time, long enough that darkness fell. It was a relief to see the stars again, to watch them wink on one by one in their familiar constellations. I sat out on deck with Isolfr, a thick woolen blanket wrapped around my shoulders. We tilted both our heads back and I told him the stories of the sky: of Brynjar and Galdur and even Rakel and Oddur, who were lovers. Telling the story made me blush, but I made it through. When I finished he smiled up at the sky and said, "That was a wonderful story, Hanna."

Hearing him say my name gave me a shiver of happiness. That was the only sort of happiness I allowed myself: the small kind, my name on Isolfr's tongue and the stars twinkling overhead. Because Lord Foxfollow still held sway here, and I knew we were sailing into battle.

It was still dark when we spotted land. Frida and Kolur brought us toward the shore on their own, with the use of Frida's magic. I didn't offer my help and they didn't ask for it, so I watched the landscape materialize up ahead. I couldn't see much of anything, only jagged silhouettes blacking out the stars, and, far, far off in the distance, a gleaming white light.

"That's the palace," Isolfr said. "That's the light of Jandanvari, and it never goes out. This late, it's the only light burning. We're actually closer to the palace than we seem."

I heard the tremor of fear in his voice and shivered.

The *Penelope II* turned and glided into the narrow channel created by the jagged cliffs. The magic-cast lanterns illuminated only patches of the stone, but in the green-tinged light I saw patterns that were clearly not formed by nature: runes and figures. Spells from an ancient magic.

"Wake your friend," Frida said, her voice close to my ear. I jumped and looked over at her. This was the first we'd spoken since I'd protected Isolfr.

She tilted her head toward the hatch leading down below. She was talking about Trystan, then. He had insisted on sleeping in the captain's quarters. "We don't want to leave him."

"I'll do it," Isolfr said.

Frida reached out toward his face as if she wanted to silence him, although she stopped, her hand hovering in midair. "Be quiet," she whispered. "Palace spies might be lurking in the darkness."

Her warning whirled around in my head. Isolfr nodded and turned to go down below. Frida looked over at me, touched her finger to her lips, and then scurried over to the ship's wheel, where she conferred with Kolur, their heads tilted together.

The cliffs loomed around us. Even in the dim lantern light I could see that they were as sleek and smooth as a polished gem, and there was no way to climb them. But we had to get onto land somehow. We couldn't attack the palace from our ship.

The *Penelope II* slowed. Water lapped up against its sides, but otherwise the night was silent. When Kolur tossed the anchor over the side, the splash made me jump, despite the sound-dampening spell he and Frida had cast over it. Frida pointed at the anchor rope. "Wait there," she whispered. "We'll be climbing down."

I did as she said. I was too numb with fear to think of much else. Isolfr and Trystan emerged from down below—I could just make them out in the darkness. I lifted one hand in greeting, and together they walked over to me. Trystan had his hands tucked under his coat, and his hair was mussed from sleep, but Isolfr lifted his gaze along the tall black cliffs.

"Oh," he said softly. "Smugglers' Wall."

"What?" I said.

"The name of these cliffs." He nodded at them. "Smugglers' Wall. They say smugglers and pirates hide their boats here before they sack the city." He looked at me sideways. "I guess they're right."

"We aren't pirates," I said, but I knew, in the eyes of Lord Fox-follow, we might as well be.

Kolur and Frida appeared beside us. Kolur leaned over the side with a magic-cast lantern and made a gesture with his hand, barely discernible in the dim light. He twisted his fingers into circles and lines, and the lantern flickered in a pattern: two long blinks, a slow blink.

Somewhere down in the depths of the sea, a light answered in turn. Two slow blinks, a long blink.

"They're waiting." Kolur said.

"Who are?" I said.

He didn't look at me—he'd been as distant as Frida, after what happened with Isolfr. "The outlaws," he said. "Our contacts here."

Of course. The outlaws. They'd seemed unimaginable when Isolfr and I were trapped in the Mists.

Kolur extinguished the lantern and set it at his feet. "Frida will go first. Climb down the anchor rope. Take care not to fall, that water will kill you." His gaze swept over Isolfr. "Most of you."

"Climb down?" Trystan said. He peered over the side of the boat, frowning. "You're quite kidding, correct?"

"I'm quite not," Kolur said. "If you don't like it, you can stay on the boat."

Trystan scowled, but I knew he would climb. He wanted to get to Lord Foxfollow too badly.

Frida tossed her braid over her shoulder, gripped the rope, and swung around over it, her movements easy and practiced. Isolfr stared at her, his eyes dark wells in his pale face. "I'll go next," he said. "In case you or Trystan fall."

I smiled at him. "I'm not going to fall." I wasn't certain of that, but I wanted to be brave.

"I, for one, appreciate the concern," Trystan said.

"Enough," Kolur said. "This chatter ends now. They won't wait forever."

That silenced us. Isolfr leaned over the edge and grabbed the rope. He swung out with the grace of the wind, his body like a shooting star. My chest tightened. He climbed down the rope— hesitantly though. It was still Isolfr.

Kolur nodded at me.

I took a deep breath. I'd never crawled down an anchor rope before, and I'd certainly never done so over a freezing ocean in the darkest of nights. But I wasn't going to let my fear get the best of me.

The rope was thick and rough beneath my bare hands. I swung my leg out awkwardly and hooked it around the rope, then let myself drop free of the boat. For one terrifying moment I thought I would fall, and I hung there, breathing hard, suspended in air. When I was certain I was stable, I began to inch down. The rope swayed in the wind, and the ocean rushed and roared beneath me. I looked back up at the *Penelope II*. Trystan was fumbling his way onto the rope. I kept my gaze focused on him as I crept lower on the rope. Blood pounded in my ears. When I was halfway down the side of the boat, I glanced over my shoulder at the water. I couldn't see anything but darkness and Isolfr. He was stationary, off to the side. In a rowboat, I decided.

I kept climbing. Trystan was still above me. I couldn't see Kolur. The silence beat at my ears.

And then, suddenly, the wind picked up, a gentle northern breeze. I closed my eyes and let it wash over me.

"Isolfr," I whispered.

You're almost there, the wind said in a dry, fluttering whisper. *I'll tell you when to jump*.

Even though the wind knocked the rope back and forth and tossed my hair into my eyes, I felt much safer with it. With *him*. Isolfr.

I climbed down, my feet slipping and sliding against the rope, my palms burning. The ocean sounded closer, but it might just have been the blood in my head.

Let go, the wind said.

I did. That was how much I trusted him. I didn't even look back.

For the span of two heartbeats I was flying. Then my feet stumbled over unsteady ground. Hands were at my waist. A spray of cold water splashed over my legs.

"You're safe," Isolfr said, in his human voice, solid and less melodious than his wind voice.

I turned toward him. His hands lingered on my hips. We were in a rowboat, just as I'd thought. Frida crouched beside the boatman, a stout, muscular man with a long beard, probably yellow in normal light, but in the light of the lantern it looked green.

"Clear a place for the others," he said in a gruff voice.

Isolfr let go of me and I felt the absence of his touch. I edged over to the stern of the boat and sat down on the bench. It was a big boat, enough for ten men at least.

I sat in silence in the darkness as Isolfr helped Trystan jump down from the rope. Kolur came next. As soon as we were all stowed onboard, the boatman dipped the oars into the water and rowed us away. He didn't even wait for a cue from Kolur or Frida.

Smugglers' Wall rose up on either side of us, reflecting the darkness back in on itself. A lantern dangled out from the bow of the boat, casting a small green circle in the water. It felt like the ocean was holding its breath.

Eventually, the boatman turned the boat and rowed us into a crack in the wall. I expected the darkness to be even thicker inside, so thick we'd choke on it, but instead the walls were veined with pale swirls of light. It reminded me of Tattersall Manor, back in the Mists. The magic felt the same.

I slid closer to Isolfr, who had come to sit beside me, and wrapped my arms around myself to stave off the cold.

"Almost there," the boatman said. "No need for silence at this juncture."

Kolur nodded, but still, no one spoke.

We hadn't been inside the wall for long when the water suddenly bumped up against a slick, black stone beach. The boatman dragged us up with his oars, then jumped out and splashed up to the beach and brought us in the rest of the way. He gave a bow to Kolur as we disembarked.

"Good luck," he said. "May Iral guide your actions."

"Thank you," Kolur said.

The boatman nodded and jumped into the rowboat and pushed off into the water.

"Where's he going?" Trystan asked. "Back out in the cold?"

"He's the ferryman and the guard," Kolur said. "It's his job. Come along. Ankia's waiting."

He led us down the black stone beach. Isolfr grabbed my hand and we held on tight to each other. I had no idea what the future was going to bring us. I didn't want to think about the possibility of death.

"Kolur Icebreak."

It was a woman's voice, bright and commanding. All of us stopped in our tracks. In the darkness the voice seemed to come from everywhere.

"Ankia?" Kolur glanced around. "You don't need to play these games."

"You've brought companions."

"I told you I was."

"There's one more than you told me about." The voice solidified. I turned around, trying to track it—and found its owner. She was tall and shrouded in shapeless gray furs, her hair tucked up under a black feather cap. A sword was strapped to her belt, but she had a pistol out and pointed at us. "Who are you?" She fixed her glare on Trystan.

Kolur looked a loss of words, but Trystan stepped forward and gave a courtly bow. "Lord Trystan of Llambric, my lady," he said. "I am a creature of the Mists, but you mustn't hold that against me. I want Lord Foxfollow dead and gone as much as you do."

Her eyes narrowed. "That's an odd thing to hear from one of your kind."

"I want to exact my revenge," he said. "Lord Foxfollow wreaks havoc in my world as well as yours. My family has fought him for generations."

She studied him. I was almost too scared to breathe.

"I will kill you," she said. "Make no mistake." And then she looked at the rest of us, from Frida to me and then finally to Isolfr. "Oh," she said when she saw him, and she dropped her pistol.

Isolfr shimmered.

"Yes," Kolur said slowly. "I wasn't aware that he was—a spirit. He'd led me to believe he was a human boy named Pjetur."

Now it was Ankia's turn to bow, and she did so deeply. "It's an honor to have you among us, North Wind. We can offer any aid you need in your mission."

Isolfr wobbled a little, looking embarrassed. "I appreciate that very much," he said.

Ankia nodded. She slid her pistol back into its holster. "All our forces are coming together," she said to him. "And you made it just in time. We've been waiting for the wedding. It's the only time outsiders are allowed into the palace."

The wedding. I felt dizzy with fear.

Isolfr, the north wind, squeezed my hand more tightly.

CHAPTER FOURTEEN

Dinner that night was loud and rowdy. The outlaws crowded around their stone tables and slammed back jugs of ale. They shouted at one another, their voices bouncing off the walls and making them sound even louder than they were. Ankia didn't participate in all that wildness, though. She was grim and quiet when she sat down at the table where Isolfr, Trystan, and I were stirring our lisila.

"North Wind," she said, "I need to discuss our plan of action with you."

"Your plan of action?" Isolfr looked up from his food and frowned at her.

"*Our* plan of action," she said. "You arrived just in time, you know. The wedding is tomorrow."

My ears started buzzing. For a moment I couldn't even hear the whoops and hollers of the outlaws—there was only that buzzing, like my head had been filled with a million insects. The wedding was tomorrow.

"No wonder they're all getting so drunk," Trystan muttered.

Ankia glanced sideways at him. "You would do well not to pass judgment, Mists-man," she said. "Your presence here is only barely tolerated."

Trystan glared at her.

"Please don't speak to him like that," Isolfr said. "Lord Trystan is the only reason Hanna and I were able to make it out of the Mists."

Ankia's expression didn't waver, but I suspected she wasn't one to be easily cowed, either. "I realize that," she said. "Which is why he's allowed to stay."

Trystan rolled his eyes and turned back to his food.

"We will be disguising ourselves as musicians," Ankia said. She spoke in a low voice, and I had to lean across the table to hear her over the outlaws. "The arrangements have already been made, but it will be easy to add two more."

"Three more," Isolfr said. Trystan looked over at him.

Ankia frowned. "No. Absolutely not."

Trystan threw his spoon to the table. "And the Sun Realms say we're untrustworthy. Isolfr spoke the truth, you know. I took them in, at great risk to myself and to my family name, so that I could see Lord Foxfollow undone—so that I could see him *killed*. He is a person of the Mists, my dear lady, and you will do well to have a person of the Mists on your side when you go to fight him."

His speech was met with silence that was crowded out by a round of slurred singing from the front of the room. Ankia fixed him with a cold gaze. Her eyes glinted like steel.

"My men won't stand for it," she said. "I feel for you, but I'm keeping you away as much for your safety as for—"

Trystan stood up, shoving away from the table. "The Sun Realms aren't the only place that have been poisoned by Foxfollow's magic," he said. His voice cracked. It took me a moment to realize that he wasn't acting out of anger, but sadness. My heart twisted for him.

Ankia said nothing.

Trystan stalked away from the table, weaving through the crowd of outlaws. They turned away from him as he passed. They cast their eyes down. It was as if they could will him away.

"That wasn't fair of you," Isolfr said. "He saved us—"

"You've made that clear," Ankia said, "and if we had more time I'm sure my men would come to trust him. But we don't have time. The wedding is *tomorrow*—"

My head buzzed again.

"—And you know as well as I that if Foxfollow marries the queen, they'll be bound together and even her death wouldn't allow us to drive him from this world. In fact, I suspect her death is exactly what he wants."

"Yes," Isolfr said quietly.

"So we go in tomorrow. Disguised as musicians, as I said. You will ride in the caravan with Frida and Kolur—stay with them, as we want our wizards grouped together."

Wizards. I was going to ride into battle as a witch. I looked down at my food and wondered if I should confess to Ankia that I'd never been properly trained, that the only times I'd ever found myself in a proper magic fight, I wasn't fighting alone.

But then, I wouldn't be fighting alone in this battle either.

"We leave at daybreak." Ankia stood up from the table, taking her bowl of lisila with her. "They tend to stay up all night drinking." She jerked her head back in the direction of the outlaws. "But I suggest you get some sleep."

It was the first time she'd spoken to me directly.

"All right," I said.

Ankia's dispassionate expression didn't change. She only nodded once and then left the table. I stared after her. I felt like I might throw up.

"She's right," Isolfr said in my ear. "You should try and sleep. Eat, too." He nudged the lisila toward me. "I imagine they made it special, since we're fighting tomorrow."

I stirred the lisila around. The surface changed colors like a rainbow. It reminded me so much of Asbera and Finnur. I'd been scared when I met them, too. But not scared like this. Back home in Kjora I could never have imagined fear like this.

"Are you frightened?" I said, speaking down into my lisila.

"I'm terrified," said Isolfr.

I sighed and pressed my face into his shoulder. He smelled of the north wind and the sea, a scent that made me think, sharply and unexpectedly, of home. Home. My family. I might never see them again, but weren't they the reason I was going to fight? Because if I stopped Foxfollow, then I had saved them.

I spooned a bit of lisila in my mouth. It tasted like ash and dirt. I knew it wasn't the fault of the lisila.

Still, I forced myself to choke it down. The outlaws' party raged on around us. Even Kolur drank enough that he started yelling like the rest of them. Across the room, I watched as he threw his arm around the shoulders of a man with a thick black beard. They sang a song I didn't recognize, about a whorehouse and a girl with yellow hair. The lyrics made me blush. They made Isolfr blush too.

Not long after that, a thin, stooped outlaw with a curved sword approached our table. He bowed when he saw Isolfr. "North Wind," he said.

Isolfr blinked up at him, the same beautiful boy I'd seen swimming in the moonlight all those weeks ago.

"Ankia has asked me to see the two of you to the sleeping room." He gave another bow. "She thinks you should both rest before tomorrow."

Isolfr and I looked at each other. I thought about Trystan, wondered if he'd be there too—I imagined the sleeping room was a sailors' barracks, row after row of cots lined up one after another.

But it wasn't. The outlaw instead led us to a small room carved out of the cavern wall. Light threaded through the stone, and a shimmering crystal hung from the ceiling. I immediately felt the magic of that crystal when I walked in—it was a protection charm, a totem, one of the strongest I'd ever felt.

"For the North Wind," the outlaw said with a bow. "Only the best."

One thing the room didn't have was a bed. Instead, a pile of thick straw covered in furs and blankets lay on the floor. Heat orbs floated around it like stars. The outlaw scurried out of the room, leaving us alone.

Isolfr collapsed down on the blankets. Bits of straw flew up around him. "I hate the way they're treating me like a hero. I'm *not* a hero."

I sat down beside him. "I wouldn't say that."

He stared up at the ceiling. Lights from the crystal danced across his face. "I don't know what I'm going to do tomorrow. What any of us are going to do. I can't believe they're not letting Trystan come—no, that's not true. I can believe it. It's just so *stupid*. Why would they turn down help from the Mists?" He threw his hands in the air.

"Well, I guess that leaves it up to us, doesn't it?" I leaned in close to him. The coolness of him was a pleasant contrast to the heat emanating from the globes. "That's what you told me back in Tulja, remember? That it was up to us. We didn't even think we'd have Trystan's help then."

He looked over at me. "I remember that."

I lay my head on his shoulder, and, after a moment's pause, he looped his arm around me. I didn't tell him everything I was thinking—I didn't tell him that the idea of marching into the castle terrified me, that I was so numb with fear I felt as if everything about myself had been emptied out, that the only thing tying me to this world was the feel of his body pressed against mine. I didn't tell him all that because I knew he probably felt it too.

"We've got our magic," I finally said. "When we work together—we're strong."

He nodded, his hair grazing my cheek. I pressed in closer to him. He was cold; I was warm. North and south. Together we were like a spring day.

I closed my eyes. My fear had me rattling inside, but at least on the outside I felt calm, comforted, safe.

Isolfr leaned back, pulling me with him. We lay together on the straw and furs, our limbs wound up in each other. We didn't speak. Both of us knew there was nothing more to say. We were scared and we were going to fight together tomorrow, side by side.

We left the caves the next morning at dawn.

As Ankia said, we disguised ourselves as traveling performers from the southerly islands—not the Kjoran style exactly, but the patterns in the fabric were still familiar to me. Ankia had developed an entire backstory about how we were a gift for the Queen of Jandanvar from the people of Lamista, how we honored her wisdom and grace and beauty and wished for her long life and prosperity in the years to come. I hoped it was enough to get us through the palace gates.

Ankia did not change her mind regarding Trystan. I saw him as we boarded the caravans, standing off to the side, a breeze blowing his hair. He smiled at me, looking sad.

"Kill him," he said, and nothing more.

It left me shaken. I didn't want to think about killing anyone, not even Lord Foxfollow.

As promised, Isolfr, Frida, Kolur, and I all rode together in a single carriage. It was small but decorated with Empire silks and Qilari rugs, and there were bits of fragmented glass hung over the windows so that in the white Jandanvar daylight, the caravan would be full of rainbows. It was a lot of finery for a ruse, but I suspected that the ruse needed to be as a detailed as possible if we wanted to pass under Foxfollow's eye.

All of us were dressed in what Ankia claimed was the traditional Lamistan style: long, colorful jackets and boots to our knees. It also allowed for women to wear trousers, which was why it had been chosen. I didn't mention to her that I would be fighting with magic, and that wasn't the sort of fighting where it mattered what you wore. But still the outlaws put me in trousers. One of them also handed me a small, slim blade and told me to keep it close.

I didn't want to think about the implications.

We rode in silence, bumping over the rocky roads. Isolfr sat close to me and let his hand drop over mine. Kolur leaned up against the carriage wall and closed his eyes, although I knew he wasn't sleeping. Frida murmured to herself, prayers for good luck. I couldn't bring myself to pray. Instead, I stared out the window, watching the grass roll by, a sick feeling lurking in the pit of my stomach.

I wasn't sure how long it was before our traveling musicians' caravan was stopped. I couldn't see anything from the window except sweeps of grass, but I could hear voices up at the front of the caravan. They were low, steady. They didn't sound like voices readying for a fight.

But then Isolfr gripped my hand more tightly, and I knew we had to be close.

It seemed like we were stopped for a long time. None of us spoke, although Frida stopped praying and glanced out the window. Kolur opened his eyes. He looked hollow and drawn. His eye sockets were sunken. Dark.

And then, just as I wasn't sure I could stand the stillness any longer, the carriage jerked forward.

"Are we there?" I whispered to Isolfr.

"We're passing through the gates," Isolfr said. "Or we should be soon." He pointed to the window. The chains of broken glass swung in time to the motion of the carriage. On the other side of it, the grass ended abruptly at a tall white-stone wall. A guard watched us drive by. I couldn't tell if he was human or Mists. He had two pistols tucked into his belt and a sword at his side, but he was kicking at the ground, not paying us any mind.

I pulled away from the window. The wall passed by.

We were inside the palace estate.

The landscape beyond the wall was no longer an empty stretch of grass, but a garden, threaded through with shimmering flowers and tall, willowy trees with white bark and crystalline leaves. A constant chiming stirred around us, a discordant, beautiful music that only set my nerves further on edge.

"Ankia's going to take us around to the back," Kolur said in a low voice. "We'll be taken to a performer's room to wait until the queen and Lord Foxfollow are ready to see us. Keep the light on. The ceremony will take place once the sun's dropped below the horizon. A Jandanvari custom."

We'd gone over all of this earlier. Ankia had laid out the entire plan. It felt too easy for me. Lord Foxfollow was not some mortal man who could be easily fooled by performers in bright clothes. He was a lord of the Mists. He had grown up in a world built of magic. Surely, he could see through our trap.

This was why it was folly that Trystan hadn't come with us. But the outlaws weren't going to listen to a half-Empire windwitch. They weren't even going to listen to the North Wind himself.

No one stopped the caravan as it pulled around to the servants' entrance of the palace. Our carriage shuddered to a stop. My heartbeat quickened. Kolur was the first to stand up. I didn't want to leave this place. The silks and broken glass were beautiful—it was a beautiful dream, and I was about to wake up into the horror of the morning.

But I still climbed out of the carriage, my hand in Isolfr's.

The caravan had circled around into a wide courtyard built of the same white stones as the palace wall. In the sun's cold light I was momentarily blinded, dazzled by the whiteout. I stepped closer to Isolfr. I wanted to be as close to him as I could during our time in the palace. If I was going to die, I wanted him to be the last person I saw.

No. I couldn't think like that. My family was waiting for me in Kjora. I would see them again. I would kiss Isolfr again, I would sail on the rich dark sea again. I was not going to die here.

"Performers!" shouted Ankia, waving a ribboned staff in one hand. "File into the palace! Master Eloy will lead you to the waiting room!"

The outlaws muttered together, playing their roles. They had disguised their weapons as musical instruments—pistols hidden away in the hollow of a guitar, harps whose strings could be snapped away for the purpose of garroting an enemy.

Ankia swooped her staff through the air the way any troupe leader would, and leaped off her carriage. We followed her inside. I'd been too frightened, really, to think about what a palace might look like on the inside—but we were in the servants' corridor, and so it looked no different from the manor houses back in the Mists. The hallway was narrow enough that we had to walk single file. I was shaking the whole time, certain that Master Eloy was leading us to our deaths, that we'd been found out long before we passed through the gate and Lord Foxfollow was toying with us. But soon enough I found myself standing in a large, bright atrium, sunlight pouring in through skylights in the ceiling.

A small, hunched-over old man held the door for us, and he gave a tilt of his head when we passed. His eyes were dark brown. Human. He must be Master Eloy.

Once we were all inside the room, he said in a thin, quavering voice, "We will call for you when Her Highness is ready. She is most looking forward to your performance."

He slipped back out into the hallway, letting the door swing shut behind him.

Isolfr moved closer to me. He'd wound a scarf around the bottom of his face, trying to disguise the qualities that made him so clearly inhuman. It mostly worked.

The outlaws muttered among themselves. They didn't talk about the attack, just little grumbles about the state of the atrium, the weather the last few days, the condition of the instruments.

Kolur looked determined. Grim. Frida stood at his side with her eyes closed. Her chest moved in and out. Readying herself. I knew I should be doing the same, gathering up the strength of my magic, but I was so frightened I wasn't sure I could think clearly enough for it.

We waited in that room forever. I watched the light in the window, afraid that it was darkening, that it was too late—

And then the door opened. It wasn't Master Eloy, but a pretty woman in a long brocade gown the color of wine, her hair twisted up around her head in braids so complicated they looked like a tiara. For one wild moment I thought she was the queen, that she had sensed Kolur somehow and come to stop him.

But she only held out one hand, gesturing toward the hallway, and said, "Her Majesty Queen Penelope of Jandanvar and her betrothed are ready for your performance."

The queen's name struck me hard between the eyes. All this time and I'd been fishing on a boat named after Kolur's biggest mistake.

"About damn time," one of the outlaws said, and Ankia hushed him and gave a broad smile to the woman.

"My apologies, my lady," she said, "but Amado here isn't used to being in the presence of such finery. We've never been given such an honor before, and—"

"It's a wedding! You should all be in better spirits." The woman looked amused. "Come, let me show you the way."

Once again, we filed out into the hallway. I was numb with fear. Isolfr walked right behind me, so close he sometimes stepped on the heels of my boots. I didn't mind. It was a reminder that he was there.

We walked, winding through the palace, past sculptures and paintings and twinkling bursts of magic.

I was afraid I would just stop breathing.

Eventually, we came to an alcove partitioned off with a curtain. Music drifted in from the other side of the curtain, along with the sound of people talking and laughing, their voices twinkling like stars. The woman in brocade slipped through the curtain. The outlaws had fallen silent. Their muscles corded up beneath their clothes. Sweat gleamed on their skin.

It was my last chance to turn and run. I could probably make it, too, if I followed the hallway back out to the courtyard, and then pretended I'd been besieged by a fear of an audience. But I glanced over at Isolfr, and he was pale and trembling but he was determined too, as determined as Kolur, and I knew I couldn't leave him like that.

"Your Majesty Queen Penelope and her paramour, Lord Fox-follow, the good people of Lamista have seen fit to grant you a gift of their finest musical performers on this most sacred of days."

The audience's polite applause turned to the buzzing of insects inside my head.

"Time to fight," Kolur whispered in my ear.

We shuffled out into the open.

The throne room was enormous, with high arched ceilings made of a polished, transparent stone that let in the diffused sunlight. The room was hung with flowers and ribbons, and the courtiers milling up against the walls wore gowns of silk and fur, their faces painted for the celebration.

And then there was the bride and groom, Penelope and Foxfollow, sitting on thrones carved of the same transparent stone as the ceiling. Penelope was older than I expected but extraordinarily beautiful. Her long brown hair was streaked with pristine white the same color as snow. She wore a tall, spiked crown that glittered like stars, and a gray gown that flowed over the steps leading up to her throne. It sparkled with jewels at the bodice and the hem. It was a wedding gown.

Lord Foxfollow wore a black suit. He looked exactly as I remembered when I called him in the in-between world.

My throat went dry. I stumbled backward, trying to hide myself among the outlaws.

Penelope gazed over us and smiled. "Musicians of Lamista," she said, her voice imbued with a kindness and warmth I would not have expected from someone betrothed to Lord Foxfollow. "Welcome to Jandanvar."

The courtiers stirred and then issued a polite ripple of applause. Lord Foxfollow stared straight ahead. His eyes were hooded, dark, unreadable. I pressed close to Isolfr, and he shrank against me, and we were in the back, where Lord Foxfollow would never see us—

"You!" he roared, his voice breaking through the whispery quiet of the throne room. He leaped to his feet and jabbed his finger toward the outlaws.

For one dizzying, stomach-sick moment I was certain he was

pointing at me, and that I would have to act when I had forgotten, in my fear, all my magic. But then Kolur drew back his hood and said, "Yes, it's me."

The queen paled. Her mouth moved but I couldn't hear what she said, not over the chatter of the courtiers.

"Intruder," Lord Foxfollow snarled. "Interloper. Guards!"

The outlaws didn't wait for a signal. They sprung their weapons free from their instruments, swords and knives and pistols. The courtiers' scandalized mutters transformed into screams, and they began trampling toward the formal entrance at the back of the room. Lord Foxfollow lifted his hands above his head and conjured a ball of light out of the air—but Kolur shot back with magic of his own, and it collided with Lord Foxfollow's and erupted into a shower of glitter that sizzled when it touched my hair and my clothes.

Guards poured into the throne room, shoving the courtiers aside. All around me was the painful clang of steel hitting steel, the pop of firearms. I whirled around, trying to find a place where I could cast magic in safety. Through the melee I saw a tapestry threaded through with flowers from the Empire. There. Perfect.

"Come on!" I shouted to Isolfr, grabbing him by the arm and dragging him across the room. He resisted at first, but a bullet whizzed past our heads and he stumbled after me. I ducked a swinging blade, toppling us both to the floor. Magic exploded in the air above the room. I smelled burning hair.

I yanked Isolfr behind the tapestry. It was dark and sickly with the scent of flowers back there, and the sound of fighting had followed us. But we at least had the illusion of safety.

"We can't just hide," Isolfr said, his voice shaking.

"We're not! But if we'd stayed out there we would have gotten ourselves killed. We need to decide exactly how we're going to fight."

Isolfr nodded. I peeked around the curtain. At first I couldn't make sense of what I was seeing—it was just a whirling storm of blades and pistol smoke and glittering magic. Penelope was bound up in a tight coil of silver thread, and she thrashed against her restraints and screamed. Kolur and Frida couldn't get to her though—Lord Foxfollow was beating them back with wave after wave of shimmering white magic that made the entire room hum like it was about to light on fire.

I jerked my head back behind the tapestry. "We need to help strengthen Kolur and Frida's spells."

"What spell is it?"

I shook my head. "I don't know."

Isolfr took a deep breath and peered around the side of the tapestry—then immediately snapped his head back in, his eyes wide and panicky. "Foxfollow's going to kill all of us if we don't stop him," he said. "That's Ansley's Folly."

I shook my head. I'd never heard of it.

"A Mists spell!" His voice edged on hysterical. "I've read about it. There's no time to explain. Just know that it will kill all of us if he keeps casting it."

"Well then, we've got to stop him." I grabbed Isolfr by the hand and then leaned over and kissed him once, quickly, on the mouth.

"Ready?" I said.

He nodded.

I yanked back the tapestry and in one solid movement, our hands still linked, Isolfr and I called down the power of the winds: the north wind and the south wind both. Everything in the room stilled—and then the air surged, wind rushing through the walls, strong enough to blow the guards and outlaws off balance. The wind threaded into Kolur and Frida's magic and there was a vast expansion of light as our spell struck the Ansley's Folly. The strength of the wind raced through me, setting me alight—but Foxfollow was pushing back, his magic cold and damp and hollow. It was an absence of movement.

In the center of the room, arcing above the battle between outlaws and guards, these two magics pummeled each other.

Lord Foxfollow let out a shout of rage, and his anger jolted through me, shuddering down deep into my bones. Isolfr gasped and his hand slipped away from me. I reached out for him, not daring to take my eyes off Lord Foxfollow—

And then Lord Foxfollow's magic collapsed in on itself. The shimmering light grew smaller and smaller until it was a dark spot in existence. Something rushed out of me. I didn't know what was happening.

Kolur shouted. It sounded like *Stop*.

That dark spot of magic slammed into Penelope, the Queen of Jandanvar. She was lifted off the ground and then slammed down hard in front of Kolur. Her bounds loosened, spilling around her like water. But she didn't move.

"You want her," Lord Foxfollow shouted. "You can have her. I can hold this palace." Then, "Guards!" He swirled one hand above his head and a wave of magic crashed over the melee in the center of the room, knocking all the outlaws to their feet. "There are easier ways to fight," Foxfollow snarled, and Kolur lunged toward him, and Frida pulled him back, and the walls were rippling and distorting with magic-sickness.

I couldn't stay there anymore. None of us could. I grabbed Isolfr by the hand and pulled him toward the doors.

"No!" he shouted. "The queen!"

"We can't get to her!" I shouted back, but I looked over my shoulder and found Kolur cradling her in his lap, his head tilted down over hers, one hand ghosting over her hair.

"She's dead!" I shouted, and pulled on Isolfr again.

"She's not! I can feel her!"

"Come *on*!"

Another burst of magic shattered in the air above our heads, and when it fell across me it sank heavily into my skin. The magic inside me crawled and shifted, threatening to transform in ways I couldn't control. Isolfr's skin was turning translucent, his hair streaking out behind like a comet's tail.

"The magic-sickness!" I screamed. "We can't stay here!"

"But the queen—"

Ankia's voice cut through the rushing in my head. "Retreat!" she shouted. "Retreat!"

Lord Foxfollow was laughing, a cold, hollow sound that struck me in the center of my chest. I grabbed at Isolfr, my hand slipping through his on the first try, on the second try, but finally latching on with the third. We raced toward the doors. No one tried to stop us. The guards were too busy with the outlaws.

We passed out of the throne room. I turned for one last look back. Frida was close behind us, her expression wild, and Kolur was close behind her.

He cradled Penelope in his arms.

I ran.

CHAPTER FIFTEEN

Isolfr turned to wind in the vast, sparkling hallways of the palace. I wasn't sure if he did it on purpose or not, if he was trying to protect himself from the magic-sickness or if the magic-sickness had forced him to change. Either way, he swept me and Kolur and Frida and Penelope up in the air and carried us out of the palace, away from the guards shooting arrows in our direction. We flew so high that the palace became a speck. It was all I was aware of, that speck of black in a sea of gray-green grass. I was too numb to notice anything else. Too numb to care about the cold comfort of Isolfr's embrace, or to think about Frida and Kolur, or to worry about Penelope.

We drifted over the landscape. Soon, Smugglers' Wall appeared in the distance, a black mass against the bright sky. The ground rushed up to meet us, and for one dizzying second I thought I was falling. But Isolfr laid me down soft and sweet at the mouth of the cave. Frida settled beside me, sprawling on her back in the sand. Kolur was next. He still held Penelope.

She wasn't moving. Her skin was pale and ashen, her eyes sunk low in their sockets. The heavy wedding dress pooled around her and Kolur. She'd lost her crown. None of that mattered anymore, I knew. I remembered what it was like when Finnur had slipped into a magic-coma, how desperate I'd been to save him. Kolur wore that desperation now. He leaned over Penelope and ran his hand down the side of her face. Murmured something I couldn't hear.

The wind—Isolfr—blew across us. It tossed strands of her hair into her face, and Kolur smoothed them away with a gentle touch I wouldn't have thought him capable of. And it struck me, hard, that Isolfr might never be able to come back to me in human form. Foxfollow's magic might have changed him completely.

"Isolfr," I whispered.

Here, said the voice of the wind. *I'll come back soooooon.*

The last word drew out into a long, mournful wail. Just wind. I closed my eyes.

"We need to get her into the cave," Frida said.

Kolur stared down at Penelope and didn't answer.

"Kolur," Frida said more firmly.

He jumped, shook his head like he was trying to clear out his thoughts.

"I know," he snapped. He brushed her hair away from her eyes. "I know." More softly this time. He was speaking to Penelope, not to us.

Then he stood up, lifting Penelope in his arms. Frida watched him, waiting until he was steady, before she led us down into the cave. The sunlight didn't reach there—everything was still lit with magic. And in the light of that magic I could see tears gleaming on Kolur's cheeks.

"Who's there?" Trystan's voice broke through the cave's echoing silence. Frida stopped abruptly.

"It's us," I called out. "Hanna and—" I stopped. Isolfr hadn't come with us into the cave. An ache shuddered through my chest.

Trystan appeared in the corridor ahead of us. He held up a magic-cast lantern. The light washed out his face. "Did you kill him?"

"No," said Frida. "No, it was a failure."

Trystan didn't move. The lantern light slid over the walls.

"We should have let you come with us," I said, my words a tumble. "Foxfollow cast Mists magic—something's Folly, I don't remember the name, but Isolfr knew it——" Tears broke through my voice. "We couldn't stop him."

Trystan moved closer. "It's not your fault. Where's Isolfr?" He stopped, his eyes following Kolur, who was half hidden by the long shining trail of Penelope's wedding gown. "Who's that?"

"Queen Penelope of Jandanvar," Frida said. "We need to tend to her. I don't suppose you could help?"

"What happened to her?" he said.

"Mists magic," Kolur said gruffly. "Not anything I've seen before. She's still alive, but she's not part of this world. Not right now."

His voice was hard, and he didn't look at Trystan as he spoke. Trystan held the light more closely to Penelope and peered down at her.

"I'll see what I can do," he said. "Lay her down in one of the sleeping rooms."

"Already planning on it," Kolur said, and he pushed past Trystan. Frida followed. Trystan and I stood in the green light, staring at each other as their footsteps turned to silence.

"I'll never forgive that Ankia for this," Trystan finally said. "You tell her that. I could have stopped him."

"I know," I said.

"Where's Isolfr?" Trystan paused. "He's not——"

"He turned to wind," I said. "He told me he'd be back." I didn't tell Trystan that I felt like the wind myself, loose and ill-defined. I hadn't noticed it until I stood still.

Trystan swung the light toward me. His eyes widened. "Calael's sword, Hanna."

"What?" His words made no sense to me. "Sword? Where?"

"No! Look——" He pulled my hand into the light. It was turning transparent in places, my veins glowing with pale white light.

"Oh," I said. "Oh, the magic-sickness—"

"You need to tend to that."

I nodded. I couldn't remember any of the things I'd learned about magic-sickness. I'd actually thought the magic had faded away from me completely during the flight out of the palace, but here it was manifesting on my skin.

"Rest," Trystan said. "Stay away from magic. Stay away from—" He hesitated, then tilted his head toward the sleeping rooms. "—The queen. She's probably radiating magic right now. Kolur shouldn't be in there. None of you should."

"You're not going to get Kolur away from her." I shuffled away from Trystan and into the calming darkness. Let him tend to Penelope. I could tend to myself.

I stumbled over a loose rock, and I threw out my arm to steady myself against the wall. Touching the damp stone helped me feel more solid. My thoughts clarified. I missed Isolfr. Missed him in his human form. And so I thought of his human form, the solidity of it, the way it had felt against my body as we lay side by side, as we kissed.

That memory, that feeling of him—I think it stopped the magic-sickness. I think it kept me whole.

The outlaws came back sometime later. I was stretched out on the pile of straw when I heard them—their heavy, defeated footsteps, the rumble of their voices. By that point my skin had largely returned to normal, and I hadn't noticed any other side effects of the magic-sickness. I was still too weak to get up, though, to see how they had fared. Not that I needed to ask to learn that our invasion of the palace had been an abject failure. Yes, we had stopped Queen Penelope from marrying Lord Foxfollow. But maybe he didn't need her hand in marriage. He wouldn't have cursed her otherwise. Maybe it was enough that she was still alive, that she still existed. He was still in her palace, and perhaps he still had her power.

I rolled over onto my side. My thoughts were thick and confused. I had tried to be Ananna and I had failed. None of the stories Mama told me ended with Ananna alone and miserable and recovering from magic-sickness. None of them ended with her handing an entire palace over to a lord from the Mists.

I pulled the blanket over my head as if that could shut out everything that had happened. Maybe if I wished hard enough, magic would transport me out of this cave at the top of the world and back into my bed in Kjora.

Footsteps echoed outside the entrance to the sleeping quarters. Soft ones, not like the footsteps of the outlaws. I pulled the blanket down. A pale figure stood a few paces away. He glowed like moonlight, the way I'd seen him the first time, swimming in the sea alongside the *Penelope*.

"Isolfr," I breathed.

I sat up—too quickly though, because the blood rushed to my head and made me dizzy.

"Hanna." He came into the room and sat down beside me. I stared at him, certain that I was dreaming, or that this was a hallucination brought on by my magic-sickness. But then I saw the wanness of his skin underneath that moonlight glow. I saw the shadows under his eyes.

"You're really here," I whispered.

He nodded.

"Are you all right?"

"I've been better." He smiled, wavering. "Just worn out. I changed back into human form as soon as I could. Maybe I should have waited, but I wanted to see you. I wanted—wanted you to see me."

Heat rose up in my cheeks. "I see you," I said, and smiled.

"I wanted to make sure you were safe," he said. "Wanted to make sure the magic-sickness hadn't—"

"I was infected earlier, but I'm fine now."

Energy sparkled between us. I wanted to kiss him, but I didn't know if I should. If it was appropriate, knowing that we had lost, that Penelope was enchanted a few rooms away. Then again, we had gone through that battle and we were both alive. Maybe a kiss was the most appropriate thing in the world, after all.

And so I leaned forward, hesitating a little. He didn't pull back. I brushed my lips against his. I expected that to be it, just a reminder that I cared for him, but he slipped his hands around my face and kissed me harder, a real kiss, long and slow and lingering. The kind of kiss that happens when you're in love.

We stayed close afterward, our noses touching. Isolfr blinked and his eyelashes brushed against my cheek. It made me smile. I leaned my head against his shoulder.

"That was a disaster," Isolfr said, after a moment's pause. I knew he wasn't talking about the kiss.

"Trystan's tending Penelope," I said. "He might be able to save her."

"I hope so." I could tell from the way he said it that he didn't believe it would happen. I didn't push him, though—I didn't want to hear his reasoning.

"Lord Foxfollow has taken over the palace."

I didn't move. That had always been my suspicion, but hearing him say it out loud, I felt a tremor deep in my belly.

"Did you see for sure?" I asked.

"I flew by when I was still in the form of the wind. I'm sure he knew I was there, but he couldn't do anything to me. Not when I'm in my natural form."

He shrugged, but I felt a twinge of guilt. He was safer as the wind. He shouldn't have to change himself for me.

"You shouldn't have changed, then," I said. "Back to human."

"What?" He looked over at me. "Oh, Hanna, no—I wanted to be close to you, and I can't—not as the wind." He took a deep breath. "Besides, we're safe here. Lord Foxfollow is fortifying the castle. He's not going to attack. He expects us to come back."

We fell into silence, but I could hear the echoes of the battle in the throne room. Swords and pistol shots.

"Are we?"

"We can't let him take the castle." Isolfr shook his head. "I wish Ankia had let Trystan come with us! I can't believe anyone thought I could do this on my own."

I threw my arms around his shoulders, trying to be a comfort. He squeezed me back, burying his face in my shoulder. "We're not safe here," he muttered. "Not for the long term. As long as Queen Penelope is still alive—and he's not going to kill her, and certainly *we* can't kill her—he could still marry her, even if he has to force her hand. He's probably enchanting her right now." Isolfr lifted his head and stared at me. "I bet that's his plan. Enchanting her so that she'll wake up and kill us all. Then she'll marry him."

I was sick with fear.

"How long do you think we have?" I whispered.

"I don't know. If Trystan can find out more about the spell— but perhaps a couple of days? A week? He has reinforced the castle's exterior, so he's certainly settling in." Isolfr paused, biting his lower lip. "Or he wants the castle ready for when he does claim the crown. Even if he controls Penelope, people will still fight back."

"And what happens if we kill him?" I said. "What'll happen to Penelope?"

Isolfr shook his head. "I don't know."

"Can't you just pull her out of the coma yourself?" I turned toward him. "Like you did with Finnur?"

"That was a different sort of spell. Different magic. Besides—" Isolfr took a deep breath. "Our first priority should be stopping Lord Foxfollow. That's more important than saving Penelope."

His voice wobbled as he spoke.

"You don't mean that," I said.

"I do." He looked down at his hands. "We may not be able to save *her*, but we can save our world. Lord Foxfollow is our priority." He paused. "That's what a queen would want, isn't it? For us to protect her kingdom?"

His words rang out in the empty room. I thought of Kolur cradling Penelope to his breast, his face blank and dispassionate in his grief.

"Kolur will never agree to that," I said quietly.

Isolfr and I sat unmoving.

"We won't be able to tell him."

I closed my eyes. I couldn't imagine going back into that palace again—and this time without Kolur's magic.

"It's the only way," Isolfr said, his voice low. "I'm sorry, I don't want to do it either, but it's the only way—"

I looked over at him. My whole body was shaking.

"I know it is," I said. "But this time, we go into the palace with Trystan."

We left under cover of nightfall. It seemed dangerous to me, but Trystan insisted it would be easier for us to break through the boundaries at night.

"Twilight," he said. "That's when we're the most dangerous to Foxfollow. We shouldn't have tried to sneak in during the day with Ankia and the others."

I wasn't going to make the same mistake as Ankia. Neither was Isolfr. So we left at nightfall with no weapons but our magic.

The three of us walked out of the cave without any trouble. Frida and the outlaws were all sleeping, snoring together in piles among the rocks, and Kolur was tucked away with Penelope. Trystan hadn't been able to do much for her—just cast a few Mists spells to try and hide her from Lord Foxfollow. Isolfr and I met him outside the room, and I could feel the magic crackling on the air, cold and strange. I also felt the queen's loss, her disorientation, drifting through the air like a miasma.

We had worked out our plan of attack over a dinner of tough salted yak meat. I'd barely been able to eat, my stomach crashing around in anxiety. Trystan had said I that needed to eat, needed to keep my strength up, but I was grateful for my lack of appetite earlier. As we marched along the black sand toward the palace, I knew that if my stomach contained food, I would have emptied it there along the shore.

Once we were clear of the caves, Isolfr transformed into the wind, his body paling and vanishing against the dark. I could feel him, though, swirling around me and Trystan. The chill of the north wind was a comfort.

He scooped us up. I was expecting it this time, bracing myself, and when my feet lifted off the ground I felt a quick thrill of exhilaration. For half a second I forgot what we were about to do.

The night soared around us. Stars sparkled in the distance, their familiar constellations a comfort. The landscape below was almost too dark to see, but I could still make out dark and light patches— buildings and roads and patches of ice. The wind lashed at my cheeks, stinging the warmth out of them. It wasn't just Isolfr, but the fact that he had taken us so high up in the air, up near the clouds where snow forms, in an attempt to hide us from Lord Foxfollow.

I glanced over at Trystan. His eyes were closed and his hair blew back away from his face. He was taking deep, steady breaths, the way Frida had done before the battle yesterday. And I was struck with the full impact of what we were doing.

There was a very real possibility that we were going to die.

Suddenly, the night lost its sparkle. I sucked in air, trying to calm myself. Isolfr's voice whispered around me:

We can do thiisss.

I nodded, although I wasn't sure if he could see me, or if I even agreed with him. It wasn't a matter of what we could do, but of what we had to do.

A dark mass appeared on the horizon. Jagged, crawling spires blacked out the light of the stars. As we grew closer I saw that the walls were covered in a churning gray mass that twisted over itself like snakes.

"Is that the Jandanvari Palace?" Trystan said, horror creeping into his voice.

"That's not what it looked like earlier." I trembled. "It had been—beautiful."

"Foxfollow." Trystan said the name like a curse. "This is what you meant, isn't it?"

I thought he was talking to me, but the wind rippled around us, and Isolfr said, *Yesssss.*

"You said he'd fortified it! Not that he'd amplified the Mists magic here!" Trystan dug the heels of his hands into his eye sockets. "You could have warned me."

"He did warn you," I snapped. "He said it had been fortified. Of course he used the magic of the Mists. What would you expect him to do?" I turned back to the castle. The gray mass slid and undulated over the palace's old lines, enshrouding it, keeping it locked away from us.

We came to a stop directly above the palace. Isolfr whirled around me and Trystan like a cyclone, holding us in place.

"You don't have to help me," Trystan said, his voice rising and falling with the wind. "I had no idea it was going to be this bad."

He was looking at me as he spoke. I wrapped my arms around myself. Here was my chance. Trystan was more help to Isolfr than I ever could be—even Isolfr had to know that. "No," I said. "I'll help. I promised Isolfr."

Thank yooooou, whispered Isolfr's wind voice, and I knew then that even as the wind, Isolfr was scared.

"Very well," Trystan said. He stared down at the palace, his expression hard. "Drop us, Isolfr."

I took a deep breath.

Around us, Isolfr began to count:

One . . .

Two . . .

Trystan reached over and grabbed my hand.

Three . . .

And then we were falling. I clung to Trystan and tried not to think about the palace barreling up to meet us. The wind howled past my ears, but it wasn't the north wind—it wasn't Isolfr. It was the wind generated by my fall, and it was cruel and dangerous and terrifying.

Over the wind's howling I could make out Trystan chanting in a language I couldn't understand, although I could feel the strength of its magic rippling through my body. *Please work please work please work,* I thought. I knew my own magical abilities wouldn't be able to help him—it was Mists magic, and too different from what I knew—but I thought I might be able to bolster its strength. And so I concentrated on that, on promising myself that this strange spell would work.

We were almost to the castle. The dark cover rippled and churned. I took a deep breath. Trystan was shouting his spell now, the words reverberating around us.

We hit.

It was like crashing into the ocean. All at once everything was dark and damp and cold, a cold that shot straight through my bones. We passed through the churning gray mass, magic crackling and sparking, and then we passed through the stone of the palace walls, sliding through like shadows.

We landed, hard, on top of a thick, lush carpet. The impact knocked the breath from my lungs, but it didn't kill me.

Trystan's spell had worked.

I stood up, shaky. The walls spun around. Everything felt muffled—my vision, my hearing, even my sense of existing. It took me a moment to realize that I was coated in the gray mass that had surrounded the castle.

I yelped and tried to scrape it off, digging my nails over my skin. But Trystan grabbed my wrist.

"No," he whispered, peering at me from the dark mask coating his face. "It will hide us from Foxfollow's spies. I just doused us in his own magic. Rather clever, don't you think?" He grinned.

I glared at him. "You said it was worse than you expected."

"And then I realized I could use it against him. It's a better spell than what I had planned originally. Unfortunately, the same trick won't hide Isolfr, so he'll just have to stay in his wind form, like we talked about. Come, let's go find him."

We skittered through the hallway. The castle had changed with Foxfollow's magic: the shadows coiled in the corners like snakes, waiting to strike, and the walls surged like sails rippling in the wind. Sometimes eyes would glow out of the darkness. They were never attached to any figures—just bright pairs of eyes, floating in midair, looking for intruders. Looking for us.

They didn't see us. Trystan's magic had worked.

We followed the hallway until we came to the servants' stairs. They were tucked away behind a tapestry, just as they had been in those great houses we visited in the Mists—but here, the figures on the tapestry moved, tiny people chasing seals across the ice, red blood splattering in the snow. I turned away, my stomach churning. Lord Foxfollow's magic had a darkness to it I had never seen before.

Trystan led the way down the stairs. They were dark, all the torches burned out, but there was enough light seeping up from the kitchen that it wasn't like it had been in the tunnel out of the Gallowglass dungeon. We didn't pass anyone else. The kitchens were abandoned as well. A great roasted boar sat in the oven, the meat and vegetables blackened and burned and the fire long since turned to ash. Crockery was spread out across the table. A cake covered in spun-sugar flowers was turned upside down on the floor.

"They left in a hurry," I said.

"Or they were killed," Trystan said.

The possibility hadn't even occurred to me. I wrapped my arms around myself and looked at the kitchen with this new revelation, trying to find clues that the chaos came from violence, rather than from fleeing.

Trystan slid open the door that led out to the courtyard. Moonlight spilled in. He stuck his head out, glanced around.

"It's fine," he said to me. "No guards."

"Why aren't there guards?"

"I don't know." Trystan stepped out into the courtyard. I followed him. The wind gusted, blowing dust from the cart path into my eyes. An easterly wind, not Isolfr.

"You don't think that's suspicious?"

"I think it's very suspicious," Trystan said. He glanced over at me. "But I couldn't tell you how exactly Lord Foxfollow does things. I only know enough to know he's up to something."

I shivered, and not from the cold. The wind howled around the side of the palace.

And then, abruptly, it shifted, spiraling up like a cyclone. Dead leaves and grass flew around in a frenzy, reflecting the moonlight. In that shimmery light, Isolfr appeared, just for a moment, in his human form. He smiled at me. A scared smile, and a brave one.

"No trouble so far," Trystan said. "Once you get in there, though—" His voice faded away.

Let me go first, Isolfr said. *I will distract them away from you.*

"No!" I cried. "You can't—"

As long as I'm like this, I'm fine.

And then he whooshed past me, an onslaught of cold and starlight. My hair flew up around my face, and I could see the trace of him as he poured into the kitchen.

"Wait," Trystan said, grabbing my wrist. "He's right. Let him draw Foxfollow's attention."

I stood trembling out in the courtyard. I hated the idea that Isolfr was in there alone, even if he was in his wind form. I hated that he could be in danger and I was standing out in the cold. Waiting.

A shriek rose out of the palace, low and mournful. It set my teeth on edge, made the hair on my arms stand up.

"Isolfr!" I lunged toward the door.

"Hanna, no!" Trystan grabbed me and pulled me back. "No, that wasn't Isolfr—that's Foxfollow's monsters—"

More shrieks filled the air. My ears ached with the sound of them. The gray mass churned over the palace walls, growing thicker and thicker.

"We're going to get locked out," I said, and I slipped out of Trystan's grip and dove inside. The kitchens were undisturbed.

Trystan slammed in after me. "We have to give him *time*," he said.

"You saw the covering! It was going to swallow up the doorway." I glared at him. "We have to get to Foxfollow. Isolfr's going to need our help."

Trystan stared down at me. But then he nodded, once.

We left the kitchen, clambered back up the staircase. I was numb with fear but I forced myself to keep moving forward, reminding myself that Isolfr needed my help. That was enough to get me to the top of the stairs and back into the hallway. The glowing eyes were gone. Just as Isolfr had promised.

"This way," Trystan said, jerking his head to the left. "I can feel him. He's amassing strength."

Amassing strength. I thought of the time I had faced down Lord Foxfollow in the in-between world, the floor a mirror reflecting us into ourselves. I had been protected there.

But here, now——I was in his domain. In a palace he had perverted to make his own.

Trystan and I jogged through the hallway. I let Trystan lead the way. He kept his head down, like a dog sniffing for scent. The shrieking started up again, and it was louder this time, and closer, and I could feel it jarring all the way down in the marrow of my bones.

The hallway opened into an entryway. Trystan and I faced a pair of wooden doors. They were carved with the faces of former queens, but in the presence of Foxfollow's magic their expressions were twisted and horrified, eyes wide and mouths open in eternal screams.

Beyond those doors was that terrible shrieking, and the roar of the wind like a storm trying to bring down a ship.

And magic. I could feel the magic sparking inside of me.

It was time.

I took a deep breath and glanced over at Trystan. He was already staring at me, waiting. I nodded, and he stepped forward and pushed the doors open.

CHAPTER SIXTEEN

Darkness flowed out of the throne and enveloped Trystan and me. The entire world blinked and for a moment I thought I had died. I wondered if this is what it meant to swim in the sea of the dead.

But then I felt Trystan's breath near my ear:

"Use your magic. It's a trick."

My magic. I took a deep breath and tried to ignore the darkness. At first all I could feel was Lord Foxfollow's magic, crawling and snaking over me. There was no way I could work enchantment with that. I needed the wind. I needed Isolfr.

And as soon as I had the thought, I felt him, distantly, the soft cold breeze of the north wind. The south wind was the north wind's sister, he'd told me, and I knew I could harness its power, his power, inside of me.

And so I did.

I reached out for him, reached out for the magic on the wind, and drew him in close. It was easier than it normally was, and I knew he was coming to me, that he was choosing to help. My bloodstream sparked and shivered as if it were turning to ice. But then there was a surge of power, and for a half-second the throne room lit up.

The walls were lined with monsters.

A wind storm raged inside.

And Foxfollow stood on the throne, feet balanced on either armrest, chanting with his hand pressed against his heart.

I gasped and stumbled back. The image blinked out, replaced by darkness. Something caught me.

"Isolfr?" I said weakly.

"No, Trystan. Can you see?"

"I did, for a moment—"

"Try harder then. He's keeping us in the dark. Seeing him is the only way we'll be able to fight."

Trystan helped me to my feet. It was disconcerting to feel his touch but not see him. Black ink oozed around us. I felt for Isolfr again. He was close, waiting. His magic threaded through me.

"Isolfr," I whispered, "help me."

Power blasted into me and magic swelled up inside my chest. I could see again. The monsters crawled over the walls, their claws digging in tightly to stop from being blown away by Isolfr's strength. They hissed and shrieked and clambered over one another. Some of them looked like the monsters that had attacked the *Annika*, thin-snouted and sharp-toothed, but others oozed like snakes or flapped thin, membranous wings like bats. Looking at them left me nauseated, and I forced my attention up to the throne.

Up to Lord Foxfollow.

He dropped his hand to his side. I moved back, unsteady on my feet. Trystan was a few paces away from me, kneeling, tracing a pattern on the floor.

Lord Foxfollow opened his eyes.

He opened his eyes and pain swelled up inside my head. I slammed back against the wall and the squirm of monsters. One of them slithered across my throat and I flew forward, hitting the ground. The pain throbbed in time with my heart.

Hanna, whispered Isolfr. *A triiiick.*

A trick. Magic. This pain, as much as it pounded inside my head, was a phantom. It was pain generated by a spell.

I screamed and forced the pain away, transforming it into a ball of light that exploded in the center of the room. The monsters shrieked and turned away from the light, scurrying into corners and behind tapestries.

Lord Foxfollow gave me a cold smile.

"Daughter of the Sun," he hissed, "did you come to aid the North Wind?"

I didn't answer him, just curled my hands into fists and concentrated on drawing in the magic from Isolfr. I needed to transform it inside of me into something that could defeat a lord of the Mists.

"Get out of Jandanvar," I said.

Lord Foxfollow looked at me and laughed. The wind swirled between us, throwing my hair up in long streaks behind my head. Magic burned inside of me. Lord Foxfollow was still laughing. Trystan—where was Trystan? I didn't dare look away from Foxfollow, but out of the corner of my eye I saw him hunched on the floor, still tracing his patterns. He needed time.

I gathered up my magic. It coalesced into a cold, searing point inside my chest, and there was so much strength there, so much power, that for a moment I didn't even feel afraid.

I murmured a prayer to the ancestors and then I shot the magic straight at Lord Foxfollow. It manifested as a column of cold blue light, and it slammed into him and threw him up against the wall behind the thrones. He'd clearly underestimated me. The monsters howled and hissed and roiled around on the wall, crawling back out of their hiding places. I collapsed on the floor, overcome with exhaustion. I felt empty. I was empty.

Lord Foxfollow wasn't moving, but the monsters were. They peeled themselves away from the wall and slunk low over the floor, a hundred different things crawling and creeping and sliding toward me. Every single one of them had their mouths pulled back to reveal long rows of jagged teeth. I couldn't breathe. Couldn't even move to sit up. I was too weak.

"Help!" I cried out, to Trystan, to Isolfr, to anyone. "I can't—"

The monsters' faces flickered. Their features were animalistic and cruel, but as they edged toward me I saw traces of humanity in them. I saw Mama and Papa and Henrik. I saw Kolur.

"Help!" I screamed. "Sea and sky! Trystan! Isolfr!"

One of the monsters leaped. All I could see was its long silver claws flying straight for my face. But then it was knocked away by a freezing blast of wind. It hit against the floor, yelping. The others hissed and swiveled their heads. Another jumped. The wind knocked it back.

I felt around on the floor, trying to push myself up to sitting, but I heard Isolfr's voice in my head:

Stay stiillllll. Rest. Recover.

I knew I couldn't do that. I wasn't going to lay out in the middle of a battle while monsters tried to kill me. It wasn't fair. It wasn't right.

With a burst of strength I sat up. The wind howled. A shadow moved past me—Trystan, rushing toward the throne, to the place where I had thrown Lord Foxfollow.

"Stay down!" he shouted, just as a gray damp magic arced through the air. It struck me on the side of the face and immediately began rioting inside my body, reacting to my own magic. I gasped and braced myself against the floor, trying to ride out the counterbalance. I could just see beside the throne, light building between Trystan's palms.

"I said get down!" Trystan shouted again, and he shot a blast of magic, that same gray dampness, at Foxfollow. He ducked. The magic splattered across the far wall and the wall turned transparent and hazy.

Foxfollow laughed. "You aren't going to get me, Lord of Llambric," he said. "We've already been through this once."

"Shut up!" Another blast of magic, another dodge. Foxfollow leaped up on top of the queen's throne and crouched there, his gaze sweeping across the room.

His eyes began to glow.

I got a sharp tug in my stomach. I scrambled backward across the floor. Isolfr was still knocking the monsters away, and they snarled and bit at the air. They had seemed to mostly forget me.

Lord Foxfollow turned his head. Stopped at me.

Fear turned me to ice.

His lips moved. The air trembled. It was distorting, shaking, changing.

"No," I whispered, and I was still crawling backward. "No no no—"

The air vibrated against my skin. A monster launched itself at me but was thrown back. Trystan was shouting something but I couldn't hear him over the distortion of the air. I just kept crawling backward, trying to get away.

And then the room went still as death.

And Isolfr, Isolfr in his human form, dropped hard against the floor.

"There," said Foxfollow. I could hear his voice buzzing inside my head. "That's a more even match, don't you think?"

Without thinking about my exhaustion or the depletion of my magic, I jumped to my feet and shot my power out into the room, not at Foxfollow but at the monsters. It blasted into them and they were flung back in a circle and my head swooned and I dropped down beside Isolfr. I was wrung out. My magic was gone.

He turned his head toward me. "Hanna," he whispered, "I'm sorry."

He reached one hand toward me, slim and pale and lovely even in the midst of all this terror. Behind him I could see Lord Fox-follow climbing down from the throne. He was walking toward us, slow and careful.

Here it was, our moment of defeat.

"No," I said, and I reached out for him, and even that one action was painful and slow, like my limbs were drying out. "I'm sorry. I couldn't stop him—"

Our fingers touched, grazing across each other, and I thought about how this was the last time I would ever touch another crea-ture in this life, and I thought about how I was glad it was Isolfr, that I wouldn't want to touch anyone else in the moment before I died.

And then—

Distantly—

Screaming.

Trystan, I thought. I was flooded with despair. I lifted my head, trying to find him. I couldn't. I only saw Lord Foxfollow.

Lord Foxfollow, doubled over one of the thrones.

He was the one screaming.

"Trystan?" I pushed myself up on one arm, ignoring the pain. Isolfr frowned at me. "Trystan?" I said, more loudly.

Trystan stepped into view.

He didn't answer because he was focusing on a beam of magic that flowed out of his fingers. It was not the damp gray magic of earlier, but something bright, as if he'd melted the stars and har-vested their light.

Lord Foxfollow's screams echoed around the room. Trystan's head was down, his eyes dark and determined.

"I told you you wouldn't win," he said, his voice barely audible over the sound of Foxfollow's screams.

I slid over to Isolfr, not taking my eyes off Foxfollow. "Trystan has him held," I said. "You need to work your magic to help. I can't, I'm too weak—"

"So am I," Isolfr whispered.

"Well then, we'll have to combine our power. Like we said. Even just a little—" I grabbed both of Isolfr's hands and squeezed them tight. He gazed up at me. His skin was washed out and dull. I was sure I looked the same, but it didn't matter. We had to stop Foxfollow.

"The count of three," I whispered. "We just have to give him a little nudge."

Isolfr closed his eyes.

"One," I said.

He furrowed his brow in concentration.

"Two."

I lifted my gaze to the throne. Trystan shot magic into Foxfollow's chest, but he was faltering, stumbling, the magic wavering. I squeezed Isolfr's hand tight.

"Three," I said.

Magic erupted out of us from the point where our hands clasped. It was only the strength of one person—one human person—but when it threaded through Trystan's magic a surge of power roared through the room. The monsters wailed and bellowed. I focused on the magic beaming out of me and Isolfr. It was the magic of our world, and when it combined with Trystan's Mists magic it created a force in the room I'd never experienced before, a shuddering strength of two worlds combined.

Lord Foxfollow let out a loud, piercing scream. I focused on the magic. My vision was starting to fade, darkness crowding in at the edges, but I didn't let go.

Beside me, Isolfr gave a gasp of pain. I squeezed his hand tighter. Lord Foxfollow was still standing—

And then power rushed through the room and Foxfollow

brightened all over, brightened like a star, and he swung his gaze over to me and I saw him, eyes wide, furious.

And then he turned to light.

It was starlight, bright and shimmering, and it erupted over the room with a dazzling glare. When the light hit the monsters' skin they screamed, their voices echoing and unearthly, and shriveled into dust.

I dropped my magic and let go of Isolfr's hand and slumped down hard on the floor. Breathing hurt. My heartbeat hurt. My entire body was shaking.

Trystan's voice billowed around the room, creating a rhythm like the pulse of the blood in my body.

"He's gone," Trystan said. "He's dead. He's dead. He's dead."

My eyes fluttered open.

I didn't know where I was. The *Penelope II*? The *Annika*? The *Cornflower*, where I'd lived back in Tulja? Except I wasn't on a ship. The world was rocking back and forth, but I wasn't on a ship. The space was too big, and the ceiling was coated in a layer of gray residue that left me anxious and unsettled.

My body burned like I'd been out too long in the cold.

I sat up, blinking. Slowly memories started coming back to me: Lord Foxfollow laughing as I tried to fight him. His monsters shrieking and scurrying across the walls. Isolfr clutching my hand so tight I thought my fingers would break—

I was in the palace. The throne room.

I got to my feet, still shaking. The room was empty, but I didn't feel any of the strange Mists magic that Lord Foxfollow had cast over the palace. I didn't even feel the after-effects of magic-sickness, although given the battle it seemed like there should be something.

I turned, dazed, and stumbled toward the exit. Why was I alone? Why had Isolfr left me here? Or Trystan—

A pain shot through my heart. I saw an image of Isolfr stretched out on the floor beside me. What if he wasn't here because something had happened to him? Because he died?

Panic drowned out my disorientation. I jogged forward, flung the door open. The hallway was empty.

"Hello!" I shouted. "Trystan! Isolfr?" My voice cracked on Isolfr's name.

Why had he left me?

"Hanna?"

I whirled around, my breath caught in my throat. Isolfr stood a few paces away, balancing himself against the wall with one arm. He lifted his free hand in a wave.

"You left me!" I shouted.

"You were asleep." His eyes were big and guileless. He didn't look so sickly anymore. "I wanted to let you rest, like I *told* you to do. Trystan and I were trying to counteract the effects of the magic-sickness. There's Mists magic that can do that."

I sighed with relief. Just wanted to let me rest. Of course.

I rushed forward and threw my arms around his shoulders and buried my face in his neck. His sweet north wind scent stirred something inside me. Hope.

"Is he gone?" I whispered.

Isolfr nodded; I felt the movement against the top of my head. "Yes," he said. "We—destroyed him. Permanently. He can't do any more harm here or in the Mists."

I pulled away from Isolfr and studied his face. He was so beautiful, so unearthly.

And he was alive. He was safe.

"We did it," I said, and I could hardly believe the sound of my own words. "We did it."

"I know." Isolfr laughed. Then he pulled me into an embrace

and kissed me. It was a kiss like the one before we fought, a kiss imbued with love. But this kiss wasn't panicked and desperate; it was slow and lingering, a celebration of our victory and a reminder that we were still together in this world.

"Oh, for love of the Mists, stop it."

Isolfr and I jumped away from each other. I glanced over my shoulder. Trystan had walked into the hallway. He grinned at us.

"Just kidding," he said.

I blushed. Isolfr looked down at his feet.

"I'm glad you're up." Trystan ambled toward me. He looked ruffled and worn out, and his hair stuck up around his head in spikes. He shoved his hands in his pockets and gave me an oddly shy smile. "What you did for me in there—I would never have killed Foxfollow alone."

Killed. He actually said the word. I snuggled close to Isolfr and tried not to think about it, that our magic had killed someone, even if that someone was a monster.

"The good news is that his fortifications all vanished with his death," Trystan went on, waving one hand around. "Palace is good as new, save for the problems with magic-sickness. But Isolfr and I should have those fixed up pretty easily."

I nodded.

"We need to go back to the caves," Isolfr said, "and tell Kolur what happened." He hesitated. "And see about the queen. I'm hoping that the spell on her broke too, but—" He frowned. "Without a ruler, Jandanvar could open itself to another attack. If Foxfollow had any allies—"

"Of course he does, although I don't know if they would move in so quickly." Trystan's eyes glittered. "Either way, the queen is our top priority. You're right. That spell was so complex, I've no idea what it might have done to her."

His words hung in the air. None of us wanted to say the worst possibility: that she might have died with Foxfollow.

I thought of Kolur cradling Penelope to his chest, his eyes glistening with tears.

I prayed to the ancestors that wasn't the case.

CHAPTER SEVENTEEN

We walked back to the caves. Isolfr was too weak to transform into the wind to carry us, and so we made our way on foot through the cold, dim dawn. It took a long time. When we left the palace, a seam of pink light had already appeared in the east, and by the time I could smell the sea again the sun was high overhead. But walking required less energy than magic, and after the battle it was enough to make me feel normal again.

Eventually, we came to the cave entrance. I'd expected to find a guard there, maybe the ferryman who'd brought us in from the *Penelope II*, but the entrance was unprotected. Isolfr stopped.

"This is odd, don't you think?" he said.

"Is it?" Trystan pushed past him. "We know Foxfollow's not here."

Isolfr and I looked at each other.

"He's right about that, at least." Really, though, I was just too weary to think about fighting anymore. I followed Trystan into the cave. The veins of light seemed brighter than usual, twinkling in the darkness like stars. I shuffled down the path, Isolfr at my side. I knew I should be more aware. I just didn't have the energy.

And then I heard music.

"What's that?" Trystan stopped up ahead and turned around to look at Isolfr and me. "Do you hear that too?"

I nodded. The music was coming from deep inside the caves. It was bright and jangling and joyful, and every now and then it was accompanied by an explosion of laughter.

"What the hell's going on?" I said.

"Well, we did just defeat Lord Foxfollow," Trystan said.

"But how could they *know* that?" I looked at Isolfr. "Do you think they had some way of—tracking him?"

Isolfr frowned. "I doubt it. Any magic those outlaws could conjure up wouldn't be able to track Foxfollow."

"I agree," said Trystan. "They were probably just drinking off their loss from yesterday and got a bit enthusiastic." He shambled forward. "I will say this: my idea of a celebration right now is more akin to a nap than a party."

I didn't like this. As far as the outlaws were concerned, they still had a second battle to plan.

"Should we find out for sure?" I asked Isolfr. Trystan had already disappeared around the bend in the corridor. "You don't think this is some kind of trap?"

"Foxfollow's dead," Isolfr said. "I know that much." He reached over and grabbed my hand. "Let's see what they're celebrating."

And so we made our way into the main room. Everything looked like a party. Magic-cast lanterns floated through the air, casting multicolored light on the gray walls. A trio of outlaws was sitting up at the front of the room, playing the instruments they had used to smuggle their weapons into the palace—I was surprised that they actually worked, and that the outlaws could actually play. The rest of the crowd was dancing and drinking. They didn't notice us walk in.

I stared at the party without comprehension. Everyone was laughing, smiling, toasting one another. Mugs of ale slammed into each other. Men whirled each other around in some kind of drunken dance.

"Well," Trystan said, materializing at my side, "I guess our efforts didn't go unnoticed."

"But how could they *know?*" I said. Beside me, Isolfr gasped.

And then I saw her.

It was the Queen of Jandanvar. Queen Penelope. She wore the shaggy furs and rough wool of the outlaws, but there was no way to disguise the aristocratic loveliness of her features. She sat at a stone table with Kolur at her side, one hand wrapped around a mug of ale. She leaned in close to Kolur, smiling. Said something to him that made him grin like an idiot.

The three of us stared at her in shock.

"When we defeated Lord Foxfollow," Isolfr said, "it just— broke her spell?"

"I'll be damned," said Trystan. He laughed. "I should have known, though. The spell seemed so complicated, it makes sense that really it was just *easy.*" Another disbelieving laugh. "Foxfollow. Crafty bastard."

Kolur glanced across the party and caught my eye. He stood up, nearly knocking his drink over in the process.

"Where the hell were you?" he shouted at me.

"What's going on?" I shouted back.

Kolur grinned again, that stupid goofy grin I'd never seen before. He took Penelope by the hand and pulled her to her feet, and she smiled up at him, then smiled at me from across the room.

"She's awake," he said. "And she says Foxfollow's dead!"

Dead. The word had a finality to it that at once made me shudder and made me want to sigh with happiness. Foxfollow was dead. We had won.

"I know!" I called back. "We're the ones who—who stopped him."

Half the outlaws in the room turned toward me. I wanted to shrink down under the weight of their stares.

"What?" said Kolur, and then he made a swatting gesture at the band. The music slowly clattered into silence.

The outlaws' raucous conversation died away. One by one they looked over at me. Looked over at *us*. Trystan, Isolfr, and me, the ones who had defeated Lord Foxfollow.

"It's true," Isolfr said, stepping forward. "We broke into the palace while you slept. We found him—"

"I killed him," Trystan said. "The only one who could do it, you know. Should have saved yourselves some trouble and taken me on the first go-round." He didn't seem exhausted anymore. Maybe the attention had rejuvenated him.

He glided forward and gave a deep bow toward Queen Penelope. "Trystan Llambric of the Llambric lands of the Mists. But don't hold that against me."

Queen Penelope tittered. She glanced over at Kolur, then back at Trystan.

"I won't," she said, her voice ringing out strangely in the echo of the cave.

"I'm always at your service, Your Highness. Your kingdom is practically a part of my world too."

She smiled. It was radiant, like sun bouncing off a glacier. "The people of Jandanvar owe you a debt. *I* owe you a debt." She lifted her face and looked at me, at Isolfr. "You two as well," she said. "Come." She beckoned us with two fingers. "I'd like to speak to all of you. In front of these witnesses." She lifted one arm and swept it out across the room, and despite the tattered clothes she looked as regal as she had when I first saw her in the throne room.

The outlaws all stared at her, silent and transfixed. Isolfr was the first to move toward her. I followed, my heart racing. We lined up next to Trystan. Queen Penelope smiled down at us.

"I owe you a debt," she said, pressing her hand to her heart. "It would be my great honor if you would agree to an old Jandanvari custom."

One of the outlaws shouted, "The Marista?"

I'd never heard that word in my life. One look at Trystan told me he hadn't either.

Queen Penelope nodded. "Yes," she said. "The Marista."

The outlaws erupted into cheers. Isolfr was beaming, his eyes shining. "What's the Marista?" I whispered to him.

"You'll see," he said.

"As Queen of Jandanvar," Penelope said, "I'm authorized— when I see fit—to grant certain wishes. They must fall within reason, of course. That is, they must be things I can *do*. But rest assured, I can do quite a lot." She winked. The outlaws cheered again. Kolur laughed. "In exchange for your service, I will grant each of you one wish." She held up her hand. "You need not choose them now. But I will complete the ceremony on the night of my wedding to Kolur Icebreak—"

I gaped at Kolur. He shrugged. "I asked, she said yes," he said. "Figured she didn't want to waste all those decorations."

Frida laughed beside him.

"Make your decision in a week's time," Penelope said. "The lands of Jandanvar thank you."

The outlaws cheered again, and then the music kicked up. Queen Penelope turned back to Kolur and he swept her up in his arms and led her out to the center of the room to dance. I stumbled over to the closest table. Frida appeared with a glass of ale, which she slid over to me.

"Don't drink it too fast," she said.

I looked past her, over to where Isolfr and Trystan were speaking a few paces away. They were both grinning, laughing. Talking about what wishes they'd have granted, no doubt.

"The Marista," Frida said. "That's an awfully impressive honor."

I took a sip of the ale. "I could tell."

She laughed and leaned forward. "What wish will you have fulfilled?"

I looked into the surface of my ale. It was dark and frothy. "I don't know," I said. "I've been wanting to go back home all this time."

"Is that still what you want?" she said.

She was staring at me, her eyes sparkling. I swirled my ale around. I thought of the adventures of the last few months. Tulja and the *Annika*, traveling through the Mists while disguised as a servant. I thought about fighting monsters and bringing Lord Foxfollow to the in-between place. I thought about Isolfr. I thought about magic.

"I'm not sure anymore," I finally said.

Just as she promised, Queen Penelope married Kolur a week later. The ceremony was held at the palace, and you couldn't even tell that a battle had taken place there. The gray mass had vanished, and the palace had returned to the pristine snow-white stone of before. Inside, everything was polished and shining. The carpets were clean, and the tapestries depicted the lineage of the royalty of Jandanvar, rather than bloody hunts. The hallways were bustling with servants and courtiers and performers.

The ceremony itself was a grand affair. It took place outside in the gardens, heat-globes drifting through the air to keep us warm. Strange trees grew out of the hard, frozen ground, their leaves transparent and sparkling like ice. Isolfr explained to me that Jandanvari weddings always took place outside and at night so that the stars could bear witness to the couple's new future together. It was a lovely idea, and I threaded my arm through Isolfr's as we strolled through the garden and wondered what the stars thought of the two of us. We were dressed in complementary outfits—I had been given a brocade dress with fabric the same shimmering white-blue as ice on a lake. Isolfr's suit was the same color, although shot through with darker blue. I laughed when I first saw him.

"We're twins," I said.

He blushed. "It's customary for couples to wear similar colors here," he said.

And that made *me* blush.

The excitement of the wedding was almost enough for me to forget about the Marista. All day I'd been watching singers and puppeteers, feasting and dancing, and all day I knew I would need to make a decision. I'd already sent a letter to Mama and Papa through the queen's personal wizard, telling them everything that had happened since I was pulled into the Mists. At the very beginning, I wrote I AM SAFE in big block letters so they wouldn't worry. I hadn't gotten a response back yet, but I knew it was too soon for one.

I told them about the Marista, but I didn't tell them my decision—mostly because when I wrote it, I hadn't made one. But when I finished the letter and sat back and read over my adventure, I knew I couldn't go back home and become a fisherman like Papa. I'd finally had a taste of the wider world, and I knew, as much as I loved my family, and as much as I would miss them, that things would never be as simple as they'd been before.

A bell chimed, echoing through the garden. It sounded like starlight. Isolfr stopped and looked at me. "It's time," he said in a soft voice.

"For the Marista?"

He shook his head. "For the marriage."

I smiled at that, trying to quell the queasiness in my stomach. After the ceremony would come the Marista, and then I would have to make my final decision—I would have to formalize my future.

Isolfr and I were given places in the front row, next to Frida and Trystan and surrounded by courtiers. He and I held hands as Penelope and Kolur promised themselves to each other. They wound silvery-white ribbons around each other's arms, and Queen Penelope sang the prayer of the bride in a voice like hot melted sugar. The priestess anointed them with scented oil and placed crowns of flowers on their heads as she spoke in a language I couldn't understand. It was a short ceremony, and beautiful, and when they finished they ran through the crowd, their white-ribboned hands clutching each other. Music spilled out of the garden and they danced together to finalize their devotion to each other, the stars twinkling overhead.

When the song ended and Kolur and Penelope kissed, the crowd leaped to their feet and applauded. Penelope held up one hand to silence us.

"Tonight is a special night," she called out. "For we are not celebrating only a wedding, but a Marista as well—a triple Marista, in honor of the three heroes who saved our world from the wiles of Lord Foxfollow."

The applause that followed her pronouncement rolled over me like thunder. I could feel it deep inside my chest.

"May the three come forward," she said, "to receive your wishes."

I looked over at Isolfr. He was smiling, as bright as starlight. I didn't share his happiness. A few moments away and I knew what I wanted to ask for, but not if I would have the courage to ask for it.

Trystan went up first, waving at the crowd. They cheered for him, seemingly not caring that he was a man of the Mists, and he basked in their admiration, soaking it up like the sun.

"Lord Trystan of Llambric," Queen Penelope said, "what is your wish?"

Trystan straightened his shoulders. He looked over the crowd.

"My greatest wish has already been granted," he said, "and that was to see Lord Foxfollow killed."

Applause so loud it threatened to call snow down from the sky.

"He destroyed my family's name because of a centuries-old feud," he said, "and took away our lands and placed them under his control. And while I've freed your land from Foxfollow's grasp, I'm afraid mine is still tainted by his influence. He humiliated me in the days before I crossed over, and it will be difficult for me to return in my damaged state."

The audience had gone silent. They watched him with wide eyes.

"All I ask," Lord Trystan said, "is a title in Jandanvar. A connection to this world I helped save, and a way for me to begin rebuilding my family's honor."

There was a pause. Queen Penelope stepped forward and placed her hand on the top of Trystan's head. He closed his eyes.

"My debt is paid," she said. "And your wish is granted."

Something seemed to flow out of Trystan. A tension, perhaps, a fear of the future. He slumped beneath Penelope's touch and sighed. The crowd roared their approval, and Trystan leaned close to Penelope and murmured something to her that I couldn't hear over the applause.

Penelope waited until the cheers died away before calling Isolfr.

"The North Wind," she said, "Spirit of Jandanvar, blessed protector."

The applause for Isolfr was more muted than it had been for Trystan—reverent, really. He walked forward. No one in this garden could mistake him for human, not in this moment. He was too beautiful.

"What is your wish?" asked Penelope.

Isolfr gazed over the crowd. I looked at him, my heart pounding. He'd already told me what he was going to ask for. It was a small thing, I thought. Nothing like the decision I would need to make.

"I don't want to ever have to do something like that again," he said.

The crowd burst into laughter, and Queen Penelope clasped her hands together and laughed too. Isolfr gave a wry smile out to the crowd.

"I mean no disrespect," he said, stammering a little. "But please——promise me you won't try to marry any more lords of the Mists. That's all."

I half expected Penelope to be angry with him, but instead she smiled and laid her hand on Isolfr's head.

"You have my word," she said. "I will not agree to marry into the Mists again. My debt is paid, and your wish is granted."

Isolfr moved aside. My face felt hot. Queen Penelope turned toward me and she was all I could see. I could not think about the audience, about the stars, about the wind spirits knocking around the leaves of the trees.

"Hanna Euli of Kjora," Penelope said.

Her words sounded far away. They were accompanied by a rumbling, thunder before a rainstorm. Applause. The audience, applauding for me.

I walked forward.

"What is your wish?" she said.

For a moment I couldn't move. Penelope smiled down at me. I looked away, over to Isolfr. I had a choice. I could wish for what I thought I'd wanted from the moment I realized that the adventuring wasn't what I expected. I could wish to go home.

Or I could wish for that thing I'd wanted since I first learned to control the wind. I could wish for a dream to become real.

Isolfr smiled at me. A spirit of the wind. Of course I'd fallen in love with him.

This time, I turned to the crowd. Their faces blurred together. I knew I couldn't make an elegant speech, like Trystan, nor could I make them laugh, like Isolfr. I could only say what I wanted.

"I wish to attend the Undim Citadels," I said, "so I can study to become a witch."

For a moment I was certain the audience would laugh at me. But they only applauded and cheered. A wind stirred around my skirts—the south wind, smelling of spices and sunlight, but also of home, of Mama's iceberry pie and Papa's hot cider.

You have my approval, the wind said, whistling in my ear. I smiled.

Penelope laid her hand on my head. I felt it like a weight.

"My debt is paid," she said.

I thought of my future. I thought of my magic, boiling up inside of me, burning with potential. The Undim Citadels. Attending was not a matter of my ability—I'd helped defeat Lord Foxfollow—but of payment. That's why it was a wish.

I knew I'd made the right decision. I didn't worry about home. Lord Foxfollow was dead. I knew I'd see my parents again. That I'd see Henrik again, and Bryn. And I also knew that the next time I saw Kjora, it would not be as a fisherwoman, but as a witch.

Queen Penelope smiled. The stars twinkled. The south wind swirled around me.

"And your wish is granted," she said.

THE END

ACKNOWLEDGMENTS

As always, I would like to thank my parents and Ross Andrews for their love and support. Special thanks goes out to all my friends-who-write: Amanda Cole, Bobby Mathews, Alexandre Maki, Laura Lam, and the members of the Northwest Houston SFF Writer's Group. Writing is such a solitary activity that it's a joy to find others willing to discuss the highs and lows in intricate detail.

Furthermore, I would like to thank my agent, Stacia Decker, for reading *The Wizard's Promise* and offering excellent suggestions for improvement, as well as for her constant hard work regarding my books and my career. Thank you to my editor, Amanda Rutter, for agreeing to take a chance on another set of stories set in this little fantasy world I made up all those years ago. And thank you to the rest of the Angry Robot staff—Mike Underwood, Lee Harris, Marc Gascoigne, and Caroline Lambe—for the wonderful support they give their authors. And I would be remiss if I did not mention the hardworking Angry Robot interns who have been wonderful about helping with marketing connections: Leah, Vicky, and Jamie.

Finally, I would like to thank the readers, reviewers, and bloggers who helped make the Assassin's Curse series such a success. Thank you, all!

SEE HOW THE STORY BEGAN IN
MAGIC OF BLOOD AND SEA.

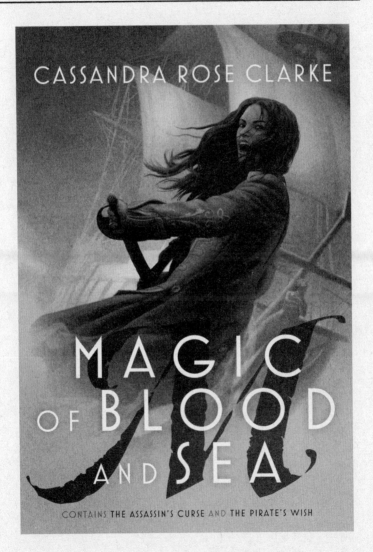

I ain't never been one to trust beautiful people, and Tarrin of the *Hariri* was the most beautiful man I ever saw. You know how in the temples they got those paintings of all the gods and goddesses hanging on the wall above the row of prayer candles? And you're supposed to meditate on them so as the gods can hear your request better? Tarrin of the *Hariri* looked just like one of those paintings. Golden skin and huge black eyes and this smile that probably worked on every girl from here to the ice-islands. I hated him on sight.

We were standing in the Hariris' garden, Mama and Papa flanking me on either side like a couple of armed guards. The sea crashed against the big marble wall, spray misting soft and salty across my face. I licked it away and Mama jabbed me in the side with the butt of her sword.

"So I take it all the arrangements are in order?" asked Captain Hariri, Tarrin's father. "You're ready to finalize our agreement?"

"Soon as we make the trade," Papa said.

I glowered at the word "trade" and squirmed around in my too-tight silk dress. My breasts squeezed out the top of it, not on purpose. I know that sort of thing is supposed to be appealing to men but you wouldn't know it talking to me. At least the dress was a real pretty one, the color of cinnamon and draped the way the court ladies wore 'em a couple of seasons ago. We'd nicked it off a merchant ship a few months back. Mama had said it suited me when we were on board Papa's boat and she was lining my eyes with kohl and pinning my hair on top of my head, trying to turn me into a beauty. I could tell by the expression on Mistress Hariri's face that it hadn't worked.

"Tarrin!" Captain Hariri lifted his hand and Tarrin slunk out of the shadow of the gazebo where he'd been standing alongside his mother. The air was full up with these tiny white flowers from the trees nearby, and a couple of blossoms caught in Tarrin's hair. He was dressed like his father, in dusty old aristocratic clothes, and that was the only sign either of 'em were pirates like me and my parents.

"It's nice to meet you, Ananna of the *Tanarau*." He bowed, hinging at the waist. He said my name wrong. Mama shoved me forward, and I stumbled over the hem of my dress, stained first with seawater from clomping around on the boat and then with sand from walking through Lisirra to get to this stupid garden. The Hariris were the only clan in the whole Confederation that spent more time on land than they did at sea.

Tarrin and I stared at each other for a few seconds, until Mama jabbed me in the back again, and I spat out one of the questions she made me memorize: "Have you got a ship yet?"

Tarrin beamed. "A sleek little frigate, plucked out of the emperor's own fleet. Fastest ship on the water."

"Yeah?" I said. "You got a crew for that ship or we just gonna look at her from the wall over there?"

"Ananna," Mama hissed, even as Papa tried to stifle a laugh.

Tarrin's face crumpled up and he looked at me like a little kid that knows you're teasing him but doesn't get the joke. "Finest crew out of the western islands." It sounded rehearsed. "I got great plans for her, Mistress Tanarau." He opened his eyes up real wide and his face glowed. "I want to take her out to the Isles of the Sky."

I about choked on my own spit. "You sure that's a good idea?"

"Surely a girl raised on the *Tanarau* doesn't fear the Isles of the Sky."

I glared at him. The air in the garden was hot and still, like pure sunlight, and even though the horrors I'd heard about the Isles of the Sky seemed distant and made-up here, Tarrin's little plan set my nerves on edge. Even if he probably wasn't talking truth: nobody makes a path for the Isles of the Sky, on account of folks going mad from visiting that little chain of islands. They'll change you and change you until you ain't even human no more. They're pure magic, that's what Mama told me. They're the place where magic comes from.

"I know the difference between bravery and stupidity," I said. Tarrin laughed, but he looked uncomfortable, and his father was glowering and squinting into the sunlight.

"She's joking," Mama said.

"No, I ain't."

Mama cuffed me hard on the back of the head. I stumbled forward and bumped right up against Tarrin. Under the gazebo, his mother scowled in her fancy silks.

"It does sound like a nice ship, though," I muttered, rubbing at my head.

Captain Hariri puffed out his chest and coughed. "Why don't you show Mistress Tanarau your ship, boy?"

Tarrin gave him this real withering look, with enough nastiness in it to poison Lisirra's main water well, then turned back to me and flashed me one of his lady-slaying smiles. I sighed, but my head still stung from where Mama'd smacked me, and I figured anything was better than fidgeting around in my dress while Papa and Captain Hariri yammered about the best way for the Tanarau clan to sack along the Jokja coast, now that the *Tanarau* had all the power of the *Hariri* and her rich-man's armada behind them. Thanks to me, Papa would've said, even though I ain't had no say in it.

Tarrin led me down this narrow staircase that took us away

from the garden and up to the water's edge. Sure enough, a frigate bobbed in the ocean, the wood polished and waxed, the sails dyed pale blue—wedding sails.

"You ain't flying colors yet," I said.

Tarrin's face got dark and stormy. "Father hasn't given me the right. Said I have to prove myself first."

"So if we get married, we gotta sail colorless?" I frowned.

"*If* we get married?" Tarrin turned to me. "I thought it was a done deal! Father and Captain Tanarau have been discussing it for months." He paused. "This better not be some Tanarau trick."

"Trust me, it ain't."

"'Cause I'll tell you now, my father isn't afraid to send the assassins after his enemies."

"Oh, how old do you think I am? Five?" I walked up to the edge of the pier and thumped the boat's side with my palm. The wood was sturdy beneath my touch and smooth as silk. "I ain't afraid of assassin stories no more." I glanced over my shoulder at him. "But the Isles of the Sky, that's another matter." I paused. "That's why you want to go north, ain't it? 'Cause of your father?"

Tarrin didn't answer at first. Then he pushed his hair back away from his forehead and kind of smiled at me and said, "How did you know?"

"Any fool could see it."

Tarrin looked at me, his eyes big and dark. "Do you really think it's stupid?"

"Yeah."

He smiled. "I like how honest you are with me."

I almost felt sorry for him then, 'cause I figured, with a face like that, ain't no girl ever been honest to him in his whole life.

"We could always fly *Tanarau* colors," I suggested. "'Stead of *Hariri* ones. That way you don't have to wor—"

Tarrin laughed. "Please. That would be even worse."

The wrong answer. I spun away from him, tripped on my damn dress hem again, and followed the path around the side of the cliff that headed back to the front of the Hariris' manor. Tarrin trailed behind me, spitting out apologies—as if it mattered. We were getting married whether or not I hated him, whether or not Mistress Hariri thought I was too ugly to join in with her clan. See, Captain Hariri was low-ranked among the loose assortment of cutthroats and thieves that formed the Confederation. Papa wasn't.

There are three ways of bettering yourself in the Pirates' Confederation, Mama told me once: murder, mutiny, and marriage. Figures the Hariri clan would be the sort to choose the most outwardly respectable of the three.

I was up at street level by now, surrounded by fruit trees and vines hanging with bright flowers. The air in Lisirra always smells like cardamom and rosewater, especially in the garden district, which was where Captain Hariri kept his manor. It was built on a busy street, near a day market, and merchant camels paraded past its front garden, stirring up great clouds of dust. An idea swirled around in my head, not quite fully formed: a way out of the fix of arranged marriage.

"Mistress Tanarau!" Tarrin ran up beside me. "There's nothing interesting up here. The market's terrible." He pouted. "Don't you want to go aboard my ship?"

"Be aboard it plenty soon enough." I kept watching those camels. The merchants always tied them off at their street-stalls, loose, lazy knots that weren't nothing a pirate princess couldn't untangle in five seconds flat.

Papa told me once that you should never let a door slam shut on you. "Even if you can't quite figure out how to work it in the moment," he'd said. He wasn't never one to miss an opportunity, and I am nothing if not my father's daughter. Even if the bastard did want to marry me off.

I took off down the street, hoisting my skirt up over my boots—none of the proper ladies shoes we'd had on the boat had been in my size—so I wouldn't trip on it. Tarrin followed close behind, whining about his boat and then asking why I wanted to go to the day market.

"'Cause," I snapped, skirt flaring out as I faced him. "I'm thirsty, and I ain't had a sweet lime drink in half a year. Can only get 'em in Lisirra."

"Oh," said Tarrin. "Well, you should have said something—"

I turned away from him and stalked toward the market's entrance, all festooned with vines from the nearby gardens. The market was small, like Tarrin said, the vendors selling mostly cut flowers and food. I breezed past a sign advertising sweet lime drinks, not letting myself look back at Tarrin. I love sweet lime drinks, to be sure, but that ain't what I was after.

It didn't take me long to find a vendor that would suit my needs. He actually found me, shouting the Lisirran slang for Empire nobility. I'm pretty sure he used it as a joke. Still, I glanced at him when he called it out, and his hands sparkled and shone like he'd found a way to catch sunlight. He sold jewelry, most of it fake, but some of it pretty valuable—I figured he must not be able to tell the difference.

But most important of all, he had a camel, tied to a wooden pole with some thin, fraying rope, the knot already starting to come undone in the heat.

Tarrin caught up with me and squinted at the vendor.

"You want to apologize for laughing at me," I said, "buy me a necklace."

"To wear at our wedding?"

"Sure." I fixed my eyes on the camel. It snorted and pawed at the ground. I've always liked camels, all hunchbacked and thread-bare like a well-loved blanket.

Tarrin sauntered up to the vendor, grin fixed in place. The vendor asked him if he wanted something for the lady.

I didn't hear Tarrin's response. By then, I was already at the camel, my hands yanking at the knot. It dissolved quick as salt in water, sliding to the bottom of the pole.

I used that same pole to vault myself up on the saddle nestled between the two humps on the camel's back, hiking the skirt of my dress up around my waist. I leaned forward and went "tut" into his ear like I'd seen the stall vendors do a thousand times. The camel trotted forward. I dug the heels of my boots into his side and we shot off, the camel kicking up great clouds of golden dirt, me cling-ing to his neck in my silk dress, the pretty braids of my hairstyle coming unraveled in the wind.

The vendor shouted behind me, angry curses that would've made a real lady blush. Then Tarrin joined in, screaming at me to come back, hollering that he hadn't been joking about the assassins. I squeezed my eyes shut and tugged hard on the camel's reins and listened to the gusts of air shoving out of his nostrils. He smelled awful, like dung and the too-hot-sun, but I didn't care: We were wound up together, me and that camel.

I slapped his reins against his neck like he was a horse and willed him to take me away, away from my marriage and my double-crossing parents. And he did.

All of Tarrin's hollering aside, we galloped out of the gar-den district without much trouble. I didn't know how to direct the camel—as Papa always told me, my people ride on boats, not animals—but the camel seemed less keen on going back to that vendor than I did. He turned down one street and then another, threading deeper and deeper into the crush of white clay buildings. Eventually he slowed to a walk, and together we ambled along a wide, sunny street lined with drying laundry.

I didn't recognize this part of the city.

There weren't as many people out, no vendors or bright-colored shop signs painted on the building walls. Women stuck their heads out of windows as we rode past, eyebrows cocked up like we were the funniest thing they'd seen all day. I might have waved at them under different circumstances, but right now I had to figure out how to lay low for a while. Escaping's always easy, Papa taught me (he'd been talking about jail, not marriage, but still). Staying escaped is the hard part.

I found this sliver of an alley and pushed at the camel's neck to get him to turn. He snorted and shook his big shaggy head, then trudged forward.

"Thanks, camel." The air was cooler here: A breeze streamed between the two buildings and their roofs blocked out the sun. I slid off the camel's back and straightened out my dress. The fabric was coated with dust and golden camel hairs in addition to the mud-and-saltwater stains at the hem, and I imagined it probably smelled like camel now too.

I patted the camel on the head and he blinked at me, his eyes dark and gleaming and intelligent.

"Thanks," I told him again. I wasn't used to getting around on the backs of animals, and it seemed improper not to let him know I appreciated his help. "You just got me out of a marriage."

The camel tilted his head a little like he understood.

"And you're free now," I added. "You don't have to haul around all that fake jewelry." I scratched at the side of his face. "Find somebody who'll give you a bath this time, you understand?"

He blinked at me but didn't move. I gave him a gentle shove, and he turned and trotted out into the open street. Myself, I just slumped down in the dust and tried to decide what to do next. I figured I had to let the camel go 'cause I was too conspicuous on him. Together we'd wound pretty deeply into Lisirra's residential mazes, but most people, when they see a girl in a fancy dress on a camel—that's something they're going to remember. Which meant I needed to get rid of the dress next, ideally for money. Not that I have any qualms about thievery, but it's always easier to do things on the up and up when you can.

I stood and swiped my hands over the dress a few times, trying to get rid of the dust and the camel hairs. I pulled my hair down so it fell thick and frizzy and black around my bare shoulders. Then I followed the alley away from the triangle of light where I'd entered, emerging on another sun-filled street, this one more bustling than the other. A group of kids chased each other around, shrieking and laughing. Women in airy cream-colored dresses and lacy scarves carried baskets of figs and dates and nuts, or dead chickens trussed up in strings, or jars of water. I needed one of those dresses.

One of the first lessons Papa ever taught me, back when I could barely totter around belowdeck, was how to sneak around. "One of the most important aspects of our work," he always said. "Don't underestimate it." And sneaking around in public is actually the easiest thing in the whole world, 'cause all you have to do is stride purposefully ahead like you own the place, which was easy given my silk dress. I jutted my chin out a little bit and kept my shoulders straight, and people just stepped out of the way for me, their eyes lowered. I went on like this until I found a laundry line strung up between two buildings, white fabric flapping on it like the sails of our boat.

Our boat.

The thought stopped me dead. She wasn't my boat no more.

Never would be. I'd every intention of finishing what I started, like Papa always taught me. But finishing what I started meant I'd never get to see that boat again. I'd spent all my seventeen years aboard her, and now I'd never get to climb up to the top of her rigging and gaze out at the gray-lined horizon drawn like a loop around us. Hell, I'd probably never even go back to the pirates' islands in the west, or dance the Confederation dances again, or listen to some old cutthroat tell his war stories while I drifted off to sleep in a rope hammock I'd tied myself.

A cart rolled by then, kicking up a great cloud of dust that set me to coughing. The sand stung my eyes, and I told myself it was the sand drawing out my tears as I rubbed them away with the palm of my hand. There was no point dwelling on the past. I couldn't marry Tarrin and I couldn't go home. If I wanted to let myself get morose, I could do it after I had money and a plan.

SAGAPRESS.COM
PRINT AND EBOOK EDITIONS AVAILABLE

THE MAD SCIENTIST'S DAUGHTER

CASSANDRA ROSE CLARKE

FINALIST FOR THE PHILIP K. DICK AWARD

"THE MAD SCIENTIST'S DAUGHTER IS A DEEPLY ENGAGING TALE BEAUTIFULLY TOLD, CASSANDRA ROSE CLARKE IS A SUPERB WRITER AND THIS SPELLBINDING NOVEL SHOULD APPEAL TO GENRE AND MAINSTREAM READERS EQUALLY."

—GRAHAM JOYCE, AUTHOR OF THE SILENT LAND